Baby Please Don't Go

A Novel

FRANK FREUDBERG

Inside Job Media
Wayne, PA 19087

Published in the United States

ISBN – 13: 978-0-9845945-3-5
ISBN – 10: 0-9845945-3-1

www.BabyPleaseDontGo.com

To my father

1

Tucked into a lush countryside of winding roads, hills and trees, and sprawling estates with their orchards and horse farms, was Red Cedar Woods—a small village in the heart of Brandywine County, Pennsylvania, thirty miles southwest of Philadelphia.

A late autumn day cast its growing darkness across the region, and a light rain began. Residents prepared for an evening at home, a night of quiet, the way folks from small towns everywhere did when winter was in the air.

It was two in the morning, and along a deserted row of antique shops, taverns, and restaurants, leaves skittered down the rain-swept streets. Lock Gilkenney—early forties, wiry and tall, and wearing a leather jacket—burst out of the front door of the only bar still open. He had always liked Foster & Zandt's on a cold night, and he thought about the last time he had eaten there, recalling the noise of the people and the sudden spill of yellow light when he opened the door. In his memory it was like a window into another world, a menagerie of people with happy lives they had worked hard for and deserved.

Lock shrugged his leather jacket up around his ears against the chill. He wanted to run toward the corner, but his legs refused. Instead, he staggered.

At the intersection, he leaned against the side of a building and drooped his head toward the pavement.

A car rolled past, and a couple, arm in arm, strolled across the street. Lock watched them go for a moment and then pushed himself away from the wall. He turned left at the corner and picked up his pace as best he could.

Midway down the block, Ivan rose up from where he had been crouched next to a mailbox, blanket-shrouded and shivering.

"Hey, Lock, that you?"

Lock was startled and lost his footing. Ivan shrugged off his blanket and hurried to help Lock back onto his feet. Lock grabbed at a stunted oak that the city had planted who knew how many years back. He steadied himself, and then patted the bark and said, "Thanks."

"Yeah, you're welcome. What's the matter, Lock? You haven't been drinking, I'm pretty sure about that," Ivan said.

Lock nodded. He started to walk away.

"You got anything I can use?" Ivan asked.

Lock turned back. "You could use a few meetings," he said with a smile.

Ivan grinned and stayed put.

Lock reached into his pocket, withdrew his wallet, and pulled out all the cash. He thrust the bills at Ivan.

"Two hundred and twenty, forty, sixty, seventy, and one, two, three," Ivan said. "You're giving me two hundred and seventy-three bucks?"

Lock nodded and hobbled off. From a dozen paces away, he paused and looked back. "Good luck with that," he said.

"You sure you're okay?"

Lock kept going.

A couple of minutes later, in the middle of a block of shops, Lock arrived at a storefront. He hesitated a moment, and with a twinge of regret, he smashed his elbow through a small plane of glass in the door and reached through the window to release the deadbolt.

Lock entered the store and kicked the door closed behind him. A piece of loose glass fell to the sidewalk and shattered. He stood in a front room that had once housed a bar, now converted into what looked something like a modest coffee shop.

The frosted glass of the window read: "Bill's Cafe and Hang-About." And under that, in smaller letters: "Liquor License Revoked by Order of the State of Inebriation."

Lock made his way through the shop and into a larger room in the rear. A couple dozen folding chairs faced an oak podium on a small stage. Next to the podium, there was a microphone on a stand. Lock stood alone in the room where he had attended countless AA meetings. He staggered up onto the stage, looked around, and switched on a lamp.

His every motion caused him pain. Even standing was taxing, and his breathing was shallow and deliberate. He leaned into the microphone and addressed the room of empty chairs.

"Is this thing on?"

His voice was scratchy and rough, and it echoed in the dim room.

"I guess not."

He found the little slide switch and turned it on. He tapped the head of the microphone and the sound reverberated, a giant fist knocking on the door of a dungeon.

"That's better."

He found an unopened bottle of water under the podium, cracked the cap, and gulped. He looked across the room. Along one side, a dry-erase board rested on an easel. Printed across the top, the name of that morning's AA meeting: "Rise & Shine ... for a Change. Next meeting – Thursday, November 24 – 6:30 a.m. Guest speaker: Lock G."

The wall clock read 2:33.

Lock leaned into the microphone and said, "Looks like I'm early."

He took a deep breath, rubbed his eyes and cleared his throat. He removed the microphone from the stand. In his imagination, Warren—the AA group leader—was on stage with him. Lock reached out and pretended to hand the microphone to him.

"Ladies and gentlemen. It is my pleasure to introduce Lock G., this morning's speaker."

Lock surveyed the room, imagining it full of familiar faces. He could see them all. He changed positions onstage and became himself again.

"Thanks, Warren," he said, and he leaned away from the microphone. He moved close to it again and said, "Most of you know Lock. Today, he has three hundred and sixty–five consecutive days clean and sober."

Lock said, "Consecutive?"

He imagined the crowd laughing.

Lock moved to the podium, hands and forearms resting on the top. Warren faded away.

"I once asked Abby how long I had to keep saying 'I'm a recovering alcoholic' when I introduce myself," said Lock. "He said until I was tired of being one." He looked around the empty room.

"Of course, Abby sometimes speaks cryptically," he said. "Anyway, for those of you who don't know, Abby is my AA sponsor and much more than that. He taught me that addiction was simply the illusion of having control, and learning that saved my life. One year ago today, he dragged me out of his office…"

Lock turned to where Abner Schlamm usually sat. Lock imagined Abby—looking every week of his seventy-five or so years—with his plaid golf cap resting on his knee, watching intently. Lock pointed to an empty seat.

"…and poured me into that chair right there."

At that moment, Lock felt a stabbing sensation in his gut and turned his face away from the non-existent audience to wince. He took a deep breath and turned back.

"Abby, you surprised to see I've logged in a full year? No?"

Lock imagined Abby's grin.

"Today is my first time being the speaker," he said. "And I'm plenty nervous. You coached me yesterday. 'Just keep it simple,' you told me. 'Just tell what it was like, what happened, what it's like now.'" Lock placed the microphone back into the stand and dropped his hands to his sides. "Okay, I'll tell you."

Lock swallowed hard. He tugged at his lower lip and said, "Abby, you know I love you. You put on the humble bit, but I know you think you're a great recovering alcoholic, that you know all the tricks. Well, you do. At least, most of them. And you're a great boss, too. No one cares more than you about the kids we're responsible for at work. And despite my messed-up past, you insisted I come to work with you. Your only requirement was that I try to stop drinking. Thank you so much for twisting my arm and getting me to come work at CPS. We do important things there. I remember on my first day, you told me, 'It's only about our kids here. We take care of them when no one else does. And when people hurt them, we track them down and put them in small rooms with steel bars.' That's why they call the staff 'Abner's Renegades'—because you encourage us to be overzealous, even overstep our authority, when it comes to protecting children."

Lock took a pull from the water bottle. He pressed his gut. Tiny beads of sweat formed on his brow.

"Now, let's talk about those kids, Abby," Lock said. "The Mannheim kids in particular."

The imagined audience was silent, watching.

"I have something to tell you, and this'll probably keep you tossing and turning for a few nights. You have world-class instincts. You started out on the right trail. Right away, you said it wasn't Wittley Mannheim who caused the crash."

Lock saw Abner blanch.

"And you said it wasn't Natalie Mannheim in it alone. There had to be someone else. Poor old Abby. You were so proud to see your boy Lochlan get clean and sober. "

Lock paused and looked around the room.

"Bad bet this time, Abby," Lock said. "You bet on me. I'm the one to blame for the Mannheim child's death. You didn't get it because you loved me too much. You didn't see what was right in front of your face."

Lock winced.

"When it came to adding it all up, you couldn't get it right like you usually do. I was in your blind spot." He pictured Abner's face draining, his cap falling to the floor. "Me. Lochlan Gilkenney. Killer."

Lock took another slug of water and grimaced.

"Take it easy, Abby. I'm going to tell you everything. You're not going to have to wonder about anything."

Lock focused on Abner's anguished face.

"Sometimes I wonder if maybe you figured out what happened," Lock said, "but not why. Well, here's why. I did it because I finally wanted to have a family and I thought I was so close. I was in love with a woman who I thought loved me back. Because I wanted someone to have children with. I never imagined anyone would get hurt. If nothing else, I want you to believe that about me. I did it because there were a couple of kids who needed a real, loving father. I wanted a pretty place to live instead of lonely rooms on the second floor of somebody's carriage house. For the first time in forty-three years, I had a decent chance of having a family—you know that's all I've ever wanted—and what happens? I get bitten by a viper."

Lock gulped sloppily from the water bottle. His elbow slipped off the podium and he nearly fell.

He heard a profanity-laced commotion from out front, and the beam of a flashlight clicked on and searched the darkness of the back room. Sergeant Jattle, her bulk exaggerated by her vest, stood in the door with her gun drawn.

"Who's in here?" she shouted. "Let's see some hands." The flashlight searched wildly.

Lock knew that voice.

"I'm getting ready to let my dog loose," she said, "and you're getting ready to get shot."

Lock, weak and slurring, spoke from the stage. "Hey Jattle," he said, "Red Cedar Woods police have K–9 now? News to me."

The flashlight immediately found Lock's face.

"Lock! You—there's broken glass everywhere. You do this?"

"Couldn't find my key, and I have to set up for the early meeting. I'm today's coffee boy. Sorry about that. I tried to be quiet."

Sergeant Jattle found the switch and flipped it. Overhead lights illuminated the room. She looked around, glared at Lock, and holstered her gun.

"You can smash a window quietly?" she asked.

She turned her head and spoke into the radio clipped to her shoulder. Lock couldn't hear much of what she said other than "Lock Gilkenney" and "AA clubhouse" and "moron."

"Don't worry about it," Lock said. "There are spare panes of glass and caulk in the storeroom. A minute to sweep up, a minute to put the pane in place, and half a minute to squirt the caulk. I can fix it fast, and it's better than dealing with twenty cranky caffeine freaks at six thirty in the morning."

"It's two thirty, Lock," Jattle said. "Four hours early to make instant coffee? Now I'm stuck writing up an attempted burglary report."

Jattle walked closer and peered at Lock. He was holding his gut and didn't look well. "What's wrong with you?" she asked, pointing to his stomach.

Lock moved his hand away.

"It's my side. I moved a heavy entertainment center. By myself. Pulled a muscle or something."

Jattle made a face. "If I didn't know you belonged here, Lock, I'd take you into custody, but I'm not going to arrest someone for being a jerk. And clean up the broken glass on the sidewalk."

Lock stood up straight, gripping the podium with one hand. He waited a couple of minutes until she was gone and then looked back into the imaginary audience at Abner. "Enough of the opening act, Abby," he said. "Here's what happened. You're not going to like it."

Lock imagined Abner clenching his teeth.

"Remember a few weeks back—November first?" Lock asked. "I fielded the Mannheim call. First thing I did was drive out to their place, out past Deep Pond Road. Unannounced, like you taught me. Around one thirty. We had an anonymous report of neglected children. No further information. I took a shot that the mom would be there. She was."

2

Three weeks earlier

On Monday afternoon, Lock drove the blue county car out to Red Cedar Woods. He wore a tailored navy blue suit. The address was an enormous farmhouse surrounded by stands of mature trees, wildflowers, and grazing horses.

The house had a vast front lawn, at least an acre. At the foot of the driveway stood a wrought-iron gate, high and ornate, flanked by two vigilant stone lions. A couple of decomposing newspapers lay on the grass. The gate was open. Lock drove through and pulled up close to the house. He got out, carrying a file folder attached to a clipboard. A kid's bike and a few toys lay on the lawn by the side door.

Lock rang the bell. He waited a full minute. No answer. He knocked loudly, and a young woman answered, wearing rubber gloves and holding a soapy dish scrubber. She shuffled her round body to music from her earbuds. Lock looked around at the spacious kitchen.

He glanced at his clipboard.

"I'm looking for Mrs. Natalie Mannheim."

The girl reached for the clipboard.

"I'll take it," she said loudly.

"Nothing to take. I want to speak with Mrs. Mannheim."

"Oh," she said, squinting at him. "Okay. I guess you can come in."

Lock stepped past her into the kitchen and set the clipboard down on the countertop. He slid the envelope out from under its clamp. He leaned against the counter, waiting for the girl to get Mrs. Mannheim.

The kitchen was immaculate but contained no evidence of use, no sign that a family spent mornings in it together. There was no fresh fruit, no hanging garlic, no plants. Sterile.

"Actually, I can take that for you," she said, nodding toward the clipboard.

"Please tell Mrs. Mannheim an investigator with the Brandywine County Child Protective Services is here and needs to speak with her."

Again, over the music in her head, the girl shouted. "Sorry, Mr. Mannheim's not home yet."

He reached toward the girl with the intention of yanking out her earbuds, but then thought better of it.

"I asked for *Mrs.* Mannheim."

The young woman scowled.

"I'm here because I'm following up on some information we received," Lock said.

A voice came from beyond a partially open sliding glass door at the far side of the kitchen. From his viewpoint—mostly obstructed by the kitchen island and the spotless pots, pans, and cooking utensils suspended over it—Lock could see someone else entering the room. Another woman, most likely Natalie Mannheim. "There's a car in the driveway, Candice. It's not Carlo, is it? We talked about that." She saw Lock and asked, "Who's this?"

"Don't know. He just came to the kitchen door," Candice said.

Lock retrieved the clipboard from the countertop, knowing it demonstrated authority. A clipboard told the people he visited that there was already paperwork—that the county had been thinking about them for who knew how long. It put them on the defensive. People didn't like the idea that the authorities had been watching them. In Lock's experience, it didn't make them any more likely to tell the truth, but their nervousness made it easier for him to spot the lies.

The woman slid the door closed behind her and took a few steps toward Lock, holding out her hand. "I'm Natalie Mannheim," she said.

She was pretty. More than pretty. She was barefoot, maybe five years younger than him and wore her hair short. She had a white shawl draped over her shoulders, just sheer enough to make Lock think she didn't have much on underneath it. Lock dropped his eyes for a moment and noticed her toes, each one bejeweled with colorful, exotic stones set in silver rings. He looked her in the eye and shook her hand.

"I'm Lochlan Gilkenney, an investigator from Brandywine County Child Protective Services."

Candice looked at Mrs. Mannheim. "I thought it was some delivery or something for Witt."

Mrs. Mannheim scowled. "This has something to do with Witt, doesn't it?" She looked Lock up and down.

"Witt is Wittley Mannheim? Your husband?"

She nodded.

"Right now, we don't know the situation. That's why I'm here," Lock said.

Mrs. Mannheim took a step toward Lock. "Get out. Get out of my house right this instant. You have no right to be here. I swear I'll call the police."

"If I don't call them first."

Mrs. Mannheim folded her arms and sighed. "There's no reason for you to be here. My kids are fine."

"There's nothing to get upset about," Lock said. "I have a few standard questions. I just need to make certain the children are okay."

"I told you they're fine."

"And as soon as I'm sure of that, I'll go. I'm sure you have a lot to do today, and so do I." Lock looked at the table and the chairs around it.

"Okay, yes. Please sit down. I'm sorry, I know you're just doing your job."

She paused, and Lock knew she had missed his name. The rich ones usually did at first.

"Lock Gilkenney."

Mrs. Mannheim nodded. "Candice, is there any coffee for Mr. Gilkenney?"

"I just washed the carafe," Candice said. She didn't offer to make more.

"Never mind," Mrs. Mannheim said. Candice lingered at the sink, wiping a dishcloth back and forth on the countertop.

Lock slid a chair out from under the kitchen table, sat down, and opened the file folder clamped to the clipboard. He removed a few sheets of paper and scanned each one quickly. She sat down across from him and folded her hands, resting them on the table.

"Okay, Mrs. Mannheim—"

"It's Natalie."

"Natalie, then. We received a report about your children," Lock said, eyes still on the forms. "Two young females, names and ages unknown. Someone says there may be a problem."

"Who says that? What kind of problem?"

Lock read, "Not getting prescribed medication, car seats aren't used. Inadequately dressed for cold weather conditions."

"That's ridiculous," Natalie said, unfolding her hands and pointing at the paperwork. "How could someone say my kids aren't getting their medicine but not even know their names?"

"Good question. Who do you think called this in?"

"Wild guess? My husband. Or his lawyer."

Lock leaned back to take a pen from his pants pocket and made a note. "You and your husband are having problems?"

"Something like that. Witt's ringing up lots of hours with a divorce lawyer. And reporting me to the authorities is part of some game they're playing."

Lock rocked back on his chair and stretched toward a photograph on the nearby refrigerator. He tugged it out from under a magnet and examined it.

"You have two children. There are three in this photo."

"The big one is their cousin from Seattle," said Natalie. "The two younger ones are mine."

Lock consulted his papers and made more notes. He looked back at the photograph and studied the faces and body language of the girls. Nothing appeared to be out of the ordinary.

"Names and ages, please?"

"Dahlia. She's two years old. And Edwina, she's four, going on fifteen. Do I have to answer your questions?"

"No. I can fax them to the Red Cedar Woods police and they can stop by to discuss it. It's up to you."

"I wouldn't have to answer them, either, would I?"

"Eventually you would, but that's not really the issue here. Mrs. Mannheim, I'm not here to cause you trouble. I'm here to make sure your children are okay. It's an inconvenience, and a little scary, I know. But if you'll answer my questions, I'll be out of your hair quicker."

"Go ahead," she said. "I wouldn't want you to write down that I'm being uncooperative."

"Thank you."

"The older one's name—Edwina—that was Witt's idea," Natalie said. "J. Wittley Mannheim, Jr.," she said in a voice like an MC at a charity award ball. "Why I went along with the name Edwina, I can't tell you—and now she's stuck with it. Edwina. Any day now, they'll start calling her 'Eddie' for short. Anyway, letting him name her Edwina is your proof that I really am an irresponsible mother." She pressed her wrists together and held them out across the table toward Lock. "Handcuff me and take me away from here. Please."

"I don't have handcuffs."

"I bet you do," she said. Lock met her mocking eyes for a second and crooked an eyebrow. He glanced away. She didn't. He caught himself starting to smile.

Natalie looked toward Candice. "Candice, can you water the ivy in the living room and check the wash?"

Candice headed out of the kitchen, but Lock stopped her. "Hold up, Candice."

She didn't hear him.

"Candice!" Natalie said, raising her voice loud enough to be heard over the music.

Candice stopped and turned around.

He raised his voice too. "Please take the earbuds out." He waited for her to do it and said, "You see the Mannheims all the time. What's your opinion of how the kids are doing?"

"I'm not here *all* the time. I'm just the nanny," she said with a smirk.

"Answer the man's question, Candice."

Candice shrugged. "The kids are fine. I make sure of it, and so does Natalie."

"What about Mr. Mannheim?"

"He's an asshole. Always yelling, always so negative, and ten times worse when he's drinking."

Natalie frowned at Candice's choice of words, but Lock didn't think she disagreed with her.

"Have you ever seen him be inappropriate with the kids?" Lock asked.

"No."

"Do you think someone saw you with the children—at a playground or store or somewhere—and called in a complaint about you?"

"I take care of Dahlia and Edwina great. Only a liar would say anything bad."

"It's true," Natalie said.

Lock made another note. He said, "What's your last name, and how long have you worked for the Mannheims?"

"Candice. Taylor. T–A–Y–L–O–R. And I've worked here almost a year."

"Thanks for your help," Lock said.

Natalie said, "Can you get my blue dress out of the dryer? It's going to wrinkle."

Candice made a face. "You're going to wear that blue-and-beige thing? Why?"

"Now, please," Natalie said. After Candice left, she turned to Lock and shrugged. "She's sassy as hell, but the kids love her."

Lock asked, "Where are the children now?"

"Locked in the basement," she said.

Lock laughed, surprised. "Well then, I think we're done here. Thanks for your time."

She smiled at him and said, "They're at Red Cedar Woods Children's Academy," she said. "The driver drops them here around three thirty." She glanced at the clock on the oven. "They'll be here any minute now."

"If they're in school, why do you have a nanny?" he asked.

"She's mostly for nights and weekends," Natalie said. "And she does some of the cleaning, too. Plus, she's the only one with the key to the basement."

Lock laughed again. She stood and said, "Sorry, I need to put something else on. I'm freezing in here. I was taking care of my flowers when you showed up, and it's almost eighty in the solarium."

Lock watched her walk out of the room, and he thought she knew he was watching her. He smiled and shook his head. She wasn't as bad as he had first thought. Bored, disappointed in her marriage, maybe, but not a bad person. He hoped that whatever he discovered during his investigation wouldn't ruin that perception.

She returned soon wearing yoga pants and a sweatshirt and went to the refrigerator. "Water?" she asked.

"No thanks. You keep flowers?" Lock said.

"Blue orchids," she said, and then, "Actually, there's no such thing as a blue orchid. It's a lie. Orchids are found in nature in every color except blue and black. The blue ones you see in a garden center or grocery store, they're dyed. Future blooms will be white. My orchids are a shade of purple as close to a blue as you can get. That's why I'm going to win the prize at the Philadelphia Flower Show in March."

He watched her pour a glass of water from a pitcher, and in the reflection on the sliding glass door, she caught his eye.

"Are you sure you're from Brandywine County?" she asked. "You dress better than I'd expect. Are you sure you're not a private investigator for my husband?"

"Practically certain."

She sat down again, and he handed her his business card. Their fingers touched for a moment. She rubbed her thumb over the gold-embossed official county shield on Lock's card.

"That complaint you have?" she said. "Probably Humphries's idea. Humphries is Witt's lawyer. It's based on nothing."

"Filing a false report to a government authority is serious business."

"I'm sure it is. I hope my husband gets in trouble. In August, we went to a marriage counselor," she said. "Witt has a thing for girls half his age. Every one of them looks identical. They usually look something like me, only younger. I just had my thirty-fifth birthday. There was this one he flirted with for hours over the counter at a mall jewelry store. He leaves Edwina in charge of her little sister on a bench in the mall. A four-year-old watching a baby not even two years old. In a mall. Someone called security, and security called the police. They couldn't find Witt for twenty minutes."

Lock made a note.

"Which mall?"

"Concord. Witt told the police he had his eye on the kids the whole time. He said it wouldn't happen again. The marriage counselor told him if that kind of thing gets to court, the judge would see that the more reliable parent gets primary custody. Witt laughed at the counselor and told her that his lawyer said it would take more than that."

"He's probably right."

"Witt does the math fast," she said. "He'd have to pay child support. Ten or fifteen thousand a month, I guess. You're here because Humphries is trying to build a case against me so Witt gets sole custody and doesn't have to pay."

"Ten or fifteen thousand?"

She shrugged. "He's not stupid. He's good at making money."

Lock made another note. "You understand that I need to see your children and I need to talk to Mr. Mannheim." He put his notes into the envelope. "I'll tell you, though, that based on what you've told me and my observations here this afternoon, I don't get the sense that your kids are in imminent danger, so..." He opened his calendar. "How's tomorrow night? I'll come back and see the children and Mr. Mannheim. Tuesday. Seven thirty?" he said.

"Sorry. Yoga practice with the instructor at his studio. No last-minute cancels, or I'm out one hundred and twenty-five dollars."

"This is important," he said.

"I know," she said. "I really do. It's fine. I'll talk to him. I've never canceled before, so maybe he'll make an exception."

Lock looked at his calendar again. "How about the night after, then? Wednesday. Seven thirty. Do you need to call your husband to make sure he'll be available?"

"He'll be here, believe me. Too much of a control freak to miss this."

There was a knock at the door. Candice came in from another room and walked past Lock and Natalie. She opened the door. The driver and two young children came into the kitchen.

"They're home," the driver said. "And look what little Edwina has to show you."

Candice took the younger child into her arms and left the room. Lock watched them leave. He had wanted to get a good look at both kids.

Edwina dropped her coat onto the tile floor, ran to her mother, crawled into her lap, and waved a brightly painted papier-mâché object in her face. The coat told Lock that at least today the kids weren't underdressed. And the way Edwina had run to her mother was at least some evidence of a loving relationship. That made him feel a kind of relief, and he knew he was allowing himself to take her side before he knew enough.

Natalie took the papier-mâché from her daughter's hand and examined it. "This is wonderful, honey. What is it?"

"You know, silly," the child said. "It's White-Mane."

Natalie looked at Lock. "That's her pony."

Lock put his pen down and turned in his seat to Edwina. He looked at the child's creation and smiled. "Is your real pony in your bedroom?"

"No!" Edwina said, laughing.

"White-Mane is out in the barn. He's real," said Natalie.

"If your pony's mane is white," Lock said, "why did you paint it blue? Is that your favorite color?"

Then Edwina pushed herself back further into her mother's lap and buried her head into Natalie's chest. Lock looked for bruises, but Edwina was wearing leggings and a sweater. Her behavior showed none of the telltale signs of abuse, no extreme shyness or clinging or crying without apparent cause.

"That's Mr. Lock, honey. He's our friend. You can answer him."

"No."

"That's okay," Natalie said.

"See you in the morning," the driver said.

"Thank you, Jackson," Natalie said. "We won't forget your coffee tomorrow morning. Sorry about that."

"That's okay, ma'am," he said, closing the door behind him.

Edwina wriggled the papier-mâché pony free from her mother's grasp and slid off her lap. She approached Lock and held the little pony out to him.

"Do you want to keep this forever?" she said. "It's White-Mane."

"Could I really? I would keep him forever, and I would feed him and brush him every day."

Edwina laughed again. "Okay," she said.

Lock took it and set it on the table and admired it. "What should I feed him?"

"Apples and oats. He even eats apples with brown spots on them. He doesn't care."

"That's good, because I don't eat the ones with brown spots," Lock said. "Thank you so much, Edwina."

"Okay, honey," Natalie said. "Go see what Candice and Dahlia are up to."

Edwina gave her and Lock another look before walking toward the other room.

"Say goodbye to Mr. Lock," Natalie said.

"Can he stay and eat dinner with us?" Edwina said.

"Not tonight, honey, maybe some other night."

Edwina pouted.

Lock said, "Thank you so much for White-Mane, Edwina."

The child skipped out of the room, and Natalie stood up. "So? Did I pass?"

"She seems fine, Mrs. Mannheim," he said, writing on a form. "She looks fine."

"My name is Natalie. Please don't call me Mrs. Mannheim. It reminds me of Mr. Mannheim."

"Natalie. Got it." Lock continued to write.

"Anything else, then?"

He looked up and they locked eyes for a moment.

"Uh, yes, a couple of things. Any chance you could call the nanny to bring the little one—"

"Dahlia."

"Any chance you could bring Dahlia back? I'd like to meet her."

Natalie nodded and called, "Candice? Can you come in here with Dahlia?"

Candice appeared instantly, holding Dahlia in her arms.

"Were you standing in the hallway listening to us?" Natalie asked.

"Not at all. I don't eavesdrop."

"Not much," Natalie said. "Give me Dahlia."

Candice handed Dahlia over, and Natalie gave the child a hug and set her down on the floor. She immediately crawled to Lock and pulled herself up into a standing position, using Lock's pant leg as a grip.

"May I pick her up?" he asked Natalie.

"Of course," she said. "You're very good with kids."

Lock smiled and said, "Best part of the job." He picked her up and sat her on his knee. He looked her over. She seemed normal in weight and height, her color was good, and there was no bruising he could see. Dahlia extended both of her arms toward Natalie and whimpered. Lock immediately handed her over, though he wished he could hold her for a little longer. He loved the contradictory lightness and solidity of little children and their moment-to-moment way of navigating each day. They met the world with no preconceptions. A child was an empty cup to pour the whole universe into. All they needed was to be nurtured and loved, and they became people. Lock had always thought that was a kind of magic, the way you could just put a seed into dirt and something wholly different grew from it.

He smiled at Natalie, and he knew from the look on her face that his smile must have reflected some sadness. He could tell she wanted to ask him a question, but he shook his head. He lived with his losses, and he thought he wouldn't mind telling her about them, but not now. This was work, not friendship.

The baby struggled to stand up in her mother's lap. Natalie helped her. Dahlia threw her arms around Natalie's neck and craned around to see Lock. He forced a smile.

"And what do you think of her? Starved and beaten?"

"I don't think it's a good idea to say things like that in front of her," Lock said.

"You think she understands?"

"Yes, I do. And no, I don't see any sign of anything wrong. She seems happy and healthy."

"I'm glad you think so. You know, you love your kids so much, it's scary to think someone is saying you don't. That you might lose them because of it."

"I understand," Lock said. "I don't want you to worry. Remember, I'm not here to find you guilty of anything. I'm just here to make sure the kids are okay. If they're okay, you don't have anything to worry about."

"You don't know my husband," Natalie said. "Money and lawyers. The whole point of money and lawyers is so that people like me always have to worry. Sorry, I know I sound bitter."

"It's okay, and I know what you mean. I've been doing this a long time," Lock said. He wrote some notes and then began to gather the papers and put them into the envelope. "All right," he said. "Here's the procedure. Wednesday night, you, your husband, the nanny, and the kids will all need to be here. I'll talk to Edwina privately for a few minutes, then the nanny can take her, and then I'll speak with their father, and then we'll all talk together. That's the procedure."

"That's fine with me," said Natalie. She looked up and caught his eye. "What if he isn't cooperative?" she asked. "What if Humphries tells him to keep his mouth shut?"

"Not likely. I'm sure he'll want to cooperate."

"Don't be so sure. Anyway, you can make a note that I'd like to cooperate fully. Anything you want."

He smiled and pretended to write. "Noted," he said.

She tilted her head, trying to catch his eye again, but he kept his eyes focused on his paperwork, busying his hands with the forms. When he was done, he gathered his papers and got up to go. She was still looking at him, a curious look on her face. Lock thought she wasn't used to her flirtations being ignored. She smiled suddenly, and he reddened, sure she knew exactly what he had been thinking. She reached out and touched his shoulder, and he shifted the clipboard from one hand to the other.

He said, "Your children are beautiful. Edwina is adorable. What a personality."

He picked up White-Mane.

"Don't throw White-Mane in the trash," Natalie said.

"I promised Edwina I'd take care of him," he said. "Maybe not the feeding and brushing part." They both smiled at that. "But I'll keep him. He's going on my mantel."

Lock saw she was about to say something, but instead she led him to the door.

"I think we're finished for now," he said. "Seven thirty. Wednesday. There may be another investigator with me, a woman. She may examine the children briefly."

Natalie extended her hand, and they shook.

"Seven thirty, Wednesday," she said.

It's a date, Lock thought, and then, *It's not a date, it's an interview, stupid.* Lock nodded and walked to his car.

As he turned the car around, he looked back at the house and saw the huge solarium. *That's "greenhouse" to you and me*, he thought. The windows were fogged over, but he could see the dim form of Natalie standing and watching him. *Ghost and her flowers*, he thought. He made sure White-Mane was safe on the passenger seat and accelerated slowly down the long drive. As young girls often did, Natalie Mannheim's kids had reminded him of his Hannah, and he felt a pang, wondering what things like White-Mane she might have given him.

He cleared his throat and shook his head and, as was his habit, let his eyes roam over the trees on the property. Trees were his infatuation. He was obsessed with trees. Reading about them, traveling near and far to see various specimens, touching them, photographing them, taking notes, imagining himself a kid climbing them. Next to White-Mane and his work papers on the passenger seat was his book, something like a birder's life list, but for trees. It was a hand-bound notebook with a scuffed leather cover, and a little pen held in place with two elastic loops, and a frayed ribbon that served as a bookmark. It was simple but well-made, and soft in the hand from years of use.

He slowed the car and squinted beyond the house at the towering tree in the middle of the backyard. He looked at it for a long moment. There were a couple dozen albino redwoods in California, huge trees with white needles, but it was hard to believe this might be one. Seeing one had always been on Lock's must-see list, but he had never made it out to California.

Anyway, he didn't think a redwood could survive north of Virginia, or maybe Maryland, and an albino needed a parent tree—they didn't produce chlorophyll, so they joined their roots to the parent in order to survive. Brandywine County was too far north, too cold, and there was no sign of a parent tree, so it must have been something else. Interesting, though, maybe even something new to him.

Most people didn't notice trees, Lock had realized years ago. They knew what a maple was, what an oak was, maybe different kinds of pines, but they were background to lives that moved quickly. Trees were too dependable and too abundant for most people to appreciate. When they saw one that was different, they may or may not remark on it, but that would be it. Few would wonder if they were seeing something unique, a zebra in a herd of horses. Lock almost turned the car around to ask Natalie if he could have a look at it, but he didn't. He told himself if was inappropriate, but deeper in his mind, he was doing the math—it wouldn't happen during the next visit, not while the husband was there. So maybe there was a reason for a visit after that.

He turned away and started the car moving again, a smile on his face. That was the thing about trees. They could surprise you if you knew to look for something different, something new.

Traffic was slow on the way back to the office. As he often did, Lock considered the case as he drove. On the face of it, it was a routine he said, she said. Lock saw it all the time. It was a sad reality that people going through a divorce often used their kids against one another. Fire and forget, like a cruise missile, never a thought given to what it did to the children.

There was nothing to it, as far as he could tell. The kids were fine. Dahlia seemed well, and Edwina was adorable. There was probably nothing to the complaint, though he was experienced enough to know that the worst child abusers often had nearly perfect social camouflage. You had to run down each case, no matter what it looked like at first, and he looked forward to doing that.

Nothing's going to happen with Natalie, he told himself. *She's from money, and it's natural for her to play nice with the guy that's investigating her.* There were a hundred reasons to forget about her. He kept thinking about her toes, though, and those toe rings. They were fancy, erotic in a way he couldn't describe. Any other time, her feet would have been hidden by shoes. Lock felt like he had seen a secret part of Natalie's life, something she did just for herself. *Or her husband,* he thought, but then shook his head. She wasn't doing anything for Wittley Mannheim anymore.

Natalie. In his cubicle, he wrote up his report about the Mannheims but didn't lay out his suspicions that the allegations were trumped up. He could add that later if further investigation supported the conclusion—a couple more visits to Red Cedar Woods, just to be sure.

3

Marked and unmarked police cars congregated in the parking lot of the Brandywine Mall Cineplex, where officers were questioning a middle-aged man wearing a windbreaker and rumpled khaki pants. About twenty yards away, other officers were talking with a gangly boy and his mother.

Abner, in a jacket, an ancient wide tie and one of his trademark caps, was there with Lock. He chewed on a sprig of licorice root, which hung out of his mouth like a cigarette. He still worked in the field despite the crushing load of his administrative duties, and sometimes he came with Lock on calls. Lock had let him take the lead on this one, which had come in late in the day. He liked to watch Abby work, and he knew Abby enjoyed calls like this one.

Abby leaned in close and poked the man in the belly with his finger.

"You should wise up," Abby said.

"Hey!" the man said, backing away from the poke. "Nothing to wise up about," he added, putting his hand over his belly.

Lock smiled. He never touched the people he was sent to interview. It was against the rules, and technically assault. But Abby had a presence about him. You just knew that if someone complained to the cops about being poked by an angry old man like Abby, the cops would figure the guy had it coming.

"This is embarrassing," the man said. "And there's a crowd now." He turned away from the gathering throng.

A teenager shouted, "Cuff him!" and his friends jeered. They couldn't have known why the man was being questioned, but that didn't stop them. It was that kind of town. Other people's misfortune was good entertainment. Lock shook his head. No doubt, thirty years before he would have been one of the kids jeering.

Abby glared at the suspect. "Of all the seats in a practically empty movie theater, you sit next to a little boy all by himself? Plus, you fit the description."

"Maybe I fit it, but it wasn't me," the man said. "And there were other people in that theater. I was toward the back and the kid was near the middle. Didn't even know it was a kid. I'm no pervert."

"Then why did the officer have to chase you?" Abby asked.

"I didn't know he was calling to me. My name's not 'Yo!' And he's in street clothes, not a uniform."

"Who has this guy's I.D.?" Abby asked.

A nearby officer stepped forward and handed Abby a Pennsylvania driver's license. Abby read it and said, "Michael Densen." He looked at Lock. Lock shook his head—he hadn't heard the name before.

Abby compared the picture to the man, then held it out to a plainclothes officer standing nearby. "Can you run this guy and see if you have anything on him?"

The cop nodded and headed back to his cruiser.

"I already told you I was in the theater. I'm not denying that."

The boy, a redhead wearing a short-sleeved shirt despite the November chill, edged closer, prodded by his mother.

Lock took over while Abby bent over and whispered to the boy.

"What do you do for a living, Mr. Densen?" he asked.

While Densen sputtered his way through an explanation of why he was at the movies in the middle of the day, Lock watched the boy crane his neck so he could see the man over Abby's shoulder. The boy nodded. Abby straightened up and patted him on the head.

"Okay, son. Thank you," Abby said, turning to the boy's mother. "We have your information. We'll be in touch if we learn anything we can act on."

"Aren't you arresting that freak?" the mother asked. She narrowed her eyes at Abby.

Abby turned back to the man, then to the mother.

"Your son says the man had a red Phillies cap and sunglasses. We had a half dozen guys searching under the seats and in trashcans. Can't find a Phillies cap or sunglasses. Nothing."

The plainclothes officer walked over from his car holding the man's license.

"Well?" Abby asked.

"Mr. Clean. But his license says he's required to wear glasses while driving."

Abby looked at the man. "What about that? Where are they, your glasses?"

The man pointed a finger at his eyes. "Contacts."

The boy's mom started to make a fuss. Abby held up a hand. Lock moved a little closer to her and put a hand on her arm to give her a sense someone was on her side. He knew Abby, and he knew he was about to pounce.

A news van pulled up, and within seconds a reporter, an assistant, and a cameraman were setting up.

"Okay, pal, you can go. But before you do, I want to tell you, this whole thing is making me thirsty."

"What's that got to do with me?"

"I'll tell you what it has to do with you," Abby said, moving closer to the man. "I've been in this business for forty-one years. I've seen hundreds of predators—and when I see one, I start getting thirsty for a stiff drink. And being here with you for just a few minutes, I'd do just about anything for three fingers of scotch."

The man's round face reddened in aggravation. "What the hell are you talking about?"

Abby reached up, removed his cap and ran his hand down the back of his head. He said, "The problem with hats is they mess up your hair. You know what I mean, right?"

"Can I go now?" the man asked. Now he looked more annoyed than scared.

Lock had seen it before—Abby liked to think out loud, and sometimes people thought he was just some crazy old guy.

"Now I notice your hair," Abby said, "and how it looks like it might have been wearing a hat, and then I look at the bridge of your nose, and I see the little red marks from glasses."

"Why would I wear sunglasses at a movie? Look, man, can I go? I already had enough crazy today. Anyway, you said I could leave."

Lock smiled at that. The guy was getting more annoyed, even aggressive. He touched the mother's arm again, and he could tell she knew Abby was getting close to something.

Abby said, "I did say that. But that was before I got this thirsty."

The man growled. "You're not making any sense. Invisible baseball cap, marks on my nose, disappearing sunglasses. I'm reporting you to the chief of police. You're babbling about whiskey. You're too old to be a cop, or too drunk."

"I'm not a cop, I'm the executive director of the Brandywine County Child Protective Services agency. I have the same privileges as the police to investigate and ask questions. And you're well-advised to answer them. We're not a law-enforcement agency, we're a social service agency. We don't carry guns and we can't arrest you, but I can make that happen fast," Abby said, pointing to a nearby uniformed officer who had been glowering at the man. The officer nodded.

Abby continued, "And if I ask him to, he'll do it. I can get a subpoena faster than you can say 'subpoena.' So don't be such a wise guy. Anyway, I'm tired of you, so you can leave..."

The man smirked.

"... with the police," Abby said. "The boy I.D.'d you, and I know a judge that thinks that's plenty to get a search warrant. What are we going to find at your house, Mr. Densen? Maybe pictures of you with a red Phillies cap on your computer? Maybe other kinds of pictures too, huh?"

Abby gave the high sign to a pair of officers, who took the astonished man into custody and marched him to a waiting unmarked police car.

"Too old or too drunk," Abby said, turning to Lock and the boy's mother and shaking his head. "Imagine the nerve of that guy."

4

A colleague nodded hello to Lock and said, "Big Boss has been paging you every thirty seconds."

"Thanks," said Lock as he kept moving. "Probably a paper jam in his printer," he said, smiling. "Huge crisis."

Under his name on the frosted glass door of Abby's office was the department's motto: "Protect the children, protect the future." Lock touched the words like he always did before entering.

Abby was on the phone, but Lock could barely see him for all the files and clutter piled high on the desk. Abby said goodbye to someone and stood up.

Just then, the phone rang again and Abby answered. He listened for a moment.

"Yes, sir. Of course I have it. It's right here on my desk." Abby rolled his eyes for Lock's benefit. "That's not a kind thing to say about my filing system. What? Okay, well, you can send her down, I'll have it ready."

"The new D.A.," Abby said to Lock as he hung up. "He wants a file that's been available for months, and all of a sudden, he's got to have it instantly."

Lock surveyed Abby's office. He'd been there thousands of times, and each time he was amazed at the amount of clutter. "You must have two hundred piles in here," he said.

"Is that all?"

"Maybe three hundred."

Abby walked around his desk to a side table with a two-foot stack of papers and folders. He ran his finger down the stack, stopped at one folder in particular, and began to tug on it. He gave up when he saw he was about to topple the whole mess.

"Steady these folders for me, son."

Instead, Lock walked over and yanked the folder out perfectly. He handed it to Abby. There was a knock at the door. It was the D.A.'s assistant, a heavyset woman with short, cropped hair.

"Here you go, dear," Abner said, holding the file out to her. "Tell your boss to enjoy himself."

She left without saying a word.

"You wanted me?" asked Lock.

Abby handed Lock a form. "Four Latino kids are supposedly living in one of those storage rental facilities in Kennett Square. Complaint came from the manager, said the kids sleep there at night. Find out what's up."

"And if they're there?"

"Standard procedure," Abby said, disappearing into his chair behind a stack of file boxes. "Get them to an E.R. right away for a medical check, then get them to intake."

Lock nodded and began to leave, complaint form in hand.

"Hey, Lock?" Abby asked. "I have two tickets to the Eagles-Dallas game Sunday. Decent seats."

"What time is the game?"

Abby walked around his desk to a pile of folders. He ran his finger down the pile again and found the folder that contained the schedule. He tried to yank it out as Lock had. Folders flew everywhere.

"Goddamned shit."

"Not sure I can go," Lock said. "Let me know what time when you find your schedule."

He left Abby's office and headed to the break room for a cup of coffee.

Back in his cubicle, Lock arranged and re-arranged some papers, but he couldn't focus his attention on work. He was distracted by the memory of a baseball game he had been excited about when he was fourteen years old.

Lock had saved up one hundred and sixty dollars—he remembered the precise amount—from cutting lawns and shoveling walks. He had planned to use the money to buy a jet-black mountain bike. But then his father invited him to go to a Sunday afternoon major league game. Upon hearing that, Lock quickly headed to the sporting goods store and bought himself a Richie Ashburn fielder's mitt, hoping that maybe he'd impress his father with his purchase and how he'd earned every cent of it himself. He didn't think his father even knew he had a lawn-cutting and snow-shoveling business. Lock fantasized about catching a foul ball right in front of his father. If that happened, that would be the greatest day of his life. For once, his father would have to say something that would let Lock know he was proud of him. That would have been something.

Another reason being invited out by his father was so important was because, while growing up and living at home, Lock never saw much of him. He was a pretty busy guy. His father wasn't one of those work-obsessed absentee fathers. It was more like he was always at this bar or that bar, this poker game or that darts tournament. He was around, all right. It wasn't like he traveled for business, or as if Lock's parents were separated. It was more that he was a drunken son-of-a-bitch, fully self-absorbed and not really giving a damn about anything other than where he could find the next job to replace the most recent one he'd been fired from, usually for showing up drunk or hungover.

On the day of the game, Lock's father was too drunk to go. Lock didn't know why, but he had been buoyed by the certainty that this time he would, for once, actually get to do something fun with his father. Instead, his father fell asleep at noon in a stupor. Lock teared up as he tried to rouse him. He'd been thinking about the game all week long. Lock tried in vain to reach into his father's trouser pockets in search of the tickets. His father woke just enough to slap him across the face and then pass out again.

Lock's mother was at work. She had been sick for years with kidney problems, and being unhappily married didn't help her regain her health. But she worked anyway. She waitressed at a Greek diner a few blocks from the house, but Lock wouldn't have told her about the slapping incident anyway, even if she were home. At fourteen, he had the sense to protect her from his father. Lock's father caused her more pain than he caused Lock by hitting him all the time. But what hurt the most was the way he ignored his son. So instead of a ball game with his dad, he sat in his room and watched reruns of *Star Trek*.

The next morning, on the way to school, Lock dropped the glove into a trashcan behind Greene's drugstore.

Fuck Dad, he thought.

Lock sat at his desk, fiddling with some papers. He pushed the memory away and tried to ignore the queasy feeling in his stomach. He knew he should go to the game with Abby, but he thought he wouldn't. It wasn't fair to Abby, who had been more of a father than his real dad ever had, but as everyone in the office knew too well, things that happened to kids echoed forward through the rest of their lives.

Enough, he thought. He dialed the phone number of the Kennett Square police and arranged to meet them in thirty minutes at the U–Rent–a–Space to look for the kids allegedly living there. When he hung up, he noticed a waiting voicemail. From the caller I.D., he recognized Natalie Mannheim's phone number.

He listened to the message. She wanted him to return that night, a day earlier than scheduled. She must have canceled her yoga lesson. At first, he didn't plan on going, but then he got to thinking about her eyes and the way she had watched him. He decided he would call her after he returned from Kennett Square. He hurriedly left the office.

When he arrived at the storage facility, the police were there. Together with the manager, they found four children, all seemingly in good shape but frightened by the authorities. The group stood outside a shed filled with sleeping bags and a mattress. The manager speculated irritably that the parents were illegal immigrants, and they were nowhere to be found. The children spoke no English, or pretended they didn't. They shrugged without speaking when one of the police officers questioned them.

Lock addressed the tallest of the children, a girl wearing a red shirt and black pants.

"Dónde está tu madre o padre?" He squatted and spoke slowly and softly.

"En el trabajo," she said.

"Dónde trabajan?" Lock asked.

"Ellos trabajan en una granja de hongos," she said. "No te preocupes, ellos vendrán aquí con la comida después."

Lock stood and turned to the police. "Their parents are working at a mushroom farm somewhere, probably Kennett Square. She says they'll be back later with food."

"Let's go lock up their parents," one of the officers said. Two of the smaller children cringed and looked at each other. Obviously those two, at least, spoke enough English to understand.

"We're not arresting anyone," Lock said loudly and clearly, for the benefit of the children. "We just want to make sure these boys and girls are okay."

The police officer said nothing. Lock turned to the children and knelt on the asphalt. "Who likes McDonald's?"

The oldest girl said something to her siblings and their eyes widened.

"We love McDonald's," she said. She barely had an accent. "And my baby brother, Miguel, likes the chalupas at Taco Bell, too." She pointed to a smiling, dirty-faced boy who looked about three.

"Well, that's good, because I know a McDonald's very close to here. All we have to do is wait for my friend who has a bigger car so we can all ride together. McDonald's will be the first place we go."

The girl translated and the kids lit up, hugging each other and hopping up and down.

After a brief stop at a McDonald's drive-thru, it took Lock most of the morning to get the children checked out at the hospital and processed into the child welfare system. Lock knew, of course, that the children would prefer to be with their real parents—regardless of the sleeping conditions—rather than be placed in temporary foster care with outsiders who would give them strange foods and unfamiliar accommodations. It bothered Lock that he was the one officiating over the separation, no matter how brief or how necessary.

He kept thinking about a gin and tonic. But why? This situation was nothing compared to some of the things he'd seen in his profession. If he had children, he knew, he'd dedicate his entire being to them, find a way to provide everything they needed. But these four? What was really better for them? He knew what it felt like to be neglected, but there were different kinds of neglect. As far as he could tell, these kids had parents that loved them, even if they weren't able to take care of them as well as they should have.

Just before noon, after a brief conversation with the temporary foster parents who would care for the kids until the matter was resolved, Lock decided to skip lunch and catch an AA meeting. Something was gnawing at him that he couldn't identify, but he knew through experience that a meeting could be a great cure-all. Meetings reminded him to seek progress, not perfection. Lock drove to the church in Media that hosted the lunchtime meetings and took a seat in the back row.

That day's speaker, a young man wearing a flannel shirt and several days of facial stubble, told how he had come to be a member of the group, explaining that after three failed suicide attempts, he decided to take a different approach to solve his drinking and drug problems. He described how two attempts to hang himself didn't work out—once, the neckties he'd fashioned into a noose broke, and the other time, he didn't make the rope short enough. On his third attempt to end his life, he thought he'd try a gunshot to the head.

"I actually missed, if you can believe that," he said. "All I did was mess up the side of my face a little." He angled his head so the audience could see a deep, angry scar at his temple and a horrifically mangled ear. "Next stop," he said, grinning, "was AA."

Lock made a mental note not to try that—not that he'd never considered ending his life. A decade or so before, after a break-up with a woman he had dated for almost a year, he did more than casually think about it. He spent hours on the Internet, visiting the Hemlock Society website to read up on the most painless and effective suicide methods. From that website, his research took him all over the Internet and into bookstores. He found a paperback, *Final Departure*, in which he read about common, non-violent ways people used to kill themselves.

One approach in particular had appealed to him. He studied the details of assembling a "helium hood" and made note of the supplies he'd need. Certain and fast, just like falling asleep. Before proceeding with his shopping list, he'd toyed with the idea of a suicide note and wondered if he really needed one, and if so, who, besides the police and the medical examiner, would ever see it. To whom would it be addressed? He had no one close to him.

He'd worked on a goodbye letter and jotted down some bullet points first—addiction, alcoholism, depression, loneliness, the unlikelihood of ever being attractive to someone decent enough to have a family with—and then wrote and re-wrote and wrote some more. He couldn't get it to say what he wanted it to say, to where it felt right. He thought it sounded like he was whining, and that was not the impression he wanted to leave.

Lock had then realized a fundamental truth—he didn't want to die. He simply didn't want to be so unhappy. He told himself he was long past due getting clean and sober, and now was the time. The right moment had finally arrived. Upon this realization, he poured his remaining supply of alcohol and cocaine into his garbage disposal and flipped the switch. In an instant, it was gone. He grinned and snapped his fingers. *Goodbye, suicide.*

He'd gone to his first AA meeting with a neighbor. It had no impact on him, and worse, he hated it. One of the first things he heard was an elderly woman joking that someone, someday, would declare that unceasing attendance at AA meetings was itself an addiction.

Lock believed she might be right, so what was the point? He thought the seats were uncomfortable, the coffee not hot enough. Nothing stuck. And he didn't like all the talk about God, which he thought was funny, because he did have confidence that there was some kind of master consciousness at the heart of the universe. He just didn't call it God.

Three days later, he was on his cellphone with his coke supplier as he drove to a bar in Philadelphia. He knew where it would inevitably end. But before things came crashing down around him, he would feel very little pain. *Hello, oblivion.*

But that was then, and although the cravings for cocaine and alcohol continued, sometimes intensely, they were less and less powerful over time. The urges weakened with each passing day. Now he had the tools acquired from AA, and he used them. He had met people he respected who were there to support him. His sponsor told him the key to success was simple—don't drink, don't think, and come to meetings. That made sense.

There had been relapses, but he had stuck with the program. Things couldn't be more different now, and they were radically better—a year of continuous sobriety and a profession he loved. The job was fulfilling, and he helped the helpless every day. He'd never felt better, and he'd been told by an admirer at work he had never looked better, either.

5

Around three o'clock, Lock drove out to see what Natalie wanted. *Bullshit,* he told himself. *You're driving out to see Natalie.* He hadn't returned her voicemail. He wanted to surprise her again.

This time, she wore cut-off jeans and a sea-green t-shirt. It went perfectly with her eyes.

She smiled and swung the door open wider. "Welcome back, Mr. Gilkenney."

"You can call me Lock, if you want."

"Okay, Lock. But probably not in front of my husband." She smiled. "Come on in."

He looked at her as she led him in. She had beautiful legs, and she wore sandals, her toe rings sparkling as she walked.

He walked in and sat at the kitchen table. He opened his clipboard, slid out a folder, and removed a notebook.

She pointed toward the sliding glass door that led to the solarium. "Why don't we talk out there?" she said. "Candice is at the mall with the kids. She won't be back until after dinner, and Witt's in New Jersey until late.

38

And I can't stand being near all these dirty dishes." She flipped her hand at the sink, which was full.

"Sure," Lock said. "I'd like to see your flowers."

He followed her, and when she turned into the solarium, Lock caught a glimpse of what he at first thought was a birthmark on her leg, but it proved to be the tattooed tail of a reddish snake slithering up her leg in the direction of her inner thigh. He made sure to raise his eyes before she looked back at him, but he knew she wouldn't mind if she caught him looking. There was something between them, that much was clear, and Lock knew she had decided—as he had—to find out what it might be.

The solarium was well-equipped. There was a hot tub, a few yards of sand that sloped down to a small built-in pond, a water cooler with an inverted plastic jug sitting on it, a laptop on a stand, and an enormous TV. His eyes wandered around the room, but kept settling on her.

Natalie gestured for Lock to take a seat. He picked the loveseat. A paperback book lay on it, face down.

"What are you reading?" Lock asked.

She picked the book up and moved it to an end table. He sat down, setting his clipboard next to him.

"It's *The Road Less Traveled*," she said. She sat upright on a lounge chair directly across from him and tucked her legs under her in some kind of yoga position. "I'm only halfway through, but it's speaking to me. I love it."

"Life is difficult," Lock said, quoting the first line of the book.

"I'm impressed."

"I always liked that idea," he said. "If you wake up each morning expecting life to be demanding, then suddenly it's not so hard."

"Exactly," she said. "And the hard part is being able to remember that when things go wrong."

Lock retrieved a pen from his pocket. "That is the hard part," he said.

Natalie draped one of her legs over the other, showing more of the snake tattoo. "I want you to hear something before you meet my husband tomorrow night."

"Okay," he said, "but anything you tell me goes into my notes, and it's all discoverable in court. I have to be totally neutral."

"Fine with me," she said, adjusting her t-shirt where it had ridden up her abdomen, exposing a tiny belly-button ring. She took a deep breath and said, "Witt is a spoiled little boy whose father left him nine million dollars. He's the kind of guy you'd think would blow it all. Anyway, we met in a bar and dated for few months. He wasn't that bad, and he made me laugh. I grew up poor. My father was the superintendent of a run-down apartment building in Newark, and we lived in four small rooms in the basement. We didn't even have windows. I never had the kind of security that money brings. We got married five months after we met. He started changing right away, and not for the better. He went from affectionate to cold overnight. Then he took all that money and bought worthless land in Florida. Everyone thought he was a fool. Especially me. Then the developers began to see the land as prime real estate. Thousands of acres. He sold out and quadrupled our money."

"Nothing wrong with money," Lock said, "but what does this have to do with the children?"

She fidgeted and looked away, then took a breath and turned back to Lock. "I was stupid," she said. "I was sick of Witt and I still am. I got bored and lonely and I found someone to hang around with. A guy. Nothing serious, and it's over. I got caught with him at the Four Seasons by some greasy little private detective Witt put on me. I was only intimate with the guy one stupid night, but Witt had something on me and that was what he wanted. And I was surprised at how hurt he was. I thought he couldn't care less what I did. I was wrong about that, too. He'll never forgive me."

Lock looked off into the middle distance, thinking about what he was hearing.

"Am I boring you, Lock?"

"No, I'm listening carefully, waiting for something relevant," Lock said. There wasn't anything else to say, really. He kept his attention on her face and waited for the tie-in to the children, though he thought he knew where she was headed.

"Well, between his lawyers and his private eye, in a divorce I'll probably wind up with something like a thousand a month. I could barely live this way on a thousand a day. My God, yoga lessons twice a week cost me that much. And if he gets custody, I'd just be a visitor in my own kids' lives."

"What's your lawyer say?"

"You mean the lawyer I don't have because I have so little money of my own I can't come up with a retainer fee? He even gives the grocery money directly to Candice. I guess he's afraid if I have it, I'll buy a pack of gum without his say-so. And he pays the yoga instructor by check each month."

"No lawyer? That seems a little naïve for someone like you. You're the one telling me how much is at stake."

"Witt explained why it's better to work it out between us, out of court."

"Better for him, maybe," Lock said. "Keep in mind that if you agree to a custody schedule now, even out of court, you're Krazy-Glued to it. Unless there's a significant change in circumstance, judges aren't wild about altering existing schedules that aren't causing major distress for the children involved."

"See?" she said, her eyes lighting up as she sat upright and leaned forward. "That's the kind of thing I didn't know. Witt's turned off my credit cards and let my checking account run dry. He knows what he's doing."

Lock made an entry in his notebook. "Get a lawyer as soon as you can. You need one. A good custody arrangement is obviously better for your daughters."

Natalie shifted in her seat and rearranged her legs. His chest thumped again, and he thought of what she had told him, that she was so done with Witt that she had found a lover.

"But," Natalie said, "he has every advantage. That's what the fake complaint to your agency is really about. To screw me. He doesn't play fair—reading my email, having people follow me. But I'm expected to stick to the rules."

"Expected by whom?"

She didn't have a ready answer for that. She hesitated. "By me…I guess. And I'll get nothing. And the kids will be with a guy who doesn't really care about them, isn't involved with them, barely knows them. I deserve half of what he's worth, but I'll take forty percent to get it over with."

Lock raised his eyebrows. "Why would he fight you?" he asked. "You say he's worth thirty or forty million. How many steaks can a man eat?"

"He doesn't care what it costs. All he wants is the win. And all I want is a quick out-of-court settlement so I can move on and focus on taking care of the girls. Like I said, not even fifty-fifty. I'm not unreasonable."

The phone rang and Natalie ignored it. "Candice told me her parents had a nasty custody fight when she was in elementary school," she said. "She says what's important to husbands and wives might not matter to a judge, but things you think are too petty to bring up in court, judges might consider crucial. So I don't know what to think or what to do."

"That's true. Judges view testimony and evidence subjectively. You never know what will resonate with them."

"I'm a vegetarian and I raise my girls that way," said Natalie. "But when Witt's alone with the girls, I know for a fact he feeds them meat. To spite me. Would a judge care about that?"

"I doubt it. Yesterday, you mentioned you suspect that your husband drives with the kids in the car while under the influence of alcohol," Lock said. "A judge would certainly care about that. But if you know your husband is drinking and you let him drive them, you're complicit. Next time you think he's DUI, call the police. Get it on record. You're allowed to build a case, too."

"All summer long, he dropped them at the pool at the club," said Natalie. "He had Candice watch them and then he played golf, got loaded, picked them up, and drove them home."

Lock made another note and put his pen down. "There you go. That's an example of what plays well in court. A judge won't like hearing that. But then again, there's a flip side. You just described a guy who's very involved with his children. A judge may care more about that than the drinking. It's tricky. That's why you need a lawyer."

"He did have a fender-bender a few months ago. While drunk. But he didn't even get a ticket—and now a Brandywine Township cop has 76ers season tickets. Our tickets."

Lock picked up his pen again and made another note. She watched him. "Were the kids with him then?"

"No."

"He gave a police officer your basketball tickets to tear up the DUI? I don't know. Bribing a cop…that happens on TV a lot more than in reality."

"All I know is he bragged about it that night. Remember, he wants to win, he doesn't care what it costs. Now that the bribe could come back to bite him, he told me he was kidding about the whole thing. I called the captain of the police department a couple of weeks ago and he blew me off. Said I didn't know the date of the accident or the name of the cop, and that no officer of his would even think about doing something like that. Then when he asked if Witt and I weren't getting along, I hung up on him. Meanwhile, we haven't been to a basketball game all year."

She fidgeted, breathing deeply. She glanced at him, then looked down. "Calling the police on him when he's driving drunk is a great idea," she said. "Thanks for that."

"Don't thank me. I'm not on your side or your husband's side—"

"I know you have to be fair, Lock. But I know you're on my side," she said, smiling and looking down.

Lock smiled and sighed, then put his game face back on. "The only side I'm on is the children's. Be smart. Don't let him take the children when he's intoxicated just so you can call the police on him. It's your responsibility to make sure your children are safe at all times. No exceptions, no games. If he's as bad as you say he is, he'll give you plenty of opportunities to get him in trouble."

"I never thought to call the police," she said.

"Really?" He met her eyes. The sun shined through the solarium's glass ceiling. He squinted.

"It's like...I don't want to be Witt, you know? He's a world-class manipulator. No matter what's going on, he's looking for an advantage. When he suggested we handle the divorce ourselves, it seemed like the logical thing to do. Otherwise, what? I'd have to spend every minute trying to screw him over. Who wants to live like that?"

Lock shrugged and looked down at his notes. "I understand, but Natalie, now's the time for you to start thinking like that. You have an idea of what's best for your children, and you need to start acting on it. Like I said, make notes, report things that put your kids at risk, build a case."

"Or maybe it's that I'm too gullible," she said. She got up and plucked a dead leaf from the stem of a magnificent sapphire-blue orchid. "I hear you. Now I feel guilty. I've been trying to take the easy way out, and that's not good for the kids, either."

"Being a parent, it's pretty much feeling guilty for something every day, isn't it? All you can do is try to do better tomorrow, right?"

"Yeah, that's exactly it. You have kids, then?"

Lock shook his head and looked down. "No."

She walked to the loveseat, picked up the clipboard next to him, and sat down. She put the clipboard on his lap. Her bare leg brushed the material of his suit. She smelled of something wonderful.

He stood up, suddenly uncomfortable and feeling like a jerk. This is what he had wanted, but it was too soon. The children came first. What if he met Natalie's husband and he turned out to be a good father? He didn't think she would lie about it, but every divorce had two sides. He couldn't start something with Natalie and still stay objective about what to put in his report.

She looked hurt, and he searched for the right thing to say. His eyes fell on the tree in the back yard. "Can I ask you a favor? Can I see the tree in your yard?"

She looked confused. "The albino? Why?"

"It's a hobby. Like bird-watching. It looks like a redwood, but they don't grow around here."

"Lock, if you don't think I'm…I didn't mean to make you uncomfortable. You just looked so sad."

"No," he said, "it's not that. You're amazing. But I can't think about that and do my job, too."

"Rain check, then?"

"Rain check." He smiled.

Her expression brightened, and she said, "Come on out back, then."

He followed her to the tree, trying to feel good about doing the right thing, but it was hard. She said, "You're right, the coast redwoods don't do well in cold places. This one's a dawn redwood, from China originally. *Metasequoia glyptostroboides*." She pronounced the name carefully. Now he was impressed.

"Not *giganteum* or *sempervirens*," Lock said. "I should have guessed that. How did it get this big, though? It has to be over a hundred years old, but with the white needles—"

"I know," she said, an angry frown creasing her brow. "It was so unique, I looked it up. The parent tree used to be right there." She pointed, and Lock saw a low mound on the lawn where the stump must have been ground out. "A branch from the other tree fell and hit the house, and Witt decided to cut the whole tree down. He did it out of spite."

"Jesus," Lock said. "Does he know that this one's going to die as a result?"

"I told him, and the tree guys told him, but Witt didn't care."

"I wish you hadn't told me that," Lock said, shaking his head.

"Harder to imagine having a reasonable conversation with him now, isn't it?"

"Yeah. A lot harder." He took out his phone and walked around the tree, taking over a dozen pictures.

Lock started his car and pulled out onto the country road. On the way back to the office, Lock thought about Natalie, about the tree, and about a look she had given him that reminded him of an old girlfriend. It was a look of determination—a small frown followed by a forced smile, the conscious decision to make the best of things. It was exactly what Dominique did when faced with life's larger difficulties.

When he was about thirty and still teaching elementary school in Philadelphia, Lock had been frantically in love with Dominique. It wasn't that she and Natalie looked alike, but he was starting to see they had many of the same qualities. Dominique had been a ballerina, and Natalie was a yoga practitioner, and their bodies were very alike. And Dominique's interest in him—what ballerina dated a teacher when she could be dating models?—gave him a similar feeling, too. *Natalie could have anyone, so why me? She tried the rich guy, and that didn't work out*, he told himself. *And maybe it'll just be a thing so she can forget Witt. Maybe afterwards she'll find someone who can give her another big house.* Even so, he looked forward to seeing her again. He admitted he was hooked now. As long as she was interested in him, he'd keep looking for excuses to see her. It had been the same with Dominique when he'd met her.

Her divorce was almost settled then, and when it was finalized, they agreed that they would live together in his apartment. It was big enough for three, and they had big, beautiful plans for their lives together.

Lock had experienced lust at first sight, and he had to admit that might have been what was happening with Natalie. But with Dominique, it had been love and devotion at first sight.

Dominique's ex, Timothy—who had walked out on her in her second trimester—had worked hard during the divorce to make her life miserable. He perjured himself repeatedly in custody hearings, claiming she was an unfit parent. He had staged photos of her medicine cabinet to give the appearance that she was a prescription pill addict. In reality, Timothy was the addict, and he couldn't be trusted to care for little Hannah, who was eighteen months old by the time the hearings took place. Dominique forgave him, even while he continued to undermine her parental rights. Lock could never understand her unconditional compassion for Timothy, and everyone else for that matter, but that was one of the things he loved so much about her.

The family court judge wasn't buying the contrived evidence and gave Timothy a hard time, punitively limiting his time with Hannah to supervised visitation for four hours once a week. The custody order was fantastic news to Lock. Timothy slouched in his chair and didn't seem to give a shit either way.

As they had grown closer and more in love, it was Lock, not Timothy, who had taken Dominique to her OB/GYN appointments and who'd spent hours rubbing cocoa butter on her bulging belly to help reduce the severity of the inevitable stretch marks. The second or third word Hannah had learned to speak was "Dada," and she used it in reference to Lock. Meanwhile, Timothy failed to show up for many of his visitation sessions. He didn't know his daughter. Lock was pleased about that, but it didn't really matter. Hannah regarded him as her father, and he loved her as his own child.

The three of them lived together happily for over a year when Dominique was struck and killed by a drunk delivery truck driver on Market Street in center city Philadelphia.

Each night during the week that followed, Lock rocked Hannah in his arms and sobbed them both to sleep.

Before Dominique was even buried, Timothy had found a new lawyer who obtained an emergency custody hearing. A different judge presided, and without paying much attention to expert witness testimony about Lock's strong paternal relationship with Hannah and their profound emotional bond, the judge ordered that Timothy would, by law, become the infant's sole custodian as Hannah's only living biological parent. Upon hearing the ruling, Timothy looked across the courtroom, grinned, and gave Lock the finger.

He saw to it that Lock would never see Hannah again, and Lock never did.

Lock thought about Witt, a man who would cut down a tree to spite his wife. A man like that would do exactly what Timothy had done—or worse.

6

Natalie, Witt, Edwina, and Dahlia sat at the breakfast table. Dahlia flailed in a highchair. Edwina plucked pieces of alphabet cereal from her bowl and used them to spell words on her napkin.

Natalie served her husband his breakfast of eggs and whole wheat toast and tended to the kids. She forced herself to put her hand on Witt's back in a cynical attempt to display affection. He didn't acknowledge the caress, too absorbed in the morning newspaper to notice or care.

"Don't count on me for dinner tonight," he said. "I'll be in Harrisburg. If my meeting runs too late, I may stay overnight. If I'm not home by ten o'clock, I'll see you tomorrow."

"What about the people from the county? They'll be here tomorrow morning."

"Screw them. Reschedule it." Witt folded the paper and set it on the table. He glanced at his watch. "Isn't there something at the girls' school this morning?" he asked. "What time does the driver pick them up?" His tone was more of a complaint than a question.

"Eight," Natalie said. He wasn't really interested in the girls. He just liked to find fault.

"He's always in my way whenever I try to back out of the garage."

"You could leave now," she said.

"And I might have to fly to Sacramento this weekend. I don't know yet."

He pays so little attention to me that he doesn't even notice when I'm being a bitch, she thought.

Witt took a quick swipe at his face with a paper napkin, dropped it on the table, and then rose and left the room. He didn't say goodbye. A minute later, Natalie heard the garage door clank open and Witt's car drive off.

Lock had just sat down at his desk when Natalie called.

"Good morning, Lock," she said. He could hear the smile in her voice. "It's me."

"Good morning, Mrs. Mannheim. What can't wait until seven thirty?"

"It's okay, I know you're at work. I need to see you," she said.

"That's what you said yesterday." Lock tapped the eraser end of a pencil against the phone.

"I meant it then, and I mean it now," she said.

"I'm sorry. I have a busy morning."

"Taking care of someone else's kids."

"That's what I do," he said, lowering his voice. No one was in the cubicles nearby, but he had to be careful. "But that doesn't mean I don't care about *your* kids."

"What if I tell you I'm beating my children with a belt? Would you come over then?"

He could hear her smiling and he laughed. "I'll see you tonight," he said.

"Wait," she said. "Witt's going out of town, and he's probably not going to be back tonight."

"Did you—?"

"I told him it was important. He said, 'Screw them.'"

"Charming," Lock said. "He's going out of town? Give me his cell phone number."

Natalie recited the number. Lock wrote it down and said, "I'll let you know what I find out."

He called her back ten minutes later. "He let it go to voicemail," he said. "I left a message saying that this is serious business and if he stands me up again, I'm going to get the police involved. I told him he has until the end of the day to return my call and make another appointment. I think I'll hear from him."

"Yes, probably," she said. "You're getting to see what a sweetheart he is."

"Yeah, I think I have a pretty good sense of him now. I'll call you when I hear."

"Thanks, Lock."

"Look for a lawyer, okay? For a case like this, I'm sure you can find someone who'll take it without getting paid up front."

"Yeah, I'll do that. Otherwise I'm going to end up like that tree," she said.

"I was thinking the same thing," Lock said.

After lunch, Lock's desk phone rang again.

"Lochlan Gilkenney."

"Mr. Gilkenney. This is Wittley Mannheim. First, let me apologize for having to reschedule our meeting. Completely unavoidable. Business crisis that's getting worse by the minute. Now, it appears that I'll be out of town for an entire week, but I am anxious to meet with you and set the record straight. Any chance we can do this by phone? I could do it today by phone, or even right now, if possible."

"It's not possible," Lock said. Mannheim sounded a little too slick, a little too ingratiating. So far, there was nothing to suggest he wasn't exactly as Natalie had portrayed him. "We need to see you in person, in your home environment, together with your wife and daughters."

"You came on a little strong with the police threat, Mr. Gilkenney. Let me assure you, I am taking this seriously. It's just that I can't be available for the interview."

"According to Mrs. Mannheim, you're not taking this seriously at all."

"You'll soon learn to take anything Natalie says with several tons of salt," said Mannheim. "Here's an example—I understand you suspect that I or my attorney submitted an anonymous report to your office. Is that correct?"

"Mr. Manheim, I can't possibly form an opinion about what is going on with the information I have right now. That's why this meeting is so important."

"I'll take that as a yes, and I'll tell you what's really going on—Natalie sent you that report. I can't prove it, but it's right up her alley. She does something wrong and then blames me. She cheated on me and broke my heart, but to hear her tell it, I practically forced her legs apart myself for that little bastard boyfriend of hers."

"Okay, that's enough, Mr. Mannheim." Lock reached across the desk for his appointment book and opened it. "When is the absolute soonest you'll be available to meet?"

"Let's see. Today is Wednesday. I'll be back late next Tuesday. I'll be in Anaheim until then, but I'll see you first thing next Wednesday morning, if that works for you."

"Ten o'clock next Wednesday. Please keep your girls home from school for the morning."

"I understand. That's fine."

"Just so we're clear, this is a favor. I'm giving you the benefit of the doubt. If, for whatever reason, you're not at the meeting next week, I will involve the police."

"Thank you, Mr. Gilkenney," Manheim said, and he hung up.

Lock felt he had kept his cool, but Manheim had made him angry, not just with his dismissive attitude, but because now Lock wouldn't see Natalie for a full week. He believed Edwina and Dahlia were happy and well cared for, and the disappointment was all about Natalie, not about the case.

He couldn't come up with a legitimate reason to see her, and for a moment he flirted with the idea of engineering an accidental meeting. Maybe if they lived in the same neighborhood it might fly, but arranging to bump into her at her local grocery store might seem like too much of a coincidence. He didn't think she'd mind, but for himself, he needed to stay on the right side of being a stalker.

Lock sat up straight when he remembered that he'd promised Natalie he'd call her once he made a new appointment with her husband. If he were being professional, he would have picked up his phone and called her then and there, but he didn't. He wanted to enjoy the anticipation of speaking with her, hearing her voice, looking into her twinkling eyes. He pictured her in the cut-offs and t-shirt, imagining her sprawled out on the lounge chair in her solarium. He wanted to be with her, and he couldn't, so he'd have to enjoy the whole experience of Natalie Mannheim through the prism of one quick, routine phone call.

He couldn't wait. He dialed her number.

Voicemail. Another disappointment. But he wasn't going to miss speaking with her by leaving a message, so he hung up.

7

Almost a full week passed and Lock didn't see Natalie, but in that week, he had crossed so far past the line of professionalism that he couldn't see it any more. Natalie had called Lock back, and after he had described his conversation with Witt, it hadn't taken much for her to get Lock's cellphone number out of him. He rationalized that she might need it in case of some emergency that involved the children. But he knew he just wanted to be in touch with her.

She called him that night, and he was delighted to hear her voice. But when she suggested they meet, he said no. He didn't want to lose his job, but mostly he didn't want to prejudice her case in the event he did discover something actionable about her husband. Any lawyer would annihilate Natalie's case if it were discovered she and Lock had had a personal relationship of any kind.

As soon as he explained that to her, he said, "I need you to do me a favor."

"What do you want?" she said.

"We can't do this on our phones. We need to end this call and get disposable, prepaid cellphones, and then only use those. If the worst happens, even this call could make it hard for you to get custody," he said.

"Throwaway phones, like spies and criminals use, right?" she asked.

"Exactly."

"I should have thought of that myself," she said. "I'm sure Witt had my phone records checked before."

"When you had a boyfriend," Lock said.

"Awkward. He wasn't a boyfriend, but yeah, that."

He smiled. "So, go get a phone and then call me at work tomorrow with the number of the new phone. I'll pick up one for me in the morning."

"I can't wait to talk to you. It's stupid, like high school." She laughed.

He laughed too and said, "I know. Tomorrow night, we'll talk as long as you want."

The next night, they talked for over three hours. They talked about when they were kids and the things they had dreamed of and the outlandish things they had believed and done. It was the same kind of talk all new lovers had, and it made Lock happy.

"So what about your family?" she asked.

He understood that she was going to let him answer that however he wanted—he could tell her more about his parents, or about Dominique and Hannah. He liked that she was so careful of him.

He said, "I was in love with a woman. Her name was Dominique, and she was a ballet dancer. She had a daughter, Hannah, and we were raising her together." He told her the rest of the story and she listened without asking questions. He told her more than he had told anyone, even the people at AA, even Abby.

He talked about how much it disturbed him not having a family he could call his own, and how he felt love was the most potent force in the universe.

"I know," Natalie said. "Before you have a family, you think you want certain things. But after, whatever those things are, they suddenly seem silly, because now there's this other thing that's bigger than anything you ever imagined."

"And when you have a family," he told her, "love is kind of just there, waiting."

"How do you deal with that?" she asked.

"Holidays hurt the most. I'm always invited somewhere for Thanksgiving, but when I go, I sit there and wonder who all these people are and I wish they'd just be quiet. All it does is remind me of Dominique and Hannah."

"I was going to say I can't imagine it, but I can. I do. That's what I'm afraid of with Witt. If he wins, maybe I'll never see my girls again."

"I'm not going to say don't worry," Lock said. "You're worried, and that's a good thing. We'll be careful, and you'll keep an eye out for anything Witt does that shows he's not a good father."

"Shit, I'm getting some kind of signal on my phone. Either the battery's dying or I'm running out of minutes," Natalie said. "Talk tomorrow night?"

"Tomorrow night."

"I love our talks," Natalie said one night, after returning home from an Orchid Society meeting and calling him immediately. "I never get bored talking to you. The more I talk with you, the more I want. I couldn't help thinking about you during the presentation tonight. I can barely remember what they were discussing. And the things you and I talk about are all over the place, but I remember everything."

"It's the pink cloud effect," he said. "We're getting to know each other. We overlook the things we might not like about each other."

"Maybe for you it's a pink cloud."

"Maybe for you, too," said Lock.

"Here we are," she said. "I'm in my bed, propped up on four pillows, and there you are on your sofa—"

"I'm in the recliner."

"—and I bet you have a fire going in your wood-burning stove."

He got up to stoke the embers with a stick he took from a pile of kindling.

"You must have a nanny-cam on me."

"Maybe I should install one. Make sure you behave when I'm not monopolizing your time."

"You're not monopolizing anything. You're my priority when I'm home."

"But not enough of a priority to meet?"

"Not going to happen. Not until your case is closed and you take care of the other stuff."

"Get divorced, you mean."

"Yeah. I'm not giving you an ultimatum or anything, but even after CPS makes a determination about your case, if Witt's lawyer finds out we're spending time together before the divorce is final, how's that going to look?"

"You'll never be able to resist me that long. I can be persuasive."

Lock smiled at that. "I don't know what gives you the impression I can be easily convinced, but I think you're going to find out you're wrong."

"We'll see."

Later on, she asked him about growing up in Philadelphia. There was a lot he didn't care to say about it, so he cast about for a good memory. "I told you about my dad. He was a grumpy man, even in his late thirties, and for most of my waking hours as a kid, he was sleeping it off. That's the bulk of my memories of my father—sleeping with his mouth open."

"Could have been worse," Natalie said softly.

"I guess so. Most of my happy childhood recollections are of my mom. Great memories. No siblings, so I got all her attention. A few times, on a Sunday when she'd be off work, she'd tell my father we were going shopping for school clothes or something, but we'd actually drive down to the ocean, at Avalon. That's where all the super-rich families vacationed, and we'd pretend we had a chauffeur drive us there. I'd call her Jeeves and she'd call me sir, and she'd laugh and we'd drive the whole way with all four windows down. When we'd start smelling the salt air, we knew we were almost there."

Natalie said, "I suppose this is the time to mention Witt and I own a home on the beach in Avalon. I didn't get to it once this summer. I kept making plans to go as a family, and Witt would reschedule at the last minute, and then summer was over."

"That's sad, having the house but not using it. It's almost worse than not having the house," Lock said. "My mom barely had enough spare money for gas and tolls. Sometimes she let me pay the tolls. I'd feel like a million bucks when she'd let me do that. Another time, on the boardwalk, I surprised her by pulling a ten-dollar bill out of my pocket—I'd earned it weeding a neighbor's backyard garden the day before—and I insisted I buy her lunch. She let me, without putting up a fight. She was great that way. I had a hot dog and a Coke—real health food—and she ordered a grilled tuna and cheese and a glass of water. I guess she asked for water to try to keep the bill down. She told me it was the best sandwich she'd ever eaten in her entire life."

"I can guarantee she was telling you the truth," Natalie said.

"Yes," he said, "she always told me the truth, and that taught me to as well. I don't like lying, not even white lies."

"What about a white lie to spare someone's feelings?"

"I used to think it was unavoidable, but now I think it's just better to tell the truth, or say nothing. I just try to be gentle about it."

"You're a rare human being then."

"My father knew how to lie. He was good at it. He'd lie for no reason at all. If you'd ask him what time it was, he'd look at his watch and see it was 5:05. Then he'd tell you it was 5:06. Just deceitful is all."

Talking with Natalie triggered memories of things Lock had forgotten—like the time he was convinced he was going to flunk fifth grade. His father had persuaded him that he was such an underachiever that the teacher and principal had discussed it and they'd decided Lock would need to repeat the year.

It had been an artless falsehood designed to get Lock to work harder in school. When Lock tearfully approached his teacher and told him of his fears, the teacher assured him that whomever had told him that was a malicious liar.

And Natalie told Lock, in the midst of their midnight phone call, that something in their conversations reminded her of the time she kicked the neighborhood bully in the nuts when he snuck up behind her and snapped her bra strap against her back.

"I don't know what made me think of that," she told him. "But my mind goes to wild places when I talk to you."

At times, their calls had the essence of phone sex—lots of lengthy silences, deep breaths, visions of what the other party was doing. The calls were innocent, though sometimes Lock would notice a long pause from Natalie's side of the line, and then he'd hear a throaty sigh. That caused him to wonder exactly what she was doing. When he asked, she said she was just sleepy, but quickly added that she didn't want to say goodnight.

The more he learned about her—her dedication to yoga, her love of reading books about personal growth, her juvenile sense of humor—she liked to pretend she didn't recognize Lock's voice and demand that whoever had answered his phone had better put him on the line immediately—the more he liked her. Her impoverished childhood wasn't the cliché he'd feared it'd be. She didn't realize she was poor at the time, and told Lock that she had been happy, with many friends and a good relationship with her parents. In her early childhood, they took her to Disney World three times before both her parents got laid off from their blue-collar jobs. When she turned seventeen a few years later, she moved out into an apartment with a girlfriend and worked three jobs to pay her rent and help her parents out.

The way Natalie talked about her girls impressed Lock.

She loved them so much, she said, and Witt's distance from them saddened her. That was one of the things about her that was so attractive to Lock. It wasn't hard for him to imagine them having children together. It wasn't hard for him to picture her being a loving mom and wife. A family was what he wanted, and Natalie seemed to fit the image of the kind of woman he ached for. He understood he knew very little about her, and he hoped he'd learn more over time, but the conflict with his job kept nagging at him.

In another conversation one night, fatigue got the best of Lock and he caught himself falling asleep as he listened to Natalie talking about being physically abused by a former boyfriend. That was a subject that would definitely interest him, so nearly falling asleep was a clear signal that he should end the call and go to bed. He waited for an opening and told Natalie that he just couldn't stay awake any longer. He looked at the clock displayed on the cable TV box.

"My God," he said. "It's almost four."

"Yes," Natalie said, "we've broken our record."

Lock yanked the handle on the recliner and it folded down into its normal position. He stood up.

"I'll let you go, then," Natalie said. "Get some sleep and save some kids tomorrow."

"It's already tomorrow," he said, "but I'll take your advice."

"Goodnight, baby," she said.

"Goodnight, Natalie."

"Just for the record," she said, wanting to extend the call, "I think I'm falling for you, so be careful with me. Be gentle."

Then he said it. It just slipped out. "I can say the same to you."

"Good," she said, sounding exhilarated by his admission, "and goodnight." He heard the click. It was the first time he'd ever let his attraction to her leak out into speech. He bit his lip and wondered how wrong it was to have said that.

Lock undressed and got into bed. Natalie was an exceptional woman, he thought, and they were quite a bit alike in some ways, while vastly different in others.

She'd worry about every aspect of her orchids' health. He'd worry about the kids he encountered through CPS. She had to have the humidity in the solarium perfect for the orchids and she didn't trust Candice to take care of them. When she would travel, she'd hire a plant expert to come in once a day to check on the flowers. And Lock didn't trust his colleagues to take good enough care of the kids under his supervision, so he rarely took vacation time. Although Lock knew all about trees, when it came to caring for plants, he resorted to his "brown method" of plant care—when some leaves turned brown and began falling, he would water the plants. And from the way Natalie instructed him on how to care for them, he realized he was alternating between killing them with neglect and killing them by over-watering.

On the other hand, Lock never would have hired Candice to care for his kids, if he'd had any. He didn't think Natalie had done adequate due diligence in vetting Candice, and he told her so. He suggested giving Candice an unannounced drug test. She laughed and said that demanding Candice submit to a test was way out of bounds. Lock countered, "Not if she's driving the kids around. And you said you thought her boyfriend was a bad influence on her. Drug testing is definitely appropriate."

"She'd quit first," Natalie said. "Then where would I be?"

"In the market for a more suitable nanny," Lock said.

It was funny, Lock thought; the more Natalie disregarded most of his advice, the more he liked her.

"Don't worry about my kids, Lock, I take care of the things I love," she said.

"So do I."

"So take care of me," she said.

"Natalie, don't push it." But he smiled and was glad she couldn't see it.

And he was crazy about her. To say he was enamored was an understatement. He began to realize she was becoming an obsession, and it reminded him of his previous cocaine habit—how it had become all-enveloping and infected every fiber of his existence. He knew he'd have to end it before it got out of control. *But good luck with that*, he thought. He was hooked, bad, and he knew it.

8

Lock knocked on the front door of the Mannheim residence. The day of their meeting had finally come, and he couldn't wait to see Natalie. He had long since quit feeling annoyed that Witt had forced him to reschedule—the week he had spent away had been the best week Lock could remember in a long time.

Candice opened the door and escorted him into the kitchen.

Witt Mannheim sat upright at the breakfast table and nodded to Lock. He was about fifty, with a slight paunch, a round face, and a receding hairline. Lock took a seat at the kitchen table directly across from him.

Natalie, dressed conservatively in dark blue slacks and a matching sweater, stood by the range while a kettle boiled water. She offered coffee or tea; Witt ignored her, and Lock politely declined.

As soon as Natalie sat down, Witt spoke up. "I'll take a cup, black," he said. Natalie got up to get it. No flicker of the annoyance she must have felt showed on her face.

"I've been thinking about this interview ever since we scheduled it last week," Witt said, pointing a finger at Lock. "The more I think about it, the more I find this whole thing intrusive. I don't see the problem here. I never filed that report with CPS, my lawyer didn't, and I haven't been negligent. So why are you wasting my time? Where's your problem?"

"I hate to agree with Witt," said Natalie, "but—"

"You're agreeing with me about something? That's a new one."

"Oh for God's sake, Witt," said Natalie, settling into a seat while sliding a mug toward him.

"Please," said Lock. "It's important for us to keep focused on the girls and why I'm here. I don't know who's playing games with CPS, but it's not funny. Whoever filed the complaint is guilty of filing a false report to authorities. I could pursue it, but I'm not interested in wasting my time. I want to be able to walk out of here feeling confident your children are all right, and as of right now, I think that's the case."

Witt took a quick peek at the business card Lock had placed in front of him on the table. "What do you think of the importance of fidelity in the grand institution of marriage, Mr. Gilkenney?"

"Let's stay on point, Mr. Mannheim. This is no light matter."

Ignoring Lock's caution, Witt continued. "Of course, I've flirted… harmlessly. Who doesn't?"

"Everyone's falling asleep, Witt," Natalie said.

"Ask her about her yoga teacher," he said. "He's taught her how to bend her body into all kinds of accommodating positions."

"That's a vile lie, Witt."

"I can guarantee you, knowing your wife is out somewhere with someone else hurts a lot." Witt made a fist and tapped his chest three times. "Especially if you loved her as much as I loved Natalie."

"I'm here to follow up on a complaint of neglect of your children, Mr. Mannheim," Lock said. "That's all. Let's confine the commentary to that. No editorializing. It's not helpful."

"Don't you want to see the kids?" Witt asked. "The sooner you see that they're fine, the sooner we can get this over with." He stood up, as if to end the interview.

Lock had seen all sorts of misbehavior during interviews like this. There was no way Witt was going to make him angry, not in his professional capacity, at least. But a part of him was fuming at the way Witt treated Natalie. *What do I think of infidelity?* he thought. *I think it's amazing she stuck with you for this long.*

Witt stood over them, removed his glasses, and rubbed his eyes.

"I still have a few questions," said Lock, looking up. *Play your power games, buddy. I'm not leaving until we're done here.*

"And I still have a few lawyers," said Witt. "You can see for yourself that there's nothing going on here that's of any interest to your agency whatsoever. Admit it."

"That's what I'm trying to ascertain. And you're right, what I need to do now is to see the kids—in the presence of you and Mrs. Mannheim."

Witt exhaled slowly, then sat back down. He scowled at Lock and said nothing.

"I need to see them now, with both of their parents," Lock said.

Witt shouted, "Candice! Get the kids."

Natalie got up to top off Witt's coffee. She flashed him a fake smile.

"I know you don't read much, Nat," he said, "but there's a book by George Orwell—*Animal Farm*—all about Big Brother. Government control. No right to privacy." He nodded toward Lock, then looked back to Natalie. "Well, right here, right now, you have an example come to life. Big Brother, right here, right now, in our kitchen. An anonymous government bureaucracy injecting itself into our lives and minding our business."

"Wrong book, Witt. All assholes are created equal, and some assholes are bigger assholes than other assholes—that's *Animal Farm*. Big Brother is in *1984*."

Candice arrived with the children. Edwina walked in on her own, and Candice held Dahlia. Lock turned, looking them over slowly, carefully. He focused his attention on the four-year-old. Candice leaned up against the refrigerator, watching. Witt and Natalie watched Edwina approach Lock.

"Hello, Edwina," Lock said, and his face widened in a warm smile. He got off the chair and, despite wearing a suit, sat cross-legged on the cool tile floor, eye-level with Edwina. "I'm Lock. You remember me. You gave me White-Mane."

Edwina, now shy, stepped back and wrapped her arm around Candice's leg, looking at Lock. Natalie and Witt watched the interaction.

Lock reached into his pocket and withdrew a packet of what looked like playing cards. He fanned them open and held them toward Edwina.

"Do you have a favorite color, Edwina?"

The child shook her head in reply.

"You don't? Wow. My favorite color is green." He removed a green card from the deck and held it up, arm outstretched. "On the front," he said, "there's a funny smiley face." He showed it to her. She shifted her gaze from Lock to the card. "And on the back there's a frowny face." Both sides of the card were glossy and colorful, and glimmered with glued-on sparkles.

Dahlia let out a small cry and lurched forward precariously in Candice's arms, reaching for the card. Candice jiggled the infant to quiet her. Witt observed quietly. Natalie watched Lock.

"Well, Edwina, if you don't have a favorite color, maybe your sister does," said Lock. "But she's too young to tell us. Do you know which color she likes? We can show her that card."

Edwina relaxed her grip on Candice's leg. She glanced at her mother and then back to Lock. "My favorite color is red and blue," she said, scanning the fanned-out cards. She took a step forward.

"Red and blue! Those are wonderful colors. And I have each one right here." Lock selected two cards and held them toward Edwina, who reached out and took them. She stepped back to Candice, beaming and examining the cards.

"What do you say, honey?" Natalie said to Edwina.

"Thank you for the smiley faces," she said to Lock.

"Thank you for telling me your favorite colors," he said. "You're lucky. You have two favorites and I only have one."

Edwina grinned. "Dahlia's favorite color is purple."

"If I give you a purple one for Dahlia, will you keep it in a safe place until she gets older? We wouldn't want her to chew on the card and eat those sparkles. They probably taste yucky."

"Yes," she said, holding her hand out expectantly. "Dahlia put my sneaker in her mouth. And Mommy's phone, too."

Lock gave her a purple card and put the rest back into his pocket.

Dahlia wriggled in Candice's arms, wanting to be set down. Candice said, "No, Dahlia. I'm going to hold you." The baby cried and wriggled more strenuously. Candice held tight.

"Which side of the cards do you like best, Edwina?" Lock asked.

Edwina showed the smiley faces.

"Feel better?" Witt asked Lock. "They look like we feed them? I have to get to the office. Anything else?"

Lock got up off the floor, brushed off the seat of his slacks, and returned to his chair at the kitchen table. He wrote for a moment in his notebook. He looked up at Witt.

"I'm finished with the girls, but there's one other thing," said Lock.

"You can take the girls to school now," Natalie said to Candice.

Lock waved goodbye to the girls. Edwina waved back, and Candice took them out of the room.

"Okay," Lock said. "Let's get this drinking and driving business resolved."

Witt gave Natalie a sharp look. "Thank you for exaggerating that, Natalie. Why don't you go shit in your bonnet?" He turned to Lock. "I was cited once, three years ago. Kids weren't with me. Blood alcohol zero point nine. What's that, half a beer over the limit? No accident, no reckless driving, stopped for weaving. Pleaded guilty. Never did it again."

"Oh, for Christ's sake," said Natalie. "Never did it again..."

Lock made a note. "And a DMV check will bear that out."

"You are correct, sir. You'll see my record is spotless."

"Driving while impaired with your children in the car," said Lock, "is wholly unacceptable. Mrs. Mannheim has stated it's happened and continues to happen. I can't close a case if I think the children are endangered."

"Mrs. Mannheim states a lot of things. My children are not in any kind of jeopardy, at least not from me," Witt said. "And any further discussion, since you're accusing me of being a serial drunk driver, will take place with my attorney present. Is that clear?"

"You have your lawyer. I have the District Attorney. We're both well represented, so it's probably not productive for us to be antagonistic."

"Whatever you say," Witt said.

Lock rose. "Thanks for your time, Mr. Mannheim," he said. "There's nothing else I need right now. This interview is over and I'll be on my way."

"I thought you were bringing a female colleague to examine the girls," Witt said.

"I determined that won't be necessary at this time. I'll write up my report and submit it to my supervisor. You'll hear from our office within ten days."

Lock shook hands with Witt, who said nothing and immediately turned and left the room. Natalie watched him walk away. Once he was out of earshot, she turned to Lock.

"That wasn't so bad," Natalie said, "and even though Witt was surly, he wasn't as obnoxious as I thought he'd be."

"I've seen a lot worse," Lock said. He stood up from the table. Now that Witt had departed, they let their guard down a bit. Their eyes met. There was a new sense of familiarity between them. Though they hadn't seen each other in over a week, to Lock it seemed much longer. Thanks to hours upon hours of phone conversations, he looked at her through new eyes, and to those eyes, she was more beautiful than he remembered.

She took a couple of steps toward him and stood there, looking at his face.

"I feel like I've known you forever," she said.

"Me too."

Her smile grew into a grin. "What happens next?" she said.

"You mean with the CPS case?"

"No." She lowered her voice. "With us."

Lock looked down. He swallowed hard and spoke slowly and softly. "I can't see how this can continue. It's just not right. It's too bad we met because

66

of a complaint. Too bad we didn't have a fender-bender and exchange contact information, then this would be fine. But that's not how it happened. And for the girls' sake, it would be better if things between you and Witt got back on track."

Natalie winced at that. Lock wanted to reach out and touch her shoulder; he wanted to reassure her that, one way or the other, everything would be okay. He couldn't do it. His eyes wandered around the kitchen while he searched for the right words.

"I have two hundred and sixty-two children to protect—not including Dahlia and Edwina—and I don't trust anyone but myself to do it as well as I do. That's one reason why I don't dare risk my job."

"Don't say that," Natalie said. She took a step closer to Lock and reached out and took his hand in hers. She squeezed. He gently pulled it away. Her shoulders slumped.

"All that we know about each other?" she said, inhaling deeply and standing up as tall as she could. She leaned her head in a few imperceptible inches closer to him. "You think you can erase that, Lock? I don't believe you can."

"Well," he said, "believe it. I know you're amazing, Natalie, I know that in my heart. The children I care for have to come first."

"But—"

"You shouldn't call anymore," he said. "This is goodbye, and I don't say that lightly."

Lock's eyes burned. He wanted to hug her, hold her, kiss her cheek, but he couldn't. He wouldn't. Instead, he gathered his things and tried to smile.

Natalie said nothing. Lock gave her a slight nod, turned, and walked to the door leading to the driveway. He opened it.

"I really wish you wouldn't leave," she said.

He stepped through the door and closed it quietly behind him.

As Lock drove off, he looked over the house at the magnificent tree in the back yard. An image of Witt's sneer came to his mind's eye. He felt the impulse to storm back into the house and hit him. Witt was everything Natalie had described and more. He ruined things because he could, because he owned them. Like the tree, and like Natalie. Both of them would wither, unable to get what they needed to live, and now Lock would, too. He was doing the right thing, but he knew that people who said what doesn't kill you makes you stronger just hadn't suffered enough. A lot of the time, a deep enough hurt could cripple you. It had happened before, and now it was happening again, to him and to Natalie.

The more he thought about it, the more angry Lock became. He drove recklessly, hating that Witt had made him an accomplice in hurting Natalie. When he was a kid, sometimes Lock had experienced a rage he couldn't control, but this wasn't one of those times. He was older now, wiser, he supposed, but at that moment he wished he hadn't outgrown his anger. It had always frightened him after the fact, even when he was young, but in the midst of it, when the world turned red after he suffered some perceived injustice, there had been a savage joy, a feeling of pure abandon.

Jimmy Rogers had been a neighbor and schoolmate, and he'd stood a head taller than Lock. They were friends the way kids that lived on the same block usually were, but Jimmy wasn't above making Lock the butt of his jokes when he had an audience. One afternoon when they were twelve, Lock was on the street, walking past the Rogers' residence, when a second-floor window opened and Jimmy's father leaned out and shouted to him to come in. Lock entered the Rogers' house and went upstairs. He'd been there a million times. Jimmy and his father were in Jimmy's room. Jimmy was trying on a new suit he'd just received for his birthday.

"Watch this," Jimmy's father said, and proceeded to put the jacket, tags dangling from the sleeve, on his son.

"Reach into your pocket now, Jimmy," he said.

"Which pocket?" Jimmy asked.

"Any one will do," his father said.

Jimmy put his hand in one of the jacket pockets and withdrew a crisp one hundred-dollar bill. He beamed and his father laughed. Lock was less excited.

"Now, try another pocket." his father said.

Jimmy reached into the jacket's lapel pocket and came out with another one hundred-dollar bill. Lock watched. The two laughed again, repeating this at each pocket in the suit until Jimmy had six or seven hundred dollars in his grip. Jimmy's father laughed even louder, took the cash out of his son's hand, and threw it up in the air, creating a shower of fluttering bills. Lock walked out, bounding down the stairs and out onto the porch.

Lock stood there thinking about what his father had given him for his birthday a few months earlier. Nothing.

"Oh, yeah, happy birthday, son," Lock's father had told him after school one evening, two days late. "I'll have to get you a little something, won't I? What would be a good present?"

Lock knew his father was perpetually broke. "Nothing much, Dad," he said. "How about a science fiction book? I like this writer named Fredric Brown. Something like that."

"Will do, son, will do. Freddy Brown. Science fiction."

After two weeks passed and his father never delivered, Lock gave up hoping for the book.

At school the next day, Jimmy approached Lock on the playground. Jimmy had the cash on him and fanned it out before Lock's face, grinning. A couple of other kids stood there watching.

"What did Mr. Drunkie get you for your birthday?" Jimmy asked, now sneering at Lock. "A box of puke?"

Everyone laughed except Lock. He reached out and punched Jimmy in the gut, and he went right down. Lock wasn't particularly strong, but his aim was good and he had knocked the wind out of Jimmy. The other kids formed a circle and started shouting "Fight! Fight! Fight!"

Lock wasn't finished. He jumped on Jimmy, grabbed him by the hair, and bashed his head several times into the asphalt until two teachers ran over and wrestled him away.

Lock had to go to juvenile court, but nothing ever came of the charges. It had been the first time he'd ever gotten in trouble, though not the first time he had uncapped the rage inside him, and the judge and social worker didn't make too big of a deal out of the fight. But Lock's father did—with a strap, every evening, for days. Every time the belt came out, Lock would look out the window at the lonely birch across the street, trying to put his mind into its wood, strong and alone and impervious to what the world served it. After that week, the tree was a kind of friend, and Lock would sometimes reach out and trail his hand over the papery bark on his way to school.

Lock hadn't seen Jimmy Rogers in more than twenty years, but he thought Jimmy had probably turned out just like Witt Mannheim.

9

As Lock made his way through the tail end of morning rush hour and got closer to his office, the images of Witt Mannheim and Jimmy Rogers faded, and thoughts of Natalie intensified. He could think of nothing but her standing alone in her kitchen as he walked out. A knot tightened in his stomach, and he felt nauseous.

He tried to push her out of his mind, but she just stood there, looking at him through hard, sad eyes. Then he began to picture himself sitting in a dimly lit bar with a bottle of cold beer sitting in front of him. After almost a full year in AA, he was able to realize he wasn't really clamoring for a drink so much as he was running from something—in this case, Natalie. The drink was merely the closest hiding place. He wouldn't give in and drink, he knew that, but he was disappointed that his goodbye moment with Natalie made him want one.

He was bigger than the craving, he told himself as he pulled into a parking spot at CPS.

He had a day filled with appointments and interviews and administrative tasks. They would keep him busy, but he knew she'd be relentlessly in his thoughts. He hadn't been to a meeting in a week and he needed one. He intended to go to an eight o'clock meeting that evening in Chadds Ford.

Lock kept his mind immersed in his work, and as the day wore on, he was surprised at how well he did at keeping images of Natalie at bay. He looked forward to being with a group of recovering drunks that night, knowing the camaraderie would provide some relief. But when he arrived home after work, the first thing he did was plug what he thought of as his Natalie phone into the outlet to let it charge.

While waiting to leave for the meeting, Lock killed time by alternating between flipping through the pages of *American Forests* magazine and watching headlines on CNN. He thought about making a sandwich just for something to do, but he wasn't hungry. He had tried to make some more notes about the albino redwood in his tree book, but it reminded him too much of Natalie, and he suddenly worried if he'd ever be able to write in it again.

When it was time to head out to Chadds Ford, Natalie still hadn't called, and she probably wouldn't. He always switched his cellphone to silent mode during meetings, and he couldn't help hoping that maybe he'd have a pleasant surprise when he'd check for missed calls after the hour-long gathering.

The meeting was crowded but uneventful, and the only thing he heard there that gave him at least some respite from his Natalie-related thoughts was when someone said, "Sobriety in AA is the first thing in my life that ever worked."

Lock could say the same thing, and knowing that made him feel better, perhaps because it gave him a sense that if all else failed, he would still have AA to fall back on. That certainly seemed logical. Practically his entire social life these days revolved around AA meetings and the friends and acquaintances he had made there. When he was alone in his carriage house, which was much of the time, he felt confident that substance abuse was solidly in his past.

The AA fellowship cautioned members to avoid the influences of "people, places, and things" formerly associated with their drinking and drugging. Lock abided by that advice, which naturally and dramatically limited his circle of friends, especially the three guys he used to hang around with—the same ones who had been there with him the night he was out of his mind at a bar in Bryn Mawr and, upon leaving, sideswiped three parked cars and nearly punched a cop.

That night, Lock had hidden a glassine envelope of cocaine in his underwear, but the police searched the car and found a half-consumed bottle of vodka and a piece of foil containing a joint. For some reason unknown, they didn't make an issue of it.

The next day, at noon, Abner escorted Lock to his first meeting. He didn't argue when his boss insisted. He knew he needed to be there. It was a relief, like pulling into the driveway after an all-night trip. That first day, Lock stopped outside after the meeting and nodded to the big sugar maple tree that stood sentinel over the building. It was how he marked passages in his life, trees like road signs to places new and places familiar. This one pointed in what Lock was sure was a good direction.

<hr />

Lock slept late the next day and the rest of the week. It was his habit to wake early and listen to the news on public radio while he cooked breakfast, but now he had trouble getting out of bed. There had been no word from Natalie. She wasn't fading from his mind as completely as he had hoped. Natalie's absence only made his thinking about her more vivid and frequent.

Deep down, Lock didn't believe Natalie was really capable of giving up on them. He didn't trust his own negative assessment of the situation, but he was beginning to accept that it must be true. If he was on her mind as much as she was on his, there was no way she'd be able to resist calling. He knew that made little sense. He hadn't called her, after all. She was stronger than he was, he concluded, and of course she had a life—her kids, her house, her orchids and her Orchid Society friends.

The fourth day since he had last seen her passed in a blur. Lock drove to the King of Prussia mall, walked around, watched people, and purchased nothing except lunch, which he ate half of. He drove back home, took a nap, watered his plants, and cleaned his bathroom.

Around ten that night, the phone rang. Lock let it ring a few times. If he didn't answer, then he wouldn't find out it was not Natalie.

But what if it was? He lunged for the phone and answered before the fourth ring began.

"Is it okay that I called?" Natalie asked.

"No," he said, "it's not okay." He didn't want her to hear the exhilaration in his tone. He paused to get his voice under control and sat on the sofa. "But don't hang up, either."

"I never want to go so many days without speaking to you again," she said. "I've been going crazy thinking about you, thinking about us, fantasizing about what it would be like if it was you, me, and the girls. I want it to be that way."

"I don't let myself think about it," he said. "But yes. I feel the same way."

"Come over. Now."

"Can't do it, Natalie. Love to, but can't."

"Yes, you can."

"Maybe I will," he said. "Maybe I'll ring the bell and Witt will open the door for me. Late on a Saturday night."

"Witt's in Avalon with the girls," Natalie said. "I'm sure his lawyer told him to do more with them so in family court he'd look like he's actually involved in their lives. Four or five years of arm's-length fathering and now he's going to erase it with a couple of trips to the beach. What a joke."

"His lawyer gave him good advice. And I'd bet he'll be presenting the receipts to the judge to prove how much he loves his children."

"I didn't think of that," she said. "I need your help, Lock. How am I supposed to do this without you? Shit, that sounded needy. You know what I mean, though. I miss you, but I'm thinking about the girls right now. What's it going to be like for them if he gets primary custody?"

Lock could see himself hurriedly getting dressed and hopping into his car.

"And Candice is off for the weekend," Natalie said. "Come over, Lock. We're not done with each other, and you know it."

"I wish I could."

"Let me ask you this," Natalie said. "Did your heart pound every time the phone rang these last few days? When you saw it wasn't me, didn't you feel it in the pit of your stomach? That's how I felt, and if you tell me you didn't feel like that, I'll quit bothering you. I know you won't lie, not even a white lie."

"Natalie—"

"But if you did feel that way, then we're not done with each other. There's a reason that's happening."

"Of course I felt the same way. Whenever the phone would ring, I knew who I was hoping it would be. But that doesn't change anything. You want what's best for your kids, and getting caught spending time with me isn't going to look good to a judge."

She snorted angrily. "And you don't want to lose your job, either."

"I don't," Lock said, "and I'm not going to apologize for that. My work is important. It's important to me, and it's important to the kids I help."

"I know, I'm sorry. It's just—"

"I want to come over, but we'd be risking everything."

"No, Lock, you have it all backwards. If you don't come over, we'll be risking everything."

For a long moment, Lock said nothing. Was she right? Could he build a life and family with her? He felt sure of it, but he knew that was irrational. Even if they were together, anything might happen. It might last a month, or ten years. It had been easy to do the right thing because he knew he wasn't thinking straight. But now, hearing Natalie say out loud what he had been thinking, something inside him began to shift, slowly, like the beginning of an avalanche.

Lock stood up. He looked around his apartment and could picture a Christmas tree and giggling kids running around. He checked the wood-burning stove. The fire was dying.

"Okay," he said. "I'll be there in half an hour. To talk. Nothing else, Natalie. To talk."

"Just talk," she said. "Hurry."

10

En route to Natalie's house, Lock's thoughts wandered to when, a little less than a year earlier, he had given up gambling at the same time he swore off alcohol and drugs.

In those first days of craps table abstinence, the hunger for escape was so intense that Lock was convinced that he wasn't strong enough to resist three powerful vices simultaneously. He knew something had to give. It was a Sunday afternoon when he rationalized that driving into Philadelphia to the Sugar House Casino was a lesser evil than picking up a drink or getting high.

After wrestling for hours with an array of cravings, Lock walked into his kitchen, opened the refrigerator, and took out a Tupperware container in which he always kept a thousand dollars in one hundred-dollar bills. The cash was "emergency funds," he had always told himself, but it was really gambling money, and rather than take a drink or a drug, he'd get into a craps game. It was safer, he thought, and the effect would be the same—near-total obliteration of whichever thoughts haunted him at the moment.

It came as no surprise when, two hours later, he returned home from the casino with practically no money left. He had sixty bucks left—he had begun his journey to Sugar House with one thousand and sixty-five. At first, he bet with 100-dollar chips and won his first two bets. Within ninety seconds, he was up $300. He took a quick trip to the men's room to clear his head and get his heart to slow down a bit.

After returning from the bathroom, he took it a little easier, betting only green, 25-dollar chips. As soon as he lost the $300 he had been up, he got more aggressive, betting $150 on each roll. He won a few rolls, but then the trend turned against him. He lost six bets of varying amounts in a row, and the thousand was gone.

He tipped the valet five bucks and drove home. His decision never to gamble again had nothing to do with the money he lost. Though he was far from rich, the cash meant nothing to him. He simply and finally realized there was no difference between cocaine, alcohol, and the green felt of a craps table. In AA, he remembered, someone once said switching vices was like being on the Titanic and demanding a different deck chair.

Now he was on his way to Natalie's place. Even though Lock's hands were wrapped around a cold steering wheel, they were sweating, and no matter how many times he swallowed, he could still feel a lump in his throat. It was the same feeling he'd had when he knew it wasn't in his best interests to be driving to the casino.

I should turn around and go back home, he told himself. *Or maybe I should stomp on the gas pedal and get to Natalie's faster. Maybe I should drive my car into a bridge abutment.*

He wanted to argue that this was love, or could be love, and that was different. But after years of addictive behaviors, he had at least learned enough so that lying to himself was almost impossible. He flashed on an image of himself and Natalie lounging in deck chairs on the Titanic, glasses of whiskey on the tables next to them. He laughed at the idea and shook his head. Aloud, he said, "Can I get another drink? Oh, and tell the captain there's an iceberg just ahead, but it's just the tip."

When drunk, high, or anchored to a craps table, the only things Lock's mind entertained were if there was enough booze, where he would be able to get more drugs, or how he'd get even after having lost so much money. Those were benign dilemmas, easier to deal with than the emotions he now sought to obliterate—especially the sense of isolation and the fear that he'd be alone, without a family, forever. *Just talk*, he thought. *That's fair. That's not too much to ask for.* But he knew that "just talk" was no different than "just one drink."

By the time he pulled into Natalie's driveway, the clamminess in his palms had evaporated.

<hr />

"Oh my God, Lock," Natalie said, rushing to him as he entered the kitchen through the driveway door.

She stepped forward and hugged him hard, closing her eyes and holding him tightly. He returned the embrace and then stepped back, holding his hands out to say "slow down." She smiled and nodded, and he smiled back.

She took him by the hand and led him to the living room, with its beige and black décor, modern furniture, and a freshly started blaze in the fireplace. He eased his hand out of hers and she nodded for him to take a seat on the sofa. He threw his jacket on an armchair and sat where she indicated. Immediately, she sat down next to him, her leg pressing against his. He slid away, only a few inches, but enough to show he intended to stick to the "just talk" arrangement.

She closed her eyes and leaned into him.

"Come on, Natalie," Lock said.

"Kiss me once," she said, "and I'll be satisfied. But I need that kiss. Nothing more, I promise."

"You promised already," he said, smiling. "Just talk."

"So? That was then and this is now. Kiss me."

He took her hand and kissed it and then folded it into his own.

"Okay, okay," Natalie said, rolling her eyes and shrugging. "You're no fun."

An easy smile came to his face. She smiled back and looked into his eyes.

"I never met a man who said he just wanted to talk who actually just wanted to talk," she said.

"I told you, I don't tell lies."

"Listen," she said, leaning back and taking a deep breath, "you're a good man. I knew that the minute I met you, and I want what's best for my girls and me. If I have to be patient—and believe me, that's not one of my talents—I'll be patient."

A gulp of beer, a line of coke, a roll of the dice. A kiss. Lock's mind spun.

"You made me think, Natalie," he said, "when you said that if I didn't come over, I'd be risking it all. I don't want to risk anything. I'm finished with gambling. I want to do the right thing."

"Coming here tonight *is* the right thing. We can take it slow, but we have to take it."

Lock looked around the room to distract himself, but he couldn't help it. He had to look back at her. "Oh boy," he said.

"I know," she said. "What are you going do? Things happen. That's life."

"Things happen when we let them happen."

"Exactly. That's how it's supposed to be. Let things happen naturally. You're trying to stifle something wonderful." Natalie ran her fingers through her short hair. "Let me ask you this. Do you want to kiss me?"

"What I want and what's best are two different things."

"So that's a yes," Natalie said.

"That's a yes."

"But you're going to resist."

"What else can I do? You're reckless," he said.

Natalie started to say something, but he held up a hand. "It's not a bad thing. It's one of the things I like about you. I used to be reckless, too. So, yeah, I want to kiss you. But once we do that, we're committed." He smiled and cocked his head. "Let's blow up that bridge when we come to it, okay?"

She laughed. "Okay, we'll do it your way." She got up and moved a few feet away to a high-backed chair across from him. "Better?"

"Yes," Lock said. "No."

"Definitely no," she said. "Let's talk about the kids. The case is still open, and I know that's part of your concern about us. I appreciate it, I really do. I know you want the best for my kids, so let's talk about them."

Lock nodded. "That works."

"So…if they're raised in a loveless home, that's bad for them, right? If they see their parents always fighting, that's bad for them, too. Right?"

"It's not ideal, no."

"If they're being carted around by a drunk driver, isn't that dangerous?" she asked.

"Yes, that's pretty bad."

"Then help me, tutor me," she said. "About things fathers do, things that matter to judges, so I can recognize it when he does it—because I can guarantee you, if it's irresponsible, Witt will do it."

Lock straightened up ever so slightly at this. "What, give you a few ideas about signs of abuse, excessive clinginess, kids getting moody for no reason? That kind of thing?"

"No, things for me to be on the lookout for, things that Witt is doing that he shouldn't be."

"Evidence for your custody case."

"Exactly. I need to know how to build a good case. I'm not Witt. I'd never invent anything, but he will, so I have to be as prepared as I can. Don't make me fight him with one hand tied behind my back."

"So I give you ideas based on my experience and help you wind up with a better custody order. A better settlement. You'd take better care of Edwina and Dahlia than Witt ever could. Right?"

"That's it. Nothing else. There's nothing wrong with that. Just talk." She smiled, and he laughed.

"Maybe you'll get better than a fifty-fifty split. And this house—"

"—and the one in Avalon, and twenty-five grand a month instead of pocket change," she said. "It's okay, I know what you're thinking."

He shrugged. "Sorry. You do this job long enough, you get a little cynical. You do deserve those things, though. It's the law, and you'd be using the money to take care of the girls. It's not like you're flying to Acapulco every weekend and leaving them home. I get it, I really do. The girls deserve the best life you can give them."

"Thank you. It's important to me that you understand the position I'm in. Witt's going to try to leave me with nothing, not even my girls. There's nothing wrong with me going for that as long as there's no perjury. It'd be stupid for me to go into this with my eyes shut."

"I don't think you're wrong. It's going to be hard. Don't fool yourself about that. But you're a good mother, and if he's still drinking and driving or whatever, getting proof of that will go a long way to making sure you get primary custody."

She stood, took a long step, and gave him a quick kiss on the cheek and immediately moved away. "Don't worry," she said, grinning. "You didn't kiss me. No violation of your professional ethics."

Lock laughed. He rubbed his cheek and said, "There. No evidence. You know, I've been thinking about your comment a couple of weeks ago about Edwina and how you hate her name. First of all, it's not that bad, I kind of like it. And second, Eddie is a great nickname. And maybe she'll like it. And if she doesn't, when she's older, she can change it. Here's something I never told you. I changed my name when I was twenty."

"Changed it to Lochlan?" Natalie asked. "From what? Elmer?"

"I didn't change my first name," he said. "I changed my last name. From Hauptmann. I'd never change my first name—my mom gave it to me. But my father and I didn't get along at all. He was a bad drunk and he was mean. I wanted nothing to do with him. I definitely didn't want to share a name with him. Then, after years of my father's abuse and neglect, my mother died. Her kidneys quit on her. Kilkenny's a county in Ireland. I altered the spelling to make the name unique and went to court and changed my last name to Gilkenney. My mom always said she wanted to be buried in Ireland, and when she was thirty-nine, she got her wish."

"That's sad."

He shook his head. "I don't know what made me think of that. I guess what I'm trying to say is that maybe Edwina isn't the name you wanted, but she'll like it, or she can change it to something she does like. Names are powerful things. Maybe the Edwina she'll experience herself as will be different from the one Witt wanted. It's like..." He looked out the back window. "Like the tree in the yard. I thought it was a *sempervirens* redwood and I was confused. I couldn't figure out how one could live in such a cold place. But it turned out to be the Chinese variant, and then suddenly it made sense."

"I get it," Natalie said. "Maybe you're right. And it's not just Witt, either. Maybe Edwina will turn into an Edwina different from the one I want or know. Someone even more special."

"I'm sure she'll be more special than either of us can imagine."

Natalie said, "So you have no parents, but you're in the making-parents-behave business."

Lock nodded. "I can't make people do the right thing, but I can try to stop them from doing the wrong thing, and I can help make children safer. And that's what I do. That's my life."

Natalie got up and moved to her original spot next to Lock. She draped her arm around his shoulders.

He cocked his head and said, "Still just talking, right?"

"Of course. You know, Gilkenney, the more I learn about you, the more I want you in my life," she said. "You've got a big heart, and there's a lot more thinking going on in there than you let on." She tapped a finger on his temple.

"Thank you. Sometimes I worry I think too much, spend too much time in my head. Here's a thought you won't like—maybe I can get this case reassigned to another investigator so that—"

"Oh my God, don't do that," she said.

"Hear me out," he said. "That would reduce the risk of our friendship compromising your case. And then, once your divorce is final, we could do whatever we wanted and know that we put your girls first."

83

"I appreciate it," she said, "I really do, but the girls are crazy about you. They're just like their mother. It's selfish, probably, but I don't want some stranger trying to figure out what's going on here. I'm sure your colleagues are competent, but they're not you."

"I'm not that special, Natalie," he said.

"Don't be stupid," she said. She leaned forward and kissed him full on the lips.

It was like feeling himself reaching for the beer, the line of coke. Without thinking about it, he put his arm around her and pulled her closer. She reached over and took his hand between hers. He hugged her and kissed her neck, then straightened up and slid away a few inches.

"Sorry," Lock said. "You know it's not that I don't crave you. But I think you're determined, and you're the kind of person who goes hard for what she wants. I don't blame you for that, but I don't want to get run over."

"I don't hurt people, Lock. I've been hurt enough to know what that feels like."

"I can't help thinking that part of you wants me because I can help you with your divorce and custody case," he said.

She let go of his shoulder and slid away. After a long moment, she said, "I don't even know what to say to that. You...do you think I married Witt for his money, and now I'm using you to get away from him? If that's what you think, maybe you were right. Let's just wait until the divorce is final and then we'll see what happens with us. I'm sorry. I shouldn't have asked you to come over."

She went to stand, but Lock put a hand on her arm. "It's not that. But I have to be careful, Natalie. We have to be careful. I don't want to lurch ahead because I have you all mixed up with a dream of mine."

"What's the dream?"

"Having a family. Like we've talked about. That's what I live for, and I came pretty close, once, a long time ago. I told you about that, and someday I plan to make it happen. And I will. So I'm almost defenseless when it comes to vulnerable women in need. Almost. I know that. I'm alert for that."

Lock shifted on the sofa. "Want to hear something funny? Years ago, I was in love with a woman pregnant with another man's child. He was basically out of the picture, and I got the idea that I had to have them as my family. I was going to marry her. I started taking care of them—the woman and the unborn child. I signed up for a million-dollar life insurance policy to protect my wife and the baby. Even before that baby was born, I was protecting them. Who does something like that? It wasn't even my child. Hilarious, isn't it?"

"No, it's not funny," she said. Lock rose. Natalie reached out and took his hand. "I'm glad you came over. If you really think it would be better to have someone else handle my case, it's okay. I trust you. Just pick up the phone when I call, okay? We can have that much."

"I will," Lock said. "I will."

Under the blackness of night, beneath leafless oaks and maples, Lock drove down a long gravel driveway pocked with shallow ditches and loose stones. He parked his car and walked up a flight of stairs to the rooms he rented on the second floor of a fieldstone carriage house.

Twenty minutes later, after reviewing his mail and pouring himself a glass of refrigerated spring water, he lay down on his bed and pictured the snake slithering up Natalie's thigh. He dozed off that way—for how long, he didn't know—until the phone rang.

He answered it.

A hang-up call. Was it Natalie? No, he decided. Not her. That wasn't her style. Probably just some telemarketer autodial.

Lock tried to fall asleep again, but he wasn't tired. He rolled over onto his side.

He was glad to be alone with his thoughts of Natalie. He was in lust, not love—he knew that much about himself. Besides Dominique, he'd never met a woman so attractive and so aggressively interested in him. Images of Natalie filled his head. He couldn't relax. He got up and looked out the window. A bright moon illuminated the ring of trees around the carriage house, and he could see some of the frozen pond beyond a stand of trees.

It was barely snowing, but the weather report predicted accumulation of half a foot. This was the coldest November in forty years, they said, with nighttime temperatures in the teens and single digits for a week straight. Snow would be great. Lock loved it when it snowed. An early November storm. When it snowed, everything got quiet, especially in the woods. He recalled when he was about ten years old, laying on his back in a neighbor's front yard under a huge holly tree, bundled in a thick wool coat, letting a heavy snow slowly cover him. White silence. What a pleasure to be warm in the snow. What a pleasure it would be to be with Natalie.

Lock turned his back to the window and surveyed his apartment, then stacked logs in the woodstove. He shivered. The carriage house had oil heat, but he paid for that. He took advantage of the free firewood the landlord provided and kept the woodstove burning as much as he could throughout the cold months. He crumpled several sheets of newspaper and stuffed them under the logs. He struck a match and the pages ignited, the nascent blaze beginning to roar. He huddled close, practically sitting on top of it, but he was still cold. Natalie ran a chill through him he couldn't shake.

The problem was, he knew, she'd lit a fire in him, too.

Usually, when something was amiss, Lock needed to get singed before he got the message. He was a slow learner. This time, though, it was going to be different, and almost definitely worse.

Lock turned on a light and read from an overdue library book—a biography of Shakespeare. He'd never read a Shakespeare play in his life, despite trying in high school and even after college, and he saw this as a significant failing, but he just couldn't penetrate the syntax. He thought that reading about Shakespeare might be the next best thing to actually reading Shakespeare.

He had reached the last few pages when the phone rang again.

"Hello?"

Another hang-up call.

That telemarketer, or maybe some idiot with a wrong number.

Thirty seconds later, there was a knock at the door. Lock didn't get many unannounced visitors, and he hadn't heard anyone climbing the steps. He got up and opened it.

Natalie. Standing there in a tight sweater dress.

"Hello, Lock."

Earlier, she hadn't been wearing any makeup, but now she was. She used it subtly and to good effect. Her eyes appeared larger than they had only a few hours before.

They stood there and looked at each other.

"I called you, but you didn't answer like you promised," Natalie said, smiling. She dialed a number on her own phone, and the answering ring came from her jacket pocket. "You left your cell phone at my house," she said.

He checked his pocket, and then looked at the charger plugged in by his reading chair. No phone. He shook his head and smiled. "Dumb of me. Sorry. Come in, you must be freezing."

Lock looked down past the hem of her coat. She wore sandals. Her toe rings glistened with tiny droplets of melted snow. She wiped her feet on the mat, kicked off the sandals, and sat on the couch near the stove.

"Tea?" Lock asked. He was almost on autopilot. Despite his reservations earlier, now that she was here, in his home, all he wanted was to make her comfortable, to get her to stay.

"Tea would be—oh!" An ember leaped out of the wood-burning stove and onto a nearby pile of newspapers. Natalie rose without hesitation, scooped up the burning papers with her bare hands, and tossed them into the stove.

Lock made tea and they sat together on the sofa, enjoying the fire. He thought, *This is better than 'just talk.' Not talking makes it easier, somehow. Probably because this is something there's no way to talk ourselves out of. Sometimes talking just confuses things.*

He set his tea down and kissed her, just once, lightly, and then sat back on the couch. She smiled and laid her head on his shoulder, and they watched the fire dance and spark for the next hour, speaking only a little, and only about unimportant things.

11

The next morning, Lock got to the office at 7:30. Besides the overnight emergency coordinator, he was the first person in. He had had a cup of coffee, but he hardly felt he needed it. For the first time in a week, he felt well rested and content.

He sat at his desk and checked his email. There was one from Natalie, and it was just a smiley face. He beamed and deleted it, then emptied the trash folder, too. The day went by quickly, despite the fact that he couldn't wait to get home and call her. A couple of his colleagues commented on his mood. Apparently he had been smiling, something he didn't do much, and even humming as he worked. Toward the end of the day, there was another email from Natalie. "I'm going to be at your carriage house tonight at nine o'clock. I'm bringing a late dinner, so don't eat much." He sent a quick "OK" and deleted both emails. *This is happening*, he thought. *Whatever this is.* He felt suddenly free, like he could step out of the window and fly. He knew the feeling intimately. It was the end of resistance, a giving in, and it felt wonderful.

Lock went to a meeting with his sometimes-friend Ivan after work. When he chose a folding chair near the back, he thought, *Deck chairs on the Titanic*, and he laughed.

Ivan said, "Something funny?"

Lock looked at him and grinned. "Yes, something is funny."

———

As she climbed the stairs to his apartment, Lock stood on the landing and watched her.

She walked past him into the living room. A fire blazed in the wood-burning stove. The light from the flames flickered on the plants and caused shadows to dance on the walls.

Natalie had on a long sweater, khaki jeans, and a navy blue thermal sweatshirt. No make-up this time.

He asked her if she wanted tea.

"Green, if you have any left," she said, sitting on one of two cushions on the floor in front of the stove. Lock opened a box and spooned loose green tea leaves into an oriental cast-iron teapot in which he'd already boiled water. He brought a tray with the kettle and two mugs and put it between them on the hardwood floor.

He sat on the other cushion. Natalie sat cross-legged with her eyes closed in an informal lotus position.

"This is perfect," she said, opening her eyes and looking around. "The darkness and cold outside, the light and warmth in here. The tea, your plants, you." Blues played softly in the background.

Lock poured tea into the mugs and handed one to Natalie, who took it and held it in both hands. They both faced the fire.

"Roads slick?" asked Lock.

"Not too bad, plus, I'm a good driver. Cautious and defensive. Never had a real accident."

"Can't say the same. Once I was drunk and didn't brake in time for a car stopped at a red light. Smacked her pretty good and she went to the hospital in an ambulance, complaining of neck pain. I learned through my insurance company that she wasn't hurt seriously, though. Plenty of poor judgment from me, anyway. But that's in the past."

She nodded, and Lock thought she was thinking of things she had done in the past she wasn't proud of. Maybe marrying Witt was one of them.

"I'm surprised you don't have any potted trees in here. Plants, but no trees."

Lock shrugged. "It's like a birdwatcher not keeping birds. I mean, maybe they do, or some of them, but I always thought it was about looking for them in the wild, and the surprise and pleasure of finding them."

"Like going on safari instead of going to the zoo."

"Something like that."

Natalie took a long sip and set the mug down on the tray. "Do you have any favorites around here? In the woods out back?"

"Nothing special, lots of cedar," he said, "but I like walking back there, especially this time of year. It's peaceful."

"Let's bundle up and take a walk. Moon's almost full, and it's snowing."

Lock looked out a window. It hadn't been snowing when he'd arrived home earlier. There wasn't much snow, but she was right. "That sounds great. Too bad there's not more snow. I like the way it smells, and the way it crunches under your feet."

Natalie smiled. "Edwina likes the smell too. Until she mentioned it, it never occurred to me snow had a smell. Do you have an extra coat or something for me?" she said. "My sweater won't do for long outside."

"I'll go get something, hang on."

Lock could hear Natalie taking their mugs to the kitchen while he found a wool trench coat in the closet. They met in the living room and he helped her put on the coat. Lock looked down and remembered her sandals.

"Wait," he said. "What about your feet? You're going to need some boots."

"We won't be out long, it'll be okay."

"You sure?"

She nodded and Lock shook his head and laughed.

"Plan on a short walk, then," he said.

Outside, Lock ushered Natalie around the side of the garage that he rarely used, though it was included in his rent. They walked between a large stack of split wood and the garage. He steered her toward the stand of frozen trees behind the carriage house.

Natalie took his gloved hand in hers. Then Lock made a decision that would change everything. He shook his hand free, but only for as long he needed to remove his glove and jam it into his jacket pocket. He took her hand. He heard her laugh, and, still moving through the woods, she turned and hugged him, squeezing hard. She immediately let go and continued walking. She was strong, despite being so slender and light. He knew that with Natalie, there would always be more than meets the eye.

A couple inches of snow had accumulated, and her feet were glistening.

For the first time in Natalie's presence, Lock was totally relaxed. As they trudged in the moonlit woods, she held his hand tightly.

A moment later, they arrived at the small pond, frozen over and dusted with new-fallen snow. Lock put his arm around Natalie. She reached out and put her arm around him, too. They stood there, watching the November night.

"Whose woods these are, I think I know," Natalie recited, "his house is in the village, though. My little horse must think it queer, to stop without a farmhouse near."

Lock grinned. "So I'm your little horse?"

"I saw White-Mane on your mantle. Sweet of you." She hugged him.

He didn't resist.

"Still not warm enough," Natalie said, her breath condensing and visible in the moonlight. "I want heat."

He put his arms around her and held her.

"That's better," she said. "That's better. Now I'm warmer out here in eighteen degrees than inside next to the fire."

She turned and looked across the pond, ringed by a silhouette of trees. She moved to the bank and tested the ice with her foot.

"Solid enough," she said. She made an effort to simulate skating on the ice in her bare feet, but the pond's surface wasn't slippery enough. The ice cracked, and she laughed and scooted back to the shore.

Natalie took his head in her hands and pulled him to her mouth.

Inside, on a blanket thrown hastily on the floor in front of the fire, Natalie sat naked and cross-legged behind Lock, her arms wrapped around his chest.

He exhaled slowly and broke what had been a long silence.

"This feels right, Natalie," said Lock. "This is perfect."

"I know."

"The only thing missing is a bunch of little kids making a racket in the next room, and us yelling at them to settle down."

"That's not that far off," she said. "We'll have to plan. We have to be smart."

"And patient."

"I hate that. I want what I want when I want it."

"Of course," he said. "Instant gratification. That's the real root of all evil."

"I thought money was the root of all evil."

"That's what they say, but money is usually used to facilitate instant gratification, so I stand by my statement."

Natalie poked Lock in his side and reached around and tousled his hair. "I was poor growing up and there wasn't anything I wanted more than the security that comes with money, and now that I have it, it's the last thing in the world I care about."

"Easy to say when you have it, though."

"True enough," she said.

"But you're not ready to march out into the world without a dime in your pocket."

"No. No one would. And Witt owes me. He owes me according to the law, and he owes me because it's the right thing to do, to pay the girls and me so we can live happy, healthy, comfortable lives. It's just a question of me figuring out what to do."

"What's there to figure out?" he asked. "You've got a good case." He turned around and looked at her.

"Not good enough. With his lawyer, he'll probably get fifty percent custody. Maybe more. How am I going to live without seeing my girls every day?"

"He's a jerk, but he's not that bad of a father," Lock said. "Unless he's still drinking and driving. Divorce is hard, and a lot of things are going to change for you."

"He *is* a bad father," she said. "He doesn't hit the kids or anything, but mostly he ignores them. That might be worse. He just wants them around because he thinks they're his property."

"Well," Lock said, "that may be true, but the court won't take that as evidence of anything."

"I know. But if Witt got caught doing something stupid again, it'd be different."

The look in her eye made him study her closely. "Something you want to tell me?"

She took a deep breath. "What if something would happen?" she began. "What if some girl was to identify Witt as the man who flashed her some-place? Indecent exposure. Something that wouldn't look too good for him in court. That would take the wind out of his sails. I don't owe him any allegiance. The prick had me followed."

"With good reason."

Natalie glared, then grinned. "Anyway," she said, "with an indecent exposure charge, even if he can get out of it, he won't want to go to court. He'd want to settle."

Lock shook his head and said, "You can't frame him. First, it probably wouldn't work. The courts see this kind of stuff all the time. Also, as much as I don't like the guy, he has a right to see his kids as long as they're not in danger or not being neglected."

She sighed, frustrated. "But he *shouldn't* have the right," she said. "Do you think he's not still drinking and driving? Witt's not going to change just because CPS came to the house."

"You still need proof."

"I just keep thinking that if I don't have some sort of plan, I might end up visiting my own kids every other weekend or something. I know he has rights as a parent, but I also know that right now he's thinking up some plan to screw me. So what am I supposed to do? I play fair and I lose. I don't play fair and I'm a bad person."

"As of right now, I don't know what to tell you," Lock said. "I wish I did."

"Primary custody's all I want. He can have lots and lots of visitation. I don't care. I know the kids need a father figure, not that he's much of that. Plus, the girls are with me most of the time as it is, so he—or they—won't be missing anything."

He held her and touched her hair. "I know it's scary, and the truth is, you might not get what you want. All I can recommend is you let the courts handle it. No matter what people say, most of the time family court judges do the right thing. Just make sure you get a lawyer, a good one."

"Oh, I did. I forgot to say. He says pretty much the same things you do, which sucks."

"How'd you find him? How do you know he's any good?"

"He's my friend's friend, and he's an aggressive lawyer, too. He helped her get primary custody in a tough situation, so I think he's pretty competent."

"Okay. As long as you think he's taking you seriously and not seeing you only as someone who's generating revenue for him."

She sighed again. "I'm changing the subject. Make love to me again."

Lock put more wood in the fire and they lay down in the warmth it shed.

12

Natalie called Lock two nights later. Witt had been home, and he knew that she didn't always have the chance to do more than send a quick text.

"Hey, it's my favorite yogi," he answered.

"Hi, Lock," she said.

She sounded stuffed up. "Did you catch that cold?" Lock asked. "Half my office has it, but I swear you didn't get it from me."

"He hit me, Lock," she said.

"What? When?" He felt his rage build. He gripped the arm of his chair and took a deep breath. "What happened?"

"He came home at lunch today all pissed off. His lawyer heard I'd retained a lawyer. I took money out of the joint account for the retainer, and he started yelling and then he hit me. Slapped me across the face. Hard. You can see the mark."

"What the hell, Natalie, are you okay? Did you call the police?"

"No," she said, and she started crying. She sniffed and said, "His lawyer's protecting him. Witt said the record will show that he was in a meeting with the lawyer at lunch. Who's going to believe me?"

"You still have to report it," Lock said.

"Why?" she wailed. "It's just going to be a he said, she said thing, and I'm going to look like a liar because he's got an alibi."

"Is that what he told you?"

"Yes! He said he'd say he thought I was having another affair and my boyfriend hit me. He's got proof of when that happened before, so what am I supposed to do?"

"Does he know about us?" Lock felt bad for asking it, because for a moment he was more worried about his job than about her.

"No," she said. "But it doesn't matter. How am I going to go to the police? And what am I going to do now? How can I live in this house with him?"

"You can't," Lock said. "You have to move out." He didn't like it, but he thought she was right. The police weren't going to do anything besides interview Witt, and if he had an alibi from an officer of the court, it probably wouldn't go any further than that.

"How? I don't have any money—Witt drained the joint account, and I can't stay with you. And what about the girls? I can't just take them—his lawyer would be all over me. What am I going to do?"

"I don't know, I have to think. Is there any way you can get away tonight or tomorrow?"

"He's leaving tonight on business for the weekend. I have no evidence, but I'm sure he's got a girlfriend stashed somewhere."

Lock despised him for it, though he saw the irony, too.

"Candice will be at your house tonight, right? Come over after the girls are asleep and we'll figure something out."

"Okay," she said.

"Okay."

Just as he was hanging up, he heard her say, "I love you, Lock Gilkenney."

He almost called her back to tell her he loved her too.

Later that night, they drank tea in front of the fire after making love.

"So?" Lock asked.

"So what?" she said.

Lock took a deep breath. ˑ

"So how's he going to get identified?"

"Don't worry," she said. "I know a girl. She'll swear to anything as long as she gets money for her crystal meth habit. She'll say they did drugs together. She'll say he made her do drugs and have sex while her two young children were present. He won't want that story to circulate."

"A false report."

"It's already all worked out," she said. "You don't need to know any more than that. I know it'll work. I know it."

"You know it. Want to know what I know? You're staging a crime, Natalie. That's a felony. And, you're bearing false witness. There's a reason that's one of the Ten Commandments. Plus, you need the girl, an addict. That's your weak link. I have a boss who's pretty smart. The first thing he'll do when he reads the report is scratch his head. Then when he learns about a divorce in the offing, he'll burst out laughing. And when he stops laughing, he's going to get mad. And when it gets to that point, he's going to call the D.A., and the D.A. will squeeze your lowlife friend until she pops—and her guts are going to splatter all over you."

"Don't be so sure," she said. "She has a good incentive to keep quiet. She's got plenty of street smarts. And believe me, I don't want to go to jail. Already did that once. When I was twenty, I spent six weeks inside for shoplifting. I had the money, sort of, to buy what I needed, but I guess the thrill of getting away with it was what I wanted."

"You're going to pay this girl out of your take," Lock said.

"It's not a take."

"Sure it is."

"It's equitable distribution," she said. "I've put up with Witt Mannheim and his abuse for six years. Raised the kids while he made tens of millions. That's not worth anything?"

He sighed. "I know how repugnant he is, I really do. It's taking all my strength not to go find him right now," he said. "And it will never work. You've been in jail. You don't want to go back, do you?"

"I'm already in a prison. Our farmhouse is just a comfortable cell."

"Maybe. But now, you get plenty of time off for bad behavior."

She smiled. It faded fast. "I can't stand him anymore. I'm nauseated when he's near me."

Lock massaged her shoulders. "I know. Let's drop this for now."

Warmed by the fire in the stove, Lock and Natalie fell asleep in each other's arms. An hour later, Natalie awoke, looked at her diamond-studded wristwatch, and cursed.

"I have to get out of here," she said, rocking Lock off her arm.

He rolled over to free her and sat up. Natalie stood and dressed quickly. She took a blanket from the sofa and placed it over Lock, handing him a pillow from the recliner. "No need to get up, Lock. You stay here by the fire. I'll let myself out." She left.

Lock went to the window and watched Natalie start her car, and a few seconds later, he watched her get out to brush snow off her windshield. He knocked on a pane to get her attention. She looked up and blew him a kiss before getting into the car and pulling out of the driveway.

What could he do? Witt Mannheim was a piece of shit, and she made a good case that he was no good for the kids, but that alone wouldn't make a strong court case. There was no smoking gun sure to convince a judge that Witt was any kind of real danger to the kids. That DUI incident wouldn't influence the court enough, and if Witt's lawyer was a scumbag, there was no value in reporting the domestic abuse. So Natalie was screwed unless Lock helped her. Who else would protect her, or her kids?

On the other hand, was it Lock's moral responsibility to do anything beyond what the CPS policies and procedures called for? If he took his desire for Natalie out of the equation, he wondered, would he be thinking about protecting her children from their father's dangerous behavior?

Was he thinking clearly? Not really. Would the relaxing effects of just one drink calm his emotions down so he could think more clearly? Maybe. But then what? Ten drinks wouldn't be enough—and one was too many. Maybe going to a meeting would give him some clarity. He couldn't get her out of his mind. He knew this was lust and infatuation, not true love, but he didn't care.

Witt was in love with his money, not Natalie, not his children. But that wasn't Lock's concern. Lock thought he loved Natalie, but maybe it was just lust, or the kind of love that lasted only weeks or months. Maybe, someday, their relationship might be more than that. Witt driving the kids while drunk was of real concern to Lock, and him hitting Natalie made him want to choke the guy. Someone was eventually going to get hurt, or worse, and that was a problem Lock couldn't ignore. The question was what to do about it. CPS and the courts weren't going to solve this, so that left Lock to fix it. He'd be giving up much of who he had become since working at CPS—an honest, by-the-rules guy, someone who believed in the system. But even while debating with himself, he knew that what he might gain—Natalie, love, a family—outweighed all that.

———✧———

Natalie and Lock lay intertwined on the floor in his living room. Logs burned in the woodstove.

"Natalie, I want to tell you something," Lock said.

She propped herself up on an elbow and faced him with a sour expression, as if she expected a lecture.

"Your plan is strictly amateur night. One hundred percent third-rate."

"Amateur or not, I have to do it."

"I'm telling you not to do it," he said. "It's a textbook loser."

"Desperate times call for desperate deeds," said Natalie as she picked a piece of lint from the blanket they were laying on.

"Your husband has no history as a deviant," Lock said. "If he was convicted, it would be a first offense. But he'll never get convicted. Your witness is unreliable. Your husband's lawyer will demonstrate that in five seconds. She'll have to make it through interrogations without flinching, not even once. And she'll fail. Then you hope to get your husband to walk into court and fold a good hand. For what? Being accused of flashing or doing drugs and a DUI? And what about his lawyer? He won't sit there sucking his thumb. They'll figure out it was your idea and that's all they'll need. You'll wind up being prosecuted. Maybe it'll stick and maybe it won't, but your divorce will drag out for years."

He took her hands in his. "Too many things to go wrong," he said. "Your idea has 'please put me in prison' written all over it. In indelible ink. Baby, you have no idea how to make it work..."

Her eyes closed and she looked away. She wrapped the blanket around herself like a cocoon. He took her chin in his hand and turned her face back towards him.

"You have no idea how to make it work," he said. "But I do."

She froze for a beat. Then she placed her hands on his cheeks and rained kisses all over his face, neck, and shoulders. He pushed her away.

"Listen," Lock said, "I've seen frames blow up in people's faces a million times. And I've seen them work, too. I know how to play the family court system and I know how we're going to do it."

She hugged him.

"Do you know what you're saying?" she asked. "Have you thought about this?"

"I can't stand here and watch you bury yourself and expose the kids to God-knows-what. And I worry about myself, too, if I'm honest. If he hits you again, I don't know what I'll do."

She held him tight. "I don't want you to get involved if—"

"Little late for that."

"Okay, Lock. Then what's your idea?"

"Don't worry about that for now," he said.

"What about Abner? You said he'll be suspicious." Natalie raised her eyebrows and looked at Lock as if to challenge him.

"He would be—if he found out about it. But he won't. I'm going to close your file as unfounded. CPS will be officially out of your lives. And whatever happens from here on in won't make it onto his radar, because the agency will no longer be monitoring the situation. We don't track closed cases."

Natalie looked at him in the living room mirror. "I love you," she said.

He sat up and said, "Me too. But you should go home. I have things to think about." He reached out and touched her breast, and he watched himself doing it in the mirror. "I have to go over this, under it, around it—and after that, we're going to go through with it. Very carefully. As I said, I don't like small rooms with steel bars. But I need to help you."

"It's illegal?" she asked as she rose.

"Well, it's a gray area," he said, knowing it wasn't. "And we have to do this soon. Right away. This week, if I can get all the details arranged."

"Tell me."

"Not now."

Natalie darted around the apartment, gathering her few items of clothing and pulling them on.

"Why this week?" she asked. "Afraid you'll lose your nerve?"

"Yes," he said. "And I'm afraid of Abby. He's in his seventies, but don't let his age fool you. He's brilliant, and worse, his instincts never fail him. We don't want him to have a shred of an idea that something's fishy. He'll be all over it."

"Why does he intimidate you so much? He's only your boss."

"We're closer than that," Lock said. "He's like my father."

"You started to explain that in one of our marathon phone calls, but then you changed the subject."

Lock intentionally hadn't told her much about Abby. He felt uncomfortable bringing Abby—whom he saw as his spiritual mentor—into a relationship that might turn out to be ill-fated. But it was too late for Lock to be that circumspect.

"I'm closer to Abby than I ever was to my own father. In his younger years, Abby was a drunk like my father, but after he quit, he changed. After I did some teaching in an elementary school in Philadelphia, I went to work for CPS. For some reason, he took me under his wing. He got me into AA and helped me quit drinking and getting high all the time. He made up for what I missed as a kid from my father. But all of this is a conversation for some other time. I need to think clearly and get some sleep."

"I'll call you tomorrow, then," she said, reaching for the door.

"No. Don't call. No more contact for now. Play it cool. Remember, small rooms."

She turned back from the door, pressed herself up against him, and hugged him hard.

"You know how we nail almost everyone who tries to scam us?" he said. "It's easy. It's because they're stupid. Even the smartest of them are stupid and overconfident, sloppy with facts, the plans, the details."

"But we'll be careful," she said.

"Right," he said. "And paranoid. Get paranoid. Real paranoid. Act as if there are a dozen investigators on you twenty-four hours a day. That way, we'll make zero errors and take zero risks. When you take risks, it's only a matter of time until you get caught. We'll take no risks at all."

She kissed him goodbye and left.

He watched her from his window.

Lock moved closer to the fireplace, but it was no use. He couldn't get warm.

The truth was, there were no details to work out—it was just working up the nerve to go through with it. He knew exactly what he needed to do, and exactly how to pull it off. But he wasn't going to worry about the rationalization he'd need for himself—that would come in time, not that there was much time. He knew if he got started in on the details of what to do and how to do it, the courage would come.

His idea was ridiculously simple. *Witt drinks too much. He drives.* One night, he'd go out drinking. That would be his contribution to his own downfall. Lock would follow him and do the rest. And when Lock was finished with him, he'd want to settle with Natalie in about two minutes. The divorce would go through and that would be that. Justice would be served and no one, including Witt, would know different.

13

For Lock, the next day was a more or less normal day in the office. Nothing out of the ordinary happened, and that helped him stay outwardly calm as he made hurried, cryptic notes on a few sheets of lined paper, mapping out the details of his plan to help Natalie and the girls. When he was finished, he read them over to help commit them to memory, then took the pages to the office shredder and watched them turn into ribbons of trash.

He couldn't sit still. He walked to the water cooler three times. Anxiety coursed through his veins. For Lock, the excitement of planning the details of the scheme was like the intoxication of drinking—knowing he shouldn't do something, but doing it anyway. Through sheer will, he quashed his second thoughts and self-doubt.

Lock had a meeting with the Latino couple whose children had been living in the storage facility. He knew only a little Spanish, so he found a Spanish-speaking co-worker who helped him lecture the couple.

The county had arranged temporary housing for the whole family. The children ran wild in a conference room nearby, loosely supervised by a staff social worker who sat with them and read a magazine. Lock could hear the kids' peals of laughter from down the hall.

He picked up a cardboard box from the floor of his cubicle and followed the sounds of the children to the conference room. He entered and they immediately recognized him. They stopped chasing each other at once and stood whispering to each other, staring at Lock.

"Good morning," he said, pulling up a chair. He turned it around to face the children and sat down. The cardboard box was filled with art supplies. "What are you guys doing? Who likes to draw?"

The oldest child, the girl, lit up, her eyes wide. "We like to go to McDonald's."

"No, not today," Lock said.

The girl turned tragically to her siblings and spoke a quick phrase in Spanish. Their faces fell. Lock opened the box and removed pads of paper and a large plastic pouch. The social worker put down her magazine and watched Lock and the children.

He placed the items on the table and the kids clambered into the conference chairs, grabbing at the paper and reaching into the pouch, retrieving handfuls of crayons, markers, and colored pencils.

"I'd like you kids to draw pretty pictures for your new apartment," he said. "Your mama and papa might put them on the wall." Lock noticed that the youngest, a girl of maybe three, was watching him instead of making something with the art supplies. He slid his chair to the table and took a sheet of paper and a marker for himself. He began drawing a simple Christmas tree with small outlines of ornaments. He held his Christmas tree out for the little girl to see.

"Can you help me fill in the colors of the ornaments?" he said. The girl looked at the picture and back to Lock, then slipped off her chair and rounded the table to get to him. She looked at her big sister and said something in Spanish that Lock didn't understand. Without taking her gaze off of her own drawing, the big sister said something to the littlest.

Then the big sister addressed Lock, again, without looking up. "She wants to sit with you."

Lock motioned for the little one to come over and helped her up so she could sit in his lap.

"What color do you want?" he asked. "We have every color. Here's blue, here's green, and here's red. Pick one." The little girl's sister gave her some instruction and the little girl took a blue crayon and began to fill in the angel shape at the top of the tree.

"That's beautiful," Lock said. "Muy bonita. You're a great artist. Una artista magnifico." He thought that was right. They continued drawing together, Lock guiding the child's hand to the outlined shapes and helping her fill them in.

Lock's enjoyment of this interaction was muted by the little girl's resemblance to what Hannah might have been like at three. She didn't look exactly like Hannah, but Lock could imagine helping to teach Hannah how to draw, praising her efforts. He forced a small smile.

This is what I want. A family. Children to nurture, a wife to love. Why has that been so impossible for me? Will it always be this tough? With Natalie, it seems in arm's reach. The thought of a drink popped up, and just as quickly, Lock banished it.

The door to the conference room opened and Abby stood there. He surveyed the room.

"Lock," Abby said, "sorry to interrupt, but I need to speak with you."

Lock lifted the little girl off of his lap and sat her down on the chair. She was too small to reach the table comfortably. She wriggled around to get up on her knees.

Lock walked past Abby and out into the hallway. Abby followed and Lock closed the conference room door behind them.

Abby, a head shorter than Lock, squinted up. "How's it going, boy? I see you haven't submitted your assessment on that Red Cedar Woods case," he said. "Why not? Is there a complication?"

"I'm still thinking about it," Lock said. "Both parents deny filing the report of neglect, and each accuses the other. I want to know who did it before I make a decision about keeping the case open."

"Well, if there's nothing to it, don't dawdle in closing it," Abby said, adjusting his necktie. "We received three new reports overnight, and I need you to take at least one of them. You're my best investigator and I need you on real cases, not out there helping damsels in distress."

"If anything, it's the husband who's in trouble—this mom is a real piranha. At least, that's my impression after meeting her twice." He hated describing Natalie that way, but he needed to put Abby off the scent.

"Well, watch out, then," Abby said. "When a piranha is hungry, it'll eat anything, including its young."

"I'll be careful. Don't worry."

Abby tried to straighten his tie again, without much success. Lock reached out and tightened the knot in Abby's tie and centered it.

"Terrific," Abby grimaced. "Rich people burning up my limited resources and using us as entertainment so they can get the goods on each other for their divorce. There ought to be a law."

"Yes. The arrogance of the privileged, isn't that what you say?"

"So," he said, "if there's nothing to this Red Cedar Woods complaint, shelve it."

Lock had already decided the case would be closed, and soon. In a day or two, he'd tell Abby he thought the culprit might be the nanny, who'd filed the report because she couldn't stand Mr. Mannheim and wanted to cause him trouble anonymously.

As the day wore on, Lock began to feel better about his decision to proceed. He couldn't leave it up to CPS, either. Too much paperwork, too many lawyers. Judges. Continuances. Half the time CPS couldn't get John Wayne Gacy convicted, he thought. Lots of times, Lock would see a man lose a custody case, and he'd know he could have shown the poor sap how to win. Bend a rule here, fabricate a little there, big deal. It was all for the greater good, and, he admitted, for his own good. Didn't he deserve a family? So many of the people he came into contact with through work didn't. He was a good man. He would give Natalie and her kids a good life. Witt had to know he was being reckless when he drove drunk with kids in his car. All Lock would be doing was providing the consequences for his irresponsible behavior.

That was exactly what Lock would do, and once closing the case was out of the way, he'd be free to move forward with the preparations for what he was going to do to Witt Mannheim. And after that, he'd be a step closer to having Natalie and the beginnings of a family of his own. Natalie already had the girls. Maybe they would have boys together. *Two boys*, he thought. That's what he had always wanted. It would be a loving family of six. He couldn't wait to get started.

14

Later that afternoon, Lock drove into Media and found a spot right in front of the café. Natalie, dressed in her yoga tights and top, was sitting there waiting for him.

He bought a coffee for himself and a green tea for Natalie. They were in take-out cups. He joined her at a little round-top table in the rear.

No kiss hello, no touching. He just sat down. She opened her eyes wide in expectation and smiled.

He looked around and leaned in close to her. "Listen carefully. It's going to happen Thursday night. A week from tomorrow. Where I told you, at the time I told you. At the curve. Eight fifty. Exactly. Got it?"

Natalie spoke quietly. "A week from tomorrow. Eight fifty. And put my car in for service so I can get a loaner."

"Correct," Lock said. "And zero contact between us. None."

"That's not fair," she said, "I can't be without you for that long." She burned her eyes into his.

"I know," he said, picking up his coffee. "I could have told you this over the phone, but I wanted to see you."

Under the table, she slipped one of her feet out of her sandal and pressed her toes into his leg, walking them up to his knee and then forward onto his thigh. He pursed his lips and grabbed her ankle, pushing it down toward the floor. She exhaled in mild disappointment.

Her hand darted out and took his. He gave it a quick squeeze and let go.

"I have to go," he said, kissing her goodbye with his eyes.

Lock's mind was full of rushing thoughts as he walked to his car in the cold November air.

But was he rationalizing? Did this plan break any of the twelve steps of AA? More like all of the steps. Was there any justification at all for violating his professional ethics, his personal code of conduct? Possibly. Probably. He admitted to himself that there was plenty he'd be getting out of all this. He knew that. He'd have Natalie. And he'd benefit from the money. He couldn't pretend that wasn't part of the equation. He would have done it anyway, but the thought of being able to live in the way she was used to, the thought of taking the kids on vacation—skiing, maybe Europe—that mattered, too. For much of his life, no one had wanted or needed him. That was about to change.

Edwina was delightful—her seemingly infinite curiosity absolutely fascinated him, and her eager affection went straight to his heart. Dahlia brought Hannah to mind, a bittersweet memory. He was glad he had known Hannah, and crushed that he'd lost her. And both of Natalie's kids were sponges, absorbing everything they experienced. Lock's elementary school teaching days came to mind. Children loved to learn, and he loved to teach. What could be more perfect?

On Friday night, Lock stayed in the carriage house and tended to two blue orchids he had bought at a Home Depot garden center. On each plant, one bud had bloomed—white—and each plant held numerous buds almost ready to burst open. He moved the pots back several inches from the cold panes of glass in the window overlooking the driveway. The window faced south, and the man at the garden center had told him orchids preferred that. He had also told Lock that the greatest myth about orchids was that they were hard to grow. Outside the window was one of his favorite trees. It was just a birch, nothing rare, and nothing on his list, but it was one of the first things he'd noticed after he had gotten sober. Going to AA had allowed him to appreciate what he had, and soon after his first few meetings he had noticed the birch—it had always been there, as if waiting for him to see it. The idea embarrassed him, but he often thought of it as his guardian angel, a sign of the new direction his life had taken.

At Home Depot, Lock had asked question after question, wanting to get it right. Did the plant need to be repotted? What kind of soil was best? Should he buy one of those jars labeled "orchid food?"

Finally, the man cut him off, saying, "The most challenging thing about raising these little fellows is understanding exactly how little water they need and how much they love to be ignored. Just get them as much sunlight as possible."

Lock bought the plants hoping to surprise—or was it to impress?—Natalie, though he expected she would howl that she would have gladly given him at least one of her prize specimens. She'd probably chastise him for buying dyed orchids. After spreading newspaper on his kitchen table and repotting the plants based on the printed instructions provided by Home Depot, and then putting them back on the windowsill, Lock sat in his living room with his checkbook in hand and flipped through a stack of bills. Unable to concentrate, he paid none of them.

He opened his refrigerator and removed a stick of butter, three eggs, a small jar of dried parsley, and an onion—the ingredients he used to make omelets. As he assembled the items, a mild wave of nausea settled in his gut. Not enough for him to consider himself sick, but enough to put him off his appetite. He shook his head and returned everything to the refrigerator.

The rest of the night, he sat in his living room and watched TV. He couldn't describe a single event in any of the shows he'd watched. Then he went to bed and watched the ceiling for a few more hours. He didn't get within a thousand miles of sleep.

Earlier that afternoon at work, the fear had begun to set in. He was thoroughly distracted, scanning his to-do list for anything that urgently needed his attention. He knew the less critical tasks were going to have to wait. He couldn't function. And after work, it was worse. He tried everything. He went to an AA meeting but didn't hear a word. The heaviness in his gut wouldn't quit. He went back home, where he found himself almost in a trance, picturing everything he was going to do. Getting the Ambien into Witt's beer would be the toughest part. But he even had that figured out.

On Saturday, after another mostly sleepless night, Lock bundled up against the fifteen-degree weather and took a long walk, past the pond and into the deep woods beyond. At first, he thought he was shivering from the cold. But it wasn't the cold. It was him. It was the whole thing.

Lock heard people approaching. A family of four, two kids and two adults, were trudging through the woods on the same overgrown path Lock was on. The kids had sticks and were busy running and whacking snow and icicles off tree branches while their parents held hands and tried to keep up.

The family brushed by Lock, and the man nodded hello. Lock nodded back. The kids kicked snow at each other and tried to hide from their parents behind a stand of scraggly young chestnut trees.

Lock walked on but soon looked back when he heard the shouts of the kids, who had given chase to a couple of squirrels. When the kids gave up, the squirrels began chasing each other wildly around a tree stump. It was a simple thing, something families everywhere experienced all the time, so often that they didn't know how precious it was. It was what Lock wanted, and he knew he would do anything to have it.

15

That Sunday, Lock spent lunch on a park bench under lightly falling snow, watching a man try to help a few animated kids launch a kite in the November breeze. The kids wore identical coats with furry hoods and were all about the same height. Lock wondered if they were triplets. Despite the frigid weather, they appeared to be having fun, more interested in bowling one another over on the hill than in actually getting their kite in the air.

Lock waved to get the man's attention and signaled for them to move to a nearby slope where he knew they'd find it easier to launch. He'd flown kites at this park years ago with a former girlfriend and remembered the slope. What had ever happened to her? He remembered she once told him she never wanted to have children, and that had turned him right off. He'd kept going out with her, but he'd known it would be a casual-only affair. He didn't even remember the details of the break-up, except that it was his idea.

He watched the man and kids move in the direction he'd indicated. A moment later, they got the kite aloft. The kids jumped up and down and shouted with delight at the kite as it fluttered wildly on the string one of the kids held. The man tipped Lock a salute. He waved back, and he felt like he was waving goodbye to his own family.

On Monday, Lock went to the office and settled into his cubicle. He called Natalie on the burner phone. He said, "I have to meet, now." He gave her the directions to the park.

Twenty minutes later, Lock arrived at the same park he'd been to the day before. It was snowing again, and the flakes came down more heavily than yesterday, the sky darkened by heavy gray clouds.

Natalie pulled up fast in her Mercedes SUV and parked next to Lock's county car. She got out, and after a quick embrace, Lock took a step back.

"I can't do it, Natalie."

He watched for her reaction. There was nothing. She looked at him, waiting for him to say more.

"It feels like I'm about to jump off a bridge," he continued. "I can't think, I can't eat, I can't sleep. The truth is, I'm too scared. I don't think it's the right thing to do."

She's listened, motionlessly, arms folded.

"Okay, Lock, okay," she said. "I get it. I understand."

"No, you don't," he said. "There's been a waking nightmare going on in my head for the past three days. I can't take it and I can't do it. I'm getting out before it's too late. I'm sorry to let you down, but that's the way it has to be."

Natalie drew a circle in the snow with the tip of her sandal. Her bejeweled toes glimmered.

"This doesn't have anything to do with that lie Witt told about me and the yoga instructor, does it?" said Natalie.

"No. Nothing at all. You said it wasn't true."

"That's right, it's a lie. He's envious and suspicious of everything."

"I'm not worried about that," he said. "I'm worried about how you're taking it—that I changed my mind."

"It's okay, baby," she said. "It was crazy anyway, to think we could have made it happen."

"Oh, we could make it happen all right. But we won't. I won't."

She hugged him tightly.

"Okay," she said. "I don't care. As long as we have each other. Don't worry. Come here."

She reached out, grasped his hand, and pulled him to her. They kissed long and deep. Soon, he pushed away, remembering they were in public.

"I have to go now," she said.

"Don't," he said.

She moved close and looked steadily into his eyes. "This changes nothing between us," she said.

"Wouldn't that be pretty."

"It is pretty. We'll figure out a way to make us work."

Snow fell on them. He shivered.

Without warning, Natalie leaped over a low parking lot rail. Lock watched her sprint to the woods. When she didn't return, Lock circled wide, a snowball in his hand.

"Huge mistake!" Lock shouted from behind a nearby oak he had crept up to. His snowball sailed through the air and beaned her, not too hard, above her ear. Snow covered the side of her face, melting and dripping down her cheek like icy tears.

She laughed. "You little prick."

Natalie wiped the wet from her hair and face and gave Lock a quick hug.

She walked to her car, got in, and started the engine. She rolled down the window and turned toward him.

"Don't worry about a thing, Lock," she said. "All's well. You shouldn't do something you're not uncomfortable with. I'll figure something out."

Natalie put her car in reverse, pulled out of the spot, and drove off. She beeped her horn a few times and Lock saw her hand dart out of the window, giving him a jaunty wave goodbye.

As he watched her drive away, he wondered what had just happened. He hadn't known what to expect—it could be difficult to predict her behavior—but having her take it so genially was not something he'd considered.

16

Natalie had prepared two excuses so that her plan to be away from home all day and night would seem logical to Candice.

"Candice!" Natalie called from the living room. "Come in here, please."

"Yes, Mrs. Mannheim. Be right there, Mrs. Mannheim," Candice shouted from upstairs.

A minute later, Candice appeared, eyes half open and looking resentful at being disturbed.

Natalie checked the dates of the home-decorating magazines on the coffee table. She removed a couple of the older ones and held them in her hand. "I have a really busy day tomorrow. I'll need you in early and you'll have to stay overnight," Natalie told her.

"I was going to go out with Carlo for Japanese," Candice said, shaking her head. "A little warning would be nice, you know."

"I'm sorry, Candice. I couldn't predict emergency dental work far enough in advance to suit you."

"Oh," she said. "Sorry. What's wrong? Didn't know something was wrong."

"Well, there is. And worse, I'm going to my sister's in Princeton right after the dentist, and Witt's in Sacramento, so you'll be on duty all day, all night, and tomorrow morning. I'll be home by eleven a.m. Then you can have the rest of the day off."

"That's like twenty-four hours straight."

"Yes. But since you're helping me out, how about if I okay it for Carlo to spend some time here? You can have him in for dinner. Just this time. And no sleepover."

Candice's eyes opened wide. "Really? Carlo can actually come in? He doesn't have to wait at the door like a delivery man?"

"No. He can come in. This time. Why do you look so surprised?"

"Uh…because you hate him?"

"I don't dislike Carlo," Natalie said. "It's just that you can do so much better."

"You don't know him. You judge him. And anyway, he has so many great qualities, I overlook his flaws."

"That's a lot of overlooking. Anyway, if anything urgent comes up tomorrow or tomorrow night, don't call my sister's number. Reach me on my cell."

<hr/>

The next morning, Natalie drove down the gravel driveway to Lock's carriage house. During the ensuing twenty-four hours, she and Lock were inseparable.

Despite Lock's request that Natalie bring warm clothes—he had told her he had a surprise for her—she arrived at his carriage house in her usual state of being under-dressed regardless of the occasion, regardless of the weather—jeans and a lightweight top. At least she was wearing boots— leather boots that reached up over her knees. When he asked her about her lack of layers, she picked up a large overnight bag and informed him it contained a sweatshirt, down jacket, gloves, and earmuffs.

"What's the surprise? I usually don't like surprises," she said before they left for town. "They usually aren't good things."

"Okay," he said, "I'll tell you. I know you're skipping yoga to spend the day with me—"

"And you took a vacation day, so we're even," she said.

"—so I thought we'd spend the day walking. We'll have a self-guided tour of the city."

"Oh! I want to see Independence Mall. I've lived near Philadelphia for two decades and I've never been there. Witt promised to take Edwina and me, but that was just a Witt promise. Written on the wind."

They walked down the stairs and out into the chilly autumn air. Natalie carried her overnight bag.

"Here's the route," he said, "and we can change it any way you want. I was thinking we start at Delaware Avenue, walk up Walnut Street to Rittenhouse Square. Go into Barnes & Noble to get coffee and then sit in the park and drink it. That's about two miles."

"But Independence Mall is down on Fifth Street, right? You have us walking right past it."

"We'll catch the Liberty Bell and the historical stuff on the way back. Hear me out."

"Okay," she said. "I love that you've got this planned."

"Then, we walk across the bridge to the Penn campus. There's a bench there on Locust Walk with a life-size bronze sculpture of Ben Franklin sitting on it, reading a bronze newspaper. There's enough room on the bench for people to sit and get their picture taken."

"Pictures of us, together?" said Natalie. "That doesn't sound like the super-cautious Lock Gilkenney I know."

"We won't be taking any pictures, I was just telling you that's what people do.

"It's not supposed to get warmer than thirty today," she said. "I'm used to it from skiing. I can take it all day long. Can you?"

"I went to school in western Massachusetts, so I can take it. And you brought cold-weather gear, so we'll be fine."

They waited at Lock's carriage house apartment until 9:30 a.m. and then drove in her Mercedes from Red Cedar Woods up 95 into Philadelphia, finally parking in a lot at Penn's Landing along the Delaware River.

Somehow, aborting the mission to frame Witt, as far as Lock could tell, had brought Natalie and him closer than ever. Natalie appeared to be more relaxed, and he was unquestionably calmer.

Once they arrived in Philadelphia and began their walk from Penn's Landing toward Old City and Center City, Natalie lost no time in talking Lock into going to Independence Mall first, rather than on their return walk.

"This way," she said once he agreed, "if we run out of time, I'll at least have gotten to finally see some actual history."

The air was chilly and the sky was gray, but there was no breeze and neither of them felt the cold.

They walked across an expanse of worn red bricks to the enclosure that held the Liberty Bell. There wasn't so much a long line as there was a large throng of people, mostly families, standing between Lock and Natalie and the entrance to the Liberty Bell.

"A lot of happy families down here," Natalie said, interlacing her arm in his and squeezing. "Look at those three."

Natalie pointed with her chin at a man and a woman who walked next to each other with a little girl between them. They held her a few inches off the ground and swung her by her arms. She giggled, and her legs pumped the air as if she were riding a tricycle. Lock watched them before they disappeared into the crowd.

As they walked along, Natalie's cell phone rang. "It might be Candice," she said, "I have to take it."

"Go ahead."

Natalie said hello, and smirked. "It's Witt," she mouthed to Lock. She continued to listen for another half minute, and then without saying a word, hung up and slipped the phone back into her rear pocket. She looked ahead.

"What was that all about?" Lock asked.

"Witt just called me a mother-fucking bitch-hole."

Lock scowled at hearing that. "Verbal abuse. Does he say things like that in front of the girls? There's something you can use in court. What's got him so upset?"

"He doesn't need to be so upset to curse at me. And who knows what's under his skin this time."

"I see that," Lock said. "When things were better between you and Witt, you must have had good days, though, right?"

"Never had days like that," she said. "Some of the days weren't horrible, but once we were married, he became a thoroughly different man. Mostly surly and always sarcastic. I think I've picked up some of that trait."

"No, Natalie, you're not that way at all. You're funny. One of the many things I like about you."

"It was Witt's idea to have kids right away. I wanted to wait, in part because I wasn't so sure about him. He must have been harboring the same concerns, but his way of dealing with it was to complicate things by having children."

"You were opposed?"

"No, I was all for it," she said. "We just differed on when would be the best time."

"He won."

"He usually does."

Natalie took a quick peek at a tour map she'd picked up at the information desk and nudged Lock toward Congress Hall across the street from the Liberty Bell.

They walked arm-in-arm. Lock asked, "How's it going with your lawyer? Is he any good?"

"Jerome?" she said. "He's been great. He cut me a break on his fees since Witt cut me off. He says Witt will be hanging himself by using all his money and influence for lawyers and private eyes while letting all my credit cards and bank accounts go dry so I can't even pay a retainer."

"Or buy clothes for the girls?"

"Yes. Right. That's going to look bad for Witt."

Natalie turned and, still arm-in-arm, walked Lock toward the street. "Let's change the subject," she said. "This is too beautiful of a day to contaminate it with Wittley Mannheim."

"Okay, but one last thing. You need to have another talk with your lawyer friend. You can't give your husband a long leash to build a case against you while you sit back and watch. You've got to protect yourself."

"I don't know, Lock. I trust the universe. Everything will work out."

"Yeah, sure. Don't forget the combat soldier's creed—'Praise the Lord, but pass the ammunition.'"

"You have to have faith, Lock. You're the one who didn't want to help me do it my way."

"Your way was a terrible way."

"I know, and yours is better. But here we are. I get that you don't want to risk anything you could get in trouble for, but that means you have to trust me, and trust Jerome. I get a good vibe from him."

"How many custody cases has he done?"

"I don't know," Natalie said. "Mostly he's done fraud cases, I think."

Jesus, Lock thought. "You couldn't find anyone else?"

"With what money? Jerome's a friend's friend, and he's helping me out. What else am I supposed to do?"

"It's just that divorce and custody...it's complicated, Natalie. You wouldn't get a divorce attorney to defend you at a murder trial, would you?"

Instead of getting mad, she kissed him. "Change of subject, okay? We're going to do the best we can. It's all we *can* do."

Lock felt like an ass. If he'd had the money, he would have given it to her, but he didn't. He had promised to help her and then backed out, and now she had some strip-mall lawyer going up against a team of whatever pro divorce attorneys Witt's lawyer could put together. *Jesus.* He had set her up to be massacred.

It started to get dark a little before five p.m., and Lock and Natalie made their way back to the car. By then, they were both thoroughly chilled.

"Let's check in to the Four Seasons," Natalie said, rubbing her hands together as Lock started the engine. "We'll get a room with a Jacuzzi and we'll warm up fast."

Even that made Lock feel guilty. Soon enough, she wouldn't be able to afford the Four Seasons. He said, "Let's go back to my place and get an inferno going in the woodstove."

When they got to the carriage house, Natalie immediately went into the shower and adjusted the water to the hottest temperature. "Lock!" she said, "Come on in. It's hot and steamy in here."

Lock popped his head into the bathroom. Her few clothes were all over the floor. "Don't take too long in there. The hot water lasts ten minutes, tops."

While Natalie hummed in the shower, Lock paced the living room in front of the fire.

What if Witt wins and Natalie gets visitation and next to nothing in child support? Shit, there's no 'what if'—that's what's going to happen. Lock tugged at his earlobe as he traversed the room, back and forth. *What if I do help her and things go wrong? Would she be worse off? Should I just stay out of this? But how can I? I have to protect her. And the girls.*

Then Lock remembered the page he'd ripped from a magazine years ago that described Ben Franklin's method of making decisions. Where was that article? He thought for a moment and then went to his bookcase, opened a scrapbook, and found the torn page. His eyes scanned it as he read it for the hundredth time. It had helped him deal with the urge to drink, and also when faced with tough decisions at work. It read:

> *My way is to divide half a sheet of paper by a line into two columns; writing over the one Pro and over the other Con. Then during three or four days' consideration, I put down under the different heads short hints of the different motives, that at different times occur to me, for or against the measure. When I have thus got them altogether in one view, I endeavor to estimate their respective weights; and where I*

find two, one on each side, that seem equal, I strike them both out. If I judge some two reasons con equal to some three reasons pro, I strike out five; and thus proceeding, I find where the balance lies; and if after a day or two of further consideration, nothing new that is of importance occurs on either side, I come to a determination accordingly.

That's the solution, Lock thought. *I'll make a list. I'll use Franklin's method, and whatever comes will come. And I'll adhere to it whether I want to or not. Whether I like it or not.*

In his head, while the sound of water came from the shower, Lock began to populate the list of pros and cons of breaking the rules to help Natalie. He had already made a decision and then changed his mind, but he had never looked at it rationally using Franklin's method.

The pros included Natalie and the girls and their legal right to live the lifestyle they were accustomed to, especially the girls. Going from a great private school to public school was no good if the public schools were like the ones Lock had attended and taught at. The next thing on the list was Lock's conviction that he would finally realize a life-long dream of having a real family and the chance to be with an incredible woman who he could easily imagine loving him unconditionally. He was equally convinced that through the knowledge and tools he acquired in AA, he had grown spiritually, emotionally, and intellectually, and knew that he deserved to be truly happy.

The cons were less ambiguous. To help Natalie effectively, he'd be breaking the law. Executing a frame-up had profound moral implications, too. Lock believed that in life, you were constantly in motion, either growing or regressing, either moving toward the light or toward the darkness. What would conspiring with Natalie amount to? Would crossing the line be justified, just this once, for a greater good? Was he being swayed by his paternal instinct, or was he in denial and yielding to garden-variety self-indulgence?

Franklin said he needed to make his list and let days go by before coming to a conclusion about the way to go, but Lock didn't have the luxury of time. He wanted an answer, and wanted it then and there.

The sound of the shower being turned off distracted him.

"Lock! There's nothing to dry off with in here."

"I'll be right there," he said, heading to the stacked washer-dryer where he usually left the clean towels until he either needed them or had to do dry more clothes. He handed her a towel as she stood dripping on the bathroom rug. He glanced at himself in the bathroom mirror, but there was too much condensation on it for him to get a good view.

As the evening wore on, Lock and Natalie sat wrapped in a blanket in front of the wood-burning stove and watched the flames consume the split wood.

"I guess it never would have worked anyway," Natalie said.

"What?"

"Framing Witt."

"We'll figure it out."

"We will, I know. As long as there's a 'we,' I'll be okay. Witt's gone a lot, so there's no reason we can't keep going on like this."

Lock's stomach did a slow roll. Sneaking around and never having the chance to be a parent? His mind raced at the thought of Natalie reconciling with Witt. *A couple of beers would be nice right about now*, he thought. He only needed a little alcohol in his system to relax. He didn't need to get stumbling drunk, just a little. And that thought gave him clarity. If imagining Natalie and the kids staying with Witt made him want a drink, he knew it was no good.

———⟫⟪———

Early the next morning, Lock got up, made coffee, and waited for Natalie to awaken. He brought a steaming mug into the bedroom when he heard her stir.

"Good morning," he said. "Sleep okay?"

"Slept wonderfully," Natalie said. "It's always wonderful to fall asleep next to you." She got out of bed naked, reached slowly to the ceiling, took a deep breath, and exhaled. She stretched her arms high and then gracefully swept them in a downward motion until her palms touched the carpet.

From her folded-over position, she spoke. "I had a dream," she said. "We were married and had twin boys. We were walking in the city and it started to rain like a madman, and you whisked us all under a restaurant's awning and kept us dry. That was the whole dream." She stood up. "But somehow that little thing left me loving you even more."

"That's a sweet dream."

"Yeah, Witt wasn't in it."

"Every time you start to think about him, replace that image with a mental photograph of Dahlia and Edwina. You'll see. It really works if you stay at it."

"Well, there's a better solution, but you don't want to help me."

"Look," he said. "Don't get mad, but I changed my mind."

"Did you. Again?" She was suspicious, and he didn't blame her.

"Okay," he said. "Okay, Natalie, I know. It's just…I need to do the right thing. Now I know helping you is the right thing. I'll make it happen. Let's move forward carefully, with extreme caution. No mistakes, no slip-ups, no small rooms. Okay?"

Natalie sprang forward and jumped up into Lock's arms. She hugged him, squeezing as hard as she could.

Lock nodded but didn't smile.

"You're doing it for the girls as much as you're doing it for me," she said, releasing him. "With your help, I'll be free. I love you. And now, I'm off to yoga." She kissed him quickly and bounded down the stairs.

Natalie, sprawled in bed next to her lawyer, Jerome Freel. She sat up, leaned forward, and fluffed two pillows behind her.

"I feel like a cigarette," she said.

"You don't smoke, Nat."

"Not anymore. Anyway, I wish you'd make the extra effort to pronounce two more syllables and call me Natalie. I've asked you that about a hundred times."

Freel, in his early thirties and muscular, got out of bed and headed toward the bathroom on the far side of his enormous bedroom. He returned a minute later holding a black, leather toiletries travel bag and sat down on the bed. He put the bag on the nightstand.

"I agree with you," he said. "There's not much that could go wrong, and if it does, I want Lock Gilkenney to be the one who's implicated. Not you."

Freel unzipped the bag and withdrew a small prescription pill vial and a short aluminum straw. He opened the vial and carefully shook out a small mound of white powder. He put the straw up to one of his nostrils, leaned over, and snorted.

"Nothing's going to go wrong," she said. "Lock's plan is solid."

Freel sniffled and held the straw out to Natalie.

Natalie shook her head. "No. I told you, it will screw up my yoga."

"Good, more for me," Freel said. "Anyway, I like his plan. Pretty clever. Sometimes I like that guy."

"Me too," she said, rolling over closer to Freel. "He brings out the best in me. When I'm with Lock, I want to be a better woman, a better mother. When I'm with you, I don't even think about my kids. I don't give a damn about anything. I want to be bad. It's like there's a light switch in my head. Flip it on, I want Lock, flip it off, I want you."

"So I'm the dark side," Freel smirked. "I love it."

"And that ludicrous drug idea worked perfectly," she said. "That was a stroke of genius. He hated it."

Freel got back under the covers and rolled Natalie onto her side and spooned up against her. He draped his arm across her chest.

"Jerome," she said.

"Yes?"

"Tell me you love me," she said.

"I thought you said I was incapable of love."

"I did. And you are. But I like it when you lie to me."

"Nat," he said. "I'm here to help you get out of a fucked-up marriage and get the most money possible. And you're here to take care of me. That's our deal, and it's working out."

"You forgot to mention your unconscionable fee. Three hundred thousand."

"Plus expenses," he said. "I told you, you owe me nothing until after you get your millions. If it wasn't for me, you'd wind up with shit. So you should look at what I'll get as a tip, not a fee. Plus, I'm looking forward to spending it all on you."

"And what about after my divorce, what will happen?"

"I don't know," he said. "You'll be a free woman. You'll do as you please. As if you don't already. I like the arrangement we have."

"Nothing more than that?"

"I know you want me to lie to you, but I won't."

"You respect me," she said. "That's funny. You make me laugh." She pushed him away from her. Then she pouted. "But on the other hand, I like you. A lot. So I guess I have to put up with what you are. Golf, sluts, coke and disbarred for insurance fraud. You know what they say—99% of lawyers give the other 1% a bad name."

"Funny," Freel said, raising a finger and grinning. "But I was suspended, not disbarred, and they couldn't prove it. Besides, my suspension is up Friday. Fully reinstated and ready to make money."

"But now you're broke and living the partying life on credit cards. You can't even pay the lease on your boat slip. I don't know why I find that so appealing, but I do." She shook her head.

"Living beyond one's means is an art, and I'm a genius at it. Plus, I'll have that three hundred grand in a month or two. And your attraction to me is just part of your low self-esteem and self-destructive behavior. I like it." Freel ran his hand over her body.

She shrugged him off. "Maybe I'll just stick with Lock," she said. "He loves me."

"Go ahead. What's he make, forty grand a year? You wouldn't put up with that for long."

"Yes, but soon I'll have all the money I need. So I can afford to be with someone who cares about me and my kids."

"Like I said, you wouldn't put up with that for long."

Freel tried to grab Natalie again, but she rolled away.

"Get back here."

"Too late," she said. She grinned at him and got out of bed. "I've got to get to yoga."

"Skip it."

"No way. Maybe I'll see you later."

Freel sat up, leaned over the nightstand, and did another line.

"For the record," he said, "I'm against anything illegal or unethical, so it's my professional advice to abandon the plan to set up your husband." He smirked again. "On the other hand, don't forget—it's Lock who has to be the one to put the sleeping pills in Witt's drink, he has to be the one who drives Witt's car into the tree, and he has to be the one who puts the baby in the back of the car. Not you. Understand? You're just an innocent bystander. He bullied you into this. That's the way it's got to appear. Remember, in court, it's not what's true that counts, it's what's believed."

Natalie pulled on her clothes and headed for the hallway.

"Yes, Jerome, I know. It's the tenth time you've told me."

17

Lock sat alone at his kitchen table, using a mortar and pestle to crush the last of six little orange-pink pills into a fine powder. He used an index card to guide the powder into a plastic drinking straw. He folded the straw in half and taped the ends closed. He tapped the straw with his thumb to see if the powder would stay put until he was ready to release it. It seemed to work, and he was satisfied that the crude device would serve its purpose.

Lock remembered the one useful thing his father had taught him—if you have an hour to cut down a tree, sharpen your ax for fifty minutes. Prepare, prepare, prepare. It was good advice, but it was ironic coming from him. As far as Lock could tell, his father spent fifty minutes thinking about sharpening the axe and then gave up and opened a beer.

But it was still good advice, and that was exactly what Lock was doing. He was thinking of everything. Every possible possibility. He had five pages of notes. Categories like things that could go wrong, places that could go wrong, people who could go wrong. Things such as Witt suspecting something, Candice suspecting something, being observed spiking Witt's beer, being seen putting Witt in his car, being seen at the curve.

Everything—even the need for Natalie to give Dahlia just a tiny amount of prescription cough medicine to insure she'd remain asleep during the execution of the plan.

Lock reviewed his notes, running his finger down the list of risks and then explaining to himself how each one had been mitigated.

The waiter seated Abby and Lock at a dinner table in Foster & Zandt's. Lock told the waiter that they were okay with water and didn't need to see the wine list. The waiter shrugged and walked away, saying that he'd give the pair a few more minutes to decide on their meals.

Abby tossed his menu aside. "So, the Mannheim file is coming back to bite us, and it's turning into quite a mess."

"Do we have to talk about work, Abby? My mind needs a break."

"Fine," Abby said. "We'll make small talk while racking our brains trying to figure out what's going on with Natalie Mannheim and her husband. Fine. Let's forget all that and talk about Phillies spring training."

"Spring training is three months away, Abby. It's just that the case is on my mind all the time. I can't shake the worry that I closed it too soon."

Abby tossed his menu aside. He looked around for the waiter, spotted him lingering by the service bar, and waved to him. The waiter sauntered over and brought a pencil point to the order pad.

"What'll it be, gentlemen?"

Abner ordered steak, medium, and Lock ordered salmon. The waiter wrote it down and walked away.

After dinner, Lock drove Abby back to his car at the office parking lot and said goodnight.

Lock drove into town, feeling unsettled. He parked at a meter and entered Jake's, a bar he had frequented during his drinking days.

He sat at the bar, drinking from a shot glass.

The bartender leaned against the counter, watching him. The adjacent restaurant had a handful of customers, but the bar was nearly empty. One lone couple, oblivious to Lock, sat at the far end of the bar, talking.

Lock caught the bartender's eye. "Another one, Billy," he said.

"Come on, man, get out of here," he said, drying a glass with a cloth. "You know I won't serve you alcohol, and drinking water like that is silly."

"Humor me."

Billy shrugged and removed the cap from a bottle of spring water. He filled another shot glass and slid it to Lock and looked him in the eyes.

"Whatever you're trying to bury, that won't do it. Why don't you get yourself to one of your meetings?"

Lock tried to stare him down. Billy held his gaze. Lock reached into his pocket and withdrew his wallet.

"Take your money back," Billy said.

Lock downed the shot, then slapped a twenty-dollar bill on the bar and stood up. He headed toward the exit. Billy called after him.

"Hey, Lock," he said. "You're really losing it."

"Can't disagree with you, Billy. I really can't."

Lock drove back to the carriage house and got into bed, and after fifteen or twenty minutes of tossing and turning, fell into a sound slumber.

When he awoke Thursday morning, he noted with some satisfaction that he had had a restful sleep, and he interpreted that to mean his conscience was clear and that his plan made sense and was justifiable. All his doubts about going forward seemed to have evaporated.

As soon as Lock arrived at CPS headquarters that morning, he was summoned to Abby's office. Several others were seated around Abby's cluttered desk when he entered the room. No one was smiling.

"What happened?" Lock asked, taking a seat.

Abby cleared his throat and addressed Lock. "One of Cohen's cases. Drumbolt family in Brandywine Village. You know the file?"

"Never heard of them," he said.

"Well, last night the father—there's no mother—got plastered. Drugs or alcohol or both, I don't know. But he managed to set the kitchen on fire. He's dead. Smoke inhalation. Fire marshal says it looks accidental. Nevertheless, we now have two children, ages seven and nine, in the hospital."

"How are the kids?" Lock asked.

"We don't have all the information yet. Second- and third-degree burns is all I know now, but I don't know how extensive. But what I do know is that we tried to get the kids removed from the residence but got blocked in court. And now, this."

Fred Cohen, the investigator in charge of the Drumbolt file, sat grim-faced, his eyes filling up. He turned to Lock. "I knew that son-of-a-bitch was a threat to the children, but there was nothing I could do. I tried. I tried." He slapped his hand on Abby's desk.

"Alright, Freddy," Abby said. "Take it easy. You're not to blame. You did an exemplary job. Unfortunately, Drumbolt had effective counsel at the protective custody hearing."

Lock walked to Cohen and put his hand on his shoulder. "Don't take it to heart, Fred. You did what you could. Too bad the judge didn't know you can't trust a drunk."

"Lock's right, Freddy. You can't trust an active drunk. They'll let you down every time."

Lock felt terrible for Cohen and the kids and wasn't unhappy to hear the fate of the father.

He couldn't help but think of Witt and the kids he would inevitably wind up maiming—or worse—unless Lock took action now. And hitting Natalie…Lock knew that kind of thing tended to escalate over time. *I'm not going to sit here someday in a meeting like this, regretting my inaction. I'm going to do it. It's the right thing to do.*

Any fleeting doubts about what he was going to do to Witt were now relegated to the trash heap.

18

The Cavern Tavern was hopping. The crowd at the bar was two deep. On a stage behind the bar, dancing girls gyrated and teased each other. Customers shouted, jeering and daring them.

One of the loudest was Witt Mannheim, holding a mug of beer. Natalie had told Lock that her husband would be there, and she was right. A curvaceous woman stood behind Witt with her arm around his shoulders. She was sloshed. He was too.

Standing a few feet away was Lock, chomping on an unlit cigar. A baseball cap was pulled down over his forehead and his jacket collar was turned up. He wore thick-framed glasses. He stole glances at Witt from under the brim of his cap and watched him in the mirror over the bar.

"Hey!" yelled the woman. "Hey, bartender!" An exasperated bartender arrived and asked for her order.

It was Lock's chance.

With the folded straw positioned carefully in his palm, Lock held a hundred-dollar bill in his fingers. He started to reach across the bar—and over Witt's mug—to ask for change. He was moments away from opening one end of the straw and dumping the powdered sleeping pills into Witt's beer.

Two rowdy customers jostled Lock, almost knocking him to the floor.

"Sorry about that, Chief," one of the men said. Lock didn't respond, and by the time he repositioned himself, the bartender was nowhere to be seen and Witt had picked up his beer.

Lock checked his watch.

———

Natalie, wearing black slacks and a yellow blouse instead of her usual cut-offs and t-shirt, shouted up to Candice.

"Candice," she said, "give Dahlia a dropperful of the medicine on her dresser. Be exact. One dropperful. Then close the bedroom door."

"I didn't know she was sick."

"Well, you're not her doctor. Give her the medicine."

Candice rolled her eyes.

"She's, like, totally asleep, Mrs. Mannheim."

"Then, like, totally give her the medicine anyway. Wake her."

Natalie tiptoed up the carpeted stairs, almost to the top, and craned her neck around the corner to watch. She saw Candice give Dahlia the medicine. Candice left the room and entered the hall bathroom. Natalie stepped up to the landing and heard water splashing in the shower.

Natalie checked her watch. In the bathroom, Candice's cellphone rang. Candice reached out of the shower and answered and said something unintelligible. Moments later, she hung up.

Natalie went back to the landing and shouted down the stairs, trying to give Candice the impression that Witt had returned home.

Louder than necessary, Natalie said, "Witt, what are you doing? What did you break?"

In the bathroom, Candice's soaking head popped out of the shower curtain.

"What? I'm in the shower."

"Not talking to you, Candice. Talking to Witt." Shouting downstairs again, Natalie said, "And look what you're doing with your fucking shoes!"

While Candice showered, Natalie quietly entered Dahlia's room, wrapped a blanket around her, and picked her up.

She checked to see if Edwina was asleep. She was.

With Dahlia in her arms, Natalie left the bedroom, careful to close the door behind her. She walked down the stairs, crossed the foyer, and purposely elbowed an empty wine glass from the kitchen counter, shattering it on the floor.

In the garage, Natalie grabbed a car seat from a workbench and belted it onto the backseat of the loaner car Lock had told her to arrange for from the Mercedes dealership. Natalie had reported a strange sound emanating from the rear axle of her own car to the service manager, knowing that they'd need to keep her car overnight. Natalie put Dahlia in the car seat.

As she was about to get into the driver's side, she heard something, a sound like something brushing up against a cardboard box. She listened for a moment, heard nothing further, and forgot about it.

She checked her watch.

Eight thirty-nine.

Natalie hurried back into the house, glancing at the shards of the wine glass shattered on the kitchen floor as she made her way up the stairs.

She walked to the bathroom door. Candice was still singing. She knocked once. Candice went silent.

"I'm late for the Orchid Society meeting," said Natalie. "I should have left an hour ago."

Candice shouted from the shower, "Okay. Will you still be back by ten? Carlo's picking me up."

"Watch out," Natalie said. "Mr. Personality's home. Drunk. He broke a glass in the kitchen, so take care of that."

A pause.

"Did you hear me?" Natalie asked.

"Yeah. Clean up his mess."

"If he's not passed out," Natalie said, "you can leave at ten. If he is out of it, that's no different than leaving the kids alone, so Carlo has to wait. And keep the baby monitor on."

Natalie went back downstairs. She looked at the wall clock in the kitchen. She needed to leave in four minutes, no sooner.

Natalie walked into the solarium and began to stretch. She raised her arms straight up and, bending slowly from the waist, reached down and placed her palms flat on the floor. She stayed in that position and took three deep breaths, inhaling and exhaling, then, just as slowly, stood up.

———————

The bar was more crowded and louder now.

Witt spoke in whispers to the woman draped over him. He followed her to a line formed at the ladies' room. The woman was trapped between the wall and his arm resting on top of a wall-mounted payphone. She laughed at whatever it was he said.

Lock watched and moved closer.

Witt set his mug on the shelf beneath the phone. Lock, cigar in his mouth, leaned forward and pretended to stumble up against the phone between him and the woman.

In a low mumble, Lock said, "Whoa. Sorry. Cell phone's dead. Trying to call home."

Lock picked up the receiver. He was closer to Witt's beer than Witt was. In an instant, he withdrew the folded straw from his pocket, flicked the tape off one end, and dropped the powder into the mug.

The beer in the half-empty mug foamed slightly. Most of the powder dissolved as it sank.

Lock had wanted to get the drug in while the mug was still full—it would be less noticeable that way. From a sideways glance, it seemed to be undetectable. No residue was apparent.

A moment later, to Lock's nervous delight, Witt reached out and retrieved his mug and, as if on cue, raised it high and drained it in one long, sloppy gulp.

———◦———

Natalie lurched out of the garage in the loaner car. The baby's car seat jostled in the rear.

A light, cold rain sprayed the windshield. She turned on the car radio. Rap. She changed the station.

She craned her neck to see if the radio had woken Dahlia, but she was still sound asleep.

As Natalie drove, she looked at herself in the mirror. In the subdued light of the car interior, she looked a good five years younger than her thirty-five. Maybe even more.

She was in a cheerful mood, not nervous at all, and her mind ran through several upbeat thoughts. She had a right, she told herself, to look younger than her years—she ate right, worked out, improved her mind through reading, and took her yoga practice seriously. When she was inspired, she thought, she was a wonderful mother to the girls.

And the best part, she thought smugly, *is that I'm about to be one huge step closer to winning everything I deserve.*

———◦———

Witt and his companion, bundled in their heavy coats, made their way across the parking lot with labored steps, like they were trudging through ankle-high mud. Witt's gait suggested he was beginning to feel the drug, not to mention the alcohol he had been drinking for more than two hours. The woman was drunk, too. They were all over each other, alternately holding one another up, laughing, stumbling, and talking loudly.

Lock stood outside, waiting in the sleet.

Witt and the woman supported each other across the icy asphalt. Lock moved closer and followed them. He could hear their slurred conversation.

"You're not driving," Witt said.

"Yes I am."

She was so drunk she could barely stand.

"At my drunkenest, I drive infinitely better than you can stone-cold sober," Witt said.

"How do you know how I drive? You don't even remember my name."

"Cindy."

"Sandy," she told him.

"Doesn't matter. You're still too drunk."

The woman leaned close and spoke into his ear as they approached his car. He leered at her.

"In that case, you leave me no choice," he said.

Whatever she'd told him had convinced him that he should let her drive.

As Witt held his keys out to the woman, Lock's hand appeared out of nowhere and snatched them from Witt's fingers.

"I don't think so," Lock said.

Lock stood half-turned away so neither of them could see him dead-on. By now, Witt was so out of it that all he did was laugh belligerently. The woman, without provocation, threw a weak punch at Witt and hit him in the arm.

"Settled," she said. "Your friend can drive us."

"I don't even know him. He might be drunker than you, sugar."

Witt looked ill, as if he was going to vomit. A rivulet of saliva dripped from the corner of his mouth. The woman saw it.

"That is disgusting," she said.

With drunken impetuousness, she marched back to the bar, teetering in her heels on the slick ground. As she reached the entrance, she slipped on the ice. She fell on her face, picked herself up, and lurched back inside. Lock breathed a sigh of relief. The story he had cooked up to get rid of her wasn't very good, and now he didn't have to use it.

Witt slumped against his car. Lock surveyed the scene. No one was there, except, at the far end of the parking lot, a running car with headlights on. Thanks to the precipitation, there was almost no visibility.

In a gruff voice, Lock asked Witt, "What's her problem?"

"Probably thinks I'm too drunk to do anything to her. She's so wrong."

"Her loss."

"And here I'm standing out in the snow with you," Witt bellowed. He half nodded off while standing there.

Lock eyeballed the path around the car to the passenger side, sized up Witt's bulk, then thought better of trying to escort him around to the other side. It would be easier to slide him into the driver's seat than to walk him to the passenger door. Once in the driver's seat, Lock would be able to shove him across to the passenger side.

He opened the driver's door and was about to heave Witt in. He stopped abruptly. The car from the far side of the parking lot eased up and stopped. It was a taxi. Lock closed the car door quickly.

"Your buddy there is out of it," the driver said to Lock. "You want me to take him home? Friends don't let friends drive drunk as hell."

"Uh..." Lock said, averting his face.

"If he doesn't live too far," the taxi driver said, "it'll be twenty bucks. Off the meter. This weather's getting bad. Pretty soon you won't be able to get a cab." The guy certainly wanted a fare.

"Nah," Lock said. "He says his brother-in-law's coming over to take him." Witt looked up from his stupor.

"No brother-in-law of mine!" he said.

The driver shrugged, put the taxi into gear and drove off, windshield wipers moving wildly back and forth.

Lock looked around. He checked his watch again. A few people exited the bar, but they headed the other way.

He walked over to Witt and propped him up with one hand as he opened the driver's door with the other. Lock dropped him into the driver's seat, took hold of the car frame above the door, and with both feet, pushed a practically unconscious Witt onto the passenger seat.

Lock leaned in and buckled the man into his seat.

En route to meet up with Natalie, the roads were dark and slippery. Lock eyed Witt's sleeping body and smiled inwardly.

He knew that what was about to happen was the riskiest part of the whole enterprise, but he felt confident everything would go as planned. The part in the bar had gone perfectly. And it was almost over. If other drivers went by when Lock was setting up the scene a few minutes from then, they wouldn't know what they were seeing. If anyone stopped, they wouldn't be able to identify him. Natalie's Mercedes SUV might have been a problem, and that was why Lock had wanted her to use a loaner. And the bad weather was a good cover. Everything was going right. And as soon as the task was completed, he'd head straight to the cabin in the Poconos and take a long, hot shower. He was cold to his bones.

Natalie arrived at her destination on the curve at precisely 8:50.

The temperature had dropped several degrees, and a hard sleet pelted her car. She pulled off the road near a couple of picnic tables. No other cars were in sight. She killed the engine.

Around the bend, headlights appeared. It was hard to see. Natalie flashed her high beams. The oncoming vehicle hit its brakes. She could see it was a FedEx truck. It drove by slowly but never stopped.

Soon after, Lock arrived driving Witt's car. He slowed down. Natalie blinked her high beams again.

He stopped alongside Natalie's car and squinted through his icy window. He opened his door, got out, and walked toward her. He took off his leather jacket. When he reached her car, Natalie lowered her window. Lock threw her his jacket.

"Overkill," she said, studying the cigar, glasses, and ball cap.

Lock tossed the cigar into the bushes. He crouched beside her and handed her his ball cap. She handed him his trapper hat, flaps down.

"This wardrobe stuff is silly," she said.

"I play the percentages," he said.

Natalie wriggled around and leaned back so she could reach the car seat holding the sleeping Dahlia. She unbuckled it and started to hand the car seat and Dahlia out through the window.

"No," said Lock. "Keep her until after I hit the tree."

"But it's only going to be a little fender-bender," she said. "She'll be fine."

"After I hit the tree," Lock said. He dashed back to Witt's car. He got in, buckled his seatbelt, and looked over at the semiconscious man in the passenger seat.

He backed up five yards and stopped. He checked the rear-view mirror. No one was coming.

From her car, Natalie had a view of the other bend, the one Lock couldn't see. She signaled with her lights. All clear.

Lock stomped on the gas pedal and drove deliberately into the mighty oak tree there—he hated to hurt the tree—slightly harder than intended. Inside the car, the front airbags burst open. Lock sustained a bloody nose and dabbed at the blood with a napkin he found in his jacket pocket. Witt appeared to be okay. There was moderate front-end damage to the car—the bumper and grille were crumpled, a headlight was smashed, and the hood had buckled.

Witt groaned. Lock released his own seatbelt, opened his door, and jumped out, keeping an eye on his passenger. Witt, in a stupor, mumbled but did not move. Lock unbuckled Witt's seatbelt and tried to lug him over into the driver's seat. He was able to move him only partway, but that would be good enough.

Lock looked over his shoulder. Natalie's car pulled up and stopped alongside her husband's car. Lock left Witt sprawled on the front seat. He turned toward Natalie.

"Don't forget to put the flashers on," he said.

She did it and then passed Dahlia, secured in her car seat, to Lock who had opened the driver's door. He adjusted the blanket to cover her exposed stomach.

Lock had anticipated that both front airbags would inflate upon impact, and he knew that would be a red flag to the police. He placed Dahlia on the passenger seat. Her weight would explain the front passenger airbag inflating, and it had the added bonus of being an unsafe place for her—another strike against Witt. He watched her as she slept soundly.

Lock straightened up and took another look at Dahlia. *I don't want to do this.*

"You'll be fine, baby," he said. "We'll be right down the road."

He shut the rear door quietly.

Lock next closed the driver's door, took a deep breath, and checked the road in both directions. He saw nothing. He hopped into Natalie's car, nodded at her, and they drove off.

"Nice and slow," he said.

He took a new prepaid cellphone from his pocket and dialed 9–1–1 to report the crash.

19

The bulk of Witt's now damaged car was on the shoulder, pressed up against the tree. Only the rear remained on the roadway. The car's single working headlight illuminated a swath of the thick woods. Steam rose from the cracked radiator.

Moments after Natalie and Lock drove off, another vehicle, a late model pickup—weaving and with windshield wipers snapping back and forth—bore down on the curve where Witt's car was.

The teenage driver's girlfriend unbuckled her seatbelt and slid closer to him. She switched on the radio. Music blared. She put her arm around him and leaned in playfully to kiss his neck. These distractions occurred at precisely the wrong moment. The pickup's right front end didn't clear the corner of Witt's car that jutted out onto the road, and they collided with a powerful impact, spinning it violently up against another tree. The pickup skidded off the road, bounced off a fieldstone wall and flipped over, landing on the passenger side.

Both driver and passenger lay there unconscious, the passenger ejected into a pile of sleet-covered gravel and the driver restrained by his seatbelt. The truck's rear wheels spun in the sleet. Steam hissed from the engine.

20

Natalie pulled into a train station parking lot about a mile up the road. The sleet came down hard. Visibility was almost zero. A couple of cars were there, waiting to pick up commuters. Lock got out. The sleet stung his face.

From his pocket he retrieved the prepaid phone, put it in front of a rear tire, and motioned for Natalie to drive over it, crushing it flat. He scattered the splintered pieces with his shoe and got back into the car. Natalie noticed a tiny trickle of blood below his nose.

She found a wad of tissues in her bag and began to blot up the blood.

"Airbag got me. Your husband's scratch-free. It's almost over."

"Let's get out of here," said Natalie. "And don't fret about Dahlia. She's fine."

"Not if I don't see the police," he said. "I told them there was an injury. They'll come even faster and they'll dispatch an ambulance. Dahlia's alone in the back of that car." Lock checked his watch. Eight fifty-four.

"Like they're not going to come," she said. "Let's go, Lock. We can't be seen together. We're so close to being safe. Besides, how do you know which direction the police will come from? How do you know we'll even see them from here?"

"This is Kennett Square jurisdiction," he said. "They'll be coming from Route 1. At least, the ambulance will."

They both sat, staring ahead. She turned the radio on.

Lock snapped it off.

"I need to hear," he said.

He looked ahead and checked his watch again. Eight fifty-six.

A police car, red and blue emergency lights piercing the falling sleet, sped past silently, heading in the direction of Witt's car.

"Satisfied?" she asked.

"There should be an ambulance any second now."

Natalie started the car.

Another police car zipped by.

"Good enough?"

"I guess."

Natalie put the car into gear.

"Nice and easy," he told her.

Natalie was about to pull onto the road. She heard a siren and saw more flashing lights.

"Brake!" Lock shouted. Natalie stopped short. An ambulance sped toward and then past them.

"Damn sirens will wake Dahlia," he said. "But thirty seconds from now she'll be safe and warm, in the arms of a paramedic."

"So what if the sirens wake her? She won't be telling them anything."

Lock gave her a hard look. She didn't seem to understand how serious this was. He wondered if living a wealthy lifestyle for so long had made her forget the world wasn't all yoga classes and orchids, but then he felt guilty for the thought. She was probably more stressed than he was—it was her daughter alone in the car.

Another ambulance passed, then another police car. Moments later, yet another police car, all moving fast in the direction of the accident.

"Five or six of them for one drunken son-of-a-bitch," she said. "And you were worried they wouldn't show."

It took Lock and Natalie almost twenty minutes along icy and circuitous back roads to get back to a convenience store several blocks from the Cavern Tavern where Lock had parked his car earlier. He had refused to let her drive back the way they came. He did not want to pass the accident scene.

Natalie stopped the car.

"You need to go straight home," Lock told Natalie, "so you'll be available when the police call about the accident."

"I'd rather go home with you to celebrate. I have my cell and Candice will call me if the police phone the house. Plus, I already set it up with Candice. She thinks I'm going to be with my sister in New Jersey."

"No, not a good idea. Plus, I'm already packed and I'm going directly to the cabin for the weekend. I'm taking tomorrow off as a vacation day."

"You don't want to be at the office when Abby learns about the crash," Natalie said. "If he learns about it."

"Oh, he'll hear about it one way or the other. No doubt about that. And you're right. There are lots of places I'd rather be tomorrow when the news breaks."

"So you drop down into a rabbit hole and I'm stuck here all alone. I won't see you for three days. That sucks."

Lock thought for a moment and checked the roads for any oncoming emergency vehicles.

"Okay," he said. "I have an idea. I was going to come home Sunday night, but I don't want to go three days without you, either. I'll come back Saturday afternoon. You find a way to break away from your house and we'll get together at the carriage house."

Natalie reached over and squeezed his hand.

"That's a good boy," she said. "I'll bring all the ingredients for my famous vegetarian chili. You relax and I'll make us an early dinner. How's that?"

"You never let me cook for you."

"Next time," she said. "I have us covered for Saturday."

Natalie gave him a quick kiss before he jumped out and got into his car. She waited while he started the engine and cleared the snow off his windshield. Like synchronized swimmers, each car drove away at the same moment and headed in opposite directions, leaving nothing but tire tracks in the snow.

A sign on the turnpike read, "Blakeslee and Mt. Pocono, 34 miles."

Lock drove, his expression grim, and he gripped the steering wheel tightly. He felt the cold night air trying to penetrate the car's windows. He had the heat on full blast but he shivered in his seat. Leafless trees flashed by as snow fell.

On Lock's way up to the mountains, he ran instant replays of everything through his mind. It was not enough of a crash—basically a one-car fender-bender—to warrant accident investigators. And anyway, it was late on an icy night and the accident scene was probably cleared already. They'd figure Witt went home in a stupor and for some drunken reason decided to take the two-year-old with him. Lock knew it made no sense for him to do that, but it didn't need to. He was a blackout drunk. They'd find the Ambien in his blood work. So what that he'd deny it? According to Natalie, Witt had a prescription. No one had seen Natalie, and only people in the bar—and the taxi driver—had seen the guy with the cigar, but who was he? Lock knew all along that as soon as the police found Dahlia and took care of her, it would all be over.

And in case they needed it, there was Candice. She would say Witt had come home, messed the place up, and broken a wine glass. She would believe what she was saying—even Witt, knowing he'd blacked out, would probably assume it was true.

Lock arrived at the small log cabin a little before midnight. The snow, which had already accumulated seven or eight inches, fell harder. Inside the dark cabin, the chill hit him. He flipped a light switch and a lamp came on. He shivered. His first order of business was to load logs into the fireplace and get a blaze going. He opened a bottle of fruit juice and took a swig. The fire warmed the cabin quickly. A half hour after arriving, Lock got into bed and was asleep in ten minutes. His conscience was clear. He had done the right thing.

As dawn began to break through the pines, firs, and junipers that surrounded the cabin, Lock's cellphone shrilled loudly in the cold air, waking him.

It was Abby. "I have calls from reporters," he said. "There's been a drunk driver accident and one of our kids was a passenger. Of course the driver is uninjured. And you know how the media is all over us whenever something bad happens and they can link it to CPS."

"Was it one of mine?"

"Yeah, it was your case," Abby said. "Before you closed it. The Mannheim case, son, out in Red Cedar Woods."

"Shit, which one of the kids was it?"

"The younger one."

"Dahlia?"

"I think that's it, yes."

"God dammit," Lock said. "I couldn't find anything to keep the case open, but I had that feeling. I should have looked harder. I swear, Abby, there was nothing there."

"Well, there's not nothing there now. Come on home. With the media all over this—well, you know, it's always CPS negligence. Always our fault."

"We'll weather it, we always do. As long as the little girl's okay, we did the best we could do."

"Well, your pal Mr. Mannheim was uninjured. It's icy and he meets up with a bad curve on Creek Road. A tough spot even if it's dry, sunny, and you're sober. He hits a tree. Minor damage. But his tail is sticking out on the highway, and now here comes another DUI around the same bend. Hits hard. See? The driver and the passenger in the second car—a pickup truck—were left unconscious. They're both critical. The little girl in Mannheim's car, the two-year-old, caught a very bad bump on her head. And a nasty gash. At least a concussion, if not worse."

Lock turned white. "Wasn't she in a car seat?"

"She was in a car seat," Abby said, "but the ass never buckled her in. And what possible difference can that make? She's injured, son."

Lock swallowed hard and tightened his grip on the phone. His knuckles turned as white as his face. He inhaled rapid, shallow breaths.

"Give this one to McHugh, could you? I'm so tired I can't see. And there must be a foot of new snow on the roads. I practically just got up here. I'll fall asleep and get killed driving all the way back home."

"I suppose that'd be CPS's fault, too. So, you be here by noon. Press conference is at one. They'll be all over us as to why that child was in a car with a known drunk. In the meantime, get a little sleep and remember, be here by noon."

Lock hung up. He stared blankly as the dying flames of the fireplace glimmered and flashed upon his face.

21

Lock couldn't sleep, so he got up and left earlier than he had planned. The drive was only an hour and a half. The storm had passed and the skies were bright as he drove south on the Pennsylvania Turnpike back to his carriage house. He was sick to his stomach.

Natalie wasn't answering her phone. He kept getting her voicemail. She was probably at the hospital. Obviously, their rendezvous was off.

Lock arrived at his office slightly unkempt, his eyes bleary. He didn't wear a suit. He could have used another six hours of sleep and a change of clothes, but Abby had insisted he be there. He entered his cubicle, sat down, and went through the motions of working, but succeeded only in doing a fairly good job of masking—not reducing—his anxiety. He shuffled papers around on his desk.

When Abby appeared behind him and spoke, Lock jumped.

"There you are." Lock swiveled in his chair and turned towards him. The old man looked him over and shook his head. "You seem well rested. Anyway, take a guess who's here."

Lock didn't like the question. There were countless people he didn't want to see.

"I'm too beat to guess. Tell me," he said.

"District Attorney Vance Jacoby."

"Jacoby?" Lock said, slapping his palm on the armrest of his swivel chair. "What's that pain in the ass want?"

"As much media attention as possible."

"What's he planning to do to get it?"

"Some Mothers Against Drunk Driving lady heard the Mannheim accident on her police scanner," said Abner. "And when it came out there was a child involved in a DUI wreck, she went berserk. Called every TV and radio station, every newspaper and wire service, saying this sort of thing must come to a stop. The media must like the story because I've been getting call after call. Jacoby's going to hold a press conference. Here."

"He's a lightweight headline grabber. I wouldn't worry about him."

Abby ignored the remark. "Apparently, the D.A.'s office has instructions out to all 911 dispatchers county-wide," he said. "Every time they get a report of a DUI with injuries, they're supposed to notify Jacoby's hotline. Count on him to make a lot of noise. I'm certain that he's the one who opened his mouth to reporters about this being a CPS case."

"I can't take very much of that guy," said Lock, getting out of his chair and tugging at his sleeves and re-tucking his shirt. He stared at the floor.

"Why won't you look at me?" Abby said.

Lock put his head in his hands and massaged his forehead and temples.

"I'm not looking at anything. I have a headache behind each eye you wouldn't believe."

Lock rubbed his face. "I was at Mannheim's home. Three times. It looked like one of the parents—the father—was case-building for custody purposes. And I closed it. That's all the press needs. We talked about it, Abby. You said close it and move on."

"I know I did, son. Let's not worry about that, let's just do what we can to make this better."

Twenty minutes later, the news conference was over. It hadn't lasted as long as Lock thought it might, and better yet, no one had asked him any questions. And CPS, it turned out, wasn't blamed for anything. Reporters and cameramen shuffled out of the crowded conference room.

A lone cameraman stopped and turned to record Abby. Lock took Abby by the sleeve, gently turned him around, and straightened his tie.

"Got to look good for the cameras," Lock said.

"Yeah," Abby said. To avoid the reporters, he feinted a move in one direction, turned, and hurried out another way.

"Abner!" Jacoby, a tall man in his fifties wearing a pinstriped suit, shouted after him. "Abner Schlamm."

Abner stopped and walked back in, giving a camera one last shot at him. A few people remained in the room. They sat around an oversized conference table.

"I just had the bartender from Cavern Tavern dragged down to the State Police barracks," Jacoby said. "He was the one pouring drinks for Mannheim last night." Jacoby cleared his throat. "I was looking for a case like this. Liquor establishment complicity is the heart of my DUI enforcement campaign. If bartenders want to serve visibly drunk patrons, they can join them in the cage. Abner, I want you to stand with me at the next press conference."

"It won't be tops on my to-do list, Jacoby, I can tell you that," Abby said. "Once is enough. Anything else?"

"Come on," said Jacoby. "This Mannheim character is my poster boy. And even though most people in county government think your case managers are cowboys, we all know this isn't a CPS screw-up. We know you're aggressive for the sake of the children. Frankly, and off the record, I applaud that. There was nothing that could have been done to head off this accident. You couldn't have anticipated it, Abner. Play ball with me. It'll be good for CPS."

"Here's my advice to you," said Abner. "Find someone already convicted of drunk driving to pummel. Your poster boy's rich and probably has big lawyers. He could beat the charges and then you look like even more of a damned fool."

Jacoby nodded. If he caught the insult, he didn't show it.

"Really? How's he going to beat it with that little girl in bad shape?"

"Sorry to break it to you," Abby said. "Our call center supervisor called the hospital last night. Just a bloody lip and a little bump on her noggin. She'll likely be home with her mama before dinner time, so, so long, Jacoby."

Jacoby furrowed his brow.

"That's not our understanding," Jacoby said. "We spoke to the hospital an hour ago. Anyway, we could use your help. The solidarity of our agencies is important. I hope you'll be with us, Abner."

"Hope makes a good breakfast but a poor supper." Abby turned and left, and Lock followed.

"What did Jacoby mean, 'that's not our understanding'?" Lock asked.

"I don't know, but I'm going to call the hospital and find out. I'll let you know."

Abby offered Lock the afternoon off to rest up, as penance for dragging him back from the Poconos. Lock took him up on it and decided to go home for the day. Before he left, he called the hospital for Dahlia's condition. Lock said he was her uncle. "Guarded," they said.

Guarded? he thought. *That doesn't sound minor.* It made him sicker. He wondered how Natalie was doing, but he didn't dare call. She was probably at the hospital, surrounded by friends.

Lock put his head down on his desk, and moments later, Abby was there.

"Didn't I give you the afternoon off? You look terrible," Abby said to the back of Lock's head. Lock turned around. "I'm sorry," Abby continued, "I had to have you here with me. You never know what questions the media will throw at us, and this was your case."

"I know," said Lock.

"You go home now, turn your phone off, pull the blinds down, and get some sleep. Call me at home tomorrow. Sharp pain behind the eyes could be a migraine. Rest up. Let me know how you're doing."

"I can tell you now, I won't be doing great."

"You have to remain professional, Lock. Stay at arm's length. You can't let yourself get too attached or you lose effectiveness, you lose objectivity, and you diminish your ability to really help the kids who need us the most."

"But I closed the case."

"Right. Just like any of your colleagues would have done. Just like I would have done. Now go home and go to bed."

Lock reached out and turned off his computer monitor. "Okay, you're right. I need to get some sleep."

"Thanks for everything, boy. You go home. Don't worry about a thing. You didn't do anything wrong."

Lock returned to the carriage house, fiddled around with the two orchids, ignored the stack of mail on the table, and took out the trash from the kitchen, which had been starting to get ripe. He dropped two tablets of Alka-Seltzer into a glass half filled with water, waited a few seconds, and then downed it in a single gulp.

The moment he got undressed and into bed, his cellphone rang.

Natalie, calling from the hospital, told him Dahlia wasn't going to be discharged. The doctors were concerned about her—they said it was a significant concussion.

Hearing this, Lock had trouble swallowing. His throat dried up. Natalie also told Lock something he already knew—Witt was being held on a reckless endangerment charge.

"I can slip away from the hospital for a few hours," she said.

Lock sat up in bed and ran his fingers through his hair. "How can you leave your child's side at a time like this?"

"Lock, I'm telling you, she'll be fine. Plus, they have her sedated, so all she's doing is sleeping."

"That's ridiculous," he said.

"You're ridiculous. I'm her mother. I wouldn't leave if I thought it was wrong. I need to see you. I have a reservation at the Four Seasons. I'll meet you there, and we'll have room service bring us lunch."

"It's too risky. If we're seen together now—"

"Who's going to see us in the privacy of our room? We'll arrive separately and leave separately. No one will notice either of us. Believe me, you need to relax, Lock. You're freaking out over nothing. Dahlia looks great. I wouldn't leave if I thought I shouldn't. Take it easy."

"But you're her mother."

Natalie laughed. "I have more maternal instinct in my pinkie than most women have in their whole bodies."

"I don't know, Natalie."

"Get to the lobby by one. I have an early check-in. When you get there, call my cell and I'll give you the room number."

Lock stood up and glanced at himself in the mirror. A haggard face looked back. He knew he should stay home and rest and get his mind right, but he felt powerless to say no. He wanted to see Natalie, and he figured that if there was any news, the hospital would call her immediately. He took a deep breath and exhaled slowly. He shook his head and, as if it was someone else's voice, he heard himself speak. "Okay, Natalie. I want to be with you, too. But only for a couple of hours. Okay? Then you get yourself back to the hospital."

"Call me from the lobby," Natalie said. "Love you."

She hung up.

Abner left the office promptly at five o'clock, something he rarely did. Usually, he could be counted on to stay behind his desk until 6:30 or 7:00 p.m., making calls and completing on-screen forms and assessment reports. But that afternoon, he was exhausted and more than a little concerned about the events of the day.

As he drove home, he noted with some pleasure that he'd had the opportunity to insult Jacoby, but that was tempered by his concern about Lock. The whole matter was exhausting everyone in the office. He couldn't wait to get his shoes off and get his feet up on the worn recliner in his living room.

A re-run of a game show appeared on Abner's television screen. He was glad the news didn't pop up. He didn't want to see any news, especially local news. He'd had enough of the media for one day.

Something gnawed at him. Something didn't seem right about the accident, but he couldn't identify it. He got up and went to the kitchen, put just enough water for one cup of instant coffee in a kettle, and turned on the burner. He opened a glass-doored cabinet above the stove and reached for a mug and the can of Maxwell House.

His eyes stopped for a moment on the unopened bottle of rare scotch he had kept there for over twenty years. *That would solve the problem,* he thought, knowing he'd never touch it. *That would solve this problem, but create many others.* He remembered what someone had once said at an AA meeting—*Alcoholism is the only disease that tells you you're not sick.*

He kept the bottle there as a souvenir of the war he'd fought with alcohol. He was stronger than the occasional urge to drink—an urge that still came after almost three decades of sobriety—and this was the kind of day when he needed to stay strong. He leaned against the sink and waited for the water to boil. While he waited, his mind gravitated to Natalie Mannheim. He didn't know why, but he knew he didn't like her. He didn't like anything about her. He made a mental note to ask Lock more about her. After all, Lock was the one who knew her best.

Abner had another thought then—she was a manipulator, and Lock was lonely. He knew that could be a recipe for trouble. He'd definitely have to have a talk with Lock.

The kettle whistled as Abner dropped a level tablespoon of coffee crystals into the mug. He started to pour the hot water and stopped mid-pour. He mustn't have added enough coffee, because, at first, the liquid in the bottom of the mug looked a lot like scotch.

22

The next day, Lock and Natalie sat in a nearly empty theater in the Art House Cinema in Old City Philadelphia.

On screen, in black and white, a man made a call from a phone booth. He spoke in low tones to a woman on the other end of the line.

At Lock's insistence, Natalie had taken a seat a row behind him. She thought that was ridiculous. They had been hissing to each other in whispers since they got there.

"She's not getting sicker, Lock," Natalie said. "She's getting better a little more slowly than they first thought. That's all."

"Abner said Dahlia's not making the progress the docs were expecting," said Lock. "And the hospital has her condition listed as guarded."

"I don't care what that old goat says. I'm her mother. I'm the one who was there all night. I'm the one who's talking to the doctors. I'm the one worried sick."

"Like right now?"

Natalie laughed, leaned forward, and gave him a quick one-armed hug. Lock stared off toward the screen. A man in a long coat was walking down a lane at night. Shadows from the street lamp fell over him.

Natalie looked away from the screen and at Lock.

"You seem a bit stressed," she said. "Dare me to sit next to you and put my head in your lap?" She leaned forward. "Right now, right here?"

Lock didn't respond. He sat stiffly upright, his fists clenched.

"Well?" she asked.

"No thanks."

They sat in silence, turning their attention to the screen. The man in the long coat sat across from a teenage girl at a restaurant table. The girl was sobbing.

They watched for a couple of minutes before Natalie broke the lull. "How are you going to get Abner off the scent?" she asked. "You say he's so smart."

"It'll be tougher now. The publicity changes everything."

"But not us, Lock. We're still rock-solid. Honey? Nothing's changed with us, right?"

"Yes, we're rock-solid," he said. Then his expression went flat. "Why are they keeping Dahlia again?"

"The doctor said something about the bump on her head making her light-sensitive. At least that's what he told me."

"What kind of doctor? And what else did he say?"

"A neurologist. They said she has MTBI."

"What the hell is that?"

"Mild Traumatic Brain Injury. It's medical double talk for a minor concussion. Nothing to worry about. And he didn't say anything else. Nothing. I'm telling you, she's fine," Natalie said. "They're being over-cautious for only one reason—so they can keep billing the insurance company."

Lock stared off into space. "Here's Abby's problem," he said. "CPS backed off a case. I was the one who closed it, and a child got hurt because of a dad we could have been monitoring. That's a problem for Abby, so it's a problem for us."

Natalie sat back.

"Being together now is too risky," he said. "We have to slow it down for a while."

"That's easy for you to say. Maybe I'm alone and scared and need you, and what do you do? You crawl under a rock and hide. How heroic."

"I thought you were cool, Natalie."

"It's horrible at the house, even though he's out on bail now and at the Sheraton. Edwina's upset, and Witt calls me about the baby twenty times a day."

"So hang up twenty times a day."

"Oh, he's so sorry. Oh, he's never going to have a drink again. He makes me nauseated."

"We have to lie low until this isn't on the news all day, every day," Lock said. "The only thing we have going for us is the media's short attention span."

"Then why the pissed-off face?"

"Abby wants a drink," Lock said.

"Can't that work out for us?" she said. "Him wanting a drink. Why can't you help him to—what do you call it—*slip*? I'm sure he's got a long way down once he starts the slide."

A picture of Natalie's snake tattoo rushed through Lock's mind. In his imagination, the snake's head came out of her throat and morphed into her head.

Lock controlled his expression.

"That would kill him, taking a drink," he said. "He wants to drink, but he won't, and the craving is his cue that something's very wrong. He'll stand there for a thousand years to figure out why he wants that drink."

She reached forward and squeezed his shoulder.

"And I'm going to help him come to a satisfactory conclusion so he stops thinking about it," Lock said. "I'm going to do it with a story that's going to taste exactly like the truth—but it will be what we need him to think. Trouble is, I've never been able to lie to him very well. I'll have to succeed this time. He knows me like a father knows his son. If he had a good a reason, he wouldn't hesitate to have himself arrested—or me."

"You have to think of something," said Natalie.

"I know. Cool is how we play it. No small rooms."

"How long do we not see each other?" she asked.

"I'm going home to think about that. Then we'll see."

"So you're taking the day off," Natalie said, "while I do nothing but sit and burn a hole in my stomach."

"You have two children to take care of."

"You have hundreds."

Lock couldn't see her face.

"Dahlia will be home from the hospital soon," he said, "and the spotlight on CPS will fade and other problems—newer, bigger problems—will pop up to distract Abby." Lock stood up. "Goodbye, baby," he said, so low she could barely hear him. "Wish I could kiss you."

"Why can't you?"

On screen, a couple argued and the man paced and made hand gestures, as if he were accusing her of something. She rushed to him.

"Stay until the movie's over. I've seen it. See how it ends."

When he left, Natalie was still sitting there, staring blankly at the couple embracing on the screen.

23

District Attorney Jacoby, bundled up against the cold and sitting on a bench in Glen Providence Park, alternated blowing into his gloved hands and shooing away hungry pigeons.

Carlo, nineteen, skinny and nervous, walked toward Jacoby, accompanied by a middle-aged woman wearing a long coat against the chill.

Jacoby gestured for the kid to take a seat and spoke a few words to the woman, who identified herself as Carlo's attorney. Jacoby produced an envelope and handed it to her. She took her time reading the document enclosed, and a minute later handed it over to Carlo. He stared at it.

From the sidewalk nearby, a police officer materialized. The kid's eyes widened when he realized an officer was going to be part of the meeting.

"What's this?" Carlo asked to both his attorney and Jacoby. "I said I'm signing, didn't I?"

"Relax, Carlo," said Jacoby. "Your lawyer won't let us pull anything."

"You both set me up—he's going to bust me," Carlo said, pointing a finger toward the officer.

"Take it easy, Carlo," the attorney said. "You're already arrested. I'm trying to get you *un*arrested."

"It's as we told you," Jacoby said to Carlo. He turned to the woman. "Okay for him to sign the statement?"

The woman looked at Carlo. "Go ahead and sign it. It's okay. Cooperating now will help you with the judge later."

The officer stood there, hovering. Jacoby handed a pen to the kid, who took it and signed the statement.

"Nice and legible, Carlo," said Jacoby, who then turned to the officer. "He's a good kid. Don't be too rough when you're testifying against him in court."

"A good kid with a half-pound of marijuana," said the officer.

"Not for distribution, just for recreational use," said the attorney. "Isn't that right, Carlo?"

"Yes, ma'am. Only to get high," said Carlo.

"That's comical," said the officer. "Anyway, what's in that statement that's so important? Arresting a kid with a half-pound looks good for me. Letting him slide looks bad. Why should I do that? Plus, I wouldn't believe a thing this kid says. He's telling you what you want to hear."

"He's a key witness in another case," Jacoby said. "And we all have to work together for the greater good."

Having witnessed the signature, the officer shrugged and walked away.

Jacoby spoke quietly to the attorney, who put her copy of the statement in her briefcase, shook hands with Jacoby, and turned to leave with Carlo. Jacoby called to the attorney. "And please, don't let your client move to Amsterdam. We need him for court."

24

Hours before dawn, Lock's eyes opened. He sat up, wide awake. He couldn't stop thinking about Dahlia. He pictured her alone and whimpering in the pediatric unit in Brandywine Community Hospital, the nurses busy with other little patients. No one to hold her. No one to comfort her.

And he imagined Natalie sound asleep in her own bed.

He got up and put on some coffee. He paced in his tiny kitchen while it brewed. His mind raced, imagining the toddler's fear and pain she experienced when the pickup truck smashed into Witt's car, the flashing red and blue emergency lights, the ride in an ambulance and being attended to by strangers in uniforms.

Lock tried to calm himself by taking a series of rapid breaths, hoping to get more oxygen to his brain. Maybe that would help him think more clearly and get his mind right. But then he worried that his mind was already right—that it was what he'd done that caused him so much distress. In all his planning, he'd never figured on this—an unforeseen crash. If he had only positioned Witt's car better.

Imagining that dark road gave him an idea. He'd go to the Poconos. Walk in the woods there. He knew he'd be able to get two or three days off. He had plenty of vacation days coming to him, and Abner would understand. He'd call him at home, but it was only five a.m., too early to wake his boss.

Lock didn't wait for the coffee to finish brewing. He turned off the coffee maker. He got into the shower and nearly scalded himself with the hot water, scrubbing himself violently with a cotton washcloth.

As he dried himself, he realized the shower hadn't worked to wash away his anxiety—the rushing thoughts returned. Running away to the mountains wouldn't help, either. He needed to get to the office and do whatever good he could. He needed to help the children whose lives came across his desk in the form of messages, memos, reports, and phone calls. That was who Lock was, a guardian of children, not a monster who intentionally put them in harm's way. It had been a horrible, horrible mistake.

He'd get to the office early, work late, and do good things. He needed to have a sense of control, and that illusion was easier to acquire at the office.

He left for CPS while it was still dark. Once there, he tore into his files. What more could he do to help the children he was assigned to? There had to be something, and he'd find it and do it.

Several hours passed before other CPS employees began arriving. Around ten, Abby called him into his office. Lock headed over to the administrative wing where Abby worked, steeling himself. Had Abby learned something else about the Mannheim case? What could it be? Would he take a look at Lock and sense something was amiss?

No, Lock told himself, *he doesn't know anything. He just wants to talk about the case.* Lock pulled himself upright and took some deep breaths. He knocked on the glass window of Abby's open door.

"Come in, boy," Abby said. He stood up from behind his desk and approached Lock, smiling. "A new day and another step closer to figuring out this Mannheim quagmire."

Lock took a couple of steps in and nodded.

"Everything is slowly falling into place," Abby said. "And I think the missus is up to her neck in this."

"What gives you that idea?" asked Lock. *Shit.* He could feel sudden sweat dripping down his back. He didn't say anything to defend Natalie. Abby was too intuitive when it came to things like this. He was thirsty, so the only way to play it was to play along.

"Mannheim hired a team of private investigators, that's what. That guy's worth a fortune. No expenses spared."

"What's he know?"

"Nothing much," said Abby, "other than Mannheim wasn't alone in his car when he left the Cavern Tavern."

"Who was he with?"

"He was with a woman in the bar, but she went back in after Mannheim left. A cabby offered a ride to an obviously drunken Mannheim and saw another man trying to take his car keys away."

"What'd the cabby say he looked like?" said Lock.

"Looked drunk as hell," said Abby.

"I mean what did the other guy look like, the Good Samaritan?

"The cabby said he didn't really see the other guy," Abby said. "He was all bundled up and it was sleeting hard. A cigar was the only thing the cabby mentioned."

Lock kept his stony face, but his heart lifted with relief.

"So now there's a loose end," Abby said, "and it's making me thirsty, I tell you. I aim to know who that man is and why he gave Mannheim his keys back. Go out there and press the bartender. And while you're at it, don't come back until you know who that woman is. If she's a regular there, the bartender should know who she is."

"You're reopening the case?"

"Yes. The D.A. and the police have their own active investigations, but I know you're not going to rest until you find out what really happened. You look like hell. I can see this thing's getting to you. Best thing to do is work it hard until we figure it out."

Lock took another deep breath. "Yeah, you're right. I keep thinking I should have done more." *Or less,* he thought. *A lot less.*

Abby patted him on the shoulder. "And now you can. Get out there and get some answers."

"Any ideas? If he's smart, he won't say anything except to the cops. He's already in trouble for serving Mannheim."

"I don't want to wait weeks for the results of a police investigation. We're going to do it ourselves. The bartender will cooperate if you play it right. Jacoby released him on bail, and he probably doesn't want to get brought in again. He'll talk to you. You're charming. You know how to play it—we're not interested in him, we just want to get to Mannheim and whoever else was involved." Abby handed Lock a slip of paper with the cabby's name and phone number.

"Alright," Lock said. "I'll get him to spill, and I'll talk to the cabby, too. Thanks, Abby. Sitting around wasn't doing me any good." *And now I'll have at least some control over what information you get.* Lock's gut twisted at the thought of lying to Abby, but "no small rooms" had been his mantra from the beginning. He didn't want to go to jail, and he especially didn't want to disappoint Abby. It'd break the old man's heart.

Lock turned to go, but Abby stopped him. "What really bothers me is Mrs. Mannheim." He cleared his throat. "They were firing nasty allegations at each other. Things that could make a big to-do at a custody hearing. Then there's an accident that gives the mom something she can really take to the bank. But she doesn't. She goes quiet. No, there's something very wrong. But what, I don't know."

"Maybe she's going for a settlement. Keep it out of court, more money for her. You didn't see their house. She lives like a queen, and she doesn't have to lift a finger. Nanny, new Mercedes, the whole trophy wife thing." He winced inside to say all that about Natalie. Not that it wasn't true, but she was more than what she appeared.

"Could be," Abby said. "The problem I'm having is this other guy. You talk to the cabby—he's saying there's no way Mannheim could have driven all the way back home that drunk and in that weather. He was barely standing when the cabby saw him. So who's this guy? To me, it looks like he was the one behind the wheel, not Mannheim."

"Yeah, but drunks—you know as well as I do, most of us have a guardian angel or we wouldn't have made it this far," Lock said.

"Point taken," Abby said, smiling. "But I'm still not seeing it. How and why does Mannheim drive home, pick up the two-year-old, put her in a car seat, get back in his car and lose control of it on the curve, drive into a tree, and then forget the whole thing?"

"He *says* he can't remember it," said Lock. "That's not the same as not remembering."

Lock swallowed hard and continued. "You're looking for something that isn't there because you feel like we let that little girl down," he said. "I feel the same way, but I have to tell you, this is starting to sound like 9/11 conspiracy stuff. A mystery man picks Mannheim up, goes to his house, grabs his kid? I'm not seeing it."

"Listen," Abby said, ticking off his reasoning on his fingers. "A. It couldn't be what it looks like. If it were that simple, Mrs. Mannheim would be rushing to cash in on her daughter's injury by screaming all over the place about Mannheim's recklessness."

Lock nodded. Too much resistance to Abby's theory would seem odd. Lock fidgeted with a pen on Abner's desk, clicking it nonstop.

"B.," Abby continued, "if she's not screaming, she's the dog that didn't bark. She's in it, one way or another. C., the Good Samaritan in the parking lot—it wasn't a coincidence he was there. Whoever he is, he's in this with her. And D., the best clue—the more I think about Natalie Mannheim, Wittley Mannheim, two car accidents, a Good Samaritan, the blackouts, and everything else, I can practically taste that Glenmorangie."

Thoughts sped through Lock's mind. Throughout his careful planning, he'd been most concerned about the power of Abby's gut instincts. But he hadn't considered the aggregate effect of several tiny inklings that Abby would latch onto. He was like a hungry dog, Lock thought, picking up the scent of hamburgers on the grill at a house down the street. The aroma would drive him crazy until he could get to it and tear into it. Every morsel.

"Stop clicking that pen," Abner said.

"Yeah," Lock said. "I'm starting to see it. But if you're right, what I can't figure out is what their real plan was. It wasn't a kidnapping. So what were they trying to do when Mannheim hit the tree? And if the mystery guy is in the car, what happened to him? Not likely he hitched a ride home. The cops would have probably seen him. And where's Mrs. Mannheim during all this?"

Abner rubbed his jaw, frowning. "Yep," he said, "if I could figure all that out, I'd have something for Mrs. Mannheim and her friend. A nice little indictment, all swaddled up and cozy, safe and sound, like a baby in a car seat."

Small rooms, Lock thought.

Abby's phone rang and he waved Lock out of his office. "I'll talk to you later. Good luck out there, boy."

Damn Abby and damn his thirst for rare scotch, Lock thought. In Lock's plan, all the danger had been in the Cavern. He had worried about Abby, but not enough. But there was still one thing keeping him safe—Abby thought the first crash was an accident. And as long as he thought that, he'd never figure out the rest. All Lock had to do was make certain that Natalie stayed cool and didn't make a move. But that thought gave Lock comfort only until his mind wandered back to the pediatric unit, and he was sick to his stomach again.

25

Lost in thought while trying to solve the crossword puzzle in Monday's *Philadelphia Inquirer,* Abner stood barefoot in his pajamas on the cold linoleum of his kitchen floor. He clenched a sprig of licorice root between his teeth.

He was stuck on the clue "peace of mind." The answer was eight letters long, and the fourth letter was an "e" and the last a "y." It was difficult for him to focus.

A short article in the local news section about the accident and Mannheim's subsequent arrest didn't mention CPS, and for that, Abner was glad. But he knew the reporters would be back on the story soon. There were too many titillating elements of the event for it to be ignored by the media.

The more Abner wondered about the identity of who he suspected was Natalie Mannheim's accomplice—and he was certain there was one—the more dyspeptic he got. Abner couldn't get comfortable with the idea that Natalie was nothing more than a collateral victim in the situation. Maybe she had succeeded in misleading Lock—Lock was smart, but everyone had a blind spot—but she definitely wasn't going to mislead Abner, or so he hoped. He hated unsolved mysteries. The unfinished crossword puzzle might ruin his whole day. Things like that always made him think about a drink.

Abner's agitated state intensified. For a moment, he explained it by thinking he was subject to a double whammy—the aggravation of the crossword puzzle clue together with his misgivings about Natalie. Then another question wedged itself into his mind. He had told Lock to close the Mannheim file as soon as he could because of the case overload, but Lock would never sign off prematurely. He usually waited thirty days, made a follow-up call, and then made his decision. Closing the case so soon was out of character—Lock would never sign off on a file if he thought there were kids at risk. He was trying to make up for his mistake now, but he hadn't come up with anything.

Lock had talked to the bartender at the Cavern Tavern, and the guy didn't say anything new, and said he couldn't I.D. the woman Mannheim had been with. Abner knew that was nonsense, and he thought he should have questioned the bartender himself. Lock said he was still waiting for a call back from the cabby, so nothing new there.

Abner had too much rattling around in his head, and his thoughts about Lock were overwhelming. Maybe what Lock needed was some extended time off—he was Abby's best investigator, and it wouldn't do him or CPS any good if he burned out. Abner didn't want to embarrass Lock or make him think he was slipping, but he thought a break was probably a good idea. He'd talk to Lock about it the next day.

His eyes wandered around the kitchen and came to rest on the sealed bottle of Glenmorangie 25-Year Highland Single Malt Scotch. He kept it there for two reasons. Having it nearby was what he called "spiritual push-ups." Seeing the bottle regularly and ignoring it, he believed, gave him the strength to resist the urges he still felt, occasionally, to drink.

He gave the bottle a long, long look.

"I'm thirsty for you, little bottle," he said. "What are you trying to tell me?"

Instead of taking time to eat lunch on Tuesday, Lock called Natalie mid-morning and arranged to meet her at noon.

"We need to talk, Natalie," he said.

"About what? Sometimes when you say 'we need to talk,' it's nothing good."

"I'm afraid this is one of those times," Lock said, doodling concentric circles on a pad of Post-It notes.

Natalie sighed. "Okay. It's pretty chilly out, but I'll bundle up. And I'll make avocado and lettuce sandwiches."

Two hours later, in the November cold, Natalie and Lock sat on swings at a playground next to an elementary school closed for renovation. A brown paper bag containing sandwiches and apples sat balanced in her lap.

Lock tapped his shoe on the frozen ground, but Natalie seemed relaxed—even cheerful—and impervious to the temperature. Lock rankled at her breeziness. She opened the paper bag and held out a sandwich wrapped in aluminum foil. He shook his head. She shrugged and returned it to the bag.

"The Old Man's going to call you in," Lock said. "You don't have to go. He can't force you to, but you should go. It's the best thing to do. He's ready to bet that you won't show. Surprise him. Call that lawyer friend of yours. You've got to drop your bid for custody and support and reconcile with Witt. It's our only chance to get Abby to relax."

"I'm not doing that," Natalie said.

"Why not? Reconciling would only have to be a temporary arrangement, just until things blow over. It would go a long way in getting Abby off your back."

"I'd rather put my hand down the garbage disposal and flip the switch than get back together with Witt. If you think otherwise, believe me, you're losing it."

"I may be losing it, but I'm not so far gone as to all of a sudden start liking small rooms."

"That's what you'd like—I get back with Witt and you're free of me."

Where did that come from? Lock wondered. *I've gone this far to help her, to be with her, so why would I bail out now?* "You've got that wrong," he said. "You're the last person I want to be free of."

He kicked at a small rock under the swing.

"We're stuck with each other," she said. "I'm not getting scared off so easy. And you don't get off so easy, either. If you want the naked truth, think about this. Dahlia getting hurt was on you. Your plan, not mine. I don't need Witt, I need *you.* Relax. And think. We haven't done anything wrong, unless it's wrong to protect my children."

Again, Lock imagined the moment when Dahlia had been jolted violently awake when the pickup truck smashed into the car.

"Get off it, Natalie."

"What are you really afraid of?" she asked.

"What I'm afraid of is Abner Schlamm. The only thing that has the slightest chance of calming him down is if you and Witt get back together," Lock said. "Otherwise he'll wonder why you're not acting hysterical and screaming for the D.A. to hang Witt for the accident."

Natalie, now expressionless, stared off into the distance. She turned to Lock. "So I'll push the police to charge him," Natalie said.

"It's too late for that. How would you explain waiting so long? That would look really suspicious."

Instead of answering the question, she said, "I'm not afraid of Abner."

"You should be. He put me on interviewing the bartender and the cabby, but I didn't dig as deep as he would have. Now he wants me to take some time off, and I don't know what he's going to do while I'm gone. If he leans on the bartender and gets the name of Witt's date, he's going to start looking really hard at me. We don't want to trigger another investigation. That'd be the worst thing that could happen. We want this to cool off, not heat up."

"You want me to reconcile with Witt? You must be insane."

"That'll be my defense," Lock said. "What's yours?"

Without another word, Natalie slid off the swing, letting the paper bag fall to the ground. She left it there as she got into her car and drove away.

Lock watched the SUV turn out of the parking lot and disappear. He got off the swing and picked up the bag. He looked around for a trashcan and saw one on the far side of the playground. He walked to it, put the litter in, and went to his car. He sat there for a long time with his eyes closed, gripping the steering wheel, thinking about Dahlia lying in a hospital bed, and questioning why Natalie would risk their cover.

He looked at himself in the rearview mirror and barely recognized the drawn face that looked back.

After Lock returned from his aborted lunch with Natalie, Abby called him into his office.

Although there was a small clearing on part of Abby's desk, his office was in more disarray than ever. Some of the piles of papers and files had been moved to one side of the room, piled there in a mountain of confusion.

Abner had about twenty more piles to move. It was clear he was trying to organize his office. Empty boxes awaited the mess.

"Oh, joyous day," Abby said. "They've ruined themselves, exactly as I told you."

Lock remained silent and tried not to react. "The Mannheim case? The mystery man?"

Abby didn't answer but pointed to one particularly large mound of clutter. "Bring that pile over and put it in this box right here, will you?" he said.

Lock took off his jacket and rolled up his shirtsleeves, happy for the activity.

"In one box? All this won't fit in one box," Lock said. He started to distribute the mess into multiple boxes.

"There's more boxes over there if you need them," Abby said, pointing. "The whole thing was a set-up all along, from the broken wine glass when Mannheim supposedly returned home from the bar, through the accident and all Mrs. Mannheim's tears at the hospital. It was a clever plan, too, but not clever enough for the call of Glenmorangie. No, not even close."

"Slow down. What are you talking about? How do you know all this?"

"The D.A.," Abby said, impatiently pointing to various piles of papers and frowning when Lock wasn't taking the initiative in the organizing activities. "Jacoby has a witness. Freak thing. Turns out the Mannheim nanny's gentleman caller, kid named Carlo, was hiding in the garage. The nanny told Mrs. Mannheim they were going to go out, but it turns out whenever they get the chance, they shack up right in the house. Carlo saw Mrs. Mannheim load the baby into the back of her loaner car a little before nine."

"What? Mrs. Mannheim put Dahlia in the car? I don't believe that."

Abby smiled. "We've got a sworn statement attesting to that."

Lock said nothing. He sat down in the chair facing Abby's desk.

"Put those in that box," Abner said, pointing to a mound of legal periodicals. "Mrs. Mannheim. She's got a partner. Her boyfriend."

Lock held his breath. He caught himself slumping in the chair and pulled himself back up.

"And get this—Mrs. Mannheim's boyfriend? It's her divorce lawyer," Abby said. "A classic. The nanny knows all about him. That's why Mrs. Mannheim told you she wasn't represented."

Lock thought quick, trying to keep the various stories he had told straight. He had never reported that Natalie had gotten a lawyer, since he had learned about it later, after they had been together.

"Jerome Freel is his name, out of Villanova. Drives a black Lamborghini. That's a quarter-of-a-million-dollar car, son, or more. In addition to all the felonies he and his girlfriend are guilty of, he'll also have one serious ethics problem to deal with. I'll see to that."

"An ethics charge from the bar association will be the least of his problems," Lock said. "If you're right, he almost got that little girl killed." Lock could barely believe he had the audacity to say that out loud.

He was having trouble focusing on Abner's words. He looked around the office again. The piles seemed higher and there appeared to be more of them, as if they were multiplying. He imagined them falling in on him.

"See, Lock, my theory goes something like this. That Ambien that Mannheim denied taking? Oh, he took it all right, only he didn't know he took it. Lover-boy Freel dosed Mannheim somehow in the bar. Slipped one past him. It was Freel who the cabby saw struggling with Mannheim in the parking lot."

"Why would Freel want the keys?" said Lock. "To prevent Mannheim from getting in an accident? A crash is what he'd pray for."

"True," Abner said. "That does bother me. Not sure about that one. I'll get back to you when I figure that out."

Lock stood up, slightly dizzy. He felt a sick heaviness in his gut.

Abner handed him a power screwdriver and indicated that he should install shelving brackets in the wall opposite the desk.

"Find the studs first, son," Abner said. Lock welcomed the additional assignment, instead of standing there and having Abner observe his facial expressions and body language. "By the way, I see you volunteered to be the guest speaker at the Wake-Up meeting at AA next week. Congratulations."

"I'm pretty nervous about that, Abby. Not so sure it was a good idea."

"It's a wonderful idea. Sharing your experience is part of the program, and hearing your story benefits others, so just relax. You'll be fine."

"I hope you're right. So how do you get from Mrs. Mannheim having a boyfriend all the way to them being involved in a plot to frame her husband?"

"Because she couldn't have done this herself. Doesn't have the brains."

"Why do you say that?"

"If she's so smart, why would she get involved in this kind of thing in the first place? She didn't think it through. She's impulsive. The sign of real intelligence, Lock, is thinking several steps ahead. Like in chess. These miscreants didn't have much of a plan."

"So Freel's the brains?"

"Freel's her partner, alright," Abner said. "But he's dumber than he thinks. Of course, he's denying it and offering an alibi that's impossible to verify. And threatening to sue us for harassing him. Who else could it be?"

Lock forced himself to look composed as his heart soared, knowing Abby wouldn't be looking for other suspects if he was convinced he knew who the guilty parties were. For Lock and Natalie, Candice's boyfriend was the real problem.

"Yes," Abby continued. "Nothing about this made sense to me until I took that bottle of Glenmorangie out of the cabinet. It was calling to me. I set it down and I looked it in the eye and I told it to talk. But it wouldn't talk. Nope, Lock. It wouldn't talk. It *sang*."

Abby sat down at his desk, satisfied. This was what Lock had been afraid of. He sat down too.

"That bottle told me the accident was all wrong," Abby said. "'Focus on what that kid Carlo saw,' it said. It told me I had to find out why the missus would put the child in her car. How and where did Mannheim get hold of the child? No, this doesn't add up, no matter how you figure it. And the Glenmorangie told me I didn't know enough about that so-called Good Samaritan. Now, let me ask you something."

Abby rose and began pacing.

Lock stood again and worked quickly at drilling the holes for the brackets. He wanted to get out of there.

Abby pointed to several shelves leaning against the wall. He wanted Lock to install them. "Are these two straight?" Abby asked, examining a pair of brackets.

"Perfectly straight. Is that all?"

"Straight is good, but I want them perfectly level, too. And no, that's not all. We have to get all these boxes on the shelves."

"We?"

"Now," Abby said, "about that crash. Phony as can be. Usually, people set up accidents for a few grand from the insurance company, and maybe a slimy personal injury lawyer's in on it. But not this time. This one was supposed to deliver a real juicy payoff."

"Mannheim's got a lot of money," Lock said. "Putting everything in boxes on shelves won't solve your problem."

"You see," Abner said, "the missus and her boyfriend wanted it to look like Mannheim was in a drunken stupor when he went home, messed the place up, and took the two-year-old for a joyride. Then he was supposed to have a little fender-bender that no one was going to pay much attention to—you know, because no one got hurt. A little fodder for a custody hearing is all. It would have been Mannheim's second DUI."

"But the first on the record," Lock said. "Mrs. Mannheim said that he got the local cops to wipe the first one out." He kept working, trying to add to the conversation and get as much information as he could, seeming to go along with Abby's theory so he didn't seem suspicious. Lock used a carpenter's level Abby handed him to make certain the shelves were seated correctly. He began loading boxes on the shelves. The brackets creaked.

"I don't know about more boxes on here," Lock said.

Abby disregarded Lock's concern and pointed toward the boxes he wanted up on the shelves. He handed Lock another box. "Don't worry, son," said Abner. "The shelves will hold just fine. So Freel goes into the bar where they know Mannheim will be and doses his drink. How exactly, I don't know, but he pulls it off. Now Mannheim goes out to his car, but he can't see straight. That's Freel's opportunity to get Mannheim's keys. See, this is what the cabby notices—and when the coast is clear, Freel drives Mannheim to that sharp curve on Creek Road. But from the police report and Mannheim's toxicology test results, we know it wouldn't have been possible for him to have gotten out of that parking lot, let alone drive to the curve two miles away—he was too drunk and drugged up. Nah, Freel had it all rigged up to look like Mannheim crashed into the tree. To prove Mannheim's a danger to his children."

"Music to a family court judge's ears," Lock said, straining the shelf with one more box.

"Precisely."

"I don't have a good feeling about this one," Lock said, hoisting a box toward the top shelf.

178

"No, it's fine. Put it up gently and be careful. Then the missus shows up with the kid in a carrier, they plant it in the car, and off they go."

"Reckless endangerment right there," Lock said. "Only they don't figure on the other drunk coming around the bend." Lock felt a surge of nausea gurgle in his stomach.

"See, that's the trouble with crossing the line between what's right and what's not, if only for an instant, son," said Abby. "The line moves on you, and you never learn that until you're too far out on the wrong side."

Lock breathed deeply.

"If Mannheim is shown to be a real danger to his children," Abby said, "and if he doesn't get custody, then the missus winds up with a big equitable distribution settlement and big alimony and big child support. Real cute. They have big dreams, Mrs. Mannheim and Mr. Freel, but what they never dreamed of was Carlo seeing Mrs. Mannheim with the baby in the garage. And they never dreamed of the other drunk driver coming and hitting Mannheim's car. That's where the line they crossed began moving farther and farther away. And something else they didn't dream about was Abner W. Schlamm and his ever-loving love of first-class scotch."

The shelves collapsed and the boxes and their contents went tumbling everywhere. The sound echoed through Abby's office.

Abby looked up for an instant but ignored the mess. He was too focused on what he was saying. "See," he said, "it's like being a recovering drunk trying to stay sober. You keep going to meetings because they keep you on your toes. That's why I still attend meetings. Keeps you from thinking you can cross the line just this once. You can't get away with anything. Yes sir, they never saw that drunk coming—or this drunk, either," he said, jerking a thumb towards his chest. "They never pictured their lovey-dovey little dream turning into a nightmare."

Lock turned his head away and swallowed hard.

With a vinegary expression, Abby examined the fallen shelves and boxes.

"Look what a mess you've made," he said to Lock, without the slightest trace of irony.

"I've got to get on a conference call," Lock said. "As soon as I'm off, I'll be back to help you clean this up."

He left the room.

At that moment, Lock could not have cared less about what Abby said. His mind was riveted on the thought of Natalie in bed with another man.

Lock returned to his desk—there was no conference call, he simply needed to get out of Abby's presence for a while. He tried to busy himself, but he couldn't work. He had no control over his mind. It went its own way and all he could do was tag along, trying to deflect one gut-churning thought after another.

Hours passed and Lock became even more distracted. He cleaned up the fallen shelves and boxes in Abby's office. He left the office and walked around the block. The cold air felt good. He returned and tried to write up his weekly activity report, but his mind went blank before quickly returning to ruminating about the crisis.

He left the office again, this time seemingly to go to lunch, but instead, all he did was drive around, not paying attention to where he was going. Then he realized he was going nowhere. He drove back to the office and took another stab at completing the reports.

It was useless. All he could think about was that Natalie had had a boy-friend all along—and he'd never considered that as a possibility. He seemed to be suffocating and took short, rapid breaths to calm himself. He felt like he'd just eaten a large, greasy breakfast. The nausea boiled inside him. And an image flashed in his mind—he could see himself being handcuffed in his living room and ushered into a police car.

It took Lock a few more seconds to realize that this whole affair had been one long con to scam him into helping her. Anyone else might have seen that from the start. Her claims of love, the extraordinary sex, the phone calls and pillow talk that would last for hours, deep into the night. The heart-to-heart talks about their future. All lies and bullshit. The sex was meaningless to her, only physical. He was simply another man she'd accommodate, for whatever reason that served her. She must have had a good laugh curling up with her boyfriend when she told him about Lock. He was heartsick. Made a fool of, swayed into becoming a criminal and a co-conspirator. *Oh, Natalie*, he thought. But that wasn't his only problem.

Abby was getting too close. He thanked God Abby thought it was Freel. That would buy Lock some time. But he had to wonder if maybe Abby was setting him up, giving him a chance to come clean. Lock knew that accepting responsibility went a long way with Abby, but he wasn't going to wait forever. Either way, he had Lock plenty nervous.

Lock had to know what else Abby knew, and he figured maybe Abby's email was a good a place to start. A while back, when Abby had gone fishing in Boca, he'd given Lock his password to check his email for him. The password was easy for Lock to remember. It was his own birthday.

Breaking into Abby's email account was a horrible thing to do, he knew. Another betrayal. But Lock persuaded himself it had to be done.

26

Natalie arrived at the Philadelphia Museum of Art—an iconic building on a hill on the eastern bank of the Schuylkill River—fifteen minutes late. She bought an admission ticket and made her way up the steps to the medieval cloister where she had agreed to meet Lock.

He was already there, seated on a stone bench, waiting, reading a pamphlet. He had arranged this meeting, wanting to speak to her face to face. The cloister, quiet and eerie in its subdued light, usually didn't get much foot traffic. It was a perfect place to meet.

Although it was colder than it had been in days, she wore no outerwear other than her long sweater.

"Hi, Lock," she said. She sat beside him. They faced the marble fountain surrounded by columns. "What's wrong? You look so unhappy."

A couple entered the room, paused to look at one of the columns, then kept going. In half a minute, they were gone.

"It's Abby," Lock said. "Now he's convinced himself it's you and someone else. And soon he might get to thinking that that someone else is me."

"He can't know it's me because it was you. Mostly."

Lock winced. Natalie continued, "All he can do is *think* it's me. And that's not enough for the D.A. to move forward with prosecution."

"It's good enough for him," he said. "He saw Witt's toxicity report and thinks it's impossible that he could have driven the car to Creek Road. Now he's wondering about the guy helping him in the parking lot."

Another visitor walked through the room, and Lock paused, lowered his voice, and continued.

"He controls the agency budget. He wouldn't think twice about making this CPS's highest priority, or asking the D.A. for help, even though he can't stand him. They would put a full detail of investigators on this, and that includes surveillance. More resources on our necks. Who knows what else they'll figure out."

"Like what?" Natalie said.

"Oh, I don't know. Maybe the guy in the black Lamborghini."

Natalie's expression changed to momentary panic—her brow furrowed and a quick grimace flashed across her face—before she consciously brought it back to neutral.

"What black Lamborghini?"

"The one your boyfriend drives."

Natalie's slumped. There was a long pause.

"Candice. She told you."

"No, not Candice. All you need to know is that I know," Lock said. "And thank you for not denying it. But I have bigger problems than worrying about a white trash cheater."

Natalie's lip curled into a snarl. "Bigger problems, such as…?" she asked through clenched teeth.

"Jacoby, the D.A. This is the kind of case he loves. And Abby's going to talk to Jacoby again—if he hasn't already—and Jacoby will bring on a lot of heat. This was made for him."

Natalie exhaled slowly.

"No matter what you think of me," she said, "you have to understand this is unraveling for both of us—not just me. We have to hang together. We'll find a way out, I know it. You're just panicking."

"The thing isn't unraveling, you're unraveling," he said. "You're not thinking straight. There's only one move—reconciliation—and you refuse to make it. And you don't know me as well as you think. When Dahlia got hurt, that did it for me. I crossed the line and there's no going back. And Abby's wrong. I'm no good. And I don't much care what happens to me."

"Then why don't you turn us in?" said Natalie. "Why don't you scamper on down to the police station with your tail between your legs and confess?"

"Because of Abby. If there's a way out of this mess where he never finds out I was behind the whole thing, then that's what I need to do. If he knew, it would kill him."

"I'll stop seeing Jerome," said Natalie. "I swear. He's nothing but entertainment for me. Can you let it go? Everyone's entitled to one mistake. Let it go. It was meaningless."

"Don't bust up with him for my sake. I don't care."

She slapped him. He didn't flinch and didn't put his hand to his check where it burned.

"Yes, you do care," she said. "I was involved with him long before you, and I didn't know how to break it off. I'm weak. You know that. Very weak. But it's you I'm crazy about, and I know you know it."

Lock stood up and looked down at Natalie as she continued to sit.

"That's hilarious," he said. "You're weak."

Natalie reached into her pocket and fidgeted with her car keys.

"All I care about is keeping Abby in the dark," said Lock. "I don't care about me, or you—not anything. I won't break his heart if I can help it."

"Maybe I started off with a rotten idea in mind, but I've changed," she said. "I'm in love with you. What about *my* heart?"

"Your heart will be fine. It's made of marble like the columns of the cloister. Cold marble."

Natalie glared. She said nothing.

"Do you know how many crimes we committed?" Lock asked.

"*You* committed."

Lock bit his lower lip. "Here they are," he said, closing his eyes. "Abduction, attempted murder, child endangerment, reckless endangerment, criminal negligence, aggravated assault, false report to law enforcement, battery, insurance fraud, conspiracy. And that's all I can think of off the top of my head. Believe me, there are others. And those are just the criminal charges. The civil charges will be as bad. We plotted the whole thing. You and me. And wait until Jacoby starts thinking about all the publicity he'll get if he can break the case."

"I don't threaten people, Lock, but I'm going to protect myself and my children, whatever I need to do."

"I know," he said. The bitterness was audible. "You always do whatever you feel like doing."

"If you don't care who gets in trouble, why should I? I don't care who gets hurt, either."

"Like Abby."

"Yes, and like me. Like you," she said.

"And Witt will have the kids while you're in jail. For a long time."

"It won't matter. According to you, I won't be getting any settlement anyway, so I may as well be rotting in jail."

"Go ahead, Natalie."

Natalie stood up and faced Lock. She looked him right in the eyes.

"Lock," she said, taking a deep breath. She reached to take his hand, but he backed up a pace. "Why are we fighting? We can get through this. It's harder than we planned. That's all. But we can do it. Together."

Lock sat back down on the bench and sighed. "What we did to your husband and Dahlia destroyed us, Natalie."

"You have to give me another chance," Natalie said. "Please. You'll see. Give me a chance to prove how good I can be for you."

He sized her up. *A pretty face on a pound of poison.*

Natalie said nothing else, then turned and walked across the floor toward the stairs that led to the exit.

Lock sat there for a couple of minutes so that he wouldn't see her in the parking lot. Once he figured she'd had enough time to start her car and drive away, he left too. The image of a craps table in Atlantic City leapt into his mind's eye, but with some effort, he dismissed it. Instead, he headed back to the office.

So there it was. On one side, Lock was being squeezed by a sociopath he was in love with, and on the other side, by Abby's thirst for the truth. All Lock wanted to do was hide what he had become from Abby. Nothing else mattered. Nothing at all. He'd never rely on anything Natalie said again, and worse, he now saw her as extremely dangerous. She could single-handedly bring down the whole scheme, crush them both, and then the worst would happen—Abby would learn the truth.

As Lock drove, he shook his head from side to side almost imperceptibly, not quite believing what he'd gotten himself into. With nearly a full year of sobriety behind him, had he absorbed nothing of the principles he'd learned in AA? Was he merely a common criminal, a fool in love, a man without even the slightest moral integrity? How could he have willingly, knowingly endangered the life of a child?

He shook his head more violently and squeezed the steering wheel so hard his hands began to cramp. He tried to cry, but the tears wouldn't come.

A drink sounded good, but at least he still had the will to fend off that bad idea.

27

As five o'clock on Thursday approached, Lock sat at his desk, organizing papers, checking the weather online, and stealing glances to monitor the end-of-day departure of his colleagues.

After a half hour, Lock couldn't sit there any longer, so he took a quick walk around the office, noting who remained. He spotted one last person— the front desk receptionist, who was putting on her coat and forwarding the phones to the night-shift coordinator, whose office was situated on the third floor. Not much chance she'd come down to the main office where Lock was. He returned to his cubicle, and by five forty-five, everyone else, even Abby, was gone.

Abby's private office was next to the break room. Lock got up and slunk in that direction. He paused at the closed but unlocked door of the office, furtively looked around, and let himself in. He stood at the threshold and his eyes fell on a silver-framed photograph of a dusty old elephant with long yellowed tusks. The photo hung on the wall behind the desk.

Abby, in infrequent displays of humor and when he was in the mood, liked to tell visitors that he had taken the picture in Zambia at the Nsumbu National Park animal preserve. When they'd praise Abby and say they didn't know his was a big game photographer, he'd chuckle and tell them the truth—he had taken the picture at 34th and Girard, inside the Philadelphia zoo.

Lock closed the door behind him and immediately took a seat at his boss's desk. He pressed the button and the computer screen lit up.

With a sweaty palm, he gripped the mouse and clicked on Abby's inbox. The program asked for the password, and Lock entered it. A long list of messages filled the screen. He scanned the subject lines of each one, and about twenty emails down, found a message titled "Confidential – Lock Gilkenney / Mannheim matter."

It was the email Jacoby had sent—at 12:55 p.m. that afternoon—to Abby. "I know you have great confidence in the professionalism of your staff," Jacoby wrote, "and so do I. But candidly, I am concerned about Mr. Gilkenney's handling of this file. It appears that he may have jumped to conclusions too quickly, and with too much certainty. My preliminary information indicates he is a single man and currently without a girlfriend. It is not lost on me that Mrs. Mannheim is an attractive woman. Those facts can sometimes lead to a conflict of interest, and this troubles the District Attorney's office more than a little. Given the implausible circumstances of the motor vehicle accident on Creek Road, I am keenly interested in Lock's whereabouts for the hours before, during, and after the accident—if that's what it was. That said, I am curious about your thoughts on this. This matter is my number one priority. Please reply as soon as possible."

Abby's reply was sent ten minutes later. "First of all, I object to your insinuation that Lochlan Gilkenney is somehow involved in any illegal activity whatsoever, or has exhibited even the slightest dereliction of his professional duties. His hunches regarding complex cases have proven correct 100% of the time. Lock is my best investigator. He is a keen observer of human nature. He genuinely loves all children. This Creek Road incident is not likely to be an exception to any of the above. Additionally, we have reviewed the file extensively and find nothing outside of our standard operating procedures—nothing at all. Furthermore, and more to the point, I have known Lock—both professionally and personally—for many, many years. I find him far above suspicion, and find your suggestion of his direct involvement in an array of felonies to be insulting, offensive, and obnoxious. I think we share the belief that attorney Jerome Freel is a bad actor, mixed up in this to some degree. Why you are suddenly focusing on Lock is a mystery to me. And to top it all off, on the evening and hours in question, Lock and I happened to be dining at Foster & Zandt's restaurant in Red Cedar Woods. I enjoyed a rib-eye, well done, with a baked potato. I recall that Lock ordered grilled salmon. I cannot remember what else he ordered. Perhaps you should charge me with obstruction of justice for withholding information about side orders. Lock picked up the check and so I cannot tell you how much of a tip he left. Perhaps your detectives can interview the wait staff and determine the amount of the gratuity and see if it meets with your approval. Respectfully yours, Abner Schlamm.'"

When Lock finished reading, he sat there, staring at the screen, amazed at getting a break—Abby had gotten confused. He was mixed up about the dates. Their dinner at the restaurant hadn't been the night of the crash, but the night before.

Finally, something other than bad news. But that didn't stop him from feeling horrible that he had betrayed Abby's trust. Even good news was ruined by the truth. He felt like he couldn't win.

⟞⟩●⟨⟝

That evening, Lock and Natalie lay in his bed, exhausted, their backs to each other, both half asleep. Neither of them wanted to be there, and Lock regretted having allowed her to invite herself over. She was just trying to keep him wound around her finger. He had known that, but at the time he thought it was Natalie or a drink tonight.

Lock got up to use the bathroom and returned a minute later. Instead of getting back into the bed, he pulled on a pair of jeans and a sweatshirt. Natalie didn't move.

When he sat on the bed to put on his shoes, Natalie rolled over and looked at him.

"We planned the whole thing meticulously," he said, "but we didn't figure on what happened next. Since then, we haven't been as careful. We've been reacting, not planning. That's where we can get into trouble."

"Like planning for what?" she said.

"Like preparing for tough questioning from the police or the D.A. Like your whereabouts on the night of the collision."

"So what?" said Natalie. "Who's going to check with the Orchid Society to see if I was really there? This isn't a murder investigation, Lock. Besides, I could have changed my mind and gone somewhere else. I don't have to answer for what I told Candice. Even if they find out I didn't get to the meeting, it will prove nothing."

"If not the Orchid Society, where else might you have gone? You're still without a solid alibi. Maybe your boyfriend could vouch for you."

"I told you, he doesn't know a thing—and things with him are through."

"Yes, Natalie, you told me already. Words are nothing but sounds that come out of your sweet mouth. You'll say anything."

"And what about you? You'll do anything to get what you want—a family. What did you say? Attempted murder, assault, abduction, fraud? More?"

Lock rose from the bed and pressed his palms against his temples, as if to massage away a headache. Natalie rolled away, again showing her back to Lock.

"If I would have known then—" he said, turning to her.

Natalie grabbed the first solid object she could reach, and a phone sailed across the bed, hitting Lock on the forehead. Drops of blood trickled down. He was speechless.

Natalie jumped out of bed and hurriedly pulled on her clothes. "So what am I doing here, then? I knew you weren't much," she said. "You live in fear of your boss and you're afraid of almost everything. You never grew up and now you're trying to bring us both down. You're not tough enough to live with what you've done. You're like a weepy little schoolgirl, Lock."

Lock felt the blood dripping; he wiped some off with his palm and looked at it. "You're deranged," he said, moving across the room and hurriedly grabbing items to pack for the Poconos, the only place he seemed to be able to clear his mind.

"You have no idea what I'm capable of," she said. "No idea."

"Yes, I do. Now Abby's not the only one I'm scared of. I'm scared of you, too."

"Pathetic. You coward."

Natalie finished dressing and left without saying another word. Lock stood there with a white sock pressed against his forehead and watched her walk out.

28

Lock had been at the cabin since just before it got dark. He brought in enough firewood to last a several days and lit a fire. The heat began warming the cabin immediately. The smoky scent filled his nostrils, and for the first time in a week, he felt a bit of calm. Apparently, his demons were as exhausted as he was.

He looked around for his overnight bag and realized he'd left it in the car. He went out to get it and took a moment to stare up at the starry sky through the topmost branches of the pine, oak, fir, and spruce trees. Normally, he might have put his things away and then walked in the woods, trying to find something new or maybe just spending time with the trees he had become familiar with over many years. But he was ashamed, as if the trees he loved might judge him for what he had done.

After a few minutes, he retrieved his bag from the trunk and climbed the three steps to the cabin's front door. He shrugged off his overcoat, put a kettle on the stove, and added just enough water for a single cup of tea. It was late, but caffeine never seemed to affect him at night.

He sat down in a rocker near the fire and closed his eyes. He waited for the water to boil. Then he changed his mind, got up, turned the stove off, and sat back down. He took long, deep breaths and consciously began to relax his body. Natalie had taught it to him, something she had learned at yoga. First, the scalp, then the forehead, the jaw, and so on. He had gotten as far as his lower back when the phone rang.

He rose and walked across the cold, wooden planks of the floor to answer it.

"Hello?"

"Lock, this is Tom, from CPS. Sorry to reach you so late. Couldn't find you earlier. There's some terrible news."

Lock's chest constricted. "What happened?"

"I just heard from the D.A.'s office. That Mannheim kid—the little girl? She suffered a cerebral hemorrhage a couple of hours ago. She died."

Lock exhaled sharply. "What? No, Tom, that's impossible. It was only a minor concussion. They're discharging her."

"Lock. Don't take this too hard. You have nothing to do with this. You did your job. Any one of us would have closed that case, too. I'm sorry to be the one to break it to you."

"Okay," Lock said, almost inaudibly. "I got it."

Then he hung up and fell to his knees, trembling. He leaned forward and pounded his already-bruised head into the floor.

Without packing or locking up, Lock jumped into his car and headed back. To where, he wasn't sure.

Lock walked into Foster & Zandt's and sat at a table close to the bar. He glanced in a mirror on the wall and saw that his face was drawn, his eyes hollow, his expression blank. The lone bartender, a new employee Lock didn't know, was cleaning up for the night.

"It's going on two o'clock," the bartender said. "We close in ten minutes. What can I get you that you can drink fast, sir?"

"You have Glenmorangie?"

"Glen what?"

"Glenmorangie. Single malt scotch. Never mind. Get me a double of the best scotch in the house."

"That'd be Highland Park Thirty Year Old. It's the boss's favorite. Forty bucks a shot. You still want it?"

"A double," said Lock.

The bartender shrugged. A moment later, he poured the drink, walked around the bar, and set it down in front of Lock.

"Drink up, sir. Savor it. They say it's delicious."

"Not as delicious as Glenmorangie."

Lock stared at the drink and handed the bartender a one hundred-dollar bill. "And a glass of water."

After the bartender delivered the water, Lock picked up the two glasses and walked them back to the furthest table from the bar. The lights in that part of the bar were already dimmed, and Lock sat in the near dark. He reached into his pocket and took out a vial of the same sleeping pills he'd slipped into Witt's beer. It was half full and held thirty or forty pills. A couple scattered to the floor when he opened the cap.

The bartender found Lock and gave him his change. Lock held the vial out of sight under the table.

As soon as the bartender walked away, Lock swallowed most of the pills. He washed them down with half the water, paused to swallow again, then emptied the rest of the vial down his throat, and finished the water. He had done research online and knew he had about twenty minutes until the drug would start to kick in. And maybe another fifteen minutes after that before he'd be unconscious.

Lock sat there, back upright, the double scotch in front of him. He stared at it, picked it up, and held it in front of his face with an outstretched arm. The low light from the ceiling fixture shone through the shot glass. He regarded the amber liquid affectionately. Only the glass separated him from the scotch. *What's in that liquid that's so damn alluring?* he wondered. He'd learned from others in AA that there were a million excuses to drink, but no valid reasons. He looked at it for a moment longer, then whipped his wrist forward and splashed the scotch out onto the floor.

He thought of Dahlia and pictured her in the morgue at the hospital. He imagined her lifeless little body on a stainless steel table in a refrigerator. Lock thought of Hannah, and wondered what she was like now, so many years later. Had she ever known there was a man named Lochlan Gilkenney who had loved and adored her and wanted to hold her hand as she grew up? Lock thought about his mother and how he missed her, how she'd always known the right thing to say when things were hard on him. And finally, he thought about Natalie—but her image was too painful to contemplate, and he booted her out of his mind's eye, the same way he'd learned to boot a craving. Lock realized how much he hated himself for what he'd allowed to happen. *Allowed?* he thought. No, he wasn't a passive participant, he was the star of the show, and the writer and director and producer, too. At his lowest low of drunkenness and drug addiction, he hadn't repulsed himself as he did now.

Dahlia was dead, and he and Natalie had killed her.

At first, it had been possible for him to rationalize his actions. Witt was bad news. He drove drunk with the kids, ignored his parental duties, and abused and battered his wife. Taking things into Lock's own hands had seemed like a good idea. At the time.

Maybe Natalie had planted the seed in his head, but that didn't matter, because he was the one who'd set it all up—the idea to put the two-year-old in the car, driving the car into the tree, the doping up of Witt, the whole catastrophe.

Last week, he had been a dedicated advocate for children in jeopardy. Today, he was a child murderer. But in an hour, it would all be over. He had no family who would mourn his passing. His only regret was how much all of this would hurt Abby.

One or two minutes passed and Lock hoped he'd soon feel the initial effects of the sleeping pills, but his mind was too active and that energized him. Until then, he'd be on his own, alone with his memories and self-judgments. He rested his forehead on the table.

Another minute passed. The bartender appeared. He saw what he assumed to be a slightly drunk Lock. He put his hand on Lock's shoulder and Lock looked up.

"Up we go, sir," the bartender said, starting to help him to his feet.

Lock shrugged to the side to shake off the bartender's grip.

"We're closing," the bartender said, backing off. "I lost you back here in the shadows. You almost got locked in."

The bartender stepped further back and stood there, glowering at Lock, waiting for him to get up and leave. A moment later, he stood up deliberately and headed to the door.

"What time is it?" he asked the bartender.

"Two twenty, friend. You okay to get home?"

"That's where I'm going," Lock said, and he left.

The cold November night air hit Lock in the face. He began walking, but he had no destination. He was still alert enough to know that if he collapsed on the street, it would be likely that someone would notice him and he'd be rushed to a hospital where he might be revived. He knew he needed to get someplace where no one would find him.

He looked up and down the street, looking for a place to go. Then, for some reason, the storage closet in Bill's Café and Hang-About popped into his head. That would be the perfect place to wait for the inevitable. It was in the middle of the night, but that wouldn't stop Lock from getting into the clubhouse. One of his AA compatriots would find him later that day. It would be a terrible scene, and a terrible thing for him to do, but did that matter at this point? He took a deep breath and kept walking—he was already headed in the general direction of the café.

He had no reason to rush, but he picked up his pace anyway. Then it hit him—he was scheduled to be the guest speaker at that morning's 6:30 AA meeting at the Hang-About. It was his responsibility to set up the room and make the coffee. People usually began arriving at the café around 6:00

a.m. In his confusion and grief, Lock thought he might be able to honor his AA commitment, or at least part of it. And he knew deep down he needed to come clean, to tell his story, to ease his conscience, to speak the truth.

But he wasn't thinking clearly—long before 6:30, the pills would have done their job.

A couple of minutes later, in the middle of a block of shops, Lock arrived at the AA club house. He needed to get in but didn't have the key. He hesitated a moment, then smashed his elbow through a small plane of glass in the door and reached through to release the dead bolt.

The door opened.

"Well," Lock said to the imaginary Abby in the audience, "I told you you wouldn't like hearing the truth, but that's what happened, and that's how I got here, half dead, and that's why I'm dying now. I'm a child killer, among other things, and I don't deserve to—"

The illusory crowd disappeared upon Lock's sudden awareness that real people had entered the room.

Abby had arrived.

He stood in the back, flanked by Ivan. Abby ambled forward slowly, his face blank. He eased himself into his regular seat, eyes steady on Lock.

"Hello, Abby," Lock said, not bothering with the microphone and sounding drunk. He spoke softly, his words barely audible.

Lock straightened up as best he could and strained to put on a smile.

"I was rehearsing what I need to tell you," he said. "'A searching and fearless moral inventory.' Isn't that what AA says? Full disclosure, kind of. And what I came up with is pure ugly. Pure evil."

Lock took another gulp of water. The effect of the pills was pronounced. He was losing his grip on the podium. "I'm so sorry."

"You're breaking my heart, son," Abby said. "I pray I'm home in bed having a terrible dream."

"I wish that's what's happening," he said, his speech nearly beyond recognition. Lock took another sip of water. "But it's not. Do me a favor."

"What, Lochlan?" Abby said.

"Don't call the police, at least not yet. Give me a few hours to be by myself."

"Too late," Abner said. "An ambulance is on its way. And you want a few hours? You don't have a few minutes. I need to know what you took."

Abby rose and took a step forward.

"Don't worry about me," Lock said. "Everything will take its natural course, I need a little more time."

"I can't let you do that."

"Let me go, please. This is the best idea I've had in a long time."

"Your best idea? Your best thinking got you right here, mixed up in a serious crime. Now it's time to let me do your thinking for you."

"An hour then. One hour is all I need."

"I don't think so," Abby said.

"You're picking a hell of a time to get tough with me."

"It's always a hell of a time."

Lock couldn't stand any longer. He slid to the floor, losing his grip on the podium. He tried to rise.

"Don't get up, Lochlan. Just sit there," Abby said. Lock watched him run his tongue over his teeth. He looked away from Lock. With a trembling hand, he took off his cap. His eyes welled up. "They'll be here in a minute," he said, moving to Lock and touching his face.

Lock struggled to get himself upright. He managed, with tremendous effort, to get to his feet. Once up, he stumbled toward the rear exit, shoved the door open, and fell out into the brick-lined dark alley and the frigid air.

Abby followed. "What are you going to do?" he asked. "Make a run for it?"

"Try to stop me."

"Run down the alley and hide behind a trash bin so you can't be found? Then curl up and die like a dog? Is that how your mother raised you?"

"Karma, Abner. You can't get away with anything."

"You have plenty coming to you, but this? Dying here? No." Tears welled in Abby's eyes.

"Dying won't get you out of this," he said. "Mannheim's been released and Natalie's been arrested. And you. You're going to get yourself patched up and face yourself and the charges against you. Then you're going to stand trial or take a plea, and they're going send you to prison for a little while. You're going to take what's coming to you. Can you hear me?"

"A little while? I'll go to prison forever. Forever. I killed a child."

Abby grimaced. "No, you didn't kill her. That story was the D.A.'s invention. He made that up for you to hear. He thought it would unnerve you, and he was right. That trick could work only on a fundamentally decent man, mind you. The child is fine, home with her father. I heard about Jacoby's ploy late tonight but couldn't find you. Thank God for Ivan. He saw you, thought something wasn't right, and called me. I figured you heard the phony story and would do something foolish. And here you are."

Lock slumped over, fading in and out of consciousness. He rolled onto his side.

Abby removed his coat, knelt down, and tucked it under Lock's head.

"Hang on, boy. They're almost here. Tell me what you took."

"To make it easier for them to save me?"

"No. For me to save you," said Abby.

Lock's eyes closed for a long moment. He opened them with an effort and tried to focus. Both men's eyes met.

"This was a tough case for you, Abby," Lock slurred. "Not one of the easy ones." He breathed heavily.

"I was praying it was Freel," said Abby. "I didn't want to rule him out—because if he was out, then you were in. But there was nothing I could do. The evidence began burying you alive in the hole you dug for yourself."

Lock's breath was slow, shallow and labored. "Got you wanting a drink, did it?" Lock asked, a weak smile on his face.

"You thought you could cross the line of what's right and what's not, and then dash back," said Abby. "But you found that you couldn't. The act of crossing the line changes the whole nature of the game."

"Disappointed you again."

"There's no time for this now."

Lock swallowed hard.

"You have to tell me what you've taken. That's an order."

"From my boss?"

"From a man who loves you," said Abby.

Lock's eyes closed for a beat, then opened. He was fighting to decide if he should answer Abby or try to get up again and run for it.

"Same thing I used on Mannheim. Ambien. Only I took a month's supply."

"What else?"

"Nothing else."

"Wash it down with a drink, did you?"

"Yes," said Lock. "Of water."

"How long ago?"

Lock was barely able to speak.

"I don't know," he mumbled. "I'm sorry I let you down."

Abby turned toward Ivan, who had followed them into the alley. "Where's that damn ambulance?"

"Let's get him up and moving," Ivan said. "Don't let him fall asleep."

They got Lock to his feet and shuffled him back into the café and into the men's room. He was unable to stand on his own.

Lock leaned over the sink and looked into the mirror, cupping his hands and feebly trying to splash water on his face. Lock's leather jacket was askew. Abby reached around and tugged it straight for him. Lock watched in the mirror, then took a long, hard look at himself.

A siren approached.

SIX MONTHS LATER

29

Chafing tires up against the curb, Abby stopped his car and put it in park a half block away from the main entrance of a long, imposing building—the dreary prison of Camp Hill, Pennsylvania, with its red brick walls and shiny, razor-wire fencing. For a reason he couldn't figure out, he didn't want Lock to know he had come early.

Any minute now, Lock would sign himself out of the prison's administrative office and open the steel doors leading to a cracked sidewalk. Abby drummed his fingers on the steering wheel and tried to formulate what he was going to say to Lock, who was being released four weeks early from his six-month prison term. During that stretch, Abby hadn't once visited him—but that had been Lock's doing. Lock had begged Abby to stay away, pleading with him not to come see him in prison garb from behind the thick Plexiglas that would certainly separate them. Lock asked instead that Abby be the one to pick him up upon his release.

Lock waited inside the prison office while a chubby guard took her time retrieving the personal articles—an all-but-empty wallet, a dead cell phone, and three or four keys on a ring—confiscated immediately upon his arrival twenty-one weeks earlier. He stood there, wearing the street clothes, now musty and wrinkled, that had been handed to him minutes earlier in exchange for his orange jumpsuit. He held a cardboard box filled with books and toiletries from his cell. He had no coat, since it had been late August when he was first imprisoned. It had taken the prosecutors and defense attorneys almost no time at all to work out a plea deal, and his sentence had started a few weeks later. Natalie had moved quickly through the system as well, working off a similar sentence that started just before Lock's. Now it was almost February, and a cold day.

After a routine handshake and a few tired words of advice from a prison functionary, Lock opened the door and walked out into the sunlight. The short-sleeved shirt he wore did very little to protect him from the bitter cold.

If Dominque were alive, she'd come get me. And Hannah, she'd be about sixteen by now. Maybe she'd ride out with her mom to see me, too.

He stood there and looked up at the sky, exhaling condensed breath. He was glad Abby was late. The more time that elapsed before he would have to face him, the better.

He felt sick to his stomach and was overwhelmed by a deep sense of shame. Where was the intense elation he'd expected upon getting released? There was none of the primal excitement of being let out of a cage. As he waited for his friend and former boss, Lock contemplated what would come next in his life. He knew he could never work for CPS again, and there was nothing else that he could think of doing. Something would turn up, of course, but at that moment, he had no idea what it might be.

Abby's car glided up and stopped in front of Lock.

They stood and sat, respectively, and looked at each other, neither one saying anything for a long beat. Lock put the cardboard box on the sidewalk and leaned down so he could see into the car.

"Abby," Lock said. Tears filled his eyes. The old man looked even older than he remembered.

Abby turned off the engine and got out of the car, moving as fast as a seventy-six-year-old with a potbelly and an arthritic back and knees could.

Lock knew by the stiff way he moved that the hour-and-a-half drive had been hard on him.

Abby walked around the car to embrace Lock. Lock stepped back after a long hug and began to speak, but he could only stammer. Abby signaled him to be quiet.

"Son," Abby said, "it's true we are nothing but our choices, and you made some terrible ones. And so have I. I've gotten better, and you can, too."

"But Abby—" Lock began. He felt utterly undeserving of Abby's trust and his kindness.

Abby ignored him. "There's nothing I can do to reverse all the hurtful, destructive things I did—except to act like a man and do the best I can with the time I have left. I've spent the second half of my life trying to make up for the drunken, wasteful things I did the first half. I work hard to protect children from the seamier side of the world, and for them, I've done a pretty good job. I'm trying to give back a little."

The sun was setting, and Lock looked into Abby's face and then looked away, up into the darkening sky. He thought, *Even if I live as long as you, I'll never make up for what I did. But I'm going to try, you'll see.*

"Let's get in the car and get the hell away from here," said Lock.

"Give me a few more minutes. I want to stretch. Sitting and driving too long gets to my back."

"Okay, but let's not stay here much longer. I'm getting the creeps."

"A couple more minutes, then we can go," Abby said. "And something else. I'm not embarrassed to say it now, no matter how you might take it. I love you, Lochlan. With all my heart. Every day you were locked up, I felt it in my gut."

Lock nodded and smiled. Abby leaned against the car.

"It's not all bad," said Lock. "Prison was the greatest thing that ever happened to me. It worked. I know it doesn't work for most people, but it did for me. I sat there every day on a crappy cot and thought about what I did and why I did it and what life could have been like had I made other decisions. Now I have a second chance, too. I'm going to take advantage of it, as you did. It's funny. Usually, people with alcohol problems go to jail, then find AA. For me, it was the other way around. I found AA, then needed jail to complete the course. Same lessons, just a different sequence. Today, I waffle between heavy depression because of what a fool I was, and powerful elation because I have a chance to start over, to take the lessons and apply them to my life."

Abby nodded and smiled.

"Don't worry about me, Abby. Yes, I have periods of regret, but most of the time, I'm excited. Not sure what my next move is, but I know I'm optimistic as hell. I've left a lot of negative things behind. I'm looking forward."

"Regret is a form of resentment," said Abby, "and as you know from the program, resentment is a shortcut to your next drink."

"Yes, you're right. I'm working on that." Lock looked up at the sky and took in a slow, deep breath. "And I thought about you, too. I know I love you more than I ever loved my own father. After I nearly destroyed my life, you wound up saving it that morning in the Hang-About when I was overdosing."

"Keep marching, one foot in front of the other," said Abby. "That's your job now. Things will get better."

The two men hugged each other again, Lock's head resting on Abby's shoulder. Lock stooped down and picked up the cardboard box and put it in the backseat. Abby wasn't so steady on his feet, so Lock gripped him by the elbow and helped him toward the passenger side of the car. He refused to get in.

"I'll drive," Lock said.

"No," said Abby, pointing to the passenger seat. "You get in. I can still drive."

Lock wanted to object, but did as instructed.

Abby got in the car, and as he shifted into drive, another car sped up and screeched to a stop in front of them, inches short of sideswiping Abby's car. Abby jammed on his brakes.

"Idiot!" Abby said, blasting his horn.

The other car was a beat-up twenty-year-old Toyota. Its creaky door opened and out stepped Natalie. Other than her attire, she hadn't changed at all.

She walked toward the passenger side of the car where Lock sat. He lowered the window halfway and immediately regretted doing so.

Natalie's huge, pregnant belly stretched the material of a not-particularly-flattering waitress's uniform. She must have been six or seven months pregnant. She wore a little makeup. Her nametag read "Nat." She held a large envelope in one hand.

"Congratulations, Lock," she said, shifting the envelope from one hand to the other and back again. "You're out." She leaned down to get a closer view of him and then looked past Lock to Abby. "Hello, Mr. Schlamm."

"Greetings, Natalie," Abby said.

She gazed at Lock for a moment. "You look good," she told him. "You don't look like you spent six months in a…a small room with iron bars." She thrust the envelope to Lock through the half-open window. He didn't move a muscle to take it, and he turned his face away from her. She withdrew the envelope.

"I almost missed you just now," Natalie said to the back of his head. "I couldn't get off work early. I drove for an hour and a half to get here."

Lock wasn't impressed. He turned toward her. "What do you want, Natalie? Haven't we had enough of each other?"

She pointed to the envelope and reached through the window and dropped it on his lap. "I spent a long time writing to you," she said. "A letter practically every day for all the months I was in prison. Never mailed them. I hoped for a day like today when I could hand them to you in person. I've thought deeply about what counts in life. You probably did the same, sitting in your cell. I've thought about what I've done wrong, all my wrong-headed thinking. It's all in the letters. And if you don't want to read them, better yet. I can tell you about it myself."

Abby turned off the engine.

"Don't do that," Lock said. "Turn it back on. We're out of here."

Abby ignored him.

"I know writing all that doesn't change a thing about what happened," Natalie said, "but there it is, anyway. Almost one hundred pages of soul-searching."

"Isn't it a condition of probation that we don't interact with each other?"

"No," said Abby. "The D.A. never asked for that. Doesn't apply to either of you. Jacoby could have gone much, much rougher on you two. Lucky for you both, he wants to be my friend, or something like that. He wasn't going to take a plea deal. I begged him to take it easy on you and got him to change his mind."

"I don't care what you have to say, Natalie," said Lock.

"You have to," she said. "We had something real and then something ugly destroyed it."

"The ugliness was there first," Lock said. He turned to Abby. "Let's go. Turn it on. Get me away from here. Get me away from her."

"And now I've changed again," Natalie said.

Abby looked at Lock, but didn't move a muscle.

"While I was in prison," Natalie said. "I got help from a great shrink and a wonderful support group. And after I got out, I went for more help. On my own. Paid for it out of my own pocket. Counseling. Another support group. I didn't have to. It wasn't a condition or anything. I wanted to. I've learned some unpleasant things about myself. I've faced them, accepted them. Now I've gotten better. And I want to live happily ever after with you and our son."

"Well, that's just fascinating," Lock said. "Terrific news. You want me to believe that baby is mine? I believe nothing you say."

"Yes, the baby's ours—it's all there in what I've written," she said, pointing to the envelope lying in Lock's lap. "Witt and I have mostly agreed on the terms of a no-fault divorce. No money for me, of course, after what I did, but I'm free and I get to see the girls. Not the worst deal in the world. And I'm evolved. I'm making it on my own—barely, but on my own. I see Dahlia and Edwina every other weekend. It's the best part of my life. And it's going to get better. Witt doesn't want primary custody anymore. His loss is my gain. Starting next month, I'll have primary custody. Witt's agreed. Too much for him, I guess. Anyway, he's volunteered to contribute more than his share to the girls. He's about to close a deal on a great three-bedroom condo for us in Stoney Springs. He'll own it, but we'll live in it rent-free. It's all in writing. He doesn't want me to get a cent, of course, but he knows if I'm impoverished, the girls will be too. Witt's turned out to be a half-decent father, after all. Still pretty much a prick, but a decent father."

"And what's all this have to do with me?" Lock said.

Natalie looked around as if she worried people were watching. She looked at Abby.

"Don't turn away," she said to Lock. "I know what kind of person you are. I corrupted a decent man. Don't laugh when I tell you I'm sorry and I've changed. And I now realize what we could have together. I pray it's not too late."

Lock felt a smirk begin to form, but managed to resist it. He picked up the envelope from his lap and started to hand it back, but instead stopped and opened the clasp. There were hundreds of pages and dozens of smaller envelopes. At a quick glance, everything appeared to be handwritten.

"So you feel guilty," Lock said. "Big deal. You *are* guilty." *Just like me,* he thought.

Abby just watched, and Lock couldn't figure out why he didn't just drive away.

"That, too, but much more," Natalie said. "Everyone deserves a second second chance."

"Goodbye, Natalie," Lock said. He turned to Abby. "Please get me out of here."

Abby gave Natalie a look and shrugged. "Sorry, dear," he said. "We knew it'd be a long shot." He started the car and put it into gear. He was hemmed in between the curb and Natalie's car.

Lock said, "You knew about this? Jesus, Abby!"

Through the open car window, Natalie said, "Please, Lock, don't drive away. Don't leave me." Tears rolled down her cheeks. "I know what I did," she said. "The past can't change, but I can. I did."

Abby turned and studied Natalie. She gripped the door handle as if to hold the car from leaving.

He put the car in park.

"Thanks anyway," Lock said. He looked at Abby. "Go."

"Don't listen to him, Mr. Schlamm."

"One thing I do want to ask you, Natalie." Lock pointed to her belly. "Whose is that? Witt's? Freel's? Some other sucker's?"

Natalie looked at him. Her lips moved a bit, but no words came out.

"Come on. Let's go. Drive," said Lock, thrusting his jaw toward Abby.

"I told you, it's ours, Lock," Natalie said. She grabbed his forearm. "A boy. I didn't want to know the sex, but they told me in prison anyway."

"Mine?"

"Yes. I'm sure. I'm positive. I know it. It has to be."

"Oh, yeah. You're sure."

Lock got out of the car, eyes transfixed on Natalie's belly. Then, for the first time that day, he really looked at her. Her face was fuller, and she looked five years older than when he had seen her last. He didn't want to admit it, but she still looked good. She looked her age. He moved closer to her, continuing to be transfixed by the bulge in her waitress attire.

"You're sure," he said. "And I'm sure too—that you're a liar. Remember, Natalie, words are just warm sounds that come out of your pretty little mouth."

The sky was darker now, and Natalie cried some more. "We can make it. We can make it if we both want it, I know it," she said. Tears rolled down her face and dripped onto the front of her uniform.

"Maybe I am a liar, by nature," she said, "but I don't lie anymore. We can all learn to resist our natural inclinations." She took his hand and pressed it against her belly. He didn't pull away. "I wasn't with anyone but you around the time I got pregnant. I'll pay for the test if that will convince you. You said you wanted a child, well, now you have one. Not that I planned it. You say you dreamed all your life about having a family. Even if you reject me, you can't reject him. It's up to you to decide how much of his life you want to be in. But he's yours, alright, and I'm due soon."

Lock stared, his hand lingering on her belly. He looked at her nametag. "I thought you hated it when people called you 'Nat.'"

"I do," she said, straightening out the tag. "But that's what they gave me. I accepted it and didn't say a word. The old me wouldn't sit still for that. But I do tell the regulars to call me Natalie."

Lock looked her in the face, then leaned down and pressed his ear against her belly. He listened for a long moment. He thought he could hear the heartbeat, and then, something poked him in the cheek. He stood straight up, with just a hint of a smile.

"Abby," he said, looking through the car window toward the old man. "I think I felt him kick."

Abby grinned.

"He's a little soccer player, alright," Natalie said. "Keeps me awake half the night. I play music for him and I swear it calms him down right away."

"What does he like?" said Lock.

"Definitely not hip-hop or show tunes," she said. "Mostly Bob Dylan. Sometimes B. B. King."

That caught Lock's attention. They were two of his favorite musicians. He couldn't recall ever telling her that. They hadn't listened to much music together.

"Don't tell me to go to hell, Lock," she said. "Meet me for coffee. Let's talk. Hear what I have to say."

"What are you going to say that you haven't just said?" Lock asked. "No thanks, Natalie. Let it rest in peace. And I doubt the baby's mine."

"He is yours. It's biologically impossible that he's anyone else's. And a simple test will prove it."

Abby cleared his throat. "Go ahead, son, meet her. Go see what she has to say. You do need to know if he's yours to have a conversation."

"Abby, please, keep out of this."

"You might be interested to hear," Abby said, "that after Natalie got out of prison, she called me. We've grown to know each other in the last couple of months. You know I'm a pretty good judge of character. I think she's learned her lesson. And she's not a bad cook."

Lock was stunned. She was an even better liar than he thought, or age was catching up to Abby. *No way has she changed. Not possible.*

"Please, Lock," Natalie said. "We loved each other."

"You loved me? I loved you. You loved what I could do for you."

"Don't you owe it to that family you've always wanted?" she asked.

Lock stared off in thought. Was she making sense, or was she conning him? Again. He didn't know. In the end, he agreed to meet just to get away from her. He didn't know how she had fooled Abby, but he knew he couldn't stand in the street for another minute.

When Abby drove away, Natalie waved, but Lock just looked straight ahead at the road before him.

———————

Lock let forty miles pass before he spoke. "There was this tree outside the fence, a white ash. The guards cut the lower branches off so no one could use them to escape, you know? But the high ones hung over the yard, the part of the yard I used to exercise in, and I could see the tree from my cell, too. That was good. I'd look out every morning and every day, and that ash would be there, and I knew soon enough I'd be outside the fence too."

Lock reached into his shirt pocket and carefully pulled out a brittle red-and-green leaf. "The leaves used to fall into the yard. You can use them to stop mosquito bites from itching, so that was a good thing. Lots of mosquitoes this year, or that's what it seemed like."

He held the leaf up so Abby could get a look at it. "This is the last one I kept. I had it pressed in a box jammed full of letters I had received, but it still got a little beat up. It was perfect, though, perfect shape, and how the colors are all there—green shading to orange and then red. Just, you know, a perfect example of something nature gives us. That's what I like about it."

Abby took a good look at the leaf and nodded.

"I don't know why I told you that," Lock said. He took a deep breath. "Now what am I supposed to do?"

"That's an easy one, boy. Go meet her. Tomorrow, noon, Main Street café, like you agreed."

Lock carefully put the leaf back in his pocket. Darkness fell and no one spoke for a while. Lock drank in his new freedom.

"There are very few right angles out here, out in the world," he said.

"What are you talking about?" said Abner.

"Compared to inside the walls, I mean," said Lock. "Everything in prison is constructed of right angles. The cell, the bars on the cell. You walk down a short hallway, and you have to turn right or left. There's nothing circular, and nothing that goes straight for very long. All these right angles you're forced to adapt to. It makes your mind think in right angles. Everything is right or left, yes or no, up or down, on or off. I couldn't think abstractly in prison."

"Not quite following you, son," said Abby. "But whatever you went through, it's behind you. Unless you drag it around in your head. It's up to you."

Abby drove only a bit faster than the posted speed limit, but as he made his way down the road, his car drifted slightly out of its lane.

"Maybe you're getting a little tired, Abby," Lock said. "I'm itching to drive. Pull over, would you?"

"I'm fine," said Abner.

"Well, if you start to feel weary, let me know. I haven't driven in almost half a year."

The image of Lock's cell flashed in his head. The cot, the sink, a few prison-approved toiletries on a stainless steel shelf, and a small stack of books and magazines. And besides the world's thinnest pillow, not much else. Then he looked around the car and into the backseat. The cabin of the vehicle was smaller than his cell, but to Lock, it offered much more freedom.

Abby cleared his throat as if he were about to say something, but he remained silent.

"I can't even begin to imagine what you see in her," Lock said. "You've read all the police and D.A.'s reports, the psychiatric evaluation, and you know what she did to me. She must have hypnotized you or something. Or she's gotten you to fall in love with her."

Abby glanced over at Lock, who was staring straight ahead at the road. "I'm too old for romantic love, and I know it. She hasn't fooled me. I feel for her. She's just a mixed-up human being."

"You could say that about most everyone in prison."

"I could say that about almost everyone walking down the street, too, and I'd be right," said Abby. "She's got her own story, like all the rest of us do, Lock. She's no better or worse than anyone else. As I always say, we are our choices, and hers were inexcusable. But I made worse when I was younger. And yours weren't anything to crow about, either."

"I know all that. But what I don't understand is how you could—"

"Befriend her?"

"Yes."

"That's another easy one, son. As you know, in AA we say the only requirement for membership is the desire to stop drinking. So when Natalie called me, I expanded that philosophy a bit and decided that the only requirement for me to help her would be her desire to grow into being a better person. And I absolutely believe that's what she wants."

"I don't know, Abby. She's a genius at manipulation."

"We drunks all have our doctorates in manipulation. She's not unique in that."

"Well," said Lock. "Just be careful. You know the scorpion and the frog story?"

Abby shrugged. "Enlighten me."

"Okay," said Lock. "One summer afternoon, a scorpion and a frog meet on the bank of a stream. The scorpion asks the frog to carry him across to the other side. The frog says, 'How do I know you won't sting me?' The scorpion says, 'Because if I do, I'll die too.' That makes sense to the frog, so he agrees. Midstream, however, the scorpion stings the frog in the neck. So the frog asks the scorpion, 'Why? Why would you do that? Now we're both going to drown.' The scorpion shrugs and says, 'Because, my friend, that is my nature.'"

Abby said nothing for a beat, then spoke up. "Natalie has a heart and a higher power, son, and you can't necessarily say the same for a scorpion."

Now it was Lock's turn to be silent. *I hope you're right, Abby,* he thought. *But probably you're just like the frog and you can't see it.*

Abby pulled into the driveway at Lock's carriage house. Lock had used his savings to keep the place while he was away. Lock leaned over and gave him a hug of gratitude. Lock picked up Natalie's envelope filled with letters and got out to get his box from the back.

"See you in the morning at the six thirty meeting," Lock said, leaning in through the open door.

"How's that make you feel?" Abby said.

"How's what make me feel?"

"Tomorrow will be the first time you're at the Hang-About since the last time."

"Since the morning I overdosed?"

"Yes. Since then."

"It will feel fine, like being home again. I'm looking forward to it. I've been looking forward to it for almost six months."

"Okay, then. Don't oversleep. I've been coming here every couple of weeks as agreed to start your car for you, so don't use a dead battery as an excuse not to show up."

"I know. I appreciate it. And when was the last time I ever tried to duck a meeting?"

Abby nodded. "Okay, you're right. You'll be there, bright and early."

"I guess the coffee is still terrible," said Lock.

"Then come with a Starbucks in hand if you've developed a gourmet attitude, now that you're used to all that excellent prison coffee."

"Good night, Abby. Thanks for picking me up. Literally and figuratively."

Lock stood in the driveway and watched the red lights of Abby's car pull away. He looked up at the stars, took a deep breath of the chilly air, and climbed the stairs to his apartment.

Inside, Lock's first instinct was to light a fire in the wood-burning stove and burn Natalie's envelope. He put his box of things down and then had a bad feeling. He had been holding the box tight against his chest while he fiddled with the lock, and when he reached for the leaf, he found it broken into a dozen pieces.

He took the biggest pieces and reassembled them on the coffee table. He looked at the puzzle he had made for a minute. Then he looked at the envelope Natalie had left him.

What if the baby really is mine? What if I'm tied to Natalie for the next twenty years? Shouldn't I at least read what she wrote? Shouldn't I give her a chance to explain herself?

Lock placed the envelope on his kitchen table, went into his bedroom, and immediately fell asleep, fully dressed, on the most comfortable bed he'd ever felt.

30

As Lock drove to the café to meet Natalie, he couldn't keep his mind off of one thing—her bulging belly.

Whose baby was she carrying? If he knew beyond a doubt that the boy was his, well, that would change everything. He'd put up with anyone to have a son—or a daughter. Pink or blue, it wouldn't matter in the slightest.

Lock had imagined he would intentionally arrive a half hour late to his meeting with Natalie, just to show her he wasn't over-anxious to see her, but on second thought he decided that would be childish.

He was at least pleased to realize he'd continued to think of it as a meeting rather than a date. He'd stay in control of his feelings if he saw it that way. Part of him wanted her back, and another part thought she was shallow, gorgeous, psychotic, ruthless, and driven to get anything denied her, all at once. That was what this might be about. Maybe she wanted him now because she thought she couldn't have him.

He had dreamed of prison the night before, of his cell and the yard and then the tree beyond the fence. Natalie's snake tattoo had been in the dream, too, and the snake was wound around the base of the tree. He didn't remember any more, but he had been wondering all morning if she still had the tattoo. It had been henna, not permanent, and she had told him it needed to be reapplied every three or four weeks. If she'd changed as much as she claimed, he guessed that the tattoo was long gone. It had been a symbol of her darker side. *It's her nature*, he thought.

When Lock drove up to the café, he wasn't surprised to see a very pregnant Natalie already there, waiting out front. She was dressed as usual—an ankle-length sweater most likely covering shorts and a colorful t-shirt that he figured would accommodate her bulging belly. Her toes didn't disappoint, either. They were bejeweled and sparkling.

"I have to admit, I thought I might get stood up," she said, walking toward him.

For the second time since he'd known her, Lock saw that she wore makeup.

"I might have canceled," he said, "but I wouldn't have stood you up. I don't do things like that."

"I know you wouldn't. I guess I'm a little paranoid when it comes to what you think of me. Thank you for coming. It means everything to me."

"Let's get a table," he said.

He held the door for her and they entered the café. It was crowded, but not too noisy. Natalie spotted two teenagers leaving a booth and claimed it immediately by putting her bag on the table. The previous occupants didn't bother cleaning off their debris. Natalie picked up two cardboard take-out coffee cups and a sandwich wrapper and threw them into a receptacle before sitting down, struggling to fit her belly between the seat and the edge of the table.

"I'm used to clearing tables now," she said.

Lock slid in and sat opposite her. He realized now how uncomfortable he'd been the day before when she'd surprised him at the prison gate.

"What do you want, Lock?" she asked, rising with some effort. "I'll go order it. I'm having decaf. Iced tea for you, as usual? Even though it's freezing out?"

"You're a good waitress," he said. "I half expect you to whip out an order pad and write it down. I bet you charm some big tips out of your customers. Yes. With lemon."

"I was a waitress long before I met Witt," she said. "Remember, I grew up poor in Jersey City."

"Then you got rich in Red Cedar Woods," he said. "My mother was a waitress, too."

She nodded. "I was an actress and living that life was playing a part. Poor growing up, burning to be rich. Cause and effect, Lock. I was infatuated with the idea of living a life of luxury. Witt bought me that Mercedes two months after we started dating—and he put the title in my name."

She took a breath and touched her belly.

"He's kicking," she said. "You know, my parents worked every day of their lives and were never able to put two nickels together. Now they're retired on social security and have nothing else. When I was with Witt, I'd send them money every month, sometimes a thousand, sometimes fifteen hundred. Snuck it out of the allowance he gave me when things were okay between us. Now I can't send them a dime, but they're fine anyway. Especially when they get to see the girls."

Lock hadn't known that. He had always imagined her spending those thousands a month on herself.

The moment Natalie stood up to get the beverages, Lock slid to the end of the bench and placed both of his hands on her stomach. He didn't look up at her face.

"He's not kicking now," he said.

"Maybe not this second, but he's been at it all morning."

Natalie walked away. She was gone a few minutes. Lock tapped his car keys on the table. She arrived carrying the coffee and iced tea and placed his drink in front of him.

"I don't want to be crude, Natalie," Lock said. "But exactly what do you want to talk about? I'm basically here so I don't disappoint Abby, who's strangely gung-ho on you."

"Whatever got you here is fine with me. It's up to me to get you to stay."

"I have to be out of here by a quarter to one. I have a dentist appointment," he said.

"Okay. Then I'll get right to it," she said. "Did you read my letters?"

"No, but I didn't burn them, either, and I don't see the point of tearing open a wound that's barely healed."

"Thanks for not destroying them, at least. Maybe you'll read them someday."

"Anything's possible."

Lock kind of liked the idea of being pursued by the woman who'd broken his heart and cheated on him. He was trying to get himself to feel sorry for her, but it wasn't working. She was still too in control, despite what Abby might think, to let herself get frantic over anything. In the midst of everything falling apart, she kept cool. Wasn't cool defined as grace under fire? When the judge had sentenced her to six months at Dauphin County, she had just smiled and thanked him. It could have been much worse, she knew. Her lawyer had warned her that a year or two of incarceration wasn't out of the question.

"You're all I have, Lock," Natalie said. "Actually, that's not totally true. I have my parents and I have the girls. And it's true I want you. But more than that, I need you. Disturbing experiences change people, sometimes for the worse, sometimes for the better. I'm one of those who's changed for the better. And I'm continuing to grow."

"I've changed too," he said. "And one thing that's changed is that I'm not so gullible."

"I need more gratitude and more humility in my life," she said. "And I work on that every day. One thing I learned in group therapy is that if I have the capacity to be honest, I'll get better, and that's happening. I've stopped being so hypercritical. Except when it comes to me. I'm too harsh on myself. I need to work on that. And I want to go to meetings with you."

"You don't drink, Natalie," Lock said. "And you don't take drugs, at least as far as I know. I admit I don't know as much about you as I thought."

"I used to drink a lot," she said. "Drinking and drugging are addictions, and we're all addicts of something or other. A substance, a way of thinking, a behavior. So, I never want to drink again, and the only requirement for membership in AA is the desire not to drink. I qualify right there."

"Another thing you don't know about meetings—there's a lot of talk about a higher power, God, and I know that won't sit well with you."

"Just so you know," she said, "I've already gone to a handful of AA meetings, some with Abby. And I like them just fine. Two women there invited me out to lunch. I didn't follow up with them yet, but I will. And Abby and I talked about the God thing. He said it bothered him, too, until someone told him that in AA, God stands for Group Of Drunks. When you look at the wisdom you get from the people at the meetings, it makes sense."

Natalie winced. She put her hand on her belly.

"You know more about me than you realize," she said. "I want to go to meetings because there's a lot to be learned there. Abby's right when he calls it the greatest show on earth. You hear some funny stories, and some heart-breakers, too. And a lot of them have happy endings. I want to attend meetings with you so we can grow together. Abby's been going for thirty years, and he says he learns something new every day."

"Abby goes to meetings because he likes to socialize," he said.

"That's bullshit. Maybe he likes to socialize, but he goes for the wisdom, too. He says it keeps him green."

"You seem to be quoting him a lot. Didn't you once call him an old goat?"

"That was before I knew him. He's quotable, what can I tell you? He's an amazing man. He's full of love and experience and he's nonjudgmental. He'd have to be to put up with me."

"He wasn't always that way."

"I know that," she said. "And so does he. He knows how he's hurt people, but that was long, long ago. All he can do now to make amends is live right, help others, and stay sober."

Lock sipped his iced tea, and Natalie stirred her coffee while toying with a napkin. A rush of customers entered and the café got noisier. Natalie and

Lock leaned in slightly to better hear each other. His hand rested on the table, and Natalie put hers on top of it. He let her hold his hand for a few seconds before sliding it out from under in order to pick up his glass. She left her hand where it was.

"You wanted to talk about us, Natalie."

"I don't know where to start," she said. "I don't want to babble. I was so afraid you wouldn't meet me."

"Well, I'm here, and we only have another half hour. Speak your mind."

"I want to talk about building a relationship and a genuine emotional connection, but there's something else that has to come out now," she said. She twirled her napkin on the table and looked into Lock's eyes.

"This is a horrible place to start," she said, "but here goes. In all of my life, from the day I lost my virginity until the last time I was in bed with a man—you—I've never been able to make an emotional connection before, during, or after sex. And until now, that was fine with me. It had always been about the physical sensation, the power, the orgasm. But recently, ever since Abby told me they moved up your release date, I've been thinking about you, and sex with you, and how one-dimensional I've been in bed. I was goal-oriented, and didn't care how I got there. But it's different now, and my feelings aren't theoretical, they're specifically directed toward you, Lochlan Gilkenney. Toward you. Not anyone else. I want more from you. I want more from us. I've never seen the possibilities before, but I can see them now. Clear as day."

Lock sipped more iced tea. "Listen, Natalie," he said, "I'm here because Abby wanted me to hear you out. But it's also true I still have feelings for you—maybe they're even stronger than I'd like to admit. And I can believe you're recovering from whatever your problems were. But that doesn't mean we should be together, and it doesn't mean we'd be good for each other. Look at how much trouble we got into before. We broke a hundred laws and we saw to it that Dahlia got hurt. That was pretty sick."

"Those are the negatives," she said. "Forgive, but don't forget—play it that way. And keep in mind, there are positives, too. We're both damaged people who've survived. We're stronger for it. See the past as winter and the present as spring. Now we can thrive. You've always wanted to be a father and have a family. Whether you believe me or not, this baby is yours. Funny, but it doesn't matter if you believe me. I wish you would, but I understand why you might not. But anyway, he's yours, and now is as good a time as any to start thinking about names."

"Baby names?" he asked, his eyes opening wide. "Isn't that getting a little ahead of ourselves?"

"Listen, Lock. I understand your lack of enthusiasm about getting together with me again. I'd hesitate, too. But I think you may be in a little bit of denial about how your life is about to change. In a month or so, you're going to have a baby. You need to get that into your head."

Natalie reached into her handbag and pulled out a folded piece of paper. She slid it across the table. He took it and unfolded it.

"It's a sonogram from my ultrasound," she said. "That grainy picture is your son at almost seven months."

Lock stared at the image. It took his breath away. He felt his heart pound.

"I think he looks just like you." She laughed. "And while you're letting that sink in, there's something else."

Lock, still lost in thought, looked at the image of what might be his son, barely paying attention to Natalie.

"Do you know what Lamaze classes are?" she continued. "They're birthing classes that help pregnant women and their partners understand and prepare for the whole process of being pregnant and giving birth. Breathing techniques, exercises, what to expect during labor, everything. You're supposed to go during the last trimester. I signed up and I've already gone to one..."

"And...?" he asked, finally glancing up.

"... and I'm the only woman in the class without a partner."

31

Natalie sat alone in Jerome Freel's waiting room. The receptionist's desk was unattended. Freel's office door was closed, but she could hear men talking.

She had only a few minutes before she had to leave for her waitressing shift, but there was something she was burning to say to Freel, something she hadn't decided to tell him until yesterday. She knew he wasn't going to like it, and that gave her a measure of satisfaction.

When she'd called and said she wanted to meet, he'd claimed he had back-to-back appointments all morning and that if she insisted on talking, she'd have to come to his office. He'd squeeze her in. *Squeeze her in?* That pissed her off.

Her round, pregnant belly made it impossible for her to sit comfortably, so she rose and paced. After a couple of minutes, the door to Freel's private office opened and he exited, accompanying a man wearing work boots and carrying a file folder.

Freel showed him out and addressed the man's back.

"Don't worry, your wife will get exactly what's she's owed—nothing," Freel said to his client. "My firm will see to that. Get me those documents as soon as you can. I'll be in touch."

FRANK FREUDBERG

The man left, and Freel motioned for Natalie to come into his office. As she walked in, he looked at the prominent bulge in her uniform without expression. She stood there while he spun his high-backed chair around and sat down behind the massive desk.

"What are you here to bitch about, Nat?" he said. "Everything's going fine with the settlement discussions. Going to jail delayed the shit out of things, but now that you're out, we're back on track. Your husband's first offer was much more generous than I expected. But I'm treating that as a sign of negotiating weakness and I rejected it out of hand. They'll come back with more. Trust me."

"What if they don't?" she asked. She started to ease herself into a chair, but a shooting pain in her abdomen hurt too much. She remained standing. "I can't take much more of 'black coffee, rye toast, scrambled eggs and well-done potatoes.' And why should I? Why can't you advance me fifty thousand until this thing settles, so I can quit this fucking job?"

"Can't do it, baby," he said. "Don't have it, you know that. And even if I did, giving you an advance on a settlement is unethical…"

Natalie snorted derisively.

"…and I could get suspended again," said Freel. "And more importantly, you not only have to look destitute for the judge, you actually have to *be* destitute. Witt is paying for the condo, and that looks good for him. It shows good faith. So we need to balance that out by having you, essentially a single mom, working your ass off for low pay. Relax. It won't be for much longer. Plus, you'll be off work when you give birth anyway."

"And where will you be then? On the ninth hole somewhere?"

Freel looked at her blankly.

"Here's what I came here to tell you, Jerome," she said. She patted her protuberance with the palm of her hand. "You see this baby? I love him. And I'm going to see to it he has the best of everything."

Freel furrowed his brow.

"You came to visit me exactly once in jail," Natalie continued. "And even though you said you came because you missed me, it was obvious you were

224

there to talk me into getting an abortion. In jail. Great. I wouldn't let those butchers near me. I'm glad I'm having our child. *Our* child, Jerome, and don't forget that little detail."

"Take it easy," he said. "All I did was advise you that being pregnant with a child other than your husband's would probably result in less—not more—of a settlement. That's all. And I told you I'm not interested in starting a family. I'm thirty-two years old and just getting back on my feet after being readmitted to the bar. Plus, I'd be a terrible father. The kid would hate me in no time. And so would you."

"You're plenty worried the baby's really yours," she said. "And I can guarantee you he is."

"I'm not worried, I just want to know whose it is. I don't want to get into the gory details, Nat, but we both know you don't really know."

"I told you, I know. I'm certain. It's you. It's biologically impossible that he's anyone else's."

Freel shook his head. "You only think you know. Don't you want to know for sure?"

"If you weren't worried," she said, "you wouldn't be spending twenty-two hundred dollars for an *in vitro* paternity test. You'd wait until he was born when it'd only cost three hundred."

"It's just better that we know. That's all. Plus, if it is mine—and that's a big if—then this isn't my fault. You guaranteed me you'd never get pregnant."

"It was an accident, and you know it," she said. "I didn't want this either, but now that it's happened, I've changed, I guess. I told you, prison transformed me."

"You didn't change a bit. You were in prison for five months. That's an easy twenty weeks. You act like you were away for twenty years of hard labor."

"You try it sometime," she said. "Anyway, my maternal instinct must have kicked in. I've accepted my pregnancy. I'm fine with it. Plus, I've always wanted a little boy."

"That's just terrific. And now you're getting your wish."

"You're right, I am."

"And I'll own up to my responsibility," he said. "If he's mine. When are you going for the test?"

"Thursday, and it's a complicated procedure," she said. "They fish a catheter up me through my cervix to test the amniotic fluid. It might hurt. All you have to do is get your cheek swabbed. Real fair."

"I'm sure they have anesthesia."

"Know what, Jerome? You're a son-of-a-bitch."

"How soon do we find out?"

"About ten days," she said, "by mail. I used your address on the form, so you'll get the news first."

"Why would you use my address? That doesn't make any sense."

"Yes, it does. You're my lawyer. I want you see the results first-hand."

"Why couldn't you just show me the document once you receive it?"

"I don't know," she said. "It seemed like a good idea at the time. Who cares? Leave me alone."

Freel shrugged and Natalie smiled inwardly. Although it was a minor detail, she thought that including Freel's name and address in the paperwork would involve him more in the situation. And she was going to need him to help her. The more entangled he was, she knew, the harder he'd work to help her. He could be a lazy bastard, and getting him more involved would motivate him to try to get her the settlement she wanted, as if his outrageous fee wasn't enough.

And proving to Freel that he was the father, if that was the case, would really prod him to find a convincing way to pin it on Lock. She knew it was only a fifty-fifty chance. The truth was she'd been with Lock and Freel repeatedly around the time of conception, and she had a bad habit of often skipping her birth control pills—they made her gain weight.

32

Two weeks later

Freel, still in his business suit after spending the afternoon in court on a personal injury case, stood in the foyer of his house and flipped through the stack of mail that had been delivered earlier in the day. Most of it was junk.

One envelope caught his attention, and he removed it from the pile. He dropped the rest of the mail on a side table and picked up the steak knife he kept there for opening envelopes. He slit it open and removed a single sheet of paper.

The letterhead read "Global DNA, Alcohol and Drug Analysis, Inc." Beneath that, there was a graph filled with a half dozen columns populated by small, hard-to-read numbers. His eyes scanned the page and came to rest on the bold-faced type below the graph. The words were clear and legible:

Conclusion
Jerome Freel: Probability of Paternity – 00.000%

Just as he'd suspected.

"Close call!" he said out loud, beaming. He'd call Natalie later. Right now he had to get ready for the golf course.

The joke's on her, he thought as he ascended the stairs to change. *She won't be able to hold this over my head. Thank you, Jesus!*

He re-read the letter to make certain he hadn't misinterpreted anything and that he was definitely off the hook. He'd have Natalie for fun and games. Let that chump Lock be the babysitter.

Later that afternoon, despite knowing that Natalie was in the middle of her shift, Freel dialed her cellphone. She was seated at a table in an empty booth and had just begun a ten-minute break. Seeing Freel's number on the caller I.D., she answered.

"What's going on?" she asked, wondering why he'd called at that hour. It was hard for her to hear him—a group of rowdy high school kids sat in the adjacent booth.

"Got some interesting mail today."

"Well?"

"I need Lock's address," Freel said.

"What? Speak up. What for?"

"Got to send him a bottle of champagne. He's going to be a proud papa," Freel laughed. "And I'm not."

Natalie pushed her cup of chamomile tea forward and rested her head on the tabletop. She said nothing for a moment, then sat upright. "Congratulations. I know that makes you very happy."

"Damn right," he said. "We're free to carry on without the complication of a baby wedged in between us."

"You're a fool and a half," Natalie said. She slid the cup back toward her. "The baby is the most important thing in my life, even before he's born. I may not have much time for you. This is the greatest news possible. And you're right, you'd suck as a parent. The baby's lucky Lock is his father."

"Lock's the sucker, Natalie." Freel laughed again.

"Maybe, but he's capable of being an awesome father. Unlike you, he has patience, genuine emotions, and a big heart."

"Yeah, sure, Nat. Good luck."

"As I said, my baby's fortunate, and so am I," she said, trying to suppress the despair in her voice. "And thanks, Jerome. That lab report made my day. And by the way, I want to see it with my own eyes."

Without another word, Natalie ended the call. Again, she pushed the cup away and put her head down on the table. She left it there for a long time.

Although she was more than eight months pregnant and pretty much exhausted all the time, Natalie was nothing if not a good actress. It was a week after the DNA test had come, and she had agreed to live with Lock. As far as he knew, she enjoyed playing house with him, and she smiled when he came home.

She bought Lock flowers, took him to inexpensive restaurants (referring to those outings as "dates"), and made him vegetarian dinners often and without outward complaint. But it was nothing more than a ruse and Natalie cursed herself. She didn't want Lock anymore, but she needed him, so she'd have to make do, at least for now.

Natalie preferred the lavish, low-stress, no-strings-attached company of Freel. She felt trapped by circumstances of her own making that were now beyond her control.

When she ruminated about how she had gotten herself into this mess, she'd remember that once she really did believe she loved Lock. Before she went to prison, she realized, her attraction to him was based on her need to use him and his expertise for her own ends.

Once incarcerated, alone with her thoughts, she believed again that she loved him unconditionally. Now she knew that had just been loneliness speaking. The reality of raising a newborn on a preposterously small budget, coupled with being with a man she didn't have much respect for, was too much. Her resentment toward Lock, once just irritating, intensified. She'd have to do something to ease him out of her life. Ease him or force him. Whatever was needed to get the job over and done with. Then she'd be free to find someone better than Lock, better than Witt or Freel. She knew she'd get her body back after the baby, and there were plenty of men looking for a woman like her.

On the last day of February, in the birthing center at Brandywine Community Hospital, an obstetrician—a tiny Asian woman with a heavy accent—finally managed to get a good grip on the baby's head and gently tugged, guiding its attempt to emerge into the world. Natalie gritted her teeth and moaned quietly but appeared otherwise calm. As the baby was halfway out, the doctor turned her masked face to Lock and said, "What is the baby's name?"

"We're calling him Augustus," Lock said, using his forearm to blot a bead of sweat from his forehead.

The doctor continued to pull, and when the baby was three-quarters out, she said, "Well, in that case, meet Augustus. Great name."

Lock exhaled slowly and saw his child. He had waited for this moment forever. An attending nurse reached over with both hands, took the baby, swaddled it, and used a sterile cloth to wipe mucous from its face and nose. She performed a cursory check of the baby's airways.

"Oh my God," panted Natalie. "That was a breeze compared to the other two. How is he?"

"He's gorgeous. Absolutely gorgeous," said Lock. "But he's not crying. Isn't he supposed to cry?"

"Let's do the Apgar," the doctor said matter-of-factly, directing her instruction to the nurse. She turned next to Lock. "Don't worry, he looks in fine shape."

"What's an Apgar? Is something wrong?" Lock asked.

Natalie spoke, and it would have been hard to tell that she just gave birth thirty seconds earlier—she was relaxed, almost detached. "They discussed it at Lamaze, if you were paying attention. It's a score of a newborn's health. They check the vitals. They're looking for difficulty breathing or heart trouble. I'm sure he's okay."

"Yes," said Lock. "I'm sure he's perfect."

The nurse examined the baby. "A good score," she said. "A nine out of ten."

Another nurse entered some information into a computer, then took the baby from her colleague and held him out to Natalie. He let out a loud, healthy cry.

"I'll take him in a second," she said. "Let Lock hold him for a minute. He's never done this before."

Lock took the baby and fought back tears. The boy was beet-red and incredible.

Then Lock frowned. "A nine? Why not a ten?"

"Hands and feet are slightly blue," the nurse said over the baby's increasingly loud wails. "But that happens all the time. He'll pink up fast, I'm sure."

Lock pressed Augustus to his chest and gave him the gentlest of hugs before handing him over to Natalie.

"I'll hold him later," she said. "What I really need now is to sleep."

33

Soon, Natalie went back to the diner.

She despised Lock for having to work, but she never showed him that side of her. And most nights, when she got home from work, she tossed her bag onto the overstuffed leather sofa that Witt had bought for them (along with all the other furniture and household items), dropped down onto the bed, and demanded that Lock massage her aching feet. It was his fault that she had to work and that her feet hurt. Lock looked forward to doing it for her, and that made her despise him even more. He still wanted her to need him. He loved their son, and he did more than his share of taking care of him. *The least he could do*, she often thought. But even the fact that he was a good father seemed to put her on edge.

In Augustus's first month of life, he appeared to be happy and healthy. He'd cry often in the night and stopped right away upon being picked up and held, and Lock was grateful every day for having a healthy child.

Before he was born, Natalie and Lock had agreed to name their baby with an "A" in memory of Lock's mother Abigail, yet they let Abby think it was in honor of him. It wasn't long before they were calling the infant Augie.

Abby, who had *carte blanche* to visit Natalie's condo when he wanted to, was nearly as excited about the child as Lock, and to a casual observer, he could easily be mistaken for the infant's grandfather. He definitely acted like it.

Having a baby to love and hold was all that Lock had hoped for. Augie immediately smiled whenever Lock held the baby's face close to his, and for Lock, nothing was wrong in the world. He loved that new-baby smell. When Augie cried out in the dark and Natalie faked being asleep, Lock sprang out of bed and was at the crib within seconds—way before the cries would have awakened Dahlia or Edwina if they happened to be there.

With Witt Mannheim's encouragement and approval, Lock and Natalie had the girls four nights every week, plus every other weekend. The girls shared the room adjacent to Augie's. Witt was a good sport, paying for the condo and all condo-related expenses—it was pocket change to him— sometimes throwing in a little extra for Natalie. He even gave Lock his seal of approval—not that Lock needed it—saying that if his girls liked Lock, then he liked him too. He stayed pretty much out of their lives.

Despite the exhilaration of finally having his family to love and worry about, Lock was often somewhat down. He was having a tough time trying to get a job that paid anything at all. He refused to label himself an ex-con, although that didn't stop prospective employers from saying so. There was no way he could return to CPS, of course, but that didn't prevent him from missing it. At least he had his own child to care for, plus he helped out with Edwina and Dahlia.

He wound up as a gofer on the evening shift at an auto parts distributorship. Ten bucks an hour. He spent his days with Augie and Natalie, when she wasn't waitressing, or he'd go through the motions of answering want ads looking for something better. He was in a bad way financially, but just thinking about his son brightened him up.

Twice in one week, Natalie and Lock asked Abby to babysit so they could go to the 6:00 p.m. AA meeting at the Hang-About. Lock enjoyed it whenever Natalie accompanied him—he liked showing her off. She made plenty of acquaintances there, and outside of the rooms, she enjoyed needling Lock when she caught him acting out of sync with the program's principles. After one of the meetings, they went to the movies, where right away Lock was infuriated by a loud-mouthed cellphone talker behind them. He was about to report him to an usher, but Natalie leaned over and whispered into Lock's ear, "There are plenty of other good seats. Let's just move." Lock adored her for the way she could bring tranquility to him.

Natalie loved her two oldest children, Lock knew that much, but it wasn't with the same intensity as she loved Augie. Maybe it was because the girls were part Witt Mannheim, maybe not. Maybe she was truly a changed person—it seemed that way—and so for the first time, she was raising a baby from her new perch, a bit banged up by life, but also presumably wiser. That wasn't the worst condition a person could be in.

Lock loved all three of the children too. He'd do anything for them. He became adept at changing diapers in almost total darkness. Natalie breast-fed Augie—a benefit neither of her two girls had had—so at first, Lock wasn't directly involved in feeding him. He read more than one article in parenting magazines and on websites about infant nutrition. He couldn't wait to make Augie an organic banana-apricot smoothie. Lock pictured most of it on the baby's face and bib, with him laughing and banging a dripping spoon on the tray of his highchair. But Lock wouldn't care. He'd clean up Augie and the rest of the mess with delight.

Natalie's tattoo had long since faded away, and Lock found he missed it. It had always given him a rush when it came into view. It didn't take long after giving birth for Natalie to become her old self in bed, and they started having sex again before the date the doctor suggested. Aggressive and demanding while somehow being submissive. It was a wonderful and odd combination. She always acted like she was really into it and she aimed to please, and she succeeded. Lust was still a strong element in their relationship, and Lock was happy for that. There was a real connection between them, and he was committed to making it grow.

It wasn't lost on him that Natalie hadn't mentioned the paternity test for weeks. That was mildly troubling, only because she had been so insistent about it when she was arguing her case for them to get back together. But the more he thought about it, the more the whole idea of a test bothered him. It was obvious Augie was their son. His eyes were Lock's—just bigger and brighter, and Lock didn't want to think about the fact that she had been with Freel while they were together. He put it out of his mind because he didn't see any point in her lying about it. Lock had nothing, and Freel was rich, or close to it. If he were the father, he'd have to pay for Augie's support, and that definitely wasn't happening.

But after the first few months of Augie's life, thoughts about the paternity test crept into Lock's consciousness more and more frequently, yet at the same time, he began to think that it would be an insult to Augie to subject him to the test. The idea of having his son's mouth swabbed to collect DNA was repugnant. And what if, by some long shot, he wasn't Lock's? Would Lock love him any less? The answer was obvious and therefore, he thought, there'd be no point in taking the test. Saving a few hundred bucks on the lab work was a consideration, too.

"Natalie," Lock said late one evening after putting Augie into his crib, hopefully for the night, "I've made a decision. I want to skip the paternity test. Augie's ours. I know that. End of story."

"Are you sure?" she said. "I have nothing to hide, so go ahead if you want."

"I don't want to. It's a waste of hard-earned money and totally unnecessary." He wanted to believe that was true.

"Whatever you say, baby," she said, sitting down on the edge of the bed and taking his hand. "It's your call. I'm happy either way."

A couple of weeks later, Natalie came home from the diner one evening, and while Lock tended to their son and reviewed with her the events of the day, she sat down at the kitchen table and emptied her purse of all of her tips. She counted the bills and coins. "Seventy-four dollars and forty-five cents," she said. "For an eight-hour shift. I'm getting tired of waiting on people, Lock. They should be waiting on me."

"You also get a check from the diner for your hours, so don't forget that," Lock said. He knew she hated her job, and he felt helpless because they needed the money.

"Yes, but since I get tips, all they have to pay me is three dollars an hour. What I earn is still a joke."

Natalie took two twenty-dollar bills and tucked them into an envelope. Lock watched her.

"What's that envelope for?" he said.

"Saving up for a surprise. For you. I need three-hundred and fifty, and I'm now thirty short of the goal."

"For me? Three-fifty? That's some surprise. Can we afford it?"

"You'll love it, honey. As much as I love you."

"What is it? Tell me."

"I can't. That's why it's called a surprise," she said.

"I hate waiting," he said. He reached into his pocket and found a ten and a twenty – almost all he had. "Here. Here's the rest." He handed her the cash. "Now, when do I get my surprise?"

"You can't pay for your own surprise," she said. She stood up from the kitchen table and hugged Lock.

"I didn't pay for it, I just rounded it up a bit so you'll have what you need."

"I'll get it soon," she said. "Just be patient. It'll be worth it."

34

The next day, a Saturday, Abby arrived at the condo to babysit for Augie. He looked pale and tired.

"You okay?" Lock asked. "I can get someone else to sit."

"No, you can't, but thanks for asking," Abby said. "I didn't sleep well, but all I need is a little Augie to make me feel better."

Edwina and Dahlia were spending the weekend at Witt's estate. A half hour earlier, Natalie had left for her day shift at the diner. Lock got ready to go into work for a mandatory weekend safety meeting. "I'll only be gone an hour," he told Abby, "two at the most."

Lock was always nervous when Abby was on his own with Augie, although that had only been twice before. The seventy-five-year-old had practically no experience caring for an infant, but he was doting, enthusiastic, not squeamish, and followed every last detail of the long notes and instructions Lock would compose and review with him before leaving. Lock wrote his and Natalie's cellphone numbers in large, blocky letters at the bottom of the instruction sheet. He drew a star next to his own number.

When the girls were there, Edwina was capable of helping, at least a little, with Augie. *Everything will be all right*, Lock thought, trying as best as he could to soothe himself. The truth was, he didn't fully trust anyone but himself to care properly for Augie. That included Natalie. In his eyes, she came up a bit short in the maternal instinct department. But she tried, he knew. She could be a good mom, but Lock believed it just didn't come naturally to her, despite her having a lot more experience.

"Call me for even the slightest problem," Lock told Abby, handing him the note. "Don't worry about interrupting me. It'll be okay if you need to reach me. Call if anything comes up, anything at all."

The one time that Natalie had been there to hand off the kids to Abby, she hadn't bothered with a note. How could she not let him know what time the baby went in for his nap, or when he might need to be fed some of the mother's milk stored in bottles on the top shelf of the refrigerator? That had irritated Lock, but he'd let it go. They were different that way. Lock kissed a napping Augie goodbye, thanked Abby again for coming over to cover for him, and left for the meeting.

Lock got a call not long into the meeting, and he rushed home.

He arrived to find police cars and an ambulance—its rear door swung open wide—parked on the street in front of the complex. He identified himself to a police officer standing by the front entrance, who asked to see his identification. Satisfied that Lock was a resident of the condo, the officer informed him that the older gentleman was deceased, possibly of a massive heart attack.

Lock hurried past the officer, up the stairs to his unit, and entered the kitchen, which was cramped with three paramedics and another policeman. The paramedics were repacking their equipment. There was no need for them to continue working on the motionless body. They had spent a quarter of an hour trying CPR techniques in their attempt to resuscitate Abby. Lock couldn't look at the body. One of the paramedics told him the body would be transported to Brandywine County Hospital to await the medical examiner.

It sunk in immediately and deeply. Lock's friend and mentor was gone, and without warning. He had a sudden memory of the albino redwood in Witt Mannheim's back yard, standing alone next to the mound where its parent tree once towered. *It must be dead by now*, Lock thought.

As Lock watched the paramedics put Abby's body on the gurney and take him out, he imagined they were carting off his real dad, the drunken, abusive one from a lifetime ago. The real Abby, the man Lock loved like a father, was still with him, in his heart. He couldn't be gone.

Lock's impulse was to call Natalie at the diner, but he decided that would be imposing upon her. Besides, what would that accomplish? She'd feel obligated to rush home, disrupting her job. There was nothing she could do, except to comfort him. That could wait until later. And maybe even then she wouldn't bother.

Lock usually never disturbed Augie when he was sleeping, but he felt a powerful need to hold him in his arms. Lock went to the baby's room and picked him up. Lock whimpered when he cradled Augie, but the baby remained sound asleep.

"Abby's gone," Lock whispered, kissing the infant on the forehead. "He loved you so much." Lock's voice cracked and his throat tightened. He sat down with Augie, holding his tiny body against his chest.

Lock thought back to that morning in the hospital, the morning he'd overdosed and had been rushed to the emergency room. Later that afternoon, Abby had showed up with, of all things, an arrangement of white roses in a glass vase. Wired up to monitors and intravenous lines, with an oxygen tube down his throat, all Lock could do was make eye contact. But that had been enough. Lock knew he was loved.

Lock began crying quietly, muffling the sound so as not to wake the baby. But within moments, the sobs came out violently, loudly, and his chest heaved and tears streamed down his face.

Abby had unconditionally forgiven him for making terrible decisions, for breaking the law, for causing Dahlia to be injured, for going to prison and for humiliating him as the director of CPS. He had hired Lock and given him a golden opportunity, and Lock had paid him back with ingratitude, insubordination, and even betrayal.

But the vital thing was that through Abby's example, Lock had been able to forgive his own father's offences, just as Abby had forgiven Lock.

———◆———

On the way home from the cemetery, Natalie sat with Lock in the rear of the funeral home's limo. She held Augie because she'd forgotten about Lock's request to bring the portable car seat, but Augie cooperatively slept through most of the day's proceedings. When the limo pulled up to discharge them at the condo, Natalie handed the baby to Lock, got out, and turned to walk away.

"Witt's really bugging me to discuss something with him," she said over her shoulder. "It's about the girls. I think something about the schedule."

"So call him," Lock said, heading up the steps to the front door. He motioned for her to join him in the condo. "Come on."

Natalie didn't follow.

"No," she said. "I promised him I'd come over. He said he wants it to be in person. It's the least I can do. You know how much he does for us."

"That's weird," said Lock. "Come in and call Witt. Tell him you can't make it today. He won't mind, under the circumstances."

"No, honey, sorry," she said, opening the door of her car. "I won't be very long. I promise. I'm sure it's much ado about not too much."

"Natalie," said Lock. "Please don't go right now. I really need you to be with me. It's not an easy day for me."

"I know you want me to be with you, and I will. Just give me a couple of hours."

Natalie started her car and drove off.

———◆———

The black clothes Natalie had worn to Abby's funeral were scattered about the room—on the floor, over the back of a chair, at the foot of the bed.

She pulled the sheet off her lithe form and slipped quietly out of the bed. She padded naked across the thick carpet to the dresser and looked at herself in the mirror. A ray of late afternoon sunlight fell through the window onto her bejeweled toes. They glittered, casting a rainbow of colors against the wall. Natalie continued to look at her reflection. She always thought she looked better without clothes.

She stepped back from the dresser. She reached high into the air and extended her arms up toward the ceiling, then out in front of her, and finally down toward the floor. She exhaled deeply through her nose and bent at the waist, placing her palms on the floor, easily, on both sides of her feet. Next, she fluidly lowered herself to the rug and executed a near-perfect *chaturanga*. She held the position for ten seconds, slowly arched her back into an upward-facing dog, and then, with a deep inhale, lowered herself into a downward dog.

"Nice view," Jerome Freel said. He was sitting up in the bed, a blanket wrapped around his lower torso.

"You should try yoga sometime," she said. "Whenever you want, I'll be your personal instructor. It's all about keeping your spine flexible."

"Not now," he said, rolling out of the bed and finding his boxer shorts in the tangle of linen.

"I can't believe I have to put this outfit back on," Natalie said. She gathered the clothes from where they had fallen when Freel tore them off an hour earlier. "The black. It's not my color. It's so morose."

Freel thumbed open the latches of his briefcase on the settee next to the dresser. From under his leather toiletries bag, he pulled an eight-by-ten glossy photograph from a folder and held it out to Natalie.

"Tell the tattoo artist to make it look like this," he said.

She examined the photo. "That's great," she said. The image was a multicolored snake. "Is that a scarlet kingsnake? I was thinking about getting that one."

"No. It's a coral snake," Freel said. "Almost the same coloration. But it's the coral you have to watch out for. A kingsnake is harmless. The coral is lethal."

"Like me." She grinned at him.

"Oh, that's you, alright. For the record, I don't much like that tattoo guy seeing you bare. It's bad enough you let Lock touch you."

By the time Natalie finished dressing, Freel had put on a robe. He sat on the settee watching her. He opened the toiletries case and took out a vial and an aluminum straw.

"That snake in the picture is a little more elaborate than I had budgeted for," Natalie said. "And it will take longer and hurt more."

"You can take it, Nat," he said. "It's just a little pain."

She rolled her eyes.

"What's a tattoo like that cost?" he asked.

"Maybe four hundred and fifty or something like that for a tat so elaborate," she said. "Maybe even five or six hundred. I've been saving up for it. Lock saw me put money in an envelope and asked me about it. I had to tell him I was saving up for a surprise for him."

"Oh, that's just great." Freel shook his head. "But don't worry about saving your tips. The tat's on me," Freel said. He reached for his trousers and removed a thick leather wallet. He counted out ten one hundred-dollar bills. "Here you go, sweetheart," he said, folding the bills in half. "Get that tattoo extra nice. And keep the change."

"That's not necessary," she said. He nodded for her to take the money. She took it and put the bills in her handbag.

"And I thought you were broke," she said.

"I'm broke as shit. I've got thirty-nine thousand left on my line of credit, and I'm burning through it at about fifteen a month. The settlement from your divorce—and my fee—can't come fast enough."

Natalie picked up the photo and looked at it again. "I can't wait to wrap that snake around your pretty little neck," she said.

Freel didn't respond. He leaned over the nightstand, picked up his aluminum straw, and snorted twice from a small mound of coke.

35

The following day, Natalie arrived at the condo in the early evening. Lock was there with Edwina, Dahlia, and Augie. All four of them were on the carpet in the living room, batting balloons at each other. Lock had blown up a dozen for them to play with. Augie, on his back on a blanket but positioned so he could see the fun, grinned every time a balloon bounced near him. Edwina gently tapped a blue balloon against the baby's forehead.

"Don't frighten him, Eddie," Lock said.

"I'm being very, very careful," she said, frowning at Lock. "He likes it."

The girls didn't look up when Natalie entered the room, but Lock did. He stood and hugged her. She flashed a smile at him, then pushed him away and sat down on the sofa. She pulled her shoes off.

"Ah. That's better," she said, wriggling her toes.

Right away, Lock noticed Natalie carried no bag that might contain the surprise she had promised to bring him.

"Did you get it?" he said.

Augie started to cry. Natalie didn't make a move to pick him up.

"Of course, honey." She got up and walked past him, putting her hand on his back and squeezing his shoulder. "You're like a child. You'll get it after the kids go to bed. It's worth the wait."

Lock bent over to pick up Augie and jiggled the infant in his arms. Augie quieted down right away. Natalie walked out of the room like no one was there. Lock shook his head. *She's just tired*, he told himself. Another part of himself said, *Tired, sure. It's her nature.*

An hour later, Lock had single-handedly completed all the chores associated with getting three children to bed. He read aloud—for the hundredth time—from *And to Think That I Saw It on Mulberry Street* as the girls clambered on his lap for the best position to hear the story and see the illustrations.

Then Lock changed Augie into a dry diaper, laid out the girls' pajamas, and examined clothes from the floor to see which could be re-worn and which needed to be thrown into the hamper.

Next, he put Augie in his crib and the girls in their beds. After kissing each child goodnight, he turned down the lights and went to find Natalie.

While Lock had been taking care of the children, Natalie had been watching a yoga video, executing an array of flawless poses. He stood in the threshold of the living room and watched.

When she saw he was finished putting the kids to bed, she turned off the video, walked past him, and with a crooked finger, gestured for him to come to the bedroom.

"Time to see your surprise," she said.

He followed her. She closed the door behind them and sat him down on the edge of the bed. She peeled off her black yoga pants and removed her top. She smoothed the clothes out on the bed, folded them, and placed them in the dresser. She opened a bottle of perfume and dabbed a few drops on her wrists and rubbed them onto her neck. She inhaled the scent and closed her eyes. Then she turned on the lamps and sat down on the comforter, naked and looking Lock right in the eye.

Lock looked back into her eyes.

"You won't find what I want you to see in my eyes, Lock," she said, her voice low.

At first, Lock didn't get it. He kept looking at her. She waited for his eyes to rove over her body, but he held his gaze.

Natalie stood up and angled her body so that the lamp's light shined on the front of her thighs.

Lock looked down, and there it was.

A stunning, glistening, multicolored coral snake writhing up Natalie's thigh, its head disappearing between her legs. The red, orange, and yellow hues, separated by thick, black, scaly bands, were kaleidoscopic and dramatically more intense than the temporary brownish henna snake that time had washed away. Her skin under the snake's body was hot and swollen from the thousands of pinholes made by the tattoo needle. Each scale on the snake's back was visible, glistening with a vibrant, iridescent pattern.

Natalie, hands on her hips, watched Lock's eyes explore the artwork.

"Well?" she asked.

"Outstanding. Just outstanding."

"Stings like hell, but the swelling will go away in a few days. I have to keep icing it. But first," she said, "I want you to take a better look. Check out his head." Natalie stood in front of Lock and lifted one foot onto the bed. She moved closer to him.

"See where he's going?" she asked, inching even closer. "Why don't you join him?"

36

Right before noon, Lock lucked out.

He found a spot in the jammed parking lot about one hundred yards from the main entrance to the annual Summer Fiesta carnival, set up on the grounds of Brandywine Community Hospital—the hospital where all of Natalie's children had been born. Over a month had passed since Abby had died, and Lock still missed him deeply. He had been looking forward to taking the kids to the carnival, but it made him sad, too. It was exactly the kind of thing Abby would have loved.

It had been a tough squeeze to get all three children into the car seats that were jammed together in the rear of Lock's old Ford sedan, but he did it. On the twenty-minute drive to the carnival, Edwina, accompanied by Dahlia, clapped their hands to their sing-song chant of one word: "Car-ni-val! Car-ni-val!" They laughed uncontrollably.

Getting the kids out of the car—Dahlia and Edwina bounced excitedly in their seats, while Augie sat contentedly—was easier than getting them in. The girls clamored for Lock and their mother to release them. Instead of helping, Natalie sat in the passenger seat doing something on her phone, so the chore fell to Lock.

He unbuckled the seatbelts and detached them from the car seats. The girls scrambled out of the car. Lock stood at the trunk, removing two strollers. Earlier, Edwina had insisted that she was big enough to walk at the carnival and refused to let Lock pack her stroller. Strollers, she'd informed him, were for little kids, like Dahlia and Augie. He closed the trunk, smiling at the memory. Edwina was growing up, and she was more formidable every day.

Dahlia—just shy of three years now—climbed into the stroller on her own while Edwina held it still. Lock watched and, seeing her caring for her little sister, wondered if she had more natural maternal instinct than her mother.

He removed Augie from his car seat and put him in the baby carrier. He loved carting Augie around that way so he could see him and touch him and point out interesting things. In a minute, they were ready to enter the fairgrounds.

"Head on in," Natalie said to Lock without looking up as she texted someone. "I'll catch up in a sec."

"I need to buy the tickets for all of us," he said. "Come with us."

Natalie snorted derisively, put her phone away, and got out.

Once inside the carnival, Lock handed Augie to Natalie and he and the girls went to the blue-and-white wooden booth and bought twenty dollars' worth of tickets redeemable for rides, though not junk food from the concession stands. The refreshments would cost him even more.

Natalie watched. "Twenty bucks won't get us far in here," she said.

Edwina looked to Lock to see if their mother was right.

"We have enough tickets for all the rides you want to go on," he said, bending down to speak to the two girls. "And if we need more tickets later, we'll get them."

Natalie shook her head and gazed up to the top of a small Ferris wheel.

"I can guarantee you I won't be getting on that thing," she said. "Go ahead if you want."

Augie burped loudly and a broad smile appeared on his face. Natalie cringed in disgust.

"Okay"—Lock grinned at the girls—"more tickets for us." Dahlia and Edwina hopped enthusiastically. "I think we can win two teddy bears at the squirt gun game," Lock told them. "Who wants to try that?"

"We do! And after that," Edwina said, "I want to ride the merry-go-round. I really want to."

"Come on, Mommy," Edwina said, walking back to where Natalie stood gazing off into space. "Lock said we're going to win teddy bears. Come on." Edwina tugged at Natalie's fingers and tried to pull her along.

"I have to find the bathroom," Natalie said. "I'll catch up in a minute. Go win your dolls." Without speaking, Natalie handed Augie to Lock, who now had to manage carrying his son while looking after two children. He didn't want the girls to pick up on his disappointment at Natalie's distant demeanor.

"Okay, Natalie," he said. "The squirt gun game is on the midway, up there on the left past the cotton candy stand. Come back soon."

Natalie didn't say a word to Lock and the girls, but turned and walked in the opposite direction.

Lock helped the girls aim their squirt guns at the moving targets—rusty metal ducks and rabbits—and succeeded in helping them win two small teddy bears. Compared to the fluffy bears as big as Dahlia on the top display shelf, the two they won were paltry, and he could see the kids' looks of dissatisfaction. Edwina pouted and Dahlia pointed to the bigger dolls.

"Anything we can do about this?" Lock softly asked the barker, who made a face. Lock slid a five-dollar bill across the counter in such a way that the girls couldn't see it.

The barker took the bill and put it in his pocket, but didn't change his sour expression.

"Buy another two games and we'll see what they win," he said.

Lock surrendered more tickets. The man flipped a switch under the counter and started the game. Both girls giggled while holding the guns and aiming at the targets. Dahlia's aim was way off and splashed the back wall of the booth. After another minute, the water stopped and the girls looked at the barker expectantly.

"Look what you two have won," he said without the slightest trace of interest. "Two bigger bears. But you have to give those two back first." He pointed at the prizes he had given to the girls before. When they didn't move, the man leaned over the counter and took the bears from them and sullenly handed the kids two more, only slightly larger than the first ones. He then glared at Lock. "That's the best I'm going to do." The girls didn't look thrilled.

Lock's phone rang. He saw it was Natalie's number, or else he might not have answered.

"Hey, can't find us?" he asked. Then he listened and his face fell. "At least come back and say goodbye to the girls," he spoke in a whisper. "And you have to be back in two hours with the car. The kids might not even last that long, and then what am I going to do?"

A few minutes later, Natalie appeared as Lock was buying the girls two paper cones of frighteningly bright red cherry water ice. Lock didn't want them to ingest the notorious red dye, but gave in at their insistence, telling himself that it would be impossible to protect them from all the world's threats. He'd have to pick his battles—and dye-in-water-ice wasn't one he chose to fight that day.

Natalie stooped down and gave each of the girls a token hug. "Mommy has to go," she said, rising. "I'll be back soon."

Edwina grabbed her mother's hand. "No, Mommy, we're going on the merry-go-round. I'm riding the white one with the golden mane. Come with us. You can hold Dahlia on your lap, because she's too little."

"Lock will hold her, honey," Natalie said.

"No!" Edwina stomped her flip-flop. "He has to hold Augie. You hold Dahlia, and I can ride the horse myself."

Natalie shrugged and, without kissing Augie goodbye or making eye contact with Lock, walked off.

"Two hours, max," Lock shouted after her. "Sooner, if you can."

She kept walking but raised her hand and backward-waved at them. All three of them watched Natalie leave. Augie was asleep in the baby carrier, his head resting against Lock's chest.

"Why is Mommy leaving?" Edwina asked, looking at Lock.

Lock felt bad but didn't want to think about where Natalie might really be going—she had told him she needed to run to the diner to settle some dispute over a check she had supposedly added up incorrectly. He wanted to believe her, but he didn't. It was apparent she didn't care to put much effort into constructing a more credible lie. That made it worse for Lock. To distract himself, he reached into the baby carrier and gently tilted Augie toward him and admired the beauty in the sleeping child's face.

"She has to go to the drug store for something, honey," he said to Edwina, "but don't worry. She'll be back soon." He realized he had just lied to her, something he had a strict policy against, but telling the child the probable truth, in this case, would have done more harm than good.

Lock turned toward the crowds of people and caught a glimpse of Natalie's back as she made her way through the throng toward the parking lot.

———

As she pulled up, Natalie saw Jerome Freel standing in his driveway, attired in the golf clothes he had been wearing all day. She liked that he was waiting for her.

He moved in close, wanting a kiss, but Natalie put her hand on his chest and pushed hard.

"Not out here," she said, and walked past him and into his foyer. He followed her in and closed the door behind him.

"How about now?" he asked. "It's not a public display of affection if we're alone in a house."

Natalie offered her cheek but wouldn't let him kiss her on the mouth.

"What's bugging you?" asked Freel, who turned and adjusted the position of his golf bag, which was leaning against the wall and looked like it was getting ready to tip over.

"Nothing. Just Lock and the kids. They dragged me to some stupid carnival and I had to miss my yoga class. And I have plenty to look forward to tonight—the eight-to-two shift of high school boys and old couples who believe in two-dollar tips."

"It won't be much longer, Nat. You know that. I tell you that every day."

Natalie sighed. "I guess you're right. I shouldn't take my frustration out on you."

"That's okay. I had a terrible day too. Shot a 107, if you can believe that."

"Yes. That's a rough thing to have to live through. But you're strong, Jerome. You'll survive."

Natalie stared him in the eyes as she tore off her t-shirt and unzipped and stepped out of her shorts—rendering herself totally naked in one graceful motion.

"Oh my Lord," he said, his eyes falling not on her body but on the tattoo of a snake slithering up her thigh. "Dazzling."

"Me?" she asked.

"That snake. Fantastic, just fantastic."

"Thanks, couldn't have afforded it without you."

Freel crouched down to see it better. "That guy knows his stuff. It almost looks like a photograph."

"I thought you'd like it."

"I do."

"So does Lock. Loves it."

Freel stood up. "Fuck you, Nat. Why'd you bring him into this?"

"Oh, calm down. What are you worried about? He's the one getting screwed over. Relax."

Freel stood there, fuming, and tried to hide it.

"Ah, poor baby," she said. "Did I hurt your feelings?" She grabbed him by the throat, pulled him close, and kissed him hard. "That make you feel any better?"

"You're getting warmer," he said, taking her hand and leading her up the spiral staircase.

———⟶⊷⟵———

Natalie kicked the sheets off her while Freel laid on his side, working to catch his breath. She checked the clock by the bedside. "I have fifteen minutes before I have to leave to pick them up. I'm taking a quick shower." She got out of bed and Freel watched.

She spoke to him from the bathroom. "You hear anything from Witt's lawyer? Like, is anyone getting any closer to writing me a check?"

"Humphries. I spoke to him yesterday," said Freel.

"I hope you have good news. I really can't play this poverty game much longer. At the carnival, the most Lock could come up with for rides was twenty dollars. Twenty dollars!"

"Yeah, well. Back to Humphries. What a dick. Anyway, the forensic accountant we hired is almost finished with her analysis, and she told me it doesn't look like Witt has concealed any assets. At least none that she could find. I was hoping he was hiding entire companies he owned. But that's not the case, and that's too bad for us. Humphries actually said, 'I told you so' to me. But the joke will be on him. And the good news is that Witt seems to be worth somewhat more than you think. Maybe three or four million more. That could be almost half yours someday in the very near future. We'll know more about that mid-week."

Natalie exited the bathroom and dried herself with a giant, dark-blue cotton towel. "I'm sorry I said that about Lock. I was teasing you, but now that I think about it, it was a dopey thing to do." She knew she had to play nice from time to time, but just enough to keep him from getting sulky. Jerome would never admit it, but he liked that she made him jealous.

"Don't worry about it," he said, opening the nightstand drawer and removing his black, leather toiletries kit. "You made it up to me."

"Just so you know, I got that snake for you and no one else. I'm sorry he gets to see it even for a little while."

He waved her explanation away and then opened the kit, removed the vial, and tapped a little mound of power onto the nightstand surface. "All will go according to plan. We just have to be patient."

"I know," she said. "But three kids and Lock? I have to say the serenity prayer all day long."

37

By the time Augie was almost four months old, Natalie had grown weary of all the demands the infant constantly made on her. Although she was good at hiding her irritation, Locked noticed but chose to say nothing.

A few times when he was sick, Augie cried off and on all night long. Natalie never once got out of bed to comfort him—it was always Lock. And Augie was an aggressive crawler—he started crawling months earlier than most babies do—and had to be watched all the time when he wasn't in his crib or his playpen.

Even though breast-feeding was supposed to reduce the risk of a child having allergies, Augie had severe reactions to the eggs, soy, peanuts, and cow's milk—ingredients often found in the recipes for homemade baby food that Lock discovered online.

"I don't know what to feed that brat," Natalie once said in the infant's presence.

"Damn it, Natalie," Lock said. "Watch what you say. You know he can sense your emotions."

Natalie laughed. "Where'd you read that? Some touchy-feely stay-at-home-dad website or something?"

Lock bristled. "And don't call him a brat," he said. "He's pure love in a diaper. And I don't know of a kid who's less whiney than Augie."

Natalie laughed again and sulked out of the room in her bare feet.

Sure, walk away, Lock thought. *That's what you do, isn't it? It's your nature.*

Late that evening, after Lock did the putting-the-baby-to-bed routine, he got into bed and tried to kiss Natalie goodnight. She was still pissed and rolled away from him.

"I just want to say goodnight," he told her. "We agreed to never go to bed angry at each other."

"That would be easier to do if you weren't acting like a dick all the time." He tried to kiss her again.

She turned her back to him. "Too bad," she said. "That's what you get for always siding with Augie and talking to me like I'm twelve years old."

Natalie fell into silence while Lock lay there in the dark with his eyes open, wondering about the woman next to him. She was asleep in minutes and didn't say a word to him when she arose the next morning and left for an early yoga class.

When she returned to the condo—much later than Lock had expected (though he said nothing to her about it)—she was ready to pick up the bad vibes where she had left them the night before.

"I'm not going to fight with you, Natalie," Lock said. "I want to love you, not battle you."

Natalie said nothing and went into the bedroom to change out of her yoga clothes.

"I want to have dinner tonight at La Tierra," she said, returning from the bedroom and wearing her cut-offs and a t-shirt. "Find a sitter, will you?"

"La Tierra and a sitter? Honey, that'll be north of a hundred and fifty bucks."

"I thought you were going to get a better job than that crappy auto parts place and that stupid shirt they make you wear."

Lock wanted to fire back that they both had jobs where wearing nametags was mandatory, but he held his tongue. "I'm working on it, Natalie, I don't like the job either. But as of now, my options are narrow."

"I know you're trying," she said, "but we hardly get a chance to go out, and when we do, it's on a small allowance we give ourselves or because I was able to shake a few extra bucks out of Witt. Movies and a cheap dinner at the Mexican place, or a picnic at Valley Forge with the kids. We don't have a night life anymore. Do you think I don't remember my sixty-dollar manicures and my hundred-and-twenty-five-dollar yoga lessons? Let's work harder at getting more money. I make shit at the diner. I need a vacation."

Lock wondered if he was devolving into the same kind of lousy provider his father had been. But something would turn up. He wasn't going to stay broke indefinitely. After all, he had a son to take care of. It was true he was struggling now, but that condition didn't trouble him nearly as much as it did Natalie.

Lock lifted Augie out of his playpen and set him on the floor. He let the infant reach up to grip his thumbs, so that Augie could pull himself up into something like a standing position. Without much prompting, Augie did so and grinned and opened his eyes wide, thrilled at his accomplishment. Lock turned to see Natalie's reaction, but she was staring out the window.

"Check this out, Natalie," he said. She glanced over, saw her baby standing, and shrugged.

"Great," she said. "Terrific. Now he can pull everything off the coffee table. What'll you teach him next? How to fire a gun?"

While Lock continued to play with Augie, Natalie said that she was prepared to go to Witt and ask him for even more money than he was already shelling out. Lock told her not to do it, but she laughed.

"I'm not staying destitute for the rest of my life," she said, examining her unpolished toe nails. "Witt's got more than he can ever spend. He'll give me more."

The next night, just after nine, Natalie, wearing her waitress's uniform, sat back up in the passenger seat of Freel's car and flipped open the mirror built into the sun visor. She inspected her makeup and reapplied her lipstick.

She ran her fingers through her tousled hair and thought about the conversation she had had with Freel earlier. She didn't know if she could fully trust him, but she did believe his affection for her—as base and superficial as it was—was sincere. She knew she could do worse than Jerome Freel.

"I'm still not clear about how we can get Lock to leave me," Natalie said to Freel. "He's too attached to his ridiculous idea of having a family. I could host a gangbang every night, and he'd stand by me. He'd be doing it for Augie. Getting rid of him won't be so easy. Definitely not as easy to manipulate as when we let him think he was hatching the plan to crash the car and frame Witt."

"I don't know why I didn't think of this before," said Freel, re-buckling his seatbelt. He rested his hands on the steering wheel and looked out the windshield at the trees illuminated by the street lamps on the other side of the deserted parking lot. "It's simple. We just tell Lock that Augie is my son, that we took a paternity test. That'll frost his balls. If he demands to see the results, you can show him. I have the lab's letterhead, so it will be easy to scan it and make up a fake test result. I'm pretty good at Photoshop."

"Don't you think there will be a little problem with that?" she said. "Just telling Lock the baby's yours? Just by showing him a piece of paper?"

"You mean his reaction?"

"Yes," Natalie said. "He's driven when it comes to Augie. He'll go crazy. He's been acting the role of father ever since Augie was born. Actually, even before that. Lock's fanatical about him. All the baby food has to be organic."

"No," Freel said, "nothing to worry about. Look at it from Lock's perspective. He's already questioning whether or not Augie is mine. It panics him just thinking about it. When the official-looking lab report hits him out of the blue, he'll be so upset he'll totally believe it. I guarantee it. He's basically a drunk, isn't he? What's he going to do besides break down and start drinking?"

"That's not true, he's a good man," she said. "He was good at his job at CPS. And he's good at being a father. I've just outgrown him." Natalie took Freel's hand. She sat there, fingers entwined with his. She said nothing. A moment passed and Freel pulled his hand back.

"That'll practically kill him," Freel said, "the poor bastard." He laughed.

"It's not funny," she said. "You're not the one who's going to tell him. You're not the one going to see his face."

"All you'd need to do is give him the news and then avoid him until he's out of the condo."

"It's that I don't love him. I never did."

"I thought you said you did."

"I might have. Once. Yes, I did. For a few days, at least. I admit I was pretty confused when I got out of prison. I must have been out of mind to think it could work with Lock."

"He's a little blue-collar for you."

"Even if he falls for the story that he's not the father, doesn't he have any legal standing?" Natalie asked. "He's been like the baby's father since Lamaze classes. That must count for something."

"He could try to make a case for being the baby's psychological father—they call it the *de facto* parent—but he won't get far with that. The kid would have to feel as if Lock is his actual parent. If Augie were seven or eight years old, it might be a different story. A court-ordered custody evaluator might interview him and make a determination that the kid thinks of Lock as his father. But as it is, your kid's too young for that legal concept to come into play. I don't think you have anything to worry about."

"He's basically a nice guy," she said. "I kind of hate doing this to him."

"I know it will bother you, Nat..." Freel said, smirking, "...for about sixty seconds. Don't forget, baby, I know you."

Freel started the Lamborghini and pulled out of the parking lot. He headed back to Natalie's diner, where he'd drive around to the rear and drop her off at her car in the employees-only parking area.

"Tell him not to feel bad," Freel said. "Tell him it's for his own good."

"How's it for his own good?"

"It would never work out with you, and he needs to know that and he needs to move on. That's why it's for his own good."

"I'm sure he won't see it that way."

"Come on," Freel said. "I want you to move in with me, in my house. God knows it's big enough. It'll be great. I'm a few months behind on the mortgage, but I'm stalling the lender, and once we get the settlement money—"

"We?" Natalie raised her eyebrows.

"Well, once you get the settlement money and I get my fee, we'll be in good shape. We have the pool and all I need to do is throw a few thou into the greenhouse to renovate it and you'll have a perfect spot for your orchids. I know you miss them since you've been cramped in that condo. We'll get a nanny for the baby and we'll take trips all over the place. It'll be terrific."

Freel slowed with the traffic on Route 1 and put on his right turn signal.

"A nanny?" asked Natalie. "That would great. That would be unbelievable."

"I told you Nat, I'm going to take care of you in high style, just like you deserve. Once we get the money."

"What about all your little sluts, Jerome?"

"If by that, you mean the paralegal—that happened exactly once. We were both drunk as shit, by the way. Obviously it was meaningless, or I wouldn't have told you about her."

"Wow. You wouldn't have lied. That's some reassurance. And what about my job?"

"Don't be coy," Freel said. "You know full well that I'm going to give you an allowance that you'll be thrilled with. But you have to move in first."

"You're broke as hell."

"I am, kind of, for now," he said. "But I have a big divorce case settling any day." He grinned. "And I've got another client—a personal injury case—where the insurance company is ready to settle. My forty percent will bring me almost as much as the fee for your deal with Witt. I'm on the verge of having a lot of working capital."

"But by then, I'll have millions myself, so why would I need you?" she asked. She smiled, squeezing his hand.

"For the good lovin'," he said, leering. "You can't get that just anywhere. Lock's not going to get violent, is he? Does he have a gun?"

"I doubt it," she said. "He's never mentioned one."

"I'm not going to worry about him," said Freel. "He's not going to do anything about it. He's too AA for that. They're a meek bunch, from what I know."

"You're right," she said. "I don't think he's capable of any real violence. He's still crying over some kid he beat up when he lost his temper on the playground thirty years ago."

"Good," said Freel. "Because if there's one thing I know, it's that when it comes to their kids, some people go insane."

38

The next day, while driving home from the mall—where all she did was window-shop—Natalie answered the mellow yoga chant that served as her ringtone. It was Freel.

"I have good news and bad news, Nat," he said. "Which do you want first?"

"Give me the bad."

"Okay," he said. "I just checked my line-of-credit balance online. I've got $23,000 left."

"How's that bad news?"

"Because thanks to my expenses and the way you spend my money, I'll burn through this in a month."

"Did you ever hear of conserving your capital?" she said.

"No, I never heard of that. Especially with you around."

"This traffic's ridiculous," said Natalie. She gunned her car onto the shoulder and, gravel flying, pulled around a slow-moving truck.

"Anyway," Freel said, "that's the bad news. Now for the good news. I just got off the phone with Witt's lawyer. The final number is nine point one million—"

Natalie shrieked.

"—and, on your behalf, I've accepted," Freel said.

"Oh my God!" said Natalie. "You did it. You did it. I love you. You're a genius."

"The papers are coming here by courier. They'll be here by two," he said. "So stop whatever it is you're doing and get over here and be ready to sign. I'll personally take the agreement to his lawyer after that. Then Witt will sign and we'll get a certified check by noon on Friday. This deal is beautiful. It's a work of art."

Natalie drummed her fingers on her steering wheel. "But that's only, like, thirty percent of his net worth," she said. "I thought you said we could get forty or fifty percent."

"Well, I was wrong," he said. "You've got almost ten fucking million dollars, not to mention $12,500 per month in child support. Take the deal, you lunatic. It's a great deal. If he wanted to, he could fight you and tie us up for three or four years, with no guarantee of anything. That's three or four more years of shit tips for you."

"Oh my God. Nine point one. I can't believe it."

"And by the way," Freel said, "I want you to quit that fucking waitress gig tonight, because tomorrow I'm flying you first class to Vegas, and we're staying in the Regal Suite at Caesar's Palace. Twenty-five hundred a night, for three nights. I'm going to spend everything I have left on you. Start making excuses to your boyfriend so you can get him to take care of the kid while you're gone."

"You're just buttering me up so I don't forget I owe you your $300,000 fee."

"Yeah, that will be nice, too."

By the time Natalie arrived at Freel's office, the courier from Witt's lawyer had come and gone. Freel, gloating and silent, handed her a pen. Without reading a word, she signed the settlement agreement at all the places indicated by little red sticky arrows stuck to the pages. Freel hovered over her.

"Witt's signature's not on any of these pages," Natalie said.

"First we sign, then he signs. Nothing out of the ordinary. Somebody has to sign first. It's standard practice."

"He'd better sign," she said, narrowing her eyes at Freel.

Barely saying goodbye, Freel grabbed the papers, shoved them into an envelope, jumped into his Lamborghini, and took off.

Natalie headed home to the condo. It didn't surprise her that Augie was sitting in Lock's lap as he held a picture book and described out loud to his son what was depicted on the pages. She gave Lock a quick kiss on the lips and patted Augie on his head. She put her bag on the coffee table and turned to Lock.

"Just got off the phone with my sister. No big bombshell, but she's in crisis mode again—one of her kids got expelled for bullying or something, and she wants me to spend a week there, holding her hand, I guess."

"A week?" Lock showed a vexed expression.

"Don't worry," she said. "I talked her into three days and she's okay with that."

Lock didn't believe her for a second. He felt sick, but then caught himself and immediately used one of the techniques he'd learned in AA—to get into the present moment and squeeze all the joy out of it, instead of projecting negatively into the future. To accomplish that, rather than picturing Natalie with another man, Lock explained to himself that Natalie's absence would mean more one-on-one time with Augie. And that meant everything to him. He felt calm again. Actually, he felt even better than he had before she'd come home.

"And when's all this?" Lock asked.

"First thing in the morning. I'll pack tonight so I don't disturb you when I wake up."

"What about your job at the diner?"

"Taken care of."

"Don't worry about disturbing me in the morning, Natalie," said Lock. "I'll be up early with Augie."

The next morning, after Freel and Natalie's limo ride to Philadelphia International, the red-and-blue Southwest Airlines Boeing 737 took off on time. Five and a half hours later, six pieces of luggage were dropped off in Freel's Japanese-themed suite at Caesar's Palace. The rooms were as opulent as Freel had promised.

"Thirteen hundred square feet and two full bathrooms," Freel said, looking around the suite. "This place is like a mansion. It's got a media room with a TV as big as a Jumbotron, a kitchen, a pool table, and a private wet bar with a perfect view of the Strip. On the other side of the kitchen, there's two extra bedrooms. And wait until I get you into the Jacuzzi. It's like a small pool."

Natalie opened the curtains wide and looked out onto Las Vegas Boulevard. "I want to walk from one end of the Strip to the other. How many miles is it?"

"No idea," said Freel. "But it will take hours. And you'll walk alone. I'm not here for exercise."

"I thought you were here to be with me," Natalie said. She began unpacking her bags and hanging clothes in a closet that was larger than most standard hotel rooms.

"I am," he said. "But that doesn't mean craps tables don't exist. Plus, we're already winning. Before we left from home, I wired in fifteen thousand to the casino. And when I checked in, the desk clerk told me our room rate dropped from twenty-five hundred to twelve-fifty. Must be a high-roller discount or something."

"I doubt fifteen thousand qualifies you as a high roller. Not these days. If they thought you were a high roller, they'd comp the whole room. And food, too."

"I have reservations at Nobu for tonight," said Freel. "Tomorrow, I've arranged for a helicopter tour of the Grand Canyon's West Rim. I had to buy the four other seats so we'd be alone. We'll fly over Hoover Dam and Lake Mead. It'll be cool."

Freel was somber the next morning. He'd lost almost twelve thousand dollars overnight in the casino. He waited as Natalie finished her half hour of yoga before they headed down to the restaurant for breakfast. She wore sandals, cut-offs, and a t-shirt.

As Natalie ordered fresh blueberries and hot green tea, her phone rang. She signaled to Freel to be quiet and pasted a broad smile on her face as she answered.

"Hi, Lock," she said. "How are my two loves?"

Freel couldn't hear what Lock was saying, but he could see Natalie couldn't wait to get off the phone. She listened as Lock talked.

"Maybe he just has a little bit of a cold or something," she said, changing her tone to sound serious. "Why don't you call the pediatrician if you're really worried? Anyway, I'll be home in forty-eight hours or so and I'll take care of both of you. My sister's shouting for me from downstairs. I need to go."

Natalie listened for another half minute. Finally, she said, "I love you too," and hung up.

After breakfast, Freel's mood improved as they headed in a cab to get to the helicopter.

"What a great idea, Jerome."

"What's a great idea?"

"This helicopter tour. And with just us. No one else, especially no noisy kids with their cellphone cameras and endless questions."

Natalie couldn't wait to get airborne. Freel couldn't wait for it to be over so he could get back to the craps tables.

———⬧———

Two days later, exhausted and completely broke, even though he had wired himself more gambling money—another ten thousand—Freel and Natalie flew home. Freel borrowed twenty bucks from Natalie to tip the limo driver.

———⬧———

Thursday night, Freel and Natalie arrived an hour and a half late at Philadelphia International. Natalie was exhausted and in an irritable mood—she was annoyed about both the flight delay and the prospect of having to deal with Lock and Augie. She could avoid them a little longer by staying with Freel, she said. Freel wanted to be alone after being so close to another human being for several consecutive days, but he didn't want to provoke her. They didn't say much as they drove on the Schuylkill Expressway, passed Boathouse Row, and went through Fairmount Park to his house.

Freel didn't know if she was disgusted with him and his bad behavior in Las Vegas, and he didn't care. He had her wrapped around his little finger. That was good, especially since Natalie was about to be worth nearly ten million. The story about the other client and the forty percent fee was a lie. Freel didn't want Natalie to think his only money came from the settlement fee from her divorce. He grinned inwardly, thinking about how he was going to offer to manage her money—after all, he had much more experience with money than she did—and if he could swing that, he'd be on Easy Street for the rest of his life. He might even have to marry her—a small sacrifice, considering.

Friday morning, while driving to his office after saying goodbye to Natalie, Freel's thoughts returned to the settlement check that, he hoped, had been delivered the day before. With his $300,000 fee and the prospect of being able to usurp some of Natalie's fortune, things were looking up. He was excited about the upcoming day.

Freel entered his office and went straight to his desk. Atop the pile of mail, placed there by his secretary, sat an unopened FedEx envelope. He examined its shipping label and saw it had indeed been sent from Mannheim's lawyer's firm. The cardboard envelope had arrived Thursday afternoon.

While standing behind his desk, holding it proudly, Freel kissed the envelope and said aloud, "The check for Natalie's $9.1 million. *Hallelujah.*

You couldn't have come a minute too soon." He held up the envelope and regarded for a moment with pure joy, then furiously tore it open.

Inside, there was a single sheet of paper. He would read that in a minute. He wanted to look at that check first, hold it, gaze upon it. It was the single biggest settlement he'd negotiated in his entire legal career, and he knew he might not have one this lucrative ever again. He wanted to savor this moment. But he didn't see the check. He looked inside the envelope, turned it upside down, and shook it. Nothing there. *They must be wiring it to my account*, he figured. He knew Mannheim's lawyer was a jerk, but honorable. A deal was a deal. There was some explanation for the check's absence, and the letter would clear that up. No worries.

Freel unfolded the letter, and as he read it, his eyes opened wide and the blood drained from his face. The only paragraph on the page stated that Mannheim had decided not to sign the settlement documents and that he'd withdrawn his offer. Furthermore, Mannheim's lawyer notified Freel that his client would immediately file an amended petition in the Brandywine County Common Pleas court and intended to "fight the extortionistic and coercive demands of his client's spouse with considerable resources, for however long it takes to prevail."

Freel slumped down into his chair, cupped his head in his hands, and groaned.

39

Lock fished in his pocket for the one loose key that wasn't on his key ring. He found it and opened the door to Abby's smallish three-room apartment.

After almost a week of procrastination—he had attended more than the usual number of meetings, worked late twice, and walked the five-mile trail at Valley Forge National Historical Park—he was there to prepare his late friend's residence for the moving company and clean-out service that would come later in the week to remove everything that Lock didn't want. So far, he hadn't been able to find a will. The furniture would be kept in storage until the estate details could be resolved. He knew Abby had no relatives, so he felt it was okay to take a few mementos by which to remember him.

He had decided to take only a couple things. For an extra fee of one hundred and fifty dollars, the clean-out service would see to it that organizations like Goodwill and Purple Heart would get the things of value—Abby's old furniture that was still serviceable, perfectly good clothes and shoes, miscellaneous household items that the less fortunate might be happy to have.

As Lock methodically moved through the apartment with a clipboard, making notes for the service, his mind drifted between a pervasive sadness over Abby's absence and disconcerting thoughts about Natalie. He didn't know what had gotten into her lately. It was as if she had gone on strike when it came to helping with the baby, and if she wasn't home shirking her responsibilities, she was out—where she went, Lock didn't know—sometimes coming home hours late, way after her shift had ended.

For someone who professed to have loved Abby, she hadn't been sympathetic or supportive of Lock. She wanted nothing to do with making the funeral arrangements. "It's too depressing," she said. And Lock had asked her to come help him that day—she had the day off—and she flat-out refused, saying she had too many other things she had to get to, and besides, she couldn't make the decisions about what to keep and what to discard.

But it was her company Lock needed, and she knew it. That she wouldn't support him made Lock suspicious. She claimed to be working extra hours, but she didn't appear to be earning more money. And there was an increasing number of excuses as to why she'd be late coming home after work. A dead battery, or someone called out sick and she had to cover the shift. He wanted to believe her, but down deep he didn't. And that left the question about where she really was. Lock didn't confront her. Maybe she'd tell him a truth he didn't want to hear.

One thing Lock definitely wanted was Abby's favorite coffee mug, made of blue ceramic. He could use it in the mornings and be reminded of him. He searched in all the logical places—the drain board, the wall-mounted rack with glasses and mugs on its shelf, the practically never-used dishwasher— but he couldn't find it. Lock checked one last place, in the glass-doored kitchen cabinet. Not only did he find the mug there, but also a pristine bottle of Glenmorangie.

Lock removed the mug from the cabinet, wrapped it in a piece of newspaper, and placed it in a cardboard box. He carefully took the bottle off of its shelf and set it on the countertop. For a moment he considered taking the bottle with him as another reminder of Abby, but on second thought decided to leave it for the clean-out crew. They would not, of course, appreciate the scotch's rarity, but that was irrelevant. Let them have it. He didn't trust himself, relatively so early in his sobriety, to respect the bottle the same way Abby did.

During the course of his search, Lock came across very few things he wanted to keep, except the only photograph of them, together at a Phillies game. The picture had been taken three years before, when Lock was still drinking. He remembered having four or five beers that afternoon while Abby simply looked at him and shook his head.

Lock also found Abby's copy of the blue Big Book—the AA bible. He noted how well-worn it was.

After an hour and a half of going through the apartment and inspecting every drawer, closet, and shelf, Lock eased himself into Abby's recliner to rest. A moment later, he sprung up, having remembered that he hadn't inspected Abby's medicine cabinet. He didn't want to leave any painkillers—Abby had recently had surgery on his wrist for a fracture resulting from a fall. It wasn't likely he would have swallowed many of the pills, fearing he might be in breach of AA's program of recovery.

Leaving a controlled substance for the taking would be irresponsible. It would also be negligent to leave Abby's .45 revolver unattended. He had completely forgotten about it.

But where is it? Lock wondered. It wasn't in the most obvious place—his nightstand drawer—and it hadn't been tucked under any of the clothes in the dresser or on the shelf in the bedroom closet. Where would he have put it?

Twenty minutes later, Lock found the fully loaded gun. He had missed it on his first pass through the articles in Abby's sock drawer. But what would he do with it? Until he could figure that out, he'd take it for safekeeping. He wasn't up on the regulations for transferring a registered firearm from one owner to the next, but finding out what to do would be solved by a call to the county sheriff's department.

Lock wrapped the weapon in a dishcloth and put it into the cardboard box. Before he left the apartment, he flushed the pills from the medicine cabinet down the toilet, put the bottle of Glenmorangie back on its shelf and closed the glass door.

In his melancholy, Lock forced his attention to thoughts of little Augie, and that brought him some relief. Images of his child eating in a high-chair, splashing joyfully in a tub of warm water, clawing at the pages of a picture book.

When his mind segued to images of Natalie, he felt worse. Was she turning on him? He was sure she was spending time with someone else, but he thought things would improve as soon as he found a better job and was better able to give her the things she said she wanted. They were both under a lot of pressure, and that never made for calm seas in any relationship.

Despite Lock's hope that the situation with Natalie might improve, it didn't. A couple mornings after he had cleaned out Abby's house, Lock noticed she had applied a little eye shadow and rouge while getting ready for work.

"Why are you dolling yourself up?" he said, standing behind her as she checked herself out in the bathroom mirror. "Makeup for work? That's not your usual routine."

"I feel like it," she said, not turning to face him but addressing Lock's reflection. "Is that a problem for you?"

Lock shook his head.

"Okay," he said. He walked out of the bathroom to get dressed.

"Actually," she said, still in front of the mirror, "there's a private party this morning at the diner—some kind of sales meeting or something—and that's why I have to be there an hour and a half early."

Lock accepted her explanation without comment and began to straighten up the living room, where the night before Augie had tossed a dozen DVDs on and around the coffee table.

He didn't feel right, but he couldn't put his finger on what was wrong. After he put the DVDs away and picked up the remaining things his son had scattered about, it hit him. He had seen with his own eyes how glibly Natalie could lie—he had been witness to her lying to Witt and Candice.

Even to the girls. And now, Natalie was lying about why she used makeup and the excuse to leave early for work. He forced the thoughts from his mind by picturing himself hugging Augie. That did the trick. Whatever Natalie was up to—if anything—would eventually reveal itself. Sometimes it wasn't good to speculate, especially without hard evidence.

Before Natalie left that morning, Lock dropped Augie off at daycare and returned home. The daycare center was only a few blocks away, and the round trip was less than twenty minutes. Only Natalie would be home—the girls had spent the night at Witt's—and Lock thought about pressing her on the makeup matter, but instead made a conscious decision to let it be. At least for now.

Back at the condo, they didn't have much to say to each other, and Lock sensed that Natalie had to force herself to kiss him goodbye before she walked out the door.

Lock waited sixty seconds and then left. He started his car and pulled out, keeping Natalie's car in sight. Instead of turning left at the intersection—the typical route she'd take to get to the diner—she went the opposite way. He lost her in traffic once, but soon saw her ahead of him, stuck in a left-turn lane. He got behind a truck to obscure her view of him. If she saw him, it didn't deter her from driving two more blocks and pulling up at a private residence. She took a parking spot on the street. In a driveway a few yards away sat Jerome Freel's black Lamborghini.

He tried to believe she was meeting him to work out the details of her settlement, but then a lump materialized in his throat, and he sat in his car for a long time and cried.

His mind filled with an array of thoughts, all of them violent and none reasonable, though perhaps justified. The worst one was the fantasy that she'd leave him and find a way to take Augie with her. His stomach churned and nausea washed over him.

Lock's fantasy of destroying Freel did not include doing any damage to Natalie. She was Lock's son's mother. Augie needed her.

Less than an hour later, Natalie, wearing her uniform and nametag, exited the house with Freel close behind. She smoothed her dress and smiled at Freel. He got into his car and lowered the window. Natalie bent over and gave him a long kiss before walking down the driveway, onto the sidewalk, and into her own car.

Lock pulled out of his parking spot along the curb behind where Natalie had parked and floored it, lurching into Freel's driveway, slamming on the brakes, and blocking the Lamborghini. He unhurriedly got out of his car, intentionally not looking toward Natalie, who was walking away from Freel toward her car. Lock approached Freel.

Freel opened his car door and began to get out. Lock used both hands to slam it closed. Freel pulled his leg back just in time.

"You can have her if you want her," Lock said. "Just lend her to me a few times a day until our baby no longer needs milk. Then you can keep her."

"Take it easy, buddy. This isn't what you think."

"It is what I think."

"You've got it all wrong, Gilkenney," Freel said. "We're working on a modification to the custody agreement for the two girls."

"What?" asked Lock. "When did you start being her lawyer again? You think I would have stood for that? With your history with her?"

Freel ignored Lock's questions.

"I don't know why Nat doesn't want you to know about it until it's finalized," said Freel. "Maybe she thinks the process will upset you. She loves you, man. She's trying to get Mannheim to cough up more money every month. I don't know why she wants it hush-hush, but that's a woman for you. Everything always has to be a secret."

"You're a lying son-of-a-bitch, Freel. I know what happened in there," Lock said, nodding toward the house. He tried to control his anger. His jaw was set, his arms hung at his sides, and his hands were clenched into fists.

Freel, watching Lock's increasingly agitated body language, was getting jumpy. "You should calm down," Freel said. "Nothing happened except what I just told you."

"Then why not at your office? Why here?"

Lock craned his neck and saw Natalie standing on the sidewalk, observing them.

"Lock!" she shouted. He ignored her and turned back to Freel.

"Maybe I should just kill you here and now," Lock said.

Freel pushed his car door open, got out, and stood up. He was Lock's height, but lighter and at least ten years younger.

"Lock," Freel said. "You just threatened me with murder. You're on probation. You're one phone call away from going back to prison. Let me give you some legal advice. For free."

"What are you charging Natalie? Exchange of services? She getting free advice too?"

"No, I'm not charging her anything. Listen to me, Lock. Get off of my property right now. Turn around and walk away from here. You're upset, very upset. I'm willing to let it go at that. Nothing happened between Natalie and me. Those days are over. Go home. Relax."

Lock stared at Freel and couldn't find any words.

"I'm not through with you," Lock said a moment later. "And I'm not through with her." He turned and began walking to his car. He looked to see Natalie, but she had driven off.

Lock left Freel alone in his driveway and then drove around, not wanting to go home, not wanting to go anywhere. He pictured Freel's dead body in the driveway, a pool of blood spreading on the asphalt. But that didn't sit right with him, not for long, anyway. Deep down, Lock knew Freel wasn't the problem. He knew who the real problem was, but that was an impossible dilemma for him to contemplate right then.

With nowhere else to go, Lock headed home, and once there, checked his AA meeting schedule. If he hurried, he could make the noon meeting in Media.

Prior to leaving, he went into the bedroom closet and reached under a pile of neatly folded bath towels. He felt for the paper bag that held a tiny, velvet-covered box. It was still there, apparently undiscovered by Natalie. He smiled and left immediately for the meeting.

40

Lock sat in the living room of the condo, mindlessly tapping his fingers on the coffee table and waiting for Natalie to return. He had plenty to talk about, but didn't know if he'd have the courage to say a word. He'd wait and see Natalie's demeanor. He'd take his cue from that.

———⋙⋘———

"That was some scene you made this morning," Natalie said to Lock upon returning from the diner. She put her handbag on the dining room table and sat down. "Nothing happened in there with him. You made a fool of yourself, and Jerome could have had you arrested. Is that what you want? To be back in a small room? Again?"

Lock looked out the window and said nothing.

Natalie emptied her purse and counted her tips. Seventy-seven dollars and a few coins.

"You lied about where you were going," he said, turning back to Natalie, "so it makes sense you lied about what you did. Why would you hide it if all you were doing was some paperwork?

She stood up tall and stiffened. "Listen, Lock—" Natalie started to speak. Her voice was loud.

"Shhh," said Lock. "Augie's asleep. He must have been tired, because he went down without a fight."

Natalie put the cash in a white envelope and returned it to her purse.

"I want to talk to you about something, Lock, and I'm not looking for another episode like this morning."

Lock swallowed hard. He had no idea what was coming, but it didn't sound good. He gazed out the window. He held his breath and looked back at Natalie. In his eyes, there was no woman more beautiful—or impossible. But before she could spout something unpleasant, he knew how to derail her. He paused for a moment, took a deep breath, and decided to make his move now and hope for the best.

"Natalie," he said. "I don't want to argue with you. I love you so much that it makes me crazy. Maybe I over-reacted this morning."

"Maybe?"

Lock slid forward from his sitting position on the sofa and down on one knee onto the carpet.

"What are you doing?" she asked.

Lock half turned back to the sofa and reached under one of the cushions and retrieved the small, blue ring box. He held it out to her.

Natalie's eyes narrowed and focused on the box. "What are you—?"

"Take it, Natalie," he said, stretching his arm forward and up toward Natalie. She took a step toward the kneeling Lock and reached out and took the box. A cruel sneer formed on her face as she opened it.

"An engagement ring?" she asked.

"Natalie. Marry me. We've had some low moments, I know, but those were glitches. Most of the time, things are perfect between us. I know we can build something great together. It will be amazing. You, me, Augie. And the girls, when we have them. We'll build a life beyond our wildest dreams. Say yes."

Natalie squinted as she continued to examine the ring without removing it from the box.

"I don't want to hurt your feelings or make you feel bad, Lock, but the truth is I didn't know they cut diamonds this small. It's really microscopic."

"It's not the cost that matters."

"Maybe, maybe not," she said. "But to even offer me something like this speaks volumes about how little you know me. How could I wear that out in public?"

"But ..."

"I have to spell it out for you?" she asked, raising her eyebrows. "The answer is no. N-O, no. Absolutely not."

With that, Natalie used her thumb to snap the lid closed. She held the box out for Lock to take, and when he didn't react immediately, she lobbed it onto the coffee table. Lock stood up and then, mouth slightly open, pale and blank-faced, sat back on the sofa.

Lock couldn't bear to look at her. He spoke so softly he was almost inaudible. "You were going to say something a minute ago?"

"Yes," she said. She stood up tall again and folded her arms across her chest. "I want to talk to you about something, Lock, and I want you to agree to stay calm."

It was hard for him to focus on her words. His eyes fell on the ring box. He decided to leave it on the coffee table, hoping against hope that she'd pick it up again, remove the ring, and put it on her finger. She's changed her mind in the past, so why not now?

"Okay," he said, still quiet. "Okay, I'll hear you out."

Natalie took a step back. "Here goes, Lock," she said, unfolding and re-folding her arms. "It's not working out, you and me."

Lock's heart thumped. He could feel it in his belly.

"At first," she said, "it was wonderful. I was out of jail and finally free. I wanted you, and I needed a father for the baby. But I guess when the stars cleared out of my eyes, I began to see this wasn't going to work. I'm more ambitious than you. You're content to live here on Witt's dime and just hang around with me and the baby. Well, I'm not content to have him support me. I hate his guts."

"What are you doing, Natalie? I've learned gratitude, that's why I'm happy with what we have. That doesn't make me complacent."

Natalie shook her head and closed her eyes for a moment.

Lock continued. "We have a great life, and things will get even better. I'm never happier than when we're right here on the sofa holding Augie between us. You can't tell me that doesn't melt your heart."

"Whatever it does, it doesn't matter. I'm unhappy, I want more, and I want out. I want a nice car and a pool. I want money to spend whenever I feel like it, and I want to go back to my old yoga instructor—the one I can't afford now. And I want to travel and go to classy restaurants where you need to dress up. I deserve more, and it makes me sick to see you so oblivious to my needs. And that's it. Don't try to talk me into anything. It won't work. My mind's made up. I'm moving on, and so are you."

"Don't do this." Lock stood up and took a step toward Natalie. He wanted to take her into his arms. He thought hugging her would bring her around. But he didn't. He stood still, sick to his stomach.

"I'm sorry, Lock. But that's the way it's going to be."

"This is about Freel, isn't it?"

"Keep asking questions. That's a good way to make this tougher on you than it needs to be. But, yes, it is about Jerome. The ugly truth is that he can give us the life we deserve and you can't."

"Us? What are you talking about? If you mean Augie, you're insane. He's not going with you and Freel. You can't just take him, he's not a football you can just pick up and run with. He's ours. Yours and mine. Ours."

Natalie fidgeted with the strap of her handbag.

"I told you, you're asking too many questions for your own good. You'll get all the answers you need in due course. All you need to know now is that you have to move out. You need to be out of here in…I'm giving you… two weeks, and that's generous. Jerome said twenty-four hours, but I want to be fair. You'll need to find a place."

"You're *giving* me two weeks? This is a joke. A sick one."

"It's my name on the lease, not yours," she said, "just the way Witt arranged it."

"You're frightening me, Natalie." Lock's breathing was deep and labored.

"No, Lock. There's nothing to be afraid of. You will be okay, I will be okay, and Augie will be fine. You gave him a great start in life, but now we're all going our separate ways."

"No, we're not," Lock said, shaking his head and pointing his finger at her. "We're both going to stay put and figure out what's wrong and fix it. That's all there is to it."

"No," Natalie said, "that's not all there is to it. There's more, and I'm warning you, stop pushing me. I have this all figured out. You're still young and handsome and you'll find someone else and have a family of your own in no time."

"I have a family of my own now, and I'm going to keep it, no matter how crazy you're acting. And even if you do hateful things to me, I don't care. I have a family and I'll never, ever give up on it. You can fight me and hurt me all you want. It doesn't matter."

"You insist on hanging on to your fantasy about us living happily ever after?"

"I love Augie, and the girls, and I love what we have together. I'm a father and I'm going to fight for my family."

"You're in denial," she said. "You must have known down deep this wasn't working. It's over."

"No it's not, Natalie. Remember what you told me—that you're a changed woman. That prison changed you for the better. You've had counseling, and you go to your group therapy and the AA women's meetings and—"

"All lies, Lock. I haven't been to a meeting in months, except a few with you. I've been with Jerome."

Lock pounded a fist once, hard, on the living room wall. "I don't care about your stories," he said, "I have a family and I'm going to fight for it."

"Your family is all in your head, Lock. I don't love you anymore. Are you listening to me? And something else. Augie is not your son."

Those last words didn't register. "What did you mean when you said I'll find out in due time?" he asked. "Find out what?"

"I told you to stop interrogating me," she said. "You'll find out in court."

"Court?" Lock, deliberately and softly, pressed his fist against the wall, trying to calm himself. "We don't need court. There's no reason for animosity. Have it your way, then. If you don't love me, I'll let you go. We'll share Augie equally. He needs his mother and his father."

"Exactly," she said, snarling. "He needs his mother and his father, not some weak, recovering alcoholic."

Lock stood up and paced in and out of the dining room. *I'm an alcoholic,* he thought, *but I'm not weak. And I'm a good father.* He took a few steps toward Augie's room to see if he was stirring. Lock wanted to see his boy, to hold him, to breathe in his baby-smell.

"You're acting as crazy as you were when we were planning to set up Witt," he said. "You're like a different person. Maybe you need a doctor and medication."

"That won't get you out of this, Lock. It's already in motion. I'm finished with you and I'm keeping Augie with me. And you have to be gone no later than two weeks from today."

"I'll never leave," he said. "And if you want to fight, you'll lose. You want court, you'll get court. I'll get the best lawyer in the world—"

"With what, your four hundred dollar-a-week paycheck? Before taxes."

"I'll get the best lawyer in the world and demolish you in court. I'll win primary custody." Lock paced frantically. "No…I'll win full custody, and then I'll be dictating your visitation rights to you. How's that sound?"

"Sounds pathetic to me. Especially since you don't know the half of it."

He returned to the sofa and sat down heavily. "Enlighten me, Natalie. Go ahead. Make it worse."

"If that's what you want," she said, "that's what you'll get." Natalie sat in a chair opposite the sofa where Lock sat, slumping. "You may as well start accepting this now." She removed the small mirror she kept in her handbag and looked at herself, fixing her makeup. "You'll have no visitation rights with Augie. Augie isn't your son. He's Jerome's. We've already done the paternity test."

Lock stood there, expressionless. "You're lying. Augie is ours and you know it. You're making that up."

Natalie reached into her handbag and took out an envelope. She handed it to him. His hands quivered as he removed the report. He stared at it for a full minute, reading it repeatedly, then crumpled it up and dropped it to the floor. He looked down, poker-faced. She looked into her mirror again and pursed her lips.

Natalie spoke. "I didn't want to have to show you that test result, but you forced me to."

Lock tried to speak, but no words came out. He felt hollow.

"Augie and I are moving in with Jerome," she said, "and he wants you out of the picture. And now. All he has to do is walk into court and file a one-page custody petition and you're gone, not to mention your death threat. And believe me, Lock, he'll do it if you give me a hard time. He loves me and he's very protective."

"Do you think he'll really love Augie?" Lock tried to make this into a bad dream. He begged God to make what was happening a nightmare and to wake him up from it.

"It's going to happen. Accept it. Get yourself to a lot of meetings. You don't want to start drinking over this."

Natalie returned the mirror to the purse and looked up at Lock. She stood up.

"Jerome told me this would happen," she said. "But I told him you've grown up and would understand. Another case of me being wrong."

"If you don't love me anymore, okay, fine," he said. "I can almost understand that. If you want to be with Freel, fine. Go ahead."

"I will," she said.

"And if you move out, I'll stay here and you'll be free of me, but we can still raise the baby together."

"Get this through your head, Lock. You can't stay here and Augie is not your son. If you love him like you say you do, you'll let him go. I know you love him, but don't feel bad. He's going to be just fine with his biological parents."

Natalie stood up, grabbed her purse, and stormed out of the apartment. She didn't slam the door. She left it wide open, and inside, Lock slumped further on the sofa.

He sat there for a long while, trying to think. He couldn't organize his thoughts. The room grew dark.

Lock thought then of Dominique and Hannah and how, back then, one tragedy had turned into two. He lost the woman he loved and then he lost Hannah. He vowed to himself that he wouldn't let that happen again. *Natalie's acting insane*, he thought. *There's something wrong with her.* He believed they could have a rich life together. *It's her nature*, the cynical part of him said. *But I don't have to be the frog.*

41

Later that day, in the interior of a darkened motel room, Freel awoke and felt for his clothes and got dressed as best he could without being able to see what he was putting on.

"I have to go," he said. "Have to be in court in an hour and I have to stop back at the office first."

"I'll miss you," she said.

"And I can't find one of my shoes," he said. "I think I kicked it under the bed. Sorry, but I have to turn the light on."

"Do I have to go back to work too?" she asked through the pillow, under which she had buried her head. "Wasn't I a good girl?"

Freel walked over to her side of the bed and cupped one of her breasts.

"Yes, you were a very good girl," he said. "And no, you don't have to go back to work. You can take the rest of the afternoon off. I'll leave you a couple hundred bucks on the dresser. Take a ride up to King of Prussia and get yourself something at Victoria's Secret. How's that sound?"

"Wow, thanks for nothing, Jerome. Leaving money on the dresser like that makes me feel cheap. Isn't that how you pay a hooker?"

Freel laughed.

"You're no whore, Jennifer. You're the best paralegal I've ever had."

42

Lock arrived at home after work looking forward to seeing Augie.

It had been a long day at the mind-numbing auto parts job and thinking about seeing his son helped time go by. Occasionally during the day, little flits of thought about the terrible things Natalie said about him not being Augie's father came into his head—but by then enough time had passed and they were easier to dismiss. She had said those things to hurt him. Why? He didn't know. But they weren't true, and he wasn't going to let them drag him down. He knew, when it served her, she didn't hesitate to say things that weren't true.

Lock bounded up the stairs to find Natalie sitting in the living room—on the sofa that had become his bed at night. He'd been sleeping with a blanket and a pillow that Natalie had shoved onto the floor. When she saw him enter, she picked up the remote and clicked off the television.

"You've let four days slip by since I told you that you need to move out and you haven't lifted one finger to pack," she said. Then she stood up. "Do I have to put it in writing and have you served with an eviction notice?"

He walked out of the room to see if Augie was in his crib. He wasn't. He looked in the girls' room. They weren't there either.

Lock didn't want to deal with Natalie immediately upon getting home, but he had no choice. "Where is everybody?"

"Have you made any plans for somewhere to stay? Are you going to Abby's?"

"Where are the girls? Where's Augie?"

"The girls are with Witt in California. We're working out a new custody agreement. Witt's relocating to Sacramento. Some involved real estate deal there. I've agreed to let him have the girls. He's already got an *au pair* on the job. All four of them are en route to Sacramento as we speak."

Lock flinched. He uttered the word *no* under his breath.

"You're giving up your girls? Natalie, you're out of your mind. You can't be that cold."

"Witt's going to pay to fly me out there every month to see them. First class. And once the details are all worked out, he's going to give me a generous allowance, too. I get sick to my stomach every time I think of that bastard, but I don't mind playing him for his money. He fucked me over by canceling the settlement, and now he's trying to be the guy who saves the day with his wallet. I'll find a way to pay him back, believe me. Anyway, all I know is that I won't have to work much longer."

"And what about Augie—where's he?"

"Augie's with his father," she said. She sat down again and turned on the television. "Jerome and I hired a full-time babysitter for Augie, someone to help me. I'll be moving in there as soon as Jerome says it's okay. He's not too good with babies yet, but he's learning. Don't worry."

Lock didn't give a damn about the words printed on the lab report she had shown him. He knew Augie looked like him and recalled how Augie lit up like Times Square when he saw him. And Augie grabbed his finger every time he got a chance. *Augie is not with his father*, Lock thought. *Because he's not here with me. I'm his father.*

He walked quickly back into the master bedroom—now Natalie's room—closed the door, and sat on the bed. *A drink would be perfect right now*, he thought, but Lock knew what he really needed was a meeting.

He found the schedule under a couple of books sitting on the dresser. There was a meeting in Red Cedar Woods in forty-five minutes. He thought of the times he and Natalie had taken the baby in his carrier seat into a meeting. Miraculously, Augie always slept through them.

Lock thought of Augie, his handsome face usually on the verge of laughing, and of his baby-smell. *My beautiful little boy.*

He dropped the schedule on the bed and rested his elbows on the dresser, his face in his palms. Tears rolled down his cheeks.

In a minute, he composed himself. Natalie already thought he was weak, and he didn't want her to see him crying—not that that would have any noticeable impact on her. He stood up and went out into the living room. She didn't look up.

He cleared his throat. "Come with me to a meeting. We have to leave in fifteen minutes. Can you be ready?"

"You're being childish, Lock," she said. "You need to move out of here. You have to make arrangements."

He couldn't hold back the tears.

"Natalie, I love you. You and Augie are my life. Don't do this. We have a beautiful family and a beautiful little boy. Forget about Freel and what you think he can give you. Think about what we have. It's real. It's very real. I'm begging you. Please don't do this."

She clicked the remote and the television came back on.

"You're a good man, Lock," she said, looking at the on-screen channel guide. "And you'll find a good woman and have your own children, and sooner than you think."

He sat on the far end of the couch. He wanted to slide over to her and put his arm around her, but that wouldn't do any good. He knew she'd shove him away. He looked down at the floor.

"Where will I go?" he asked.

"I already told you. Stay at Abby's," she said. "You have the key, and there's a few more weeks left on his lease. That'll give you time to make more permanent living arrangements."

Natalie stood up and turned off the television. She grabbed her handbag and car keys and started to walk out the door. As she began to pull it shut behind her, Lock called out, "Natalie. Wait."

"I'm late," she said.

"No!" he said.

"I told you I'm late."

"Baby, please don't go."

Natalie didn't reply; she closed the door and was gone.

Lock said nothing else.

He walked into what he was now painfully aware of as her bedroom—not *their* bedroom—closed the door behind him, and fell onto the bed. In no time, he fell into a deep and dreamless sleep.

⟶⟶✦⟵⟵

The next morning, Lock searched every square inch of the condo for that paternity test report, but couldn't find it. He tore open drawers and rummaged through closet shelves like a burglar. Where would she have put it if it wasn't where he had dropped it? He couldn't think clearly. All he could remember was reading those stomach-churning words and crumpling the paper into a ball.

He had to find it. It was fake, he was sure of that, but he had to have it in his hands in order to convince himself that it really was bullshit. He continued his search, ransacking the condo in the process, searching the floors, under beds, in wastebaskets, in the kitchen trashcan, everywhere. It was nowhere to be found. He checked every place, even in places he knew it couldn't be.

In his desperation, Lock was reduced to calling Natalie, though it was fruitless. There was disgust in her voice when she answered, and she claimed to have no idea where it was. He figured she was lying when she said he was the last person to have seen it. She said it didn't matter where the report was because facts were facts. Then she hung up on him. Lock decided Natalie had to have picked up the crumpled sheet from where he dropped it and then taken it. That would be just like her.

The lab's name and phone number were what Lock was after. He cursed himself for not being able to recall it. He wanted to contact them and ask about the accuracy statistics of paternity tests. If he had to, he'd get a lawyer and force Natalie and Freel to do another test. They were flat-out liars and he wasn't going to let them get away with it. Make them prove it.

Or was he kidding himself? Why would a lab issue a false report? In his heart, Lock knew that the words printed on the report spoke the truth. But he couldn't fully admit that to himself, and so he continued his search.

He tried to call Natalie again. She'd probably remember the lab's name. But she didn't answer, and he guessed it didn't matter anyway. What were the odds there was a mistake at the lab and that it was Lock, not Freel, who was Augie's biological father? Slim to none. He took a deep breath. He had to be realistic. He thought of another AA slogan, but this time it gave him no solace—*Know the truth and it shall set you free.* He'd have to find a way to accept that the results were correct. He'd have to find a way to accept that Augie was not his son. But he'd never stop loving him, he'd never stop trying to get him back, to be his father.

Around lunchtime, with hunger nowhere in sight, Lock read through innumerable websites and online forums discussing paternity testing. He read for hours, carefully noting the names of lawyers in the area who were mentioned in the conversations.

He picked up the phone, and within an hour, he had spoken with three lawyers and left messages for two others.

The outcome of the first call was profoundly disappointing. The lawyer rushed Lock off the phone after telling him that he'd have an insurmountable battle in light of an existing paternity test that proved another man was the child's father.

"DNA test results are deemed by courts to be 99.99% reliable," the woman told him.

"What if I get my own test, what about that?" he asked.

"You'd need a court order," she said, "and plus, you have no standing to get one. Any semi-competent attorney would see to it that such a test would never occur. No judge would order a test because the mother will say she was never intimate with you, and all she has to do is file a complaint about you being a stalker or someone with an axe to grind, and you'll get laughed out of court in no time. If the mother was my client, you'd never get near that child, sorry to say."

Lock's head began to spin and nausea percolated in his gut.

The second call was more discouraging than the first—as soon as that lawyer heard the facts of situation, he couldn't hang up fast enough. And the third lawyer gave essentially the same story, but added, "It's worth a shot, though this could take a year or two to shake out—and I'll need a $25,000 retainer to get started and see what we can do."

Lock said he'd think it over and hung up. He stared at the phone. He pictured Augie being driven away in a car seat in Freel's Lamborghini. He couldn't breathe.

Again, the thought came to him—*Accept the truth, Augie's not yours.*

But how could that be? He knew he wasn't dreaming, but the texture of his reality felt like any number of nightmares he'd had in recent years. They seemed so real, but he always woke up and the terror quickly abated. A good nightmare would stick with you for a while, he reminded himself, but it would always fade with time. He had to give it time and not do anything rash. Lock fought back at dark ideas—suicide, homicide, absconding with Augie—as they advanced on him. He pushed them away but knew they still lurked, lying in wait for the right time.

Even if he's not my biological child, no one will keep me from Augie, he thought. *No one.*

43

After an aggravating shift at the diner—food being sent back left and right, lousy tips, and the lecherous leer of the night manager—Natalie sat fuming in the living room at Freel's house.

"What's eating you, Nat?" he asked as he padded across the carpet in his underwear. Natalie exhaled through her nose.

"Maybe you can help me find someone to rough up Witt.'

Freel shook his head and sneered.

"As revenge for backing out of the divorce settlement," she said. "I'd think you'd be all for that puke to feel some pain, too."

"And what do you gain by that?" asked Freel as he sat down next to her and used the remote to turn on the Golf Channel.

"Satisfaction, pure and simple," she said.

"I can think of a better way for you to feel some gratification," he said. He turned to look at Natalie and smirked.

"Don't flatter yourself," she said.

"I could find someone to help you out in no time, but why should I?"

"You do me a favor and I'll do you a favor." Natalie approached Freel and ran her fingers through his curly hair. "How about that punk you get your coke from?" she asked. "He's pretty much a low-life. He'll come up with someone who wants to make a few bucks."

"That's exactly who I'm going to call."

"Wow. Thanks."

"Right after I get my favor."

"Oh no, you don't. Whores always get paid up front. You should know that."

"You're too much, Nat. That's why I love you." Freel grinned.

"You'll get yours after you seal the deal."

Freel walked into another room and made a call. Natalie couldn't make out the words.

"Nat, get me something to write on!" he shouted. She found a pen and scrap of paper in a desk drawer and hurried in and handed it to him. He motioned her out of the room.

A minute later, he returned to the living room and handed her the scrap of paper. On it was the name Marcus and a phone number. She smiled at him and put the paper into her bag.

"I don't know if that's such a good idea, but that's for you to decide. Don't you think Witt will figure it's you?"

"With all he's doing for me? Paying for the condo, taking the girls, offering to fly me first class to California? I'm the last person he'd suspect. Plus, I'm going to tell the guy to make it look like a robbery and kick him, hard, in the face. Then I'll go visit Witt and be able to enjoy seeing the damage while acting real sympathetic."

"Oh, man, you're sick. What do you get out of it again?"

"Knowing that he got beat up will make me feel much better. Speaking of which, what's this going to cost?"

"I have no idea," said Freel. "My man said work it out with the guy yourself. You're street-smart. Don't accept the first number he says. He's probably a drug addict and will do anything for peanuts. And for Christ's sake, don't mention my name, whatever you do. I'm not involved in this. As your attorney, I'm not recommending this course of action."

"And as my lover?"

"Bang him up good. The prick cost me three hundred thousand dollars. Now that I think about it, you work out the deal and I'll pay for it."

The following afternoon, another overcast and cold November day, Natalie drove into Philadelphia to a creepy part of the city's Grays Ferry neighborhood. There, she was to wait in front of a plumbing supply warehouse on Vare Avenue. She was surprised at herself for feeling so anxious. Was Witt really that bad? Did he deserve to get beaten? Then she thought about the long and tedious night shift she'd be working later and decided that yes, he really was that bad.

The person she was scheduled to meet turned out to be a skinny man who looked like he smelled. He tapped on her window. She didn't open it.

"Marcus?" she said through the glass.

"That's me, alright," he said. "Let's talk in my car."

"Bad idea. Let's sit in mine," she said. She leaned across the passenger seat to unlock the door of her old Toyota for him. He shrugged and got in the passenger side.

He put out his hand to shake hers. "They call me H.M.," he said. "Word is your boyfriend's a nice guy, and your husband slaps you around pretty good."

"That's not the half of it," Natalie said. "I need him to know what getting hit feels like. If I could do it myself, I would."

"That's why they call me H.M.," the man said. "Stands for Hurt Man. I don't kill people. I'm not a hit man. I give people a good talking-to, get their attention. My step-father taught me all about that. I can also deliver a personal message for you. No extra charge."

"No," Natalie said. "No messages. I don't want him to know this came from me. Make him think this is a robbery. FYI, he usually has a lot of cash on him. Take his wallet, and whatever's in it is a bonus for you."

The man nodded appreciatively.

"I do have one concern, though," said Natalie. "No offense, but you don't exactly look like a powerhouse. You're kind of skinny. My husband's no weakling."

"Lady, don't worry about that. I'll get the job done. I employ the element of surprise. Works every time."

Natalie rolled her eyes and regarded him warily. "What's something like this cost?"

"Oh no," he said. "You have to make me an offer. Then I'll turn it down and tell you it's more. That's the way it goes."

"I could get you three hundred."

He grunted. "For three hundred, I'd give him a kiss. You'll have to do much better than that."

"I can give you three hundred right now," she said, "and another three hundred after. Six hundred. That's it. That's all I have."

"You're still not even close." Her max was a thousand, but she wasn't going to let on about that.

"Come on," she said, "I'm a waitress. I work for tips."

"I don't," he said. "Eight."

"Six-fifty or get out of my car." Natalie glared at him. She wasn't intimidated in the least. H.M. looked away.

"Holy shit, you're scary, lady." He looked her over slowly and then grinned. "I have an idea. How about we trade?"

"Okay," she said. "You're done. Get out."

H.M. put up his hands in mock surrender.

"Okay, tough guy," he said. "You win. Six-fifty. Up front."

"Three now and the rest afterwards."

His watery eyes widened. "You win again." He put out his hand.

Natalie reached under the floor mat and retrieved the three hundred in twenties she had counted out earlier, and handed them to him, being careful to make sure she didn't touch his filthy hand and disgusting fingernails. Then she reached up to the sun visor and found a piece of notepaper.

"He's usually out of town, but he'll be back here on business Saturday night," she said. She handed him the note. "Here's the address of a bar where he'll be. My advice would be to hang around in the parking lot and sucker-punch him when he comes out, which should be around ten or eleven. Nothing more than one good sock. No messages, no nothing. Got it?"

H.M. examined the paper.

"Red Cedar Woods? How the fuck am I going to find this place?"

"I don't know. Go get yourself a GPS. Remember, nothing life-threatening, nothing that would put him in the hospital. Just a good punch and a good scare. Oh, and only if he's alone. You don't want any witnesses."

"Okay," he said. "I guess."

"Oh. You'll need this." Natalie handed him a photo that had been torn in half. It was a shot of Witt. He wore a tux and was smiling broadly. Whoever had her arm around him couldn't be seen.

H.M. looked it over and jammed it in his pocket along with the twenties. "I got everything I need."

"Thank you," she said, "and don't forget about his wallet. It could be more than you expect."

Without either of them saying another word, the man exited her car and she drove off. He stood in the parking lot and watched her leave.

Natalie headed home on I-76, the radio cranked up to drown out doubts about sending someone to attack the man who had been, at least recently, so good to her. She made the music even louder and rolled down the windows. She needed some cold air.

—————

Natalie's shift flew by that day, her mind occupied with images of Witt being punched and knocked to the ground in the parking lot of the Cavern Tavern. Witt lived in fear of losing his wallet and having to contact all of his credit card companies, get a new driver's license, and all that. She'd been in a good mood ever since she struck the deal earlier in the day. If this worked out, maybe she'd be able to get H.M. to get back at some other people with whom she had scores to settle. No, she told herself, don't get carried away. Just sit back and enjoy. She smirked, knowing big-shot Witt would soon feel some of the pain he loved to dish out.

She was about to deliver a check to her last table—three high school boys who had been whispering about her as they watched her walk away to fill their order—when the bell chimed at the front door of the diner.

Natalie had to look twice at a group of people entering the diner to be sure it was who she thought it was. Yes, it was definitely him, H.M., with a woman and two other men. All of them, even H.M.—who now looked clean and professional—were wearing suits. They spoke to the manager, who turned and scanned the dining room. When he spotted Natalie, he pointed to her. The group looked at her.

"Nat! Get over here," the manager said. Natalie set the check down at the high schoolers' table and headed to the cashier's counter. The three men and the woman stood next to the manager, watching her approach.

"You need to see me about something?" she asked Nikos, the manager.

"Natalie Jeanne Mannheim?" the woman said, stepping forward.

Natalie squinted at her. "Yes, I'm Natalie."

The woman and one of the men each took one of Natalie's arms.

H.M spoke. He looked at a form. "Natalie Jeanne Mannheim, you are under arrest for criminal conspiracy, solicitation of the commission of a felony, and solicitation to commit aggravated battery. Turn around."

Natalie did as ordered, and found two uniformed officers behind her. Her heart pounded so loudly she thought everyone could hear it. A nauseating dizziness affected her balance. The two officers at her sides held her tightly as she wobbled.

Then one of the policemen walked behind her and handcuffed her. The dining room fell silent. Everyone in the restaurant turned to take in the scene. Natalie looked down toward the floor. She would have covered her face if she could have.

The detectives' sedan pulled up to the Brandywine County Municipal Services building and parked illegally at the sidewalk closest to the entrance. Natalie was ushered out of the cart and walked like a zombie, prodded rudely by the woman officer.

They escorted Natalie to an interrogation room.

"Are you certain you don't want to contact an attorney?" the officer asked as he uncuffed Natalie and pointed the chair she was to occupy. "We've read you Miranda twice now. If you want to explain yourself, let's get going."

"I didn't do anything except talk to someone about my ex-husband. Anything else your partner says is hearsay. You said he didn't tape the conversation."

"I tried," H.M. said, grinning. "Not my fault if department-issued recording equipment sucks." One of the detectives narrowed his eyes at H.M.

"Do you realize how serious this is?" another of the detectives asked. He sat down, removed his glasses, and rubbed his face. A pen lay on top of a yellow-lined notepad. "The D.A. wants to charge you with attempted murder."

A video camera on a tripod stood on the floor next to the desk where Natalie sat facing the detective.

"Murder?" she asked. "That's ridiculous. Is that camera on?"

"No," the detective said. "Not unless you give me the okay to record. And if you have nothing to hide—"

"I only asked the undercover guy to rough him up a bit. I even specified nothing serious, nothing that would put him in the hospital. I said that. Those exact words. Just a good scare. My ex has ruined my life and he thinks there are no consequences."

"How could you have been certain the man you hired wouldn't have gotten carried away and killed him? One good punch can kill a man. You know that. That's attempted murder."

"Actually," Natalie said, "I thought your officer was an addict who would just rip me off for the three hundred and never lift a finger and hurt my ex. That's it," she said, getting a second wind and feeling better. For the first time that evening, she sat up tall and relaxed. "I never had the slightest intention of any of this coming to pass. It was just some sick game I was playing with myself. To make me feel better."

The detective picked up the pen, pointed it toward her and started to say something, but then stopped. He dropped the pen on the pad and sat back. He smiled at Natalie.

"Now you're getting cute because you think we have nothing on you because the recorder screwed up. Well, think again. It would have been helpful to have it, sure, but we can make do very nicely without it. Detective Abramovitz's testimony will be believed. Your best bet is to call your lawyer so we can get a confession from you that he won't challenge later. But if you want to play games, fine. We'll talk more."

Natalie took a deep breath and tried to stare down the detective, who just relaxed his smile and shook his head.

"Maybe I will call my lawyer," she said. "Can I think about it?"

"Sure," the detective said. "You think about it all you want while I call the D.A.'s night desk and see what else we can charge you with."

"That's fine," Natalie said, holding out her wrists, assuming she was about to be handcuffed again and taken to a holding cell.

One of the officers advanced with cuffs in hand. The detective waved him off. "We don't need to handcuff Mrs. Mannheim. Just give her a seat in the hall. She wants time to think."

"Thank you," she said. "I appreciate the courtesy."

"Oh," he said. "I'm not being courteous. I want you to think about telling the truth and making the inevitable easier on all concerned. You're on probation, and the D.A.'s recommendation to the sentencing judge counts for quite a bit. I'm giving you a chance to think about things and do the right thing. That's a full confession. I can guarantee you the D.A. will smile kindly on that. He's a busy man, and your admission will save him time, money, and human resources. That's your best value. Think about it."

Natalie sat on a hard bench in the hallway outside of the interrogation room. Her finger traced the lines of graffiti marked on the wall behind the bench. The nausea returned, and she felt so dizzy that she leaned across the bench to lie down, her head painfully up against the wall. She couldn't get comfortable, and after a few moments more she stood up, walked a few paces to the interrogation room door, and knocked.

The head detective opened the door and motioned for her to come in.

"I'll give you your statement," she said, "but first I better talk to my attorney. I'll make sure he doesn't talk me out of it. I want to cooperate and get the best deal I can. I'm no fool."

The detective looked around at the other police in the room and winked.

"Good move, Mrs. Mannheim. I wasn't playing good cop. You make this easier on us, and we have no motive to make things worse for you."

"Yeah," said H.M. "We don't need to make things worse for you. You're pretty good at doing that for yourself."

"Shut up, Abramovitz," the detective said. "Clock out."

Abramovitz said nothing and walked out of the room, passing close enough to Natalie to shoot her a malicious grin. She said nothing, but she felt quite ill. She hoped she wouldn't puke.

Three days later, the county prosecutor told the judge that Natalie had believed that the Hurt Man was a convicted felon and that she knew or should have known that it was a clear violation of her probation to meet with him.

Whether or not she would eventually be convicted of the criminal conspiracy and solicitation charges, the judge ordered her to be remanded to the custody of the state without bail while awaiting trial.

Freel looked at Natalie and shrugged as she was being led away. "Don't worry," he said to her, shouting halfway across the courtroom.

Natalie wouldn't look at him. She blamed him for being arrested. His dealer had been busted for distribution and was ratting out everyone left and right and cooperating with the police. She should never have trusted Freel. He was as stupid as every man she had ever known.

Back in his office after his unpleasant experience in court, broke and overwhelmed, and not interested in caring for Augie (Natalie had lied to Lock about having a full-time babysitter), Freel contacted a nanny who advertised her services on Craigslist and, after a ten-minute interview with the first candidate provided, hired her. He was too busy to check her references.

How he'd find the money to pay her in two weeks was another matter.

44

Several days later, Freel drove three hours out to the State Correctional Institution in Muncy, Pennsylvania, where he would meet with Natalie. Acting as her attorney, he would be able to meet with her in person, not separated by Plexiglas, and talk confidentially.

Once inside, he was shown to a small conference room, sparsely furnished with a few chairs and a beat-up wooden desk. An oversized American flag hung limp on a stand in the corner. After fifteen minutes, Natalie was brought to the room. She seated herself at the table. Freel had a small pile of file folders and a notepad on the desk.

Without greeting her, Freel assumed the persona of humorless, all-business attorney. He got right to the point and spoke so softly Natalie had a difficult time hearing him.

"There's a lawyer in upstate New York who specializes in connecting birth mothers with high-net-worth couples looking to adopt," Freel said. "The birth mothers like it because they get to feel warm and fuzzy about the affluent lives their brats will have."

"How do you know this guy?" Natalie asked. Her prison uniform draped baggily over her body.

"I read about him when he was accused of being a middleman in the sale of babies. They couldn't prove it. He's still in business and was thrilled when I told him your situation. Mostly thrilled by the high fee he's going to collect from the adoptive parents."

"And what's the situation you told him about?" Natalie asked.

"Don't worry about it," said Freel.

"What about Lock? How about if he goes to court or something to find out where the baby went?"

"He can't," Freel said, smirking. "The state adoption agency—which will okay the adoption once you and the kid's new parents sign the forms—would never reveal the identity of the adoptive parents. There's a law against it. Plus, Lock can't prove he has any legal standing to make the request."

"So there's no way he'll ever see the baby again," she said.

"The only way that could happen would be if the baby grows up and wants to find his biological parents. He'd probably have to sue to get that information, but he'd probably prevail. But don't worry about it. None of that's going to happen, and even if it does, it will be decades from now, and what will you care?"

Natalie drummed her fingers on the tabletop.

"Okay, how illegal is this?" Natalie asked. "I want to get out of here someday. And I know enough to know you can't sell a baby to the highest bidder. Isn't that human trafficking?"

"Who's selling a baby? You're not. I'm not. Adoptive parents are not allowed to pay birth mothers anything other than legit medical expenses and rent and food and things like that, and only during the pregnancy. So, they won't be paying you a dime."

"I know you have a way around that."

"The money that can be paid to birth mothers is highly scrutinized. We can't make any money that way. On the other hand, the fees paid to attorneys—that's kind of a gray area."

"Gray area?"

"That's right," he said. "I can show a lot of hours and expenses I put into finding the adoptive parents, and by agreement, they're going to pay my fee."

Natalie exhaled as if she was blowing smoke from a cigarette. "So you're going to collect a fee from the adoptive parents for your so-called work in placing the baby? How much are you getting?" Natalie lowered her voice and whispered, "And how much of that will I get?"

Freel shook his head in impatience. "Listen, Nat. We're in a tough spot. I've got like five cents left. The mortgage on my house is overdue. Rent on my office is due. I've got to pay the nanny. The Lambo needs to go in the shop, and I've got a million other expenses. We have to do something. And keep this in the forefront of your mind—this adoption is going to be best for your son. He'll get a real chance in life from parents who will absolutely dote on him. Don't worry, we're not going to get into any trouble. Guaranteed."

"Who got disbarred after his third year as a practicing attorney, Mr. Guaranteed?"

"I did, but that was different. I was an idiot then, but now I'm smarter. The attorney's fees for adoptions—it's definitely a gray area, meaning it's okay. I'm getting eighty-one thou for my professional activities."

"You? You're getting?" Her eyes opened wide.

"We're getting," Freel said.

"And what are those so-called professional activities you're billing me for?" Natalie asked.

"I set it up this way. You hired me to do a ton of work to find adoptive parents, help you identify a suitable couple. And by the time I did, I had racked up one hundred and eighty hours. At $450 an hour, that comes to eighty-one thou. The adoptive parents have already agreed. No one could prove how much time I spent actually working, but it doesn't matter, and anyway, no one's going to ask any questions. This is a clean deal. The New York lawyer assures me the Pennsylvania state adoption agency will rubber stamp an uncontested adoption between parties."

"If he's wrong," Natalie said, "we're screwed. Selling a baby is probably a million years in jail."

"Forget about it, Natalie. All you need to know is we're getting eighty-one thousand dollars. Split two ways. Relax."

"How fast can this happen?"

"We can hand the child over in seventy-two hours," he said. "The legal adoption process is a bit longer, maybe a couple of months. But I'll get my fee right away."

"Who's taking care of Augie in the meantime?"

"Got a nanny. Checked her out. The baby's fine. It's better for you to stop referring to him by name. Just call him the baby. That's what the New York lawyer told me. He said there can be separation issues for the birth mother. I doubt that will be the case here, but let's take his advice on that one."

Freel stood up and gathered his files. No guard was in the room, and he and Natalie embraced, hugging each other quickly. He broke away from her, turned, and left. But he did try a sincere smile on the way out.

"Don't worry, baby," he whispered. "Things are a little rough right now, but I've got your back, and we'll be together sooner than you think."

———◦●◦———

The next afternoon, Lock made the same trip Freel did. He intended to visit Natalie and beg her to influence Freel to let him just see Augie. He meticulously rehearsed everything he was going to say. He wanted to believe Natalie might still have a shred of affection or respect for him and agree to his request.

As he drove through the rolling hills of central Pennsylvania, a light snow started to fall. Lock loved that. The snow lifted his spirits. He worked on the words he'd use to convince Natalie to see it his way.

Listen, Natalie. No matter whose son Augie really is, the truth is, at least as of now, your baby thinks of me as his father. I know that has to come to an end, but before it does, he must be—he has to be—in some kind of emotional turmoil, not seeing either of us. It's impossible for you to hold him while you're locked up, but I can. I can give him real, genuine, heart-felt love. I just want to hold him, and I'm certain he wants to be held. I'm begging you to tell Freel to let me see him—even just once—and I promise I'll leave you alone from now on. In the name of what we once had, please help me make this happen. Please, Natalie. Just this once.

He walked quickly and joyfully through the parking lot and stated his business to the desk clerk. The clerk told him to take a seat.

Lock rehearsed those words again and again. He had his speech down pat and promised himself he wouldn't let his emotions get the best of him while speaking with Natalie. He knew he could do it without tearing up, and he knew Natalie's maternal instinct, buried deep as it was, would recognize the truth of what he would say. After all, didn't she love Augie too?

He would soon be holding Augie in his arms again. A rush of delight shot through him.

A few minutes later, a guard approached Lock, who stood up expectantly.

The guard spoke loudly, "Yup, you're on the visitor's list, all right, but she refuses to see you today, buddy. You'll have to leave. Immediately."

Lock didn't sleep much that night. He got up early and went to the 6:30 a.m. Rise & Shine meeting at the clubhouse.

Afterward, he drove into the parking lot of Freel's office. He walked to the door slowly and deliberately.

There was no receptionist, and Freel's office door was wide open. He walked in and saw Freel on the phone. When Freel looked up, his mouth dropped open and he hung up. He set his pen on his desk and stood up. Freel scanned Lock, looking for a sign that he had a weapon. He saw nothing that alarmed him.

"What do you need, Gilkenney?" asked Freel.

Lock stepped forward.

"Look, Freel, I'm only going to say this once. I know Augie is your son, but I've been a father to him since before he was born. I went to Natalie's

Lamaze classes with her, for the love of God. I got up in the middle of the night for months to feed him and change his diapers. I held him and sang to him. I learned how to make him laugh. I can accept that I've lost him, but please. All I want to do is hold him, to see him again. One more time. Let me hold him. Just for a minute. Let me say goodbye to him. You're human, man. Make that happen and I swear you'll never see me again."

Freel stared silently.

"I'm begging you, Freel. Let me say goodbye to the one person in this world I love more than anything."

"Wish I could help you, Gilkenncy, but I can't."

Lock's bluster left him and he stood there deflated and dizzy. "You can if you want to. What harm would it do to let me say goodbye?"

"You have no say in Augie's life," Freel said. "I'm sorry, but that's the way it has to be."

"Please, Freel." Lock's voice cracked.

"I gave you good advice before," Freel said, "when you were flipping out in my driveway a few weeks ago. And remember, I never called the police on you, though I could have. And now I'm going to give you some more advice. You should go about your own business. Natalie and I decided the best thing for the child—for our son—would be for him to be with a more traditional type of family than we could offer him."

"What do you mean?" Lock swallowed hard and felt his eyes burning.

"This will be hard for you to hear, Lock, but Augie's been adopted."

"What?" He lowered himself into a chair.

"I'm not heartless," said Freel. "If the kid were around, sure, I'd let you hug him goodbye. But that's not the case. We arranged a private adoption through an attorney who represents the adoptive parents. Augie's already with them. Out of state. Natalie and I both signed the Termination of Parental Rights documents. It's all over. We don't even know where he is, and we'll never know. That was one of the terms the adoptive parents insisted on. They don't want us to change our minds and come looking for the baby. We couldn't change our minds even if we wanted to. The release is final and unconditional. It's a *fait accompli*. And what should make you happy is that what we did is what's best for the boy."

Lock's face turned red. He couldn't look at Freel. "Where's my son, you son-of-a-bitch? I'll kill you." Lock stood up and took a step toward Freel. Freel spun around and retrieved a putter from a black, leather golf bag behind his desk.

"Get out, Lock," he said. "I could take you out right now and it'd be self-defense. I'm not going to tell you to leave again."

Holding the club in one hand, Freel pressed a button on his speaker-phone. A dial tone could be heard throughout the room. Freel dialed 911 with a quivering finger.

Within a second, the dispatcher answered. "Brandywine County 911, what is your emergency?"

"Okay, okay," Lock said, raising his hands. He turned and walked out of the office.

"911. What is your emergency?"

"My mistake, operator," Freel said. "I misdialed."

Lock reversed out of the parking spot. He was on autopilot, observing the rules of the road but not really conscious of where he was headed or what he wanted to do. A thousand scenarios played themselves out in his head. He couldn't have felt any worse had he received news that Augie was dead. Actually, maybe this was worse.

He fantasized about breaking into the adoption lawyer's office to steal the records that would reveal the identity of the adoptive parents—although he had no way of learning who that lawyer was or where he or she was located.

If Lock were ever to find a powerful enough excuse to drink again, this was it. He had enough experience with alcohol to know that he could, in fact, use it to successfully quash the burning emotional pain coursing through his body and mind. But AA kept jabbing itself into his thoughts. *There's no problem bad enough that a drink can't make it worse.* That was true, he knew from his own experience. And Lock knew that if ever there were a time to keep his wits about him, it was here and now. He'd stay strong for Augie, or he'd die trying.

If he was smart enough, he knew, he could solve this near-impossible situation and get to see Augie again. And did it matter who the biological father was? Lock didn't give a damn.

On the other hand, people did become drunks, and often for good reasons. Maybe he would buy a bottle. After all, some of the world's great artists and writers and musicians were alcoholics and half-insane, if not more, and they often claimed they did their best work while drunk. Maybe finding Augie would turn out to be the defining challenge of his life, and maybe he could solve it drunk. God knew, nothing else had worked so far. He knew this was a convenient justification, but it was one he desperately wanted to believe.

As he drove, he gradually came back to his right mind and could think more decisively. Yes, he was going to take a drink, no question about that. It took a certain strength to resist the temptation, and he no longer had it. And maybe while drunk he'd get a workable idea to get the boy back. That alone made it reasonable to get drunk. At the very moment he decided to buy a bottle—he wouldn't dare take Abby's Glenmorangie—he had the simultaneous realization that he'd left his wallet back at Abby's apartment where he had been staying since moving out of Natalie's condo.

Without being fully aware of the act of driving, Lock pulled up to Abby's, only to be greeted by a cleaned-up, presentable, and healthy-looking Ivan, the former homeless panhandler and current assistant manager at a West Chester Wawa convenience store.

"Lock, you look like you got run over," said Ivan, rising from the stoop he had been sitting on. "What happened? You're whiter than cream cheese."

"I'm getting a drink. Don't want to be a bad influence on you, but I'm going in to get my wallet and then I'm on my way."

Ivan, thinking Lock was joking, laughed. "Yes," he said. "Let's go to the Beer Yard and get a keg."

Lock turned his back on Ivan, found the door key, and let himself in. Thirty seconds later, he was back outside, carrying his wallet. He bounded down the steps and got into his car. Ivan followed him and stood in front of the car so Lock couldn't drive away. Ivan leaned his palms on the hood of Lock's car.

"Turn that engine off and talk to me," said Ivan.

Lock was hunched over the steering wheel, sobbing wretchedly. So much so that it was a simple task for Ivan to reach into the car past Lock, turn off the ignition, and remove the keys.

Lock got out of the car. He was so distraught, he could hardly stand. But before he could speak, Ivan embraced him with a huge bear hug. Then Lock really broke down, sobbing harder than he had in the car.

"Let me drive," Ivan said, after the men had finally let go of one another. Lock barely nodded. They got into Lock's car, with Lock as the passenger.

"Okay, wherever you want," Lock said.

"I'm pretty sure we're heading to a meeting," said Ivan. "As a matter of fact, I'm willing to bet on it."

45

Lock was asleep, and in his dream he was in Natalie's condo. It was early on a Sunday, on a glorious November morning, after a lousy night's sleep. He reached out to feel the other side of the bed for Natalie. The sheets were cool, and no one had pulled most of the covers to her side of the bed during the night.

He walked into Augie's room. No Augie, either. That was no surprise, of course, but it stabbed at him. And knowing that he'd have to move out of the condo soon made it all the worse.

When am I going to wake up from this? he asked himself from deep within his dream.

The condo was a nightmare of fear and grief and memories of his devastated family. An image came to mind of the time he and Natalie took Augie to a playground for the first time and how they laughed uncontrollably at his expression of pure amazement as he took his first ride on a swing. Lock could get that back. He could rescue it. He knew it.

It was hard for him to breathe, and though, in the dream, he hadn't eaten for a day and a half, he felt queasy. He went back into Augie's room and picked up the Winnie the Pooh baby blanket. He pressed it to his face and inhaled deeply. He could smell Augie's scent. Lock picked up the baby's silver, soft-bristled hairbrush and plucked at a strand of hair and wept.

He woke up on the sofa in Abby's nearly empty apartment.

Hours later, Lock left Abby's and got into his car. He drove around aimlessly for an hour. He wasn't headed anywhere, but he did avoid nearby places—the playground, the supermarket, the car wash that he had been to countless times with Augie.

He thought about going to a meeting, but then had a different idea. No, he told himself, forget the scotch, forget the oblivion. Focus on the problem and then solve it. Nothing else mattered.

Instead of ruminating, he killed an hour driving around, consciously pushing depressing thoughts from his mind by focusing on the portrait in his head of him and Augie together, playing in the park.

He wanted to see that laughter on the swing again. He ached for that.

After about an hour, he exited his car near a church in Malvern where a meeting was about to start. He entered with high hopes of finding some solace there, maybe even a nugget of wisdom that he could carry with him the rest of the day to help keep the demons at arm's length. He recognized a few people, but kept to himself and took a seat in the back row, sometimes referred to by old-timers as Denial Aisle.

Fifteen minutes later, he left, irritated by the boring drunkologue from the meeting's speaker. He knew it wasn't the speaker, but his own mind's relentless focus on Augie.

I'll go to Freel's house, kick the door in. I'll find that the adoption story was a lie and that Augie is really still at Freel's. I'll take Augie back to the apartment with me, where he belongs. I'll be in and out of Freel's in moments. Their mouths will still be hanging open, and I'll already be back in the car with my baby. They can't get away with this.

But then reason penetrated Lock's grief-filled head. The consequences of that act would be catastrophic. No, he wouldn't do it. But what would he do? He certainly wasn't going to do nothing.

It was so early in the afternoon. There was so much day left and no plan on what to do. The sky was deep blue, and a few thick clouds floated up high. A lovely, joyous day for most. Lock couldn't bear to think about spending the rest of it feeling the way he did. He drove off.

Lock soon found himself parked in front of Abby's apartment. He got out of the car and walked up the stoop and entered the apartment.

Abby, if you were around, you'd know what to do. Even though you're gone, tell me anyway. I need help like I've never needed it before. He eased himself into Abby's recliner, fully feeling his fatigue. He felt older than his years and could only sit there and shake his head in utter dejection. As he looked around the room from Abby's former vantage point, his eyes focused on the objects that triggered memories of his late friend. Things like Abby's TV remote that had fallen apart and been duct-taped into working order, or the stack of *National Geographic* magazines that he had kept on a corner of the kitchen table.

He thought of Abby's one regret, stated every now and then throughout the years—of never having visited Africa and going on a photography safari. Lock had never understood that, because Abby had no experience taking pictures, and as far as he knew, he hadn't even owned a camera. But that was his friend. Lock told himself that someday he'd be in better circumstances and be able to take Augie on a safari. He pictured the child as a young teenager, full of excitement about riding in a Range Rover and shooting wildlife with a sophisticated camera that Lock would buy for him. The boy would have studied up on Africa and its animals and environment and would be spouting facts and opinions that would amaze the adult members of their tour. Lock would be so proud.

But when he came back to the present, the heavy blanket of hopelessness fell on him with a suffocating thud. His eyes filled, but he didn't cry. He kept exhaling without inhaling. Then he gasped for air and burst into tears.

Where's my beautiful child? What's he doing now? He must think I abandoned him.

That last thought was what drove him over the edge. Imagining Augie's emotions and feelings of bewilderment. The baby could certainly feel emotional pain, and Lock believed he could end it, if only he could figure out how. In the meantime, Lock needed to find a way to kill his own debilitating agony.

Then there was the bottle of Glenmorangie, sitting quietly on the shelf, waiting for the inevitable. Keeping the scotch on a shelf so nearby had been a tool for Abby, but Lock wasn't that strong, and his sobriety wasn't yet fully entrenched in his heart and mind. Sometimes it took much longer. He understood that, but he took the bottle off the shelf nevertheless.

He knew he would open it and drain it, and he didn't care. He didn't care about blowing his sobriety, he didn't care if he died trying to rescue Augie from a fate designed by contemptible people who saw the child as nothing more than a prop in their scheme for money and comfort. He didn't care about anything.

The throbbing dread and agony he felt to his core had to be obliterated, and the scotch would do the job. His mind would settle down, he thought, and then he'd come up with the solution. It would be something like Freel getting Natalie and him getting Augie. That would be the solution, but how could he make it happen?

Lock sat in Abby's recliner with the bottle in one hand and a glass in the other.

With one abrupt turn of his wrist, he peeled the thick foil from the cork and yanked it out of the bottle. He held it up to his nose. He inhaled slowly and deeply. He envisioned pouring a couple of inches into the glass and holding it up in the air, the translucent, light-amber liquid swirling and beckoning. He could imagine the sharp taste that would be the first sip, and the gentle warmth of drunkenness that would shortly ease its way into his body and mind. He'd feel the first signs of intoxication in the mild numbing of his hands and feet, and then in a subtle lightheadedness, it would finally overwhelm his whole being. And the pain would be gone, at least for a few hours. It would be worth it.

I can't do this here, sitting in Abby's chair. What would he think? I'd be breaking his heart again.

Lock smacked the cork back into the bottle and set the glass down on the side table. Holding the bottle by its neck, he got up and left.

Without thinking about it, Lock drove to the park where he had met Natalie so many times before prison, and where they had taken Augie while they were all living together.

He sat on the bench where they had sat and held hands and played with the baby and watched the snow falling. Augie used to look up into the sky and blink furiously as the flakes landed in his eyes, flailing his arms and laughing madly.

Those memories needed to be erased. Lock opened the bottle, raised it to his lips, and took a sip of the fiery liquid. His two years of sobriety, officially at an end.

Then he took not a sip, but a gulp, a mouthful. Heat on his tongue and heat in his throat and nose and stomach.

In less than fifteen minutes, Lock had guzzled a quarter of the bottle, and at first, he felt nothing. But when he stood up from the bench, he knew he had been drinking. His hands were tingling, and he couldn't see clearly in the distance. He wasn't too steady on his feet, but he didn't think twice about getting behind the wheel. He knew he was already too drunk to operate a car, and he didn't care. He needed to get something. Driving back to Abby's apartment drunk was more of a challenge than he had anticipated. He had trouble keeping the car between the white lines. Lock believed he had once been an expert impaired driver, though he knew that was a common conceit of drunks. He didn't want to get stopped by the police, so he consciously drove the speed limit and was on the lookout for yellow traffic lights.

Then he could proceed with his plan—to get in Freel's face and tell him what a kidnapping piece of shit he was.

46

Natalie was in jail, Lock thought, but even if she were free, he would never harm her. She was Augie's mother. But Freel was a different matter. Lock planned to point a gun in his face the next time he saw him. He wanted to threaten Freel into helping him get Augie back, and he wanted Freel to fear him. He wasn't going to wait around and hope to bump into Freel somewhere. And Lock had a convincing prop. He had Abby's revolver.

It took him all morning to find Freel. Lock went to his office. He wasn't there. Lock drove to his house. His car wasn't there. Maybe it was in the garage. Lock rang the doorbell and banged on the door. No answer. He tried one last place—the country club. First thing Lock saw in the parking lot was Freel's car.

Bingo.

Lock stopped and opened his car's door. He placed his foot on the asphalt. He tried to stand up, but lost balance and fell back into the driver's seat. He paused to collect himself and then swung his other leg out and raised himself again, this time with more success. He lurched forward, neglecting to close the door behind him. He was able to follow the signs to the course and knew enough to avoid the clubhouse and the employees who certainly wouldn't recognize him. As he walked and inhaled the crisp air, he sobered up slightly—enough to make him a bit steadier on his feet.

Where's that son-of-a-bitch? He better be here somewhere. He can't hide from me. He's got my baby. He imagined a frog transforming itself into a crocodile and devouring a scorpion in one loud, snapping bite. *He's evil. It's his nature.*

Lock walked right up to the first-hole tee. It was abandoned. The border of the course was lined with cedars. They seemed impossibly thin and tall, like giants. Or judges. Lock ignored them. He didn't care what they thought. *I love my boy. It's my nature.*

He walked the next three holes and finally caught up with Freel and three of his buddies on the fourth. One of them was teeing up, and the others stood around watching. Freel's back was to the approaching, unsteady, disheveled Lock.

"Freel, you son-of-a-bitch," Lock slurred. "You sold my son. You're a dead man." Lock took the revolver from his coat pocket. It dangled in his hand

Freel spun toward him and the others froze, each one staring at Lock, eyes wide, mouths open. Freel pasted a weak smile on his face and put his hands up as if to say, *Relax, pal, let's discuss this.*

"Gilkenney, you're crazy," Freel said when Lock was ten feet away. Freel talked fast. Lock knew what Freel saw—an enraged drunk who needed to be placated.

Let's hear this lie. I'll let him sputter and beg before I end his life.

"Don't feel bad, man—no one sold Augie. We put him up for adoption, that's all. But think, man. It's a better deal for the kid. Natalie and I would make rotten parents. As a matter of fact, we made arrangements with the new parents for you to visit with him. I did that on my own, to help you out. I got a fax confirming that this morning. Didn't my secretary call you? I swear I gave her explicit instructions to reach you."

Lock smiled. He knew Freel would lie. *It's his nature.* "You're a god-damned liar, Freel."

He raised the gun and tightened his grip. One of the golfers screamed, then covered his mouth with his palm. The others stood there breathing heavily, afraid to move.

Freel's face was as white as the sand trap he stood next to. "Don't shoot, Gilkenney, please. If you do, you'll never see Augie again. Please, man, put your gun away. We can work this out. Put your gun away. I swear you can walk away and I won't say a word. None of us will. I didn't get you in trouble the last time, remember? Put your gun away."

Freel's friends wildly nodded in agreement. "Not a word, we swear," one of them said.

Lock raised the gun and aimed it at Freel's chest.

"My God," Freel said, staggering back a step. "Don't do it, my God, please don't kill me. What will that get you?"

Lock straightened his arm and tightened his finger on the trigger.

"Why not, Freel? You killed me. You and Natalie. You took the only thing that mattered."

"No. No I didn't. It was Natalie's idea, but I arranged it so you can visit Augie. The people who adopted him? Turns out they live nearby, in Gladwyne. That out-of-state stuff was bullshit. They're open to letting you visit him. They even said it would be good for him to see you. Don't do this, Lock. Don't do this."

"You're a bad liar, Freel. You and your girlfriend." *It's your nature*, he thought, *and being a father is my nature. And a father would do anything for his son.*

Lock took a step closer and kept his aim on Freel's heart. Killing Freel, he told himself, was the right thing to do. But what if Freel was telling the truth? A million-to-one shot, but Lock couldn't take the risk. He had to hold Augie again. That was all that mattered.

"Prove it, Freel."

"Prove what?" Freel said.

"Prove they've agreed to let me see him."

"Okay, okay. I can. I can do that. But please, put your gun away. You're upset, it could go off accidentally."

"When it goes off, it won't be an accident. How can you prove it?"

"Put the gun down. We'll go to my office. Right this second. I'll show you the fax. I know exactly where it is. Then you'll see."

Freel looked at one of his friends but said nothing, then looked back to Lock.

"And what's to stop your friends from calling 911?"

One of the others spoke. "We won't. We understand what you're going through. Jerry already told us about the fax this morning. He's telling you the truth, sir."

"Here," said Freel. "We'll give you our cellphones so you'll know we won't call the police. I promised you we won't, and we won't."

Freel and the others reached into their pockets and held out their phones to Lock. He didn't take them. He stared at them blankly for a few seconds, then looked up at Freel.

"I want to see Augie again. I don't care about that fax, you just make that visit happen, and you do it today. If you're lying, I will find you and kill you. No matter where you try to hide."

Lock turned around and walked away. He had sobered up during the confrontation, but was feeling the scotch again as he made his way shakily over the greens towards the parking lot.

He got into his car, started the engine, and drove off. He didn't have a clue as to where to go.

47

Lock pulled up to Abby's apartment a little while later and could still feel the effect of the scotch. The three-quarters-filled bottle sat on the seat next to him. Anyone could have seen it, but Lock paid it no attention. He had better things to think about—like the soon-to-be reunion with Augie.

Should I bring a toy or something? No, just me. That will be more than enough.

He sat there thinking. He didn't want to go into Abby's apartment still drunk, so he started the car again and pulled out into traffic. He began to turn on the radio but realized he had a lot to think about and didn't want the distraction of the all-news station. All he could think about was seeing the baby.

Freel wouldn't have the guts to lie to a man pointing a gun at his heart. He was afraid of me, and fear can bring out the truth from those generally reluctant to speak it. I will get to see Augie. I know it.

Lock rolled down his window and took a deep breath of the cool autumn air. His mood soared.

He imagined himself holding Augie and kissing him, hugging him, enfolding him in his arms. It was all he wanted. His joy sobered him up.

He had never needed anything as much as he needed to love that child. And he knew Augie needed the same.

As Lock drove, weaving slightly but not as badly as before, he saw a father pushing an infant in a stroller along the sidewalk. Lock, stalled in traffic, watched with genuine pleasure as the man stooped to pick up a toy duck that the child had dropped onto the cement. Lock smiled at his realization that he had done the same for Augie many times.

But something tugged at him and he couldn't identify it. Then it hit him. No way would Freel have—of his own volition—made the effort to set it up so that Lock would be able to see Augie. That couldn't be true. It was something Freel had thought of on the spot to diminish Lock's rage and protect himself from Lock's menacing behavior. Something that would give Freel a chance at survival. *God dammit*, he thought. *Too drunk. Stupid.*

That was it. Sickening thoughts took over, and they made more sense to him.

Lock's dream imploded and he dry heaved. He swerved into the first side street he came upon, pulled over, a tire up on the curb, and eyed the bottle. The chilling truth was exploding in his head.

He had had enough.

I'll never see Augie. He'll never reach out and grab my finger again. Never.

Lock dry heaved again.

He reached over and opened the bottle. In one desperate motion, he guzzled half of what remained.

He knew what he had to do, and turned on the ignition and headed back to the country club. He sped recklessly and arrived in less than ten minutes. How he kept the car on the road was anyone's guess. The fresh surge of alcohol hit him hard.

Lock stopped the car haphazardly across three parking spots and stumbled out.

Through blurry eyes and double vision, right away he saw Freel and the others huddled next to the Lamborghini. They were absorbed in their conversation—probably talking about whether or not to call the police—and didn't see him.

Lock got out of his car, walked over to Freel, stood at arm's length, and shot him twice in the face with the .45.

Freel's friends ran, but Lock didn't.

He had nowhere to go, but, for the first time in a long time, he didn't feel bad.

18 YEARS LATER

48

Rockview, Pa.

Late one cold and overcast December morning, eighteen years after he had shot and killed Jerome Freel, Lochlan Gilkenney walked out of the State Correctional Institution at Rockview in Bellefonte, Pennsylvania, a free man at the age of fifty-nine.

Almost two decades earlier, as Lock's lawyers prepared to argue that the shooting was a crime of passion, the Brandywine County District Attorney came to the conclusion that he might fail to secure a first-degree murder conviction. Instead of proceeding to trial, he offered a plea-bargain agreement that changed the first-degree murder charge—with its potential death sentence—to voluntary manslaughter and its twenty-year max.

Lock was advised by counsel to take the deal, and he did. Later, his twenty-year sentence for voluntary manslaughter was reduced to eighteen years as a result of good conduct during incarceration.

As he stood on the sidewalk in front of the prison waiting to be picked up, Lock shifted his weight from foot to foot and peered down the road for the car that would be there at any moment. He walked over to the Japanese maple trees that had been planted along the parking lot years ago. From his cell, he had watched a landscaping crew plant them, and after several years, he had been selected as one of the trustees who watered and pruned them.

Under his arm he clutched a cardboard box full of letters that, in recent years, arrived at his cell almost every week. One letter had come from Natalie, who told Lock that after her prison term she had moved into a studio apartment in northeast Philadelphia and worked part-time in a podiatrist's office and every now and then taught a yoga class. She mentioned she hardly ever got to see Edwina, who married young, or Dahlia, who was in college. Natalie wrote that she lived a solitary life and was deeply sorry about everything that had happened and hoped that he'd someday find a way to forgive her. Lock never replied, and months later received a postcard from her that said, "I'm free and you're still in a small room with steel bars—rot in hell."

But most of the other letters in the box came from a teenage boy who had acquired an all-consuming interest in Lock's case and who, beginning at age thirteen, started to correspond with him. The letters led to phone calls, and Lock and the boy's lengthy conversations were genuine and candid. The boy confided in Lock, and Lock always responded with as much wisdom and advice as he could muster. The two soon grew to respect each other. When he was old enough to travel by himself, and with the blessings of his understanding parents, the boy made the four-hour bus trip from New York City several times to visit Lock in Rockview.

The boy—now a young man, who turned eighteen a month prior to Lock's scheduled release—was adamant about driving to Rockview to pick him up.

Lock shivered and checked his watch, looking down the road again, eager to get out of the chill and away from the prison. Although his ride was twenty minutes late, he wasn't worried in the least.

After all, if Lock could count on anyone in this world to be there for him, he could count on Augie.

ABOUT THE AUTHOR

Frank Freudberg is a journalist, ghostwriter and novelist. He has contributed to the Associated Press, Reuters, United Press International, *USA Today*, *Los Angeles Times*, *Der Spiegel*, *Christian Science Monitor*, *Newsweek*, *The Guardian*, and others. His novel of revenge *Find Virgil* has received international critical acclaim and is celebrated as a cult classic. Freudberg lives near Philadelphia.